Donation   17.95   4/18/18

Y0-BGH-613

No Longer Property of
Wellington Public Library

DECLARED DEAD
A Thriller

WELLINGTON
PUBLIC LIBRARY
WELLINGTON, CO 80549

Also by DJ Steele

Dead Ringer (eBook short)

DECLARED DEAD

A Thriller

BARb,
Thank you for The
support!
Enjoy Elke
DJSteele
2017

DJ Steele

SWITCHBACK
PRESS

DECLARED DEAD. Copyright ©2017 by DJ Steele. All rights reserved. No part of this book may be used or reproduced in any manner whatsoever without written permission of the publisher/copyright owner except in the case of brief quotations embodied in critical articles and reviews. For information, please contact Switchback Press, info@switchbackpress.com.

DECLARED DEAD is a work of fiction. Names, characters, places, and incidents are products of the author's imagination or are used fictitiously. Any resemblance to actual events, locales, or persons, living or dead, is coincidental.

Edited by Chuck Barrett
Cover by Chuck Barrett

FIRST EDITION

ISBN: 978-0-9985193-0-2 (Print)
ISBN: 978-0-9985193-1-9 (Digital eBook)
Library of Congress Control Number: 2017930181

Steele, DJ.
      DECLARED DEAD / DJ Steele
      FICTION: Thriller/Suspense/Mystery

Published by Switchback Press

www.switchbackpress.com

For Chuck:
Without his support and encouragement this novel would still be ideas
scribbled on a notepad

For Derick:
The inspiration for the fictitious character Derick Carver

For our Armed Forces:
A special thanks for your service and sacrifices

WELLINGTON
PUBLIC LIBRARY
WELLINGTON, CO 80549

APR 1 8 2018

"Through rock and through stone
The black wind still moans
Sweet revenge
Sweet revenge
Without fail. ...Sweet Revenge"

—John Prine

PROLOGUE

Riga, Latvia
Twenty-three years ago

HE WAS LATE.

And she was not a patient woman.

The only reason she'd stayed this long was the significance of flipping the Russian wanting to defect—a high-ranking KGB officer. Less than twenty-four hours ago, her informant had relayed that the Russian was turned away at the American Embassy. Now, she wondered if the time she spent traveling to the small country in the Baltic region of Northern Europe was wasted.

Outside the corner coffee bar, snow was piled along the sidewalks. The frigid temperature outside seemed to match the building's Soviet-era exterior. She watched as men and women passed by the frosty windows bundled in heavy overcoats, their breath rising in visible puffs, and she was glad she was inside.

This operation was not sanctioned.

She knew that the American Embassy had struggled dealing with the recent flood of Russian exiles fleeing the crumbling Soviet Union. U.S. intelligence could not screen all the Soviet walk-ins seeking asylum in the West. Not all at once. Many were escorted out and told to come back up to six months later. It was because her informant had been so reliable in the past that she agreed to meet with this Russian at all. Her informant believed the idiots at the embassy had made a grave mistake turning the KGB officer away.

Perhaps the American Embassy did not trust the KGB officer. The KGB had been known to play rough and use deceptive measures to infiltrate their enemies. The intelligence services might have been concerned the Russian was attempting a fake defection with the true intention of spying on the United States from within. Her expertise in counterintelligence was the reason that she was contacted.

After she listened to what the KGB officer had to offer, she would determine if he was sincere. When she asked how she could identify the Russian in the coffee shop, the only description was that the man would be carrying a suitcase.

Fifteen minutes past the scheduled meeting time, she doubted the KGB officer would show. Signaling the waiter for her check, she noticed a scruffy looking man walk inside the cafe carrying a suitcase and scanning the room.

The man's clothes, not much more than rags, made him look like a street peddler bundled in a heavy wool overcoat. A tattered scarf wrapped around his neck covered his chin. His slumped-shoulder posture certainly not that of an officer. The older man had thinning hair, bushy eyebrows, a mustache, and wore thick lenses in black plastic frames. She untied the red scarf wrapped around her neck and put it in her lap. This was the signal she was told to use.

The Russian walked over to her table and sat down across from her. To confirm their true identities, they each placed a half of a dollar bill on the small table and matched the tear line.

His English was broken so they spoke in Russian. After

he ordered coffee, he told her he attempted to defect at the American Embassy, but officials told him he was just a librarian and his handwritten documents were fake.

She understood why the CIA might not believe this man was serious. He opened his suitcase next to her. Hidden amongst his dirty underwear and socks were files marked classified. He explained he was no longer an officer for the KGB, he was a senior archivist at the KGB's foreign intelligence headquarters. The archivist claimed that for more than a decade he secretly took files home from headquarters and hand copied them. He alleged these files contained a list of the real identities of KGB *illegals* living under deep cover abroad, many of whom were residing in the United States. He also claimed to have documents showing locations where weapons, explosives, and equipment caches were hidden near several major European and American cities. He told her those caches would be used by sleeper agents in the event of war with the Soviet Union.

If what this Russian archivist claimed were true, then he was a goldmine of information for the Western world. She informed him she would be required to verify the documents and, if they were indeed genuine, then and only then would her government provide him sanctuary.

The man gulped his coffee, clasped his hand on top of hers and pleaded, "I risk my life to give this to your country. If KGB finds out, they hunt me down and kill me." He paused. "You understand?"

She gave him a stiff nod. "I have a source in Riga who will provide you with a safe place to stay. Give me forty-eight hours. If your documents check out, then my government will set you up with another identity to live out a comfortable life in America."

On the plane trip, back to the United States, she settled in her seat and began to read the documents. She was glad to finally be headed back home to Fort Collins after being in Europe for two weeks. She had a long weekend planned, and hoped to take her granddaughter to City Park. The little girl loved to feed the ducks at the lake in the park and she wanted to squeeze in as much time as possible with her. Maybe, she should take more time off and cancel her meeting next week with the CIA director in Washington, D.C.

After reading most of the documents on the long flight, she knew that she would be able to determine if the briefing with the director could be delayed or not.

Two hours later, she laid her head back against the seat, closed her eyes, and reflected on the last two pages of the document she had just read.

Her pulse began to quicken.

She knew now she would have to catch an early flight for D.C. on Monday morning.

A briefing with the director could not be delayed.

CHAPTER 1

Washington D.C.
Present Day

HER THREE-SIDED vertical enclosure was identical to the others in the large room.

Cubicles of four, ergonomically arranged in a swastika pattern for maximum productivity. Each pod with an L-shaped desk and overhead storage.

Her earplugs muted the keyboards' clicks and phone conversations of co-workers in the bullpen. Although her job title was Internal Auditor, most people called her a bean counter since her degree was a Masters in Accounting. Her job was to identify potential land mines in the company's compliance infrastructure. A mundane task to most, but one she enjoyed. A detective searching for evidence in business practices that could affect the reputation of the company.

Julia Bagal studied the documents on her computer screen when the instant message appeared. *How did it go with Vinny last night?* It was from Krystyna, an intern and good friend.

Julia was buried in paper work and did not need a distraction right now. And Krystyna could be a big distraction at times.

She first met the intern when Krystyna arrived at the company five months ago. Her cubicle was located directly behind Julia's. She was close to Julia's age, late twenties, and at

5'11", taller than most men. Tall women typically wore flats, not Krystyna, she usually wore heels. High heels. Drab navy or grey suits were the norm for most employees at the conservative firm; however, Krystyna wore vibrant colors with flashy scarves draped around her neck. Her dark red hair, cut with bangs, hung straight to her shoulders outlining her ivory oval face. At first impression, she was not a good fit for the company. But business models change and after administering the Meyer's Briggs test to all their employees, upper management realized they needed more personality diversity in the work force. And that was exactly what Krystyna provided.

Julia liked the rebellious nature of the new intern. She was smart, quick-witted, and brash. The intern's anecdotes provided needed comic relief for the overly serious atmosphere at the firm. They became good friends immediately. The only problem with her new friend was Krystyna lacked focus and always seemed bored.

She knew if she didn't reply to the instant message soon, her friend would keep hounding her. Agitated she typed, *His name is not Vinny. It is Alvin. It was okay. Busy. Talk later.* Of course, another message appeared on her screen.

Alvin. Wow. That is WAY cooler than Vinny. LOL. Drinks tomorrow night after work. El Centro?

She responded quickly. *Sorry tomorrow night I pick up my grandmother. Bingo night.*

The last message seemed to work at ending the interruptions from Krystyna. Just as she got back in the zone preparing to wrap up a project that had been dragging on for weeks, Krystyna's head popped over the top of her cubicle wall.

She pulled out her earplugs and let them hang on her shoulders. She started to protest when Krystyna said, "We need to talk, let's go to lunch."

"It's only 11:15 and I planned on working through lunch to get caught up. Besides, you know how the bitch feels about going to lunch before noon." She referred to their temperamental supervisor.

"I've already talked to her and told her we needed time to troubleshoot the Leaner file." She gave an impish smile.

There was no Leaner file.

Only Krystyna could have swayed management to bend the rules. No use protesting, just go and let her vent about whatever she needed to talk about. Then Julia would be able to get back and wrap up this project that was already past the deadline date. If she hurried she might manage to get home before eight p.m. and eat something besides ramen noodles for dinner.

She straightened her workspace, placed her files in the file cabinet, and put her empty coffee cup in the top drawer of her desk. All the clutter on her desk was now gone.

"Okay," Julia said, "just pick some place close so I can get back and finish this project before I get fired."

"Geez, do you ever have fun? You need to get out and live a little. How about Clyde's? It's walking distance." Krystyna spoke rapid fire, never giving her a chance to respond.

Her friend was right, her life consisted of work, a daily jog, cleaning house, and off to bed. Most of her friends were married with children and had moved in different directions. Too many of the guys she knew or met either lived at home, did drugs, were gay, or were just losers. All she wanted was to meet a responsible man who had a job. A real job. Was that too much to ask? That was why she agreed to go out with Alvin. He had a real job as a CPA for a large accounting firm in town.

He was nice. She should give him another chance.

Clyde's café was a favorite in Georgetown. Great food and fast service. She was glad her friend suggested it. Her stomach was already growling.

They were seated at a cozy booth directly across from the oak bar. The décor consisted of a French limestone fireplace and antique aircraft and sports memorabilia. The young female waitress brought water with a slice of lemon.

"Ready to order?"

"Yes, we are on our lunch break," she hinted in hope of speeding up lunch.

After they ordered, Krystyna stared at her and frowned.

"You always have to live by the rules, and look where it's gotten you. A date with Vinny and bingo night with your grandmother. You live in a one-star duplex and stay in most nights. Your clothes blend in with the office cubicles. Blah. Blah. Blah." She opened her mouth and pointed inside with her finger. "Gag. Your idea of fun is cleaning your duplex. You are way too young to be swallowed by boredom."

"I live within my means. By the way, his name, once again, is Alvin, and he is a nice guy with a good job," she said with an intense glare at her friend.

"Do you know how many times you have said he is a nice guy?" her friend shot back. "Nice guy makes him sound boring." She emphasized the last word by saying it slowly.

The waitress came over and refilled their glasses with water. She looked at Krystyna with a flirtatious smile and said, "Your order will be out shortly."

Krystyna returned the smile. "Thank you, Kelly."

When the waitress was out of earshot Julia asked, "You know her?"

"Not yet. Her name was on her badge. I was being polite."

"Please, tell me you are not going to get her number."

"Maybe I will, maybe I won't. Perhaps you should get her number," Krystyna said with an exaggerated grin. "Might spice up your life some."

"You are the one who likes women, not me."

"I like women and men. I like leaving my options open, you know. You on the other hand like nice men. Come on, Julia, step out of your comfort zone. Makes life more interesting."

"Let it go. I like my life the way it is. I'm not you." She started to continue when her cell phone rang.

She answered.

"May I speak to Miss Julia Bagal please?" The voice sounded familiar, but she couldn't immediately recall who it was.

"This is she."

"I'm so sorry to bother you. This is Mrs. Adams from Harmony Assisted Living Facility. I know you're probably at work, but we have a problem."

Julia's heart sank like a boat sinking beneath the ocean making her hands tremble. Mrs. Adams was the manager of the assisted living home where her grandmother lived. What could Elke have done now?

"What seems to be the problem?" she asked.

"Your grandmother is missing."

CHAPTER 2

THE NOISE IN the restaurant grew louder.

At least it seemed to grow louder. Surely, she misunderstood the woman on the phone from Harmony Assisted Living.

Holding a finger in one ear and her cell phone tight against the other, she asked, "Would you please repeat what you said? It sounded like you said my grandmother is missing."

Krystyna looked at her mouthing *what* as she raised her hands, palms up.

The woman's business-like voice explained, "When she didn't appear in the dining room for breakfast, we assumed she was not hungry and wanted to sleep in, even though it was a bit unusual for her. We didn't check on her right away since our residents are free to wake up and eat whenever they want. We explained this to you before you placed her with us."

The painful words were like a jellyfish releasing a tentacle of poison on her consciousness. "Yes, yes. But, why do you think she is missing?"

The waitress delivered their food as Julia glanced up and made a check mark in the air to tell her to go ahead and bring the bill.

After a few more minutes of conversation, Julia thanked the woman on the other line. "Please, keep me informed."

"Is this the same grandmother who thinks she's a spy?" The excitement on Krystyna's face was borderline drunk. Grinning, she began to chuckle.

"Yeah, that's right, Krystyna. My bingo packing grandma thinks she's a spy. Her dementia had gotten to the point where I put her in an assisted living facility." She tried to convince her friend it was the right thing to do. "We need to hurry up, eat, and get back to the office. I have to wrap up my project and go to Harmony to figure out what's going on. I should have put her in a more secure facility."

"Do you think she will go to your place?"

"I control her money, so she couldn't call a cab. Yet my gut tells me she will find a way to get there."

"This could be the most excitement you've had in a while, Julia."

"No. What this could be, is a nightmare."

Julia ate half of her sandwich, gulped down her water and handed Krystyna money for her share of the bill. As she snatched her purse from the seat, her friend grabbed her arm.

"Do not leave me out of this. I am here to help."

"I'll keep you up to date," she lied to her friend.

The project took more than two hours to finish. It was a rush job, but she found herself distracted and unable to fully concentrate on her project. There were more important things on her agenda. She was surprised Krystyna didn't bother her again at work. Perhaps her friend did have a little empathy in her. She silently laughed. Always a good listener and genuinely interested in her life, Krystyna never showed concern for the rest of her co-workers when they experienced problems in their lives. She was a strange one—a duck out of water. A popularity contest was something she wasn't interested in. Everybody knew to go to Krystyna for a straight answer. She had the respect of her co-workers as a *tell it like it is* woman.

After explaining to her annoying supervisor there was a family emergency and agreeing that leaving early would be counted against her leave, she walked by Krystyna's cube on the way out of the office. It was empty. Staring at the empty cube she shook her head. *Shit.* Krystyna was still on a lunch break and probably getting the waitress's phone number. *I desperately need to learn how she manipulates people.*

She rode the subway to the terminal where her car was parked. Her anxiety kicked in as she realized her beloved grandmother might be in harm's way. Wandering the streets could be dangerous, especially for a sixty-three-year-old woman with dementia. *Come on Elke don't do anything stupid. Call me.*

Damn. That was it. She gave Elke a phone last month when her grandmother started complaining the landline in her room was tapped. There was a built-in GPS on the phone. It was Krystyna's idea to get the GPS tracking app, so before she gave her grandmother the phone, she installed a third-party tracking app. Right now, she wished she could kiss her friend.

Rummaging around in her large Hobo bag, she found her iPhone. She quickly located the app and used it to track her grandmother. Staring at her phone, she felt confused. The pin showed her grandmother was about thirty miles from Harmony. She needed to alert the facility and, instead of going home and changing clothes, get her car and go find her grandmother.

Departing the subway station, she walked across the street and located her car in the terminal parking lot. After jumping in her car, she started to speed dial the facility, but decided to check the locater app again. The app showed the pin moving. *Where is that woman going?* Suddenly she knew, her grandmother was headed back to Harmony. A sigh of relief was mixed with aggravation. Her grandmother knew the facility policy was to sign out when you left the premises and sign in when you returned. She must have charmed another resident to take her somewhere. Her grandmother enjoyed stirring up trouble.

Emotionally exhausted, Julia decided to go home instead. She called the facility to let them know her missing grandmother had been located and was headed back to Harmony. She directed them to let her know the moment her grandmother arrived. Later she could decide what to do with her.

It was a twenty-minute drive from the terminal to her home. Sinking down in the driver seat, exhaustion began to zap her energy and mental alertness. Driving to her safe retreat, her mind was preoccupied with her grandmother. Elke was the only family she had left in this world. Now the old woman's brilliant mind was being robbed by the hideous effects of dementia. Approaching an intersection, she failed to see the stop sign at the four-way intersection. A split second, a horn blaring from a driver in the perpendicular direction snapped her out of her mental fog.

The other car's tires squealed against the pavement as it swerved. She hit the brakes hard, skidding toward the middle of the intersection. She white knuckled the steering wheel and braced for the impact from the vehicle approaching the driver side of her car. She prayed that her airbag would deploy on impact. The oncoming car turned sharply, continuing around the front of her car, missing a collision by a mere two feet. The man shouted obscenities and gave her the finger as he continued through the intersection. *Shit, I almost died.* Composing herself, she let off the brake and eased the gas pedal. Her body was shaking from the adrenaline.

Thank goodness she left work early or this could have been disastrous. This time of day, commuter traffic was not heavy.

After her nerves finally settled, she noticed a car in her rear-view mirror. She held her gaze a few beats and realized it was the same car that had been behind her for the past three blocks. She slowed below the speed limit and watched the car behind her match her speed. *Am I being followed?* To make sure she wasn't wrong, she used the odds of probability, something her grandmother taught her many years ago. She turned right at the next street, drove two blocks and made another right turn. At the next intersection, she put on her signal and turned her wheel right. Next block she made the last right turn. Four right turns. Driving toward the river she slowed at the intersection as the green light turned yellow and then just before it turned red gunned the accelerator racing through the light. Now she was certain.

She was being followed.

CHAPTER 3

THE CAR BEHIND her made the same four right turns.

When the traffic light had turned yellow, she slowed to test the theory. As she accelerated through the yellow light, she was on high alert and concentrated on the car behind her. It would catch the red light.

But, the car didn't stop. It blasted through the red light nearly t-boning a crossing minivan.

Certain she was being followed, she reached in the passenger seat to grab her pocketbook, but the seat was empty. Lying on the floorboard, with all the contents scattered on the car mat, was her pocketbook, her phone buried somewhere in the rubble. She checked her rear-view mirror and recognized the vehicle as a black Volvo. There was only one person in the car; that individual appeared to be a man wearing dark glasses. *I need to call 9-1-1.* Looking for a safe place to pull over, she spotted a man in uniform walking down the sidewalk on her side of the road. Pulling to the curb, she slammed the car in park and jumped out. She raised her arm to flag the man in uniform as she bolted toward him.

The black Volvo sped past.

The man in uniform turned out to be a security guard at a neighborhood housing project. The security guard told her he was late for his shift and could not help her. He needed the job. *Just call 9-1-1.* In her haste to get the attention of the man she thought was a policeman, she failed to read the tag number. There were a lot of black Volvo's in this city. Reporting what she suspected was not enough; she needed more details. Calling 9-1-1 and telling the dispatcher she thought somebody was following her might have worked if she was driving and the car was still behind her and she could report the tag number.

Returning to her car, she collected all the scattered items on the floorboard and put them back in her pocketbook. She placed her cell phone in the cup holder beside her. Time to take a different route home just in case the car was waiting to pick up her tail. Nervous, she sped toward home and checked her rear-view mirror every few minutes. After fifteen minutes, she began to wonder if she was just tired from all the excitement of the day or if the car was following her? Maybe it was a different car on the third turn. Elke was right about always paying attention to her surroundings. It had been a long day. All she wanted to do was go home and rest.

As she approached the driveway to her duplex there were no unfamiliar cars in sight. Just the neighbors' cars parked on the street. She let out a sigh of relief. The turmoil from the day's events made her feel light-headed. Chasing down her crazy grandmother, running a stop sign and then convincing herself she was being followed. Her mouth lifted into a smile thinking her friend Krystyna would love every moment of this. They were so different.

She slid the key in the lock on her door, clicked a turn and pushed it open. An aroma filled her nostrils. Memories from her childhood began to emerge. The smell was so familiar. Leaving the door wide open, she tiptoed toward the light in the kitchen. Krystyna was a practical joker. Sneaking up and scaring her would serve her right.

In the kitchen doorway, she froze. Her eyes widened, jaw dropped when she saw the woman standing in front of her stove cooking. The older woman did not turn around and kept her attention on the stove.

"So Julia, I did not expect you home so soon." The woman's voice wasn't feeble sounding at all. Her once long-flowing brown hair, now pearl white, was upswept into a French bun and secured with a dragonfly shaped clip. Her grandmother still had eyes in the back of her head.

"Elke, how on earth did you get here? I thought you were headed back to Harmony."

The older woman turned revealing her seasoned face with pale lips surrounded by a wrinkled mouth from years of smoking. Her almond shaped eyes were still sparkling blue and bright as the Caribbean Sea. The woman let her smile widen and her eyes beamed.

"Come give me a hug, honey," her grandmother demanded. "I have had a long day."

The two embraced. It was a relief knowing her grandmother was safe. The other feeling welling inside her was the overwhelming urge to fling herself to the floor in a screaming tantrum.

"Elke, what is going on?"

"First let's eat and then I can tell you all about my escape."

Escape?

The word sent a chill down her back. This was not going to be good.

Elke made the best Wiener Schnitzel.

Julia's favorite food was the veal dish.

"That meal was wonderful, Elke. It tasted the same as when you made it for me growing up." Julia wiped her mouth and placed the napkin on her empty plate. "Now we need to talk. Why did you leave Harmony?"

Elke gazed out the window and corrected her, "I escaped."

"Okay. Why did you escape?"

"I knew they were on to me." She turned back around and stared directly into Julia's eyes. "They know I am a spy. I got out in the nick of time. People were dying almost every day."

Of course, they knew you were a spy. You told anybody who would listen. "Elke, it is an assisted living facility," she emphasized the words. "Old people live there, eventually they die. Nobody was harming them."

Elke stared out the window again as if she was deep in thought. Julia had a lot more questions for her grandmother.

"How did you get in my house? I always keep the door locked."

A chuckle erupted from her grandmother. "That fake rock by the sidewalk? I'm surprised you haven't already been robbed."

Julia's brows creased together. "I tracked your phone and it showed you left and then returned to the facility. How is it you are here?"

"I know all about the GPS in phones. Warren told me his son put one of those trackers on his phone. So, when Warren's son came to pick him up at the facility, I slipped my phone in his pocket. Then I called a cab from the kitchen and when nobody was looking, climbed out my window and here I am." She sat up straight with a smug look on her face.

"Elke, where did you get the money for a cab? I control

your social security."

"Yes, you do, but I have my other money for emergencies."

Julia was getting ready to continue her interrogation when her cell phone rang.

Caller ID showed it was Krystyna.

Elke stood up, a weary look on her face, "I am tired and need to go to bed now. Just leave the mess, I will get it in the morning." Her grandmother walked toward the guest bedroom.

She nodded and answered the phone.

"Is the bingo spy there yet?" Krystyna asked.

"How did you know she was here?"

"You told me at lunch she would find a way to come to your place. You promised to keep me in the loop. What excitement did I miss?"

Julia held her voice low, recounting her day to her friend. She told her about Elke slipping the phone to her friend in the facility to keep from being tracked back to her house. When she told her about running the red light and the man's road rage, her friend laughed and told her *at least he didn't shoot you.* Then she described the supposed vehicle following her.

Krystyna interrupted, "A car following you and a spy in the family can mean only one thing."

"What?"

"This is a pivotal moment for you, Julia. Your life is about to get a lot more exciting."

After their phone conversation, she began cleaning up the kitchen and thinking about what her friend had said to her. Her life was exciting in many ways. For her last vacation over a year ago, she drove down to Richmond, Virginia to visit a good friend. They went out to some great restaurants and did the tourist thing. There were so many historic sites and museums in Richmond. Excitement for her was not the same as for Krystyna.

Exhausted from such a trying day, she went to bed early. Tomorrow she would figure out what to do with her troublesome grandmother.

† † †

She didn't know how long she had been sleeping. Her heavy eyelids barely opened, she glimpsed a human silhouette bending over her. Groggy and trying to come out of the dream state, she gasped. The dark figure was holding a gun. The cold hand covering her mouth muffled her panicked scream. The hand slowly pulled away. Her eyes focused on the face.

"Oh my God. Elke, what are you doing?"

"Shhh." Elke put her finger to her lips. "There is somebody outside in a car watching the place. I went to pee and saw the car outside the window parked across the street."

"People park on the street all the time." She glanced at the clock on her nightstand. 11:00 P.M. "Please, put that gun away," Julia pleaded as she sat up and rubbed her eyes. "Wait. Is that my pistol?"

"Yes. I told you last time not to keep it on the bookshelf in that hollow book," Elke scolded her like she was still a child. "How can you protect yourself when you don't carry your weapon with you?"

Her grandmother pulled Julia out of bed by her arm. Then she instructed her to stay low. Crawling on all fours with her grandmother leading the way, they moved to the window. Julia suddenly realized she was acting as crazy as Elke. She would humor the old woman for now and then in the morning she would talk to the management at Harmony about moving her to the more secure unit.

"Now Julia, very carefully look out the side of the blinds." Elke's voice was barely audible.

Julia rose to the side of the window and pulled the blinds back just enough to peek out. The dim streetlights illuminated cars parked on the street. "Okay. I do see cars parked on the street. They are usually there every night. Now can we go back to bed?" She started to let go of the blinds when something else caught her attention. A shadow moved in a car. Next, a tiny orange glow highlighted a face, followed by a billow of smoke through the cracked car window. She strained a look at the car and jumped away from the window.

The black Volvo was parked across the street.

CHAPTER 4

Shelby Township, Michigan

"IS HE DEAD?"

As he pushed himself up from the pavement, those were the words he heard his friend say to him.

The blow he had delivered to the large man's face caused him to lose his balance. He remembered to roll into the fall and land on his right buttock and thigh. Using his powerful arms and upper body strength, he transferred his weight to his good leg while rising. Falling was something he always tried to avoid—especially while fighting.

Derick Carver had the body of the young legendary bodybuilder, Arnold Schwarzenegger, with one exception. His left leg was missing.

Now it was replaced with a prosthetic leg.

"No," Carver replied. "He's still alive. I didn't hit him hard enough to kill him. Might be missing a few teeth, though. That'll teach the son of a bitch to keep his mouth shut." Carver's powerful arms and fists hung by his side as he stood in the dark alley.

"You got to control your anger, bro. You almost killed him."

"I know how to kill people. I was trained by the best. If I had wanted him dead, he would be dead."

His friend raised his hands. "Cool with me, man. Just got

worried there for a moment. I mean, he did say the wrong thing."

"Shut up, Tony, I don't need your fucking approval."

Tony was more than a drinking buddy and good friend; he was a brother.

A fellow soldier who had served with him.

The man on the ground moaned. Carver walked over and looked down. "Don't ever fuck with a paratrooper." He wiped the blood on the corner of his mouth with the back of his hand, turned, and left the alley without saying another word.

As they crossed the street Tony looked at Carver. "You want to go to another bar and get a drink?"

"Yeah. How about Dooley's?"

The walk to Dooley's Sports Bar took less than five minutes. Once inside, Carver and Tony sat on stools at the dark oak wood bar. Behind the bar were a row of taps for an inordinate selection of beer. Above them, bottles lined a glass shelf. The walls were covered with flat screen TVs, each tuned to different sport stations. Back in the corner was a pool table with three women and a guy shooting pool. The place was crowded with guys trying to pick up women. A jukebox in the back played eighties music.

Dressed in a plaid shirt with sleeves rolled up and a white cloth draped over his shoulder, the young bartender walked over. "What'll it be fellas?"

Carver and Tony both ordered a Budweiser on tap.

"You guys military?" The bartender reeked of cigarette smoke.

"Army. 82nd Airborne Infantry Division," Tony answered.

"Where did you serve?"

"Last tour was Afghanistan. That's where my brother lost

his leg. He was my platoon leader. We were on a dismounted patrol when the Taliban ambushed us. There were seven 107mm rockets detonated in the middle of our formation. I was only feet away from him," Tony nodded at Carver and continued, "when he was hit by an IED. I dove to the ground, scared shitless. He patted Carver's shoulder. This guy, unable to move, kept shouting commands."

Carver didn't want pity from people and especially not tonight after what had just happened. He flashed Tony a cold, hard look.

The bartender squinted at Carver, "Sorry, man, I didn't mean to pry. I have a buddy stationed in Afghanistan. I'm proud of the soldiers who protect our country. Beer is on the house."

People's attitude toward soldiers had changed drastically since Vietnam, thought Carver. His grandfather was a Marine who did four tours in Vietnam. He came home to witness war protests, people spitting on soldiers, and calling them baby killers. After twenty years of service, his grandfather died a slow, painful death from the effects of exposure to Agent Orange. Now, on the bar in front of him was a free beer. Ironic.

"My girlfriend has a friend she wants you to meet," Tony said. "You would like her."

Carver took a swallow of beer and didn't respond.

"How long you gonna stay like this?"

"Like what?" Carver shot back.

"Cut the bullshit, Derick. Ever since you were released from Walter Reed, you spend your time alone. We are both lucky to be alive."

"Lucky to be alive? Funny, but I remember telling our commander we needed to wait. All he said was *rock, paper, rank, go give the patrol brief.* We should never have gone in."

"You said it yourself, a mission is a mission. We were soldiers, we knew the danger," Tony declared dryly. He took a sip of beer. "Now, you spend all your time at the gym or holed up in your apartment."

A moment of silence and then Tony pleaded with Carver again, "I'll give Kristie a call and she can get her friend to meet us back at my place."

"Not tonight." Carver downed the rest of his beer. "I need to go home and check on Parker Brown."

"You mean you would choose Parker over a hot chick?" Tony had a wide-eye gaze as he popped his forehead with his hand. "Brother, I am seriously beginning to worry about you."

Carver stood, jaw tightened, as he faced Tony.

"Parker Brown is always there. He's never let me down. That's more than I can say for most people in my life."

"Parker Brown is a dog, Derick."

Carver walked alone back to his truck, enjoying the feel of the cool night breeze brush across his face. Tony was right about Parker Brown. He was a dog. But that was the only thing he was right about.

CHAPTER 5

THE BLACK VOLVO was parked across the street from the duplex.

She was certain the movement in the car was that of the man she saw in her rear-view mirror while driving home. Slumping to the floor, her heart pounded. Adrenaline rushed through her body dramatically heightening her senses.

"It's him. He followed me earlier today." Julia's breathing sounded like Darth Vader.

"Somebody followed you? Why didn't you tell me?" Elke sounded irritated.

"I wasn't certain I was being followed. You didn't need to be worried. Stay down," Julia instructed, "I will get my phone and call 9-1-1."

Staying low on the floor, Julia crawled back around the bed toward the nightstand. She found her cell phone and started to dial the emergency number when she eyed her grandmother raising the window and pointing the pistol toward the street.

"No," she shouted, jumping across the bed tackling her grandmother.

Elke fell backward and the pistol discharged striking the windowsill. Lying on the floor beside her grandmother she felt pain and pressure on her chest, shortness of breath and heart palpitations. It took her several minutes to regain enough composure so she could think.

"What the hell were you doing? You might have killed somebody."

"No. I was just going to scare him. He had binoculars. The pistol would let that stalker know we were onto him. You, on the other hand, almost got yourself shot. I'm worried about you."

Worried about me? I must be having a nightmare. "Give me that." Julia took the pistol from her grandmother and stood up beside the window to peek out. The black Volvo was gone. The loud noise and muzzle flash from the Smith and Wesson *Airweight* .38 Special must have spooked him. Hopefully her neighbors didn't hear the noise. Her ears still rang from the blast. Her grandmother moaned and mumbled something as she got off the floor.

"Are you okay Elke? I didn't mean to tackle you so hard."

"He'll be back, you know."

"Elke, this has gotten out of control. I don't understand why somebody might be following me. Maybe it's just a coincidence." She felt her delusional grandmother had made her paranoid.

"Did you do the *odds of probability* like I taught you?"

"Yes. Yes, I did."

"And the car was still behind you as you drove home and tonight the same car is parked across the street with a man sitting inside at this wee hour. It is not a fluke, child."

Deep down, Julia knew her grandmother was right. Growing up she was taught to trust her instincts. She felt like her organized quiet life was falling apart and she didn't like it. Julia forcefully shook her finger toward the couch in the living room and commanded her grandmother to go sit down so they could talk. Her grandmother didn't protest. She walked out of the bedroom and sat on the sofa. Julia looked out the bedroom window again to make sure the Volvo had not returned and then walked into the living room to join her grandmother. She could not believe what she saw. There on the couch was her grandmother lighting a cigar with a butane lighter. Slowly puffing on the cigar while rotating it around the flame, she toasted the outer portion to expose the filler.

"Elke, the doctor told you to quit smoking. Those things will kill you."

Elke frowned at Julia, "We are all on the clock, my dear. As soon as we are born, the clock starts ticking. We all have the same ending."

She hated when her grandmother tried to be philosophical. It grated her nerves. It always sounded so…condescending.

"I'm tired. And I'm not going to argue about life expediency. This is my place and I don't want to smell your second-hand smoke." Julia walked over, laid the pistol on the coffee table stretching her hand palm up toward the cigar. Her grandmother's sulking face studied the cigar as if saying goodbye to an old friend, then released the lit cigar to her granddaughter. Julia went to the kitchen handling the cigar like it was a piece of hazardous waste. *A gun, cigar smoke, what else will she use to kill me?* She doused it in the sink and tossed the soggy cigar in the garbage.

Back in the living room, she sat down on the couch next to her grandmother. "Now we need to talk and settle some issues before tomorrow morning. You cannot handle a weapon any more. At your age, you must be careful about these kinds of things. I will report the incident of the car following me and be more prudent about checking my surroundings. I do remember everything you taught me growing up." Julia lectured her grandmother as if the roles of adult and child were suddenly reversed. Her grandmother nodded until Julia mentioned the living arrangements.

"I am not going back to Harmony." Elke's eyes filled with defiance and she crinkled her brow obviously perturbed by what Julia had said. Pursing her lips, Elke spoke in an even tone. "I do not like it there. I only went because of you. You worried too much about me so I just went along with your plan to pay my bills and put me in that loony bin."

"You were in the retirement section at Harmony where everything is done for you," Julia corrected her grandmother. "And if I remember correctly, you were insistent on going to this particular place. Why, I never understood."

"It was my cover for the time being. I have a new assignment now, so I needed to leave. Only the damn place has too many rules. I hate rules. I should've been able to leave without having to jump through so many hoops and all the red tape."

Cover. Assignment. Maybe she should have put her grandmother in the dementia unit.

Her grandmother switched subjects abruptly, "By the way, this couch is very uncomfortable." She pushed down on the mustard yellow cushions trying to demonstrate the lack of support in the couch Julia bought from Goodwill.

Her grandmother's dementia was causing too many problems in daily life. Especially in Julia's daily life. She could not remember when her wonderful fun loving grandmother's mind began to slip. Now, Elke lived in a fantasy world of make believe.

"Elke, we need to figure out where you are going to live. You need somebody to check on you periodically," Julia said as she tried to reason with her. "I work full time and live in a very small duplex."

"You are right. This is a tiny duplex. We can look for a bigger place this weekend." Her grandmother's eyes brightened.

Gritting her teeth, Julia was about to respond when she heard a rapid knock at the front door. Their heads turned toward the door and quickly swung back to face each other, eyes questioning what should they do.

"Open up. Police," the voice on the other side yelled.

"Could be a trick," her grandmother warned.

Julia picked up the pistol on the coffee table, gestured with her other hand for Elke to stay put. Getting up from the couch she firmly held the pistol downward with a two-handed grip, her trigger finger extended against the frame of the gun to avoid accidentally pulling the trigger. She moved cautiously toward the front door. Using one eye pressed against the peephole she saw two uniformed police officers.

"Let me see your badge," she yelled through the door.

Both officers held up their badges.

"We had a report of a gunshot being fired from the premises," the officer yelled back. "Now please open the door so we can talk."

She unlocked the deadbolt, removed the chain and cautiously opened the door.

The police officers immediately stepped back and drew their weapons.

"Ma'am, I need you to put the gun down on the floor and raise your hands." The officer and his partner kept their weapons aimed at her.

"Now," the older officer commanded.

She didn't think about the weapon in her hand being a threat.

Oh, my God, they think I'm dangerous.

She lowered the pistol to the floor, raised her hands and stepped back, allowing the officers to use his foot to open the door wider. Her grandmother on the couch smiled greeting them like they were longtime friends.

Julia described the events leading up to the pistol being fired to the officers. Lastly, she showed them the bullet hole in her bedroom windowsill. After she had satisfied all the officer's questions, he returned the weapon to her. She placed the pistol on the nightstand while listening to him lecture her on the danger of weapons and what if she mistook her sweet grandmother for a burglar. He advised her to get a gun safe.

She lied to the officers telling them a noise outside scared her and when reaching for her pistol on the nightstand it had accidentally discharged. She was afraid to tell him the sweet grandmother was crazy and was the one with the pistol readying to fire at the man in a car across the street.

Voluntary manslaughter would be the verdict making me an accessory to the crime.

Returning to the living room, the officer spoke to her grandmother still sitting on the couch, "What is your name, ma'am?"

"Elke." She tilted her head with a wide-eyed innocent look.

"Are you okay? You look scared."

"Oh yes. I'm okay. It was quite a scare when I heard the loud noise. I was sound asleep."

"Well, you make sure your granddaughter goes tomorrow and buys a gun safe. Will you do that for me?"

"I will, officer. I never did like guns," her grandmother said as she batted her eyes.

Julia shook her head in disbelief at how effortlessly the lies flowed from her grandmother's mouth. Now she felt like an idiot for endangering a sweet, innocent, lying old woman.

She explained to the officer about the car following her earlier in the day and parking across the street from her duplex. He noted the vague description she gave, telling her to call and let the police handle it if she saw the car again.

She waved and thanked the officer for his advice while closing the front door. When she turned around she was ready to put her foot down and tell her grandmother she could not live with her. But, her grandmother was gone. The couch was empty. The door to the spare bedroom closed.

Opening the bedroom door, she saw her grandmother tucked in for the night.

"Elke, we need to talk."

No sound.

"I know you aren't asleep, Elke. Now, sit up and let's talk about what to do going forward," she begged her grandmother.

"I am too tired, child. Tomorrow we can talk. It has been an exhausting day for me."

The bedside clock showed the time 11:50 P.M. Julia was exhausted too.

"Okay, Elke. But we will talk tomorrow after I get home from work."

She went back to her bedroom and started to climb into bed when she noticed something was wrong. Shit. She got up and padded across the duplex to where her grandmother was sleeping. Hands on her hips she looked down at her grandmother and wondered how she could look so damn innocent.

"All right, Elke, hand over my pistol."

CHAPTER 6

**Capitol Hill
Washington D.C.**

THE MAN IN the dark navy business suit strode across the sidewalk in the largest residential neighborhood in Washington, D.C. Cumulus clouds dotted the early morning blue sky. Dawn's first rays of sunlight struck the cotton-like clouds contrasting their dark base. His neatly-combed blond hair ruffled in the stiff breeze. At least an hour before commuters jammed the streets, he enjoyed the solitude of his short walk to work.

In his left hand, he carried a leather briefcase full of files along with his laptop. Legislative files for floor consideration needed to be reviewed along with the legislative calendar agenda before today's session. His office was walking distance from his rented historic row house. He decided not to take a taxi to Capitol Hill since the remainder of his day would be spent sitting in meetings and working long hours behind his computer. The exercise would be good.

His eyes absorbed his surroundings, always alert to any sign of trouble. One of his constituents had received a threatening letter about upcoming controversial legislation. The man knew the danger of being in the public spotlight. Threats and intimidation against Congress members were not uncommon.

He had a job to do and refused to let fear dictate his life.

He joked with his constituent that the real danger wasn't the isolated crazies, but the toxicity of partisan politics. The polarization of Congress affected the whole country.

Inside the Rayburn House Office Building, he greeted Security and then made his way down the long hallway. He did not have to pass through the metal detectors like everybody else when they entered the building. This early in the morning, there were no long lines of people waiting to meet with their state representative or get a tour of the excess marble lining the inside of a rather unimpressive building.

The Rayburn House Office Building was a congressional building for U.S. House of Representatives on Capitol Hill. The building, named after former Speaker of the House Sam Rayburn, was completed in 1965, and with over two million square feet, it was the largest of the congressional office buildings. It was a place where a congressman could live if he so desired. It had everything a person needed. Amenities included a cafeteria, Library of Congress book station, recording studio, gymnasium and facilities for the press and television. There was even a subway tunnel with two cars connecting the building to the Capitol.

Alan Wagner, a tall, thick man with deep-set blue eyes had become a top dog on Capitol Hill and turned heads with his impressive work ethic, intellect, and ambition. His fast track to the No. 2 job in the House of Representatives was due to his political skills for forming and maintaining relationships. Wagner worked hard to amass support across the rank and file for his authored bills, while serving Florida's 2nd congressional district. Many of his colleagues, though, criticized him for not being tough enough to succeed in the cloak and dagger world of politics. However, his new leadership role was a clear sign his colleagues trusted him with their vision for the party.

He continued to his first-floor office suite inside the Rayburn House. His office had an oversized 19th century antique mahogany desk with a high back leather chair behind it. There was a picture on the desk of him and a friend standing barefoot in the sand on a beach in the Caribbean. Another picture showed him and the President shaking hands at a political event. A landline black phone covered with speed dial buttons was within easy reach of the high back leather chair. Papers stacked in neat piles surrounded a gold-based lamp located on the far corner of his desk.

It resembled the offices of most of his constituents except for what was missing. No pictures of a wife, children or family vacations.

He was a bachelor.

The media touted him as the most eligible bachelor on Capitol Hill. Long workdays and stress took a toll on his personal life. His former secret lover wanted nothing to do with the constant scrutiny of politicians living under the microscope, and he knew her background would hinder his rise to the top. From the beginning, their clandestine relationship was destined for doom.

In a stand, next to his desk was an American flag, a present from the Speaker of the House on Wagner's inauguration. A bison leather couch with matching facing chairs and a coffee table occupied one side of the room. He spent many nights sleeping on that couch after working late. Twelve and fourteen hour days were his norm.

On the other side of the room stood a bookshelf filled with trophies from his college football days, books on law, a private collection of rare books on war strategies left to him by his late father, and assorted political memorabilia. Among the items on the shelves was a picture of him campaigning to cut waste in the federal budget and an unopened bottle of Wild Turkey, a gift the distillery had sent to him.

He heard a light knock on the door as it opened. "Good morning, Mr. Wagner."

"Good morning, Megan. You're early." Alan liked Megan. She was a highly skilled and intelligent assistant who loved her job. He worried she would burn out like most of the grossly underpaid staff workers.

"I knew it was destined to be a long day." She stood in the doorway holding a cup in her hand dressed impeccable with her businesslike attire. The deep violet color of the skirt and jacket complemented her rich, dark skin. The young woman knew how to dress for success. She often gave him advice on the suits and ties he wore. Being a bachelor, he welcomed her input. Megan walked over to his desk and handed him a tall cup of coffee. "I had them add an extra shot of espresso."

"Thank you," he said. "I don't know what I would do without you."

"I'm sure there would be plenty of staffers lined up for this job."

"That is very kind of you to say. Not sure it's true."

"All staffers know their careers are tied to the members they work for, and you, Mr. Wagner are already dubbed one of the young guns of the GOP." Even though he told her it was okay to call him Alan in private, Megan insisted on addressing him as Mr. Wagner.

She was right. If a young staffer wanted to climb the office ladder on Capitol Hill, they needed connections.

Especially women.

Megan was an African-American woman in her mid-twenties. She was not naive. She knew the score. The number of women in top positions of congressional offices was thin. Congress was still a good ol' boy system.

Both he and Megan were type-A personalities. Her desk did not have a picture of a husband, boyfriend or children. He imagined she lived with several roommates in a small run-down apartment on the wrong side of town. She used public transportation and did not own a car. Just like him, Megan could not worry about a work-life balance. Her job was her life.

Wagner wondered if, unlike him, Megan had a choice of careers. Even before he graduated from high school, his strict parents pushed him into a career of politics. They told him it would be an honor to your country to work on Capitol Hill. He could not disappoint them.

He wanted to tell Megan to leave the job. She was too young to sacrifice so much for a life in the lion's den of politics. One day he should talk to her about her future. But, not anytime soon. He wanted Megan around. She was a beautiful woman and he found himself attracted to her, despite the obvious issues of age and…well, the fact that many political careers had been ruined by affairs with Congressional aids. Yet, she was a very desirable woman.

Right now, more than anything, he *needed* her. She was the most competent assistant he'd ever had. The talk would have to wait.

"Hold my calls. Cancel my meeting at ten with Dan Quatterman."

"Do you want me to give him a reason for the canceled meeting and should I reschedule?"

"Tell him that his damn—" He stopped. He realized he might say too much. Megan had the balls to repeat verbatim what he said.

Megan's face brightened as she grinned. "I will give him the standard excuse and reschedule."

"Thanks."

She left the room and closed the door.

Congress's partisan divide had led to several legislative dead ends and many wasted weeks with no significant action taken on any legislation. The man responsible for a big part of the problem was Dan Quatterman. Amendments were needed for most of the proposed bills, but Quatterman did not want his members to be held accountable by the voters.

Wagner sat back in his leather chair and swiveled it around to look out the window of his office.

Quatterman is a damn fool.

Admiring the view from his window, he sipped his coffee. A lot of staffers and lawmakers who walked to work complained about the ascent to the congressional offices on Capitol Hill. Wagner thought they must not have an office with a view. He did not have a lot of time to look out his window since he was usually staring at the computer screen. But, when he needed a moment to unwind and reflect, he would gaze out his window at the unobstructed view over all southwest Washington, including the Potomac River, and the Nationals baseball stadium. Sometimes, when he worked late, he would turn off the lights in his office and watch the sky light up with fireworks over the stadium.

Wagner needed a moment to pause.

A moment to be prepared.

Then it happened.

His cell phone screen lit up.

Looking down at the phone in his hand, he saw the incoming call.

It was her.

CHAPTER 7

Shelby Township, Michigan
Bayonet Crossfit

THE SLOGAN PRINTED on back of his t-shirt read *You'll Pass Out Before You Die*. The Bayonet coach and athlete stood facing the five Crossfitters who were preparing to do the *Workout of the Day* (WOD). The high intensity training was the Grace WOD. Thirty clean and jerks, to be done as fast as possible. It was a sprint with a barbell. This was Olympic lifts—snatch, clean and jerk—one of the most difficult Crossfit movements. The barbells in front of the two men had a weight of 135 pounds and the three women barbells weighed 95 pounds each. A Crossfit center was not called a gym, it was called a *Box*. Basically, a bare bone gym without all the bells and whistles.

After a pep talk, the Bayonet coach pointed to the motto stenciled on the wall in the box and said, "If it doesn't challenge you, it won't change you." He recognized their determination. He also understood the fear in the eyes of one of the young men. Fear that the man might not be able to complete the challenge. The young man was also an amputee. He had lost his left leg in a motorcycle accident.

Determination and fear.

The same expression the men in his platoon had after he gave the mission-prep instructions in Afghanistan. He lowered his head as the vivid memory of that day took control of his mind.

Closing his eyes, he could only see dust. He felt himself somersaulting in the air, heel-over-head. Counting four. Four somersaults. Tasting the explosives. The loud ringing in his ears. He wanted to yell "IED," but his men already knew.

"Derick, you okay? interrupted one of the Crossfitters.

Triggers.

The therapist told him to recognize and avoid what triggered the memories. Shit. They just crept up on you like the damn Taliban.

He slowed his breathing, returning his attention to the Crossfitters in front of him.

"Let's do this," he commanded.

Two hours later, the center had cleared and only a few people were left working out in the box. Motivating himself to do his workout, Carver prepared to do his one-arm snatch with 135-pound barbell. An employee stood nearby watching the Bayonet coach.

"Derick, did you know in the early 1900s circus performers would perform one arm snatches to draw crowds with their impressive strength?" The employee was a coach at the Crossfit box and a good friend. Kurt always shared a lot of trivia knowledge. A lot of useless, annoying trivia knowledge.

"No shit? Well, did they do a one-arm snatch with one leg?" he countered.

"Just pointing out that you being a beast and all, could bring in more clients."

Carver ignored the remark. His CrossFit business was growing. Just not fast. Most people wanted instant results without sacrifice. Instant gratification. The new generation.

He started the business to help other wounded veterans build strength, confidence and a sense of self-worth. Last night, Tony was wrong. Carver had not given up on life. A soldier fights. Always. No matter what happened to him in life.

Carver gripped the bar with one hand and then exploded using his hips to raise the loaded bar above his head. He held it for a few short seconds before letting gravity slam it to the padded gym floor.

He noticed a young woman on the side of the box who stopped to watch him.

Kurt nodded. "Derick, looks like you got a fan. Her name is Karen. You should go talk to her after your workout. Better yet, before you start to stink."

"Been there, done that. I got the only companion I need right now."

Kurt laughed. "You mean Parker Brown? Your dog, Parker Brown? Dogs are man's best friend but they can't— "

Carver leveled a deadly look at his coach friend. Karen turned and continued her workout.

Kurt walked back toward the front desk next to the office where people check in and ask questions. His friend just didn't know when to keep his mouth shut.

Carver continued to load the barbell for his deadlifts. He had an hour before Marvin arrived.

Marvin was a three-month recruit. His progress at CrossFit was inspiring to Carver. The young Marine had both legs amputated at the knee after stepping on a roadside bomb in Afghanistan. Working with disabled veterans was what motivated him and he enjoyed watching their progress.

He lowered his hips so his thigh was parallel to the floor. Looking straight ahead he straightened his back and stood using his hips and shoulders keeping his abs tight while lifting the bar close to his body. He came to a standing position with upright posture and shoulders pulled back. Then he let go of the bar and the 450-pound barbell bounced against the bumper plates on the floor. When he placed his good foot on the bar to stop the bouncing, Kurt walked up.

"Derick. There is some guy at the counter who wants to talk to you."

"See what he wants," Carver said. "I need to finish my work out before Marvin arrives."

"I already tried. The guy was insistent, said he has strict instructions that he can only talk to you. Told me he is a truck driver and on a deadline." Kurt had a quizzical look.

Carver walked toward the middle-aged man dressed in baggy jeans, plaid shirt with long brown hair sticking out from a ball cap waiting at the front desk. The truck driver had a dark tanned weathered look with deep wrinkles on his face and a beer gut. Too many hours behind the steering wheel of a truck. Not enough time in a gym.

"You must be Derick Carver," he said without any introductions.

"I am."

"Thought so." He noticeably glanced at Carver's prosthetic leg. "I was given a full description of you." The truck driver held out his hand. "Damn proud to meet you. Not sure why this was so damn important that it had to be hand delivered." With his other hand, he held out a sealed manila envelope and handed it to Carver.

The truck driver turned and walked out the door without saying another word.

Casting his eyes down at the envelope, Carver silently read

the words scribbled on the outside.

Time to pay up.

CHAPTER 8

WORDS ON THE outside of the envelope clued him to the identity of the sender. It had been a long time since he last saw her.

Seated behind his cold metal desk in his office, he stared down at the manila envelope lying in front of him. The words printed on the outside of the envelope were the last words she spoke to him.

He did not open the sealed envelope.

When the truck driver gave him the envelope and left, his first instinct was to rush into his office, shut the door, and rip it open. What could the woman want from him after so many years?

He was not ready to read her words. Not yet, anyway.

Not from fear of what she would want from him, but from the memories.

Memories of the time he'd spent with her during his recovery at Walter Reed Army Medical Center. Triggers. He needed a moment to reflect.

The place was a nightmare. The hospital was overrun with critically wounded soldiers on the verge of giving up. Suicides were not unheard of. During his fourteen months of recovery, he loathed when people felt sorry for him.

She was different.

Working as a volunteer at the Walter Reed Army Medical Center, she never felt sorry for him. Direct and to the point was her style. He was surprised how she could break down the walls he had built due to his social anxiety.

Their first meeting was at the Military Advanced Training Center Physical Therapy clinic. MATC PT as they called it, which specialized in the treatment of lower limb amputees. The large room was full of soldiers who were once at the peak of their physical ability, but now needed to be repaired—both physically and mentally. Repaired was the right word. Not healed. One never truly healed from this type of traumatic injury.

He wondered if the people in the nation's capital, responsible for sending these brave soldiers to war had ever seen a recently wounded veteran. During his recovery, he remembered one young politician who seemed to give a damn. The politician visited him numerous times during his recovery and they even shared drinks after his release. The injured soldiers didn't want pity, they wanted to regain the highest degree of functional independence possible.

They wanted to be repaired.

On the other side of the large rehabilitation training room, he noticed a woman about 5'6", in good shape, studying the amputees working on core strength, balance, and stability. She wore slim black slacks, flat shoes and a white button down shirt. The physical therapist who had been assigned to him walked over and handed her a clipboard. The therapist appeared to review information on the clipboard with her. At one point, they stared in his direction. Her expressionless eyes fixated on him. Her stone face gave him a bad vibe. He hoped she was not going to be part of his recovery team.

The physical therapist and the woman stopped talking and together they strolled across the room toward him. Her good looks and air of confidence told him she had turned a lot of men's heads in her lifetime.

The physical therapist stopped in front of him and held out his hand.

"Good morning, Derick."

"Morning." He could not recall the man's name.

"Derick Carver, this is Addy Bravo." The therapist gave a slight turn of his head to acknowledge the woman standing next to him. "She will assist you in your rehabilitation at MATC."

The woman stuck out her free hand. "Nice to meet you, soldier."

"Aren't you the lucky one?" Carver replied in a sarcastic tone as he shook the woman's hand.

The woman tilted her head slightly as if startled by his sarcasm. She grinned at him and replied, "Bullshit, Carver. *You* are lucky to have *me*."

He liked her immediately.

During the long days in rehab, he never heard her complain about helping set up and clean equipment or fetch water for the patients. As the weeks went by their conversations became more intimate. She was good at extracting his true emotions. Bullshit was always her reply whenever he tried to skate around questions he was not ready to deal with. Her commanding nature was sometimes difficult, but it was not unlike his. The process of dealing with the traumatic effects of the explosion challenged him more mentally than physically.

He had a team consisting of a physician, prosthetist, physical therapist and a psychologist. Addy's role was assisting the team. She was a volunteer.

Rehab was long and painful. Some shrapnel from the blast could not be removed from his body. Just like the memories of the day it happened could not be removed from his mind.

Never one to beat around a topic, she asked him, "How is the shrink therapy going?"

He shrugged his shoulders. "Okay, I guess." He did not think it was any of her damn business.

"Bullshit. Does the shrink have a bowl of candy on her desk and let you have a piece after every right answer? You're a soldier, Derek. A paratrooper. A badass. You did not come back from Afghanistan the same man as when you left. You feel victimized by fate. Life is unjust. To cope, you go mentally numb, sleepwalking through life, you are unable to feel your emotions." She never flinched speaking to him in such a direct way.

The words were a bulls-eye into his mental psyche. It pissed him off when she held up a mirror and forced him to look, especially in the beginning.

As the weeks went by, he began to understand the woman who happened to enter his life at the right time. She shared her past with him. He discovered they were two people who carried emotional wounds. They had gone through anger, denial, and depression caused by their personal tragedy. She told him it didn't matter what life circumstances brought about the grief, what mattered was refusing to let the trauma cripple you and putting your life back together. She explained that some people never recovered from their trauma, but some would become stronger. During their talks, he sensed she was hiding something from him. He often wondered if she had left her past behind and moved on. Carver looked forward to seeing

Addy every day at Walter Reed Medical Center. He pushed past the pain as he learned to walk with his prosthetic. She was his drill sergeant and cheer leader rolled into one. Then one day she told him, she had to leave. He still had months of rehab remaining. "Addy, you have been my life line during rehab. You saw me at my worse and never walked away or gave up on me. I need you to stay."

"Bullshit. You are going to be just fine. I spoke to the doctors and they are impressed with your progress." He thought he saw a tear in the corner of her eye.

"Where are you going?"

"I have business I must attend to." Addy looked away.

"I want to somehow repay you for all you've done for me."

She turned, cupped his face with her hands, "I'll let you know when it's time to pay up." She smiled, turned, and left.

That was the last time he saw or heard from her.

Until today.

He picked up the envelope and opened it. A letter inside was written in short concise sentences.

Dear Derick,

Remember your promise!

I cannot give you details. I need someone I can trust. Someone with your training and background. There is an envelope with instructions and money inside. You know my past. This will likely be dangerous.

As always,

Your devoted Addy Bravo

When the office door opened, it startled him. He turned

the letter upside down on his desk and looked up. Kurt was standing in the doorway.

"Marvin is here," he said. "You ready to work with him?"

"Change of plans, Kurt. I need you to coach Marvin and look after the Box while I'm gone. I need to leave town for a few days. Something has come up that I must attend to."

"Does this something have to do with that letter?" Kurt pointed to the letter on the desk. "You aren't in trouble or anything, are you?"

"Nope. Just need to be gone for a few days to help an old friend. You mind taking care of Parker Brown till I get back?"

"Well, for you to leave me in charge of the business and take care of your mangy dog, she must be pretty damn important."

"Yeah." He sat back in his chair. He relaxed as he envisioned her face saying bullshit to his guarded answers. "She saved my life."

CHAPTER 9

His iPhone vibrated in his hand. He waited several seconds before he swiped his finger across the screen to answer the call. Wagner wanted the woman to know he had a life of his own and wasn't going to sit around at her beck and call.

But he always would.

The conversation was short. She used the ploy he *was doing a great job in Washington* in a lame attempt to pump his ego. This was her way of manipulating him. Her motive was transparent. He wanted to tell her if she wanted to pump up his ego, she could come over and share his couch on late nights at the office.

But he never did.

It would not be wise to let her know his true feelings. He knew when he agreed to go to work on Capitol Hill, it would be a lonely job. Wagner knew what he had signed up for. One day he would be remembered for the many great things he had done. That would be satisfaction enough.

After ending the call, he swiveled his chair back to face his desk.

Megan was right. Today would be a long day and he needed that extra shot of espresso.

He opened his briefcase and removed his laptop and several folders. The most pressing project would be scheduling legislation for floor consideration and then consulting with members to gauge the goals of the majority party.

He had worked hard honing his skills to bring proposed bills across the finish line. The most daunting challenge was trying to unite a divided House of Representatives. It would not be easy to quell conservative rebellions in the caucus, but it was important to know how to play the game. After two years, as Majority leader, he had to swiftly contact lawmakers to lock in their support before the competition could rally. His rapid rise to the top was due, in part, to his amazing ability to memorize obscure facts about his constituent's families, such as children names, favorite sports and their political needs. His continuous efforts cultivated ties to his constituents.

Wagner often joked that politicians had to have an array of qualities, which at times could mirror a psychopath's personality. They had to be ruthless and ambitious, all the while having a superficial charm.

Politics was not for the weak or thin skinned. One mistake in your personal life or one word out of place could kill a career. He thought at times about leaving politics, but he knew it was not an option. There was too much at stake. People counted on him to get the job done.

Wagner worked tirelessly to keep his goals and ambition on track with what he believed. He was building a program of policies linked to his party's values. Policies guaranteed to win elections. Policies guaranteed to get him noticed.

The noise outside his office alerted him to the impending situation. Dan Quatterman's adenoidal voice was so loud it echoed though the closed door. Megan was doing a good job at keeping the motor mouth from barging in, but even she had to surrender when the towering man bullied his way inside his office.

As the door swung open, Megan apologized for the interruption. "I am sorry to interrupt you, Congressman Wagner, but Congressman Quatterman says it is an emergency."

"Does he need you to call 9-1-1, Megan?" She put her hand to her mouth to suppress what sounded like a giggle.

Everything was an emergency for Dan Quatterman.

"Very funny Alan. You are a regular comedian."

The man had a slightly flat broad nose and a face scarred from a bad bout with teenage acne. The eyes behind his black-framed glasses had heavy lids. He dyed his hair jet black to cover the gray. It made him look ridiculous with the gray hair growing out of his ears. His body looked flabby with his shirt tight around his midsection. Quatterman hired a personal trainer about the time he dyed his hair. Obviously, she was not doing a good job helping him get in shape. Rumor was she was good at other things with several politicians on the hill. Weight loss was not one of them.

"Thank you, Megan," Wagner said, "you can leave us alone."

Quatterman's eyes followed her as she walked out of the office.

"Megan still single?" Quatterman asked after she closed the door.

"Yes. But you are not." Wagner hoped the seriousness in his tone would let Quatterman know not to go any further with the inquiry about his assistant.

"What is it you need to talk to me about? I am in the middle of reviewing the proposed legislation to give the president the green light if talks fail with Iran. I want this on the floor for consideration this week."

"That bill won't make it out of Congress. We both know that."

"The intent of the bill is to show we are not weak on foreign policy."

"Shit. We both know the U.S. influence remains strong, but is declining in terms of economic output compared to China, India, Brazil, and Russia. After World War II the United States established dominance around the world. Today, there are signs everywhere it is collapsing."

He knew what the outspoken man said was true. The feeble response to the Russia-Ukraine and Syrian crises, along with the problems in North Africa and the Middle East, were signs of democracy retreating. The panic, Americans had over the spread of communism during the Cold War had been replaced with a new generation concerned with domestic issues.

"We need a strong President who recognizes we cannot become complacent in our Foreign Policy," Wagner said.

"Damn straight," Quatterman confirmed. "But, the reason I needed to see you immediately is to give you the good news."

Wagner raised his eyebrows. He despised the man in front of him. Good news meant he had just stabbed another politician in the back. He wielded power due to his uncanny ability to find dirt on other lawmakers.

"I just heard scuttlebutt Mark Thompson has some skeletons coming out of his closet," Quatterman said.

Mark Thompson was the current Speaker of the U.S. House of Representatives. Thompson was also Wagner's friend. The Speaker was the most powerful and influential legislator in both houses. He was literally two heartbeats away from president.

"There is an ethics investigation into his business dealings. He has been using federally funded vehicles and planes for his personal business ventures."

Many of the lawmakers used federal funds for business

travel and would tack on a vacation while there or conduct personal business. It sounded like a drummed-up allegation to dispose of the Speaker. Thompson had made many enemies while holding his current position.

"So how is this good news? Thompson is an influential Speaker. He has ensured passage of much needed foreign programs advocated by our party. Am I missing something? I don't think our party needs another scandal now," he glared at Quatterman and then continued, "there are no innocent people on the hill. We all have skeletons. Are you saying you don't have any secrets you don't want leaked?"

The man squirmed in the chair as several beads of sweat rolled down his over-sized head. Wagner knew the man across from him wanted to get up and run. His career would be over if people knew what kind of man he was. Quatterman's wife and children would be devastated. His past would make an ethical allegation seem like a joke. The man on the Hill had a reputation for chasing women. Maybe he regretted his past. Maybe it was a one-time thing. The Hill was a hard place to keep secrets, and yet only four people seem to know about his dirty little past.

Quatterman knew.

Wagner knew.

Wagner's ex-girlfriend knew.

And the young Page who Quatterman was involved with, he knew.

CHAPTER 10

WAGNER ENJOYED WATCHING the lawmaker squirm. A clap of thunder outside the window made the nervous man jump and land with a thud back in the leather chair.

"It's just a thunderstorm, Dan. We could use the rain after a month of drought," he said.

"Uh-huh. We need rain not lightning. I need to get back to my office." The color was returning to the man's face. He stood and looked directly at Wagner as he stated in a businesslike tone, "Thompson will resign his position. He won't want a scandal to scar the party. I am going to nominate you to be the succeeding Speaker of the House."

Before Wagner could react, Quatterman left the room. He did not like the man, yet he knew the man wielded power in the House. Blackmail was a powerful bargaining chip. How did the man know Thompson would not fight the allegations? He could not deny that he wanted to be the Speaker of the House. Any ambitious lawmaker would want that job. Now he understood the earlier phone call. She knew the scuttlebutt also.

Why did she not just tell him what was going on?

How did she find out so soon?

Next phone call he would ask her. But now he needed to contact Thompson to express his support and concern. The

Speaker's number was on his landline's speed dial list. He started to press the button then stopped. He rubbed the nape of his neck and closed his eyes as he took deep breaths to relax. Quatterman probably knew as soon as he walked out of the office, he would call Thompson. Devastated, Thompson would be doing as much damage control as possible. He needed to be cautious, not appear too supportive of a man others wanted brought down on ethics charges.

He decided to delay the call to Thompson. Not because he was a coward. It was important to know the best way to proceed. He did not want to be caught in the crossfire. Right now, he needed more information about the situation unfolding in the House. He quickly pushed the speed dial button number five. Within a minute the door to his office opened.

"You need to see me, Mr. Wagner?" Megan said as she held her iPhone in one hand. No longer did an assistant need to take short hand or carry a memo pad. She used her phone to take notes. It amazed him to watch her thumbs dance across the screen of the phone as he dictated notes. He had an iPhone and knew how to text, Snapchat, Facebook, Twitter and all the other things you could do with such a small device. Yet, he did not use it like the other congressmen. This small invention had ruined many careers. He preferred the old fashion communication, face to face.

"I do. I need your help learning more about the situation with Congressman Thompson."

"What can I do?"

"I need you to find out what gossip is being whispered in the corridors. Any dirty laundry *Roll Call* has gotten on the Speaker of the House."

Roll Call, a newspaper published in Washington, D.C. covered the U.S. Congress. When *Roll Call's* gossip blog exposed the ethic charges against Thompson, it would be like cancer had spread to the lymph nodes. Not only would Thompson's career be over as Speaker of the House, but his career in Washington would be dead as well.

"Right now, I'm a little shocked by all this," Wagner continued. "I knew there was an ethics investigation against Mark. But, I assumed he would survive any witch hunt. The enmity against Mark is his bullish style of leadership in his two years as speaker. He had to be tough to force members to pass major bills. Mark deserves a lot of credit for fighting against partisan polarization. If he does decide to resign, then Congressman Quatterman said he will nominate me for speaker." He saw no surprise look on the young woman's face.

"This is good news for you, isn't it, though?" She smiled weakly.

"Sure, politically speaking. I just hate that it will happen on these terms."

"I know you have a lot of respect for him. I will find out as much as I can."

"Thanks Megan. You are a good sounding board."

When she turned, and opened the office door, she literally ran into the Speaker of the House. Her cell phone tumbled from her hand.

"Excuse me. I am so sorry Congressman Thompson," Megan said as she reached down to retrieve her phone. "I did not expect you to be coming in as I was leaving,"

"Don't apologize. It was my fault. I can be like a charging bull once I know where I am headed."

The words captured the perfect description of the man entering his office. When Thompson wanted to get something done, he ruled the house with an iron fist to get it done fast.

"Alan, we need to talk," Thompson said.

Thompson was five foot six inches with the lifts he put in his shoes to make him taller. Even at sixty-seven years, he still had plenty of gray hair. His unruly busy eyebrows made him look like Andy Rooney from *60 Minutes*. The unmistakable stench of cigarette smoke permeated his clothes.

Out of respect, Wagner rose from his chair behind his desk and motioned with his hand toward the leather couch. "Please, Mark, have a seat. Can I offer you something to drink?"

"Quit the sympathy shit, Alan. Has your office been checked for bugs?"

"Bugs? You think my office is bugged?"

"Let's talk in the cafeteria," Thompson said with a deep raspy voice.

The cafeteria was in the basement of the building. Once inside they sat at a table away from other patrons.

"You know," Wagner began, "I am sorry about the ethic charges being drummed up against you, Mark. We both know next to other legislatures you seem like a choirboy."

"Yeah. Somebody has an agenda, all right. That is what bothers me. Some of the dirt they dug up was impossible to find."

"Mark, it is not impossible or even hard to find records or people who know you used federally funded vehicles and planes for personal trips."

"Shit, Alan. I gave them that dirt for the ethics violation. I had to throw them a bone. I needed a way out."

Surprised, Wagner asked, "What are you saying? You framed yourself?"

"Twenty-five years ago, I was a young naive aspiring lawyer

who wanted to change the system. I hated seeing the rich filling their pockets by supporting politicians. I wanted to clean up politics. What I needed to succeed was votes and money to win elections. It was not an easy battle. I lost more elections than I won."

Wagner listened to his friend and thought he knew what Thompson was getting at. *Money and power can corrupt even a good man.* "Are you being bullied by a big supporter? We can fight this. You don't need to let them win." But, what his friend and colleague said next could never have been predicted.

"It is not like what you think. My skeleton has blood on its hands. I did not expect my past to hold me hostage. By stepping down on the ethics charge, I am breaking the bondage. I can't tell you the details. It was a long time ago. I only tell you this now as a warning."

"Warning?" Wagner was perplexed. "What are you talking about? We need to face this thing, whatever it is."

"Don't be stupid Alan. Just be careful who you trust in life. You have no friends when you have power."

CHAPTER 11

FRIDAY THE 13TH was considered unlucky in some cultures. Although Julia was not superstitious, she had a premonition this was going to be a bad Friday. After yesterday's events, she was unable to concentrate on her job. Her supervisor, *the bitch*, had asked her if everything was okay at home. She managed a weak smile saying her grandmother was having a few health issues, but otherwise everything was fine. There was a grain of truth in what she said. Telling her supervisor all the details might not be the best course for now. She stayed tight-lipped, not giving the woman ammo to use against her. Her supervisor was the office drone. A spy, gathering information to use against employees for upper management. The woman, only a few years older than herself, had brown-nosed her way up the corporate ladder. Ingratiation and flattery, along with tattletales on co-workers, was her recipe for success in this company. Her supervisor could only look good by making others look bad.

The eight-hour workday was passing too slowly. She needed to figure out what to do with Elke. Tonight, she promised to take her to bingo, yet they needed to talk. Julia pulled out her planner and began to make notes. At the top of the page she wrote, *Emergency Action Plan* with numbered steps.

1. *Take Elke to doctor and get a medical evaluation*
2. *Call Harmony to discuss new living arrangements*
3. *Figure out financially how to pay for....*

In her peripheral vision, she saw the head pop up and glare down at her.

"I'm busy, Krystyna. I have too much on my plate now to talk."

"Honestly, you don't look good. Your hair looks like a bird nest and you have dark circles under your eyes. And now you are writing down a very depressing bucket list. What happened last night?" Her friend was not known for tact.

"I'm not sure what is happening." Julia shook her head. She started to fill her friend in on last night's events when Krystyna instantly put her finger to her lips and dropped out of sight.

A man in a business suit walked up to her cube opening and said, "Good morning, Julia." It was the audit manager of the company. She was surprised he remembered her name. "I want to congratulate you on the Johnston audit. Very good work."

"Yes, stellar work, Julia." The backstabbing tattletale drone standing behind the manager appeared. She was doing what she does best, sucking up to management.

"Thank you, Mr. Stephens. Your compliment means a lot."

"I hear you are having family issues," he said. "I want you to know if you need personal time to handle them, that won't be a problem for the company."

"I appreciate your concern." Julia felt her blood pressure rising. The tattletale drone did not waste time telling the manager about her taking time off to care for her grandmother. "It is nothing serious. My grandmother is fine now." She could not even think of a good lie.

"Glad to hear it."

"Yes, we are happy she is fine." The bitch sounded like a parrot.

"We have a big project coming up from one of our largest

clients and I need to know I can count on you."

Julia quickly closed her planner and feigned a smile. "Absolutely, Mr. Stephens. You can count on me."

The two strolled away as she sunk in her faux leather swivel chair. "I know it. I'm going to get fired."

She expected to see the head pop up but Krystyna walked around and stood in the doorway of her cubicle. She climbed to over 6 feet in her cork accented beige heels. Her curves were hard not to notice in the fitted tribal print dress short enough to let her long legs catch everybody's attention. Her red hair, subtle make-up, and bold red lipstick made her model material. Julia stared at her friend and sunk lower in her chair. It was a moment when she secretly hated everything around her, including herself. "Damn, Krystyna. Why don't you become a model? Why are you working in this pathetic place?" Julia let her insecurities loose.

"Quit whining, Julia. Don't let that office suck-up get you down. Tonight is Friday night. Bingo night. I know you are tired because you look like shit, so why don't I take your grandmother to bingo and let you have time to rest?" Her friend tilted her head to the side as her eyes sparkled.

Julia thought for a second about her friend. *If I were a lesbian, she could be my girl-friend. Not only is she beautiful and smart, but now she wants to take Elke to bingo.*

"Ordinarily, I would put up an argument. I do need some time to regroup and decide what to do with Elke. However, I'm not sure if the old geezers at the bingo parlor can handle it if you stroll in looking like that." Julia laughed.

She filled her friend in on last night's events without interruption. Krystyna seemed concerned when she mentioned the gun. She asked if she knew how to handle a gun, what model it was, and if she bought a gun safe. Reassuring her friend that the gun was in a safe place where her grandmother couldn't get to it made Krystyna act relaxed.

"Just call me if you get scared," Krystyna said, "I don't live that far from you."

"Thanks. Right now, I need a good friend. Can you come over around 6:30 tonight? Bingo starts at 7:30. You can meet my grandmother and if you decide she is too wacko for you, then I can take her."

"Funny. Some people think I'm the wacko."

Julia added, "Because you are." They laughed.

The thought of Krystyna waltzing into bingo night at the Baptist Church creating a frenzy of gossip from the blue haired old ladies gave her a chuckle. If she wasn't so tired, she would be tempted to go with Elke and Krystyna just to witness the commotion her friend would stir up.

She was glad her friend offered to take her grandmother to bingo. Elke was obsessed with the game. It seemed odd that her grandmother enjoyed playing bingo. Growing up, her grandmother hated playing games of any kind.

Walking to Metro Center after work, she cautiously monitored her surroundings. No Volvo in sight. Her gun was tucked in her bag. Just in case. She did not share the fact her gun was in her pocketbook with Krystyna. A weapon at work was against company policy. She was a rule follower, yet circumstances forced her to take a chance. If she had the gun with her, then her grandmother could not get to it and if she was in danger the weapon might be the equalizing force she needed.

After boarding the subway, she noticed a man close to her age getting on. He was a bit short of 6 feet, dark buzz-cut black hair, intense dark brown eyes, and a strong jawline accented by a close-cropped beard, more like a 5 o'clock shadow. The man was wide-shouldered and big armed making the leather jacket fit snug. Remembering earlier what Krystyna said about how she looked, Julia hung her head down pretending to look for something in her pocketbook. The disinterested man never looked her way making her feel like an idiot for staring at him. *He's probably a loser. A good-looking loser.*

The twenty-five-minute ride to Forest Glen Metro gave her enough time to catch up on reading her emails. She made a few notes in her phone on what she needed to discuss with her grandmother tomorrow after she was rested and ready to confront the difficult problem. Departing the subway, she walked across the platform to the elevator, which carried her up to street level. Forest Glen Metro was too deep to have escalators. There were a handful of people walking to the parking lot to retrieve their cars and head home or to a local bar after work. She didn't see the dark featured man she had spied on the subway.

Driving home, she continuously checked her rear-view mirror to ensure there was no black Volvo tailing her. In fact, there was no car following her. Elke taught her to be cautious and always aware of her surroundings. The woman taught her many things that most children never learned. How to shoot a gun, self-defense, defensive driving, and reading body language were among the skills she mastered. Her grandmother always worried something bad would happen just like the untimely death of her parents. Elke never seemed to fully recover from the loss of her daughter.

Walking up to the front door of her duplex, Julia hoped to experience the wonderful smell of dinner being cooked in her kitchen. As soon as she opened the door, she knew there would not be a hot meal tonight unless she cooked it herself. On the small round dining table were two plates with what looked like sandwiches and chips. One glass filled with milk set by a plate and another glass with wine next to the other plate.

"Julia you're home. We need to eat and get ready to go to bingo. I can't miss tonight." Her grandmother was rushing around putting everything on the table.

Julia smirked remembering all the sandwiches she had consumed as a child. Her grandmother was a wonderful cook, but did not do it often. "Looks great, Elke, let's eat."

During dinner, she told her grandmother about her friend wanting to meet her and go to a night of bingo. The sparkle in her grandmother's eyes faded. "Bingo night is our time together," Elke reminded her.

"It usually is, but my friend offered to go with you." She covered a yawn and continued, "I'm exhausted and need to rest. We will have many more bingo nights together. You'll like her. She is very colorful, just like you."

The doorbell rang as her grandmother protested going to bingo without her. She held up her hand to silence Elke and sauntered over to the door. Opening the door, she stared with an expression of stunned surprise at the sight of her friend standing there.

Krystyna's flamboyant attire was not only toned down, it was gone. Her friend wore black yoga pants, a white button down shirt, flats, and the bright red lipstick was now clear lip gloss. In her hand, she had Julia's favorite wine, Terra Barossa.

Krystyna stepped around Julia and walked over to her grandmother extending her hand.

"It is a pleasure to finally meet you, Elke. My name is

Krystyna. Julia has told me so many wonderful things about you. You are an amazing woman." Krystyna sounded sincere. Julia turned and shook her head in disbelief at what was unfolding before her. Her grandmother enjoyed the flattery. Elke's face lit up.

"Well, thank you, my dear. I hear you are taking me to bingo so we can give Julia a break. That is very sweet of you. Sit down so we can talk while Julia cleans up the kitchen. We have about twenty minutes before we need to leave."

Krystyna held up the bottle of wine, "Would anybody care for a glass of wine? This is Julia's favorite and I hoped you would like it also."

"Yes that would be lovely." Her grandmother held up her empty glass.

Krystyna took the empty wine glass from her grandmother and winked at Julia as they both headed to the kitchen.

Her friend was a miracle worker. This was going to be a glorious evening.

"I want you to relax tonight Julia and after a soaking bath, sit in your ratty old chair and have a glass of your favorite wine." Krystyna put her arm around Julia. "I worry about you."

"I owe you big time for this favor," Julia said with conviction in her tone. "You are a wonderful friend."

"All I want is you to promise me that you will relax tonight and, while drinking your wine, think of me yelling bingo. I plan on cheating."

Julia could not help laughing at her friend. "I promise. You and Elke together tonight will make headlines."

Cleaning up the kitchen, she heard Krystyna and Elke talking about her and snickering. She was glad Elke seemed to like her friend, but wished they would change the subject.

Maybe tomorrow her grandmother would be more reasonable about moving out of her place. She wanted her quiet bland life back. Almost thirty years old, she needed her routine.

Julia finished cleaning the kitchen and walked into the dining room. She glanced at the clock on the wall and said, "You two better get going, so you aren't late for bingo."

Krystyna stood up and excused herself to go to the bathroom. As soon as she closed the bathroom door, her grandmother leaned over and whispered in her ear, "I am not going anywhere with your friend."

"What?" she asked with irritation in her voice. "What are you talking about? I heard you from the kitchen and it sounded like you two hit it off."

"Did you know that she is Russian?"

"Oh, good grief, Elke," Julia answered. "Her parents are from Russia. She was born in the United States. Which makes her an American citizen."

"You know how I feel about Russians."

"Elke, the Cold War is over. It ended in 1989. If you think Krystyna is a Russian spy, then keep your friends close and your enemies closer." She pointed her index and middle fingers toward her eyes and then at Elke's eyes.

"Maybe you are right, dear. We do need to keep close tabs on her."

Julia heard a flush, water running and then the bathroom door opened. Krystyna said enthusiastically, "Ready, Elke, to win the big bucks?"

After they left, she took a long hot bubble bath and then slipped into her comfy pajamas. She went into the kitchen and poured herself a full glass of the red wine Krystyna had brought over, ambled over to her comfy chair and curled up.

She took a sip of the wine while she continued making notes in what Krystyna said was a depressing bucket list. Lists helped organize her thoughts. The list would let her figure out how to handle the situation with her grandmother. She hoped Elke would not be a problem for her friend.

After fifteen to twenty minutes, her drowsy state made it hard to concentrate. She took a few more sips of wine and began to feel overwhelming fatigue. The words on the notepad were blurry making it impossible to read what she had just written. Her body was so relaxed; she could not manage enough strength to raise her arms. Her head dropped back against the chair, her mind disoriented.

It was a struggle to keep her lids from closing. The room went in and out of focus. She felt a detachment from her body and her physical surroundings. Closing and opening her eyes, a dark figure moved toward her. The man standing by her chair bent down and she could smell his bad breath. His face near hers, she recognized Volvo man as he began to grip her shoulders from behind.

Suddenly, the man let go and turned around catching a blow to his face. She managed to lift her head in time to see Volvo man fall to the floor. Another man with massive arms walked over to her, picked up the wine glass and lifted it to his nose. Then he reached down taking her face in his hands and said in a deep voice that sounded like an echo, "Julia, are you okay?" It was the man from the subway. The dark-haired man. Her mind kept repeating, *how does he know my name?* Her eyes blinked several times seeing a movement behind the dark-haired man. Volvo man was pointing a gun at him. She screamed, but no sound was heard. The dark-haired man turned, grabbed the arm holding the gun, and pulled it toward him. An arm twist and the gun dropped to the ground. Volvo man, using his other hand, hit the dark-haired man in the face causing him to stagger backward. Volvo man reached down to get his gun as the other man grabbed him from behind. The man's massive arm wrapped around Volvo man's neck as the other hand struck him in the side. She saw the intense determination as the arm tightened around the man's neck. Then the body being strangled went limp. Volvo man slid slowly to the floor and did not move.

She struggled to hold her head up. Her mind was going numb. A strong arm wrapped around her shoulders and beneath her legs. She felt the hardness of his chest against her body and a tingle of excitement that came with it. Her body relaxed more. The deep voice in her ear was soothing. She drifted into a deep slumber.

CHAPTER 12

THE NEXT DAY, Julia awoke in her bed. She had no recollection of getting into bed. The memories of last night were blurred and fragmented. Placing her hands on her temples, she moaned. Her head throbbed. When she stood, her legs were unsteady so she held on to the nightstand for a moment. She never could hold her liquor.

Stumbling into the living room, she kept blinking her eyes and massaging her temples as she scanned the room. She looked hard at her cozy chair and had disconnected flashbacks of last night.

There was no evidence of a fight or a dead body. The dream seemed so real. She noticed the door to her grandmother's room was open. Peeking inside she saw the bed was made and her grandmother was not in there. Thinking Elke must be in the kitchen, she turned and wobbled in that direction when she heard several rapid knocks on the back door. The noise startled her since people did not come to the back door very often and especially not in the morning. Cautiously, she approached the constant knocking and stood to the side of the kitchen window glancing out the blinds. It was Krystyna. She jumped back. Her heartbeat sped up pumping enough blood to help clear her foggy mind as panic set in.

Oh, my God. Something has happened to Elke.

Quickly turning the deadbolt, she unlocked the door and

swung it open. Before she could speak, Krystyna almost breathless said, "Get dressed, you have got to get out of here."

"What happened? Where is she?" Elke must be in harm's way.

Krystyna stepped inside putting both hands on her arms like she was trying to steady Julia before she spoke. "I got a call this morning from Oleg."

"Oleg? The janitor from work?"

"Yes. He said Lynda was found dead at the office."

"Lynda, our supervisor? The spying work drone?"

"Yes."

"Oh, no." Julia squeezed her friend's arms. "How did she die? A heart attack?"

"No." Without flinching, Krystyna said, "She was murdered."

Julia stepped back befuddled as if her friend had said she had seen an alien space ship.

"I can't believe this. Just yesterday I talked to her."

"Well, I haven't told you the worst part. Do you know where Oleg found the body?"

"I don't understand, Krystyna, why would Oleg call you? Are you still sleeping with him?"

"He called me because he knows you and I are good friends and Lynda's body was found in your cubicle."

"That can't be. Why would she be in my cubicle?"

"That is why you have to get out of town now. Everybody knows you hate her. We need to hide till we figure out who did this."

"I am confused. What's happening? Where's Elke?" She felt her knees trying to buckle. "I have to sit down, look for Elke, and get a lawyer." Krystyna helped her to the sofa in the living room where she sat down.

The knocking on the front door drew both their attention. "Don't answer," Krystyna blurted out. "It's probably the police."

She felt disoriented and grumbled, "Why the hell are the police at my door?"

She knew it was a good chance the police were back. Especially if a dead body had been found in her cubicle. This did not make sense. A feeling of doom overcame her. She heard Elke's voice telling her that when things were tough, "Batten-down-the-hatches and figure it out." Damn she hated when her grandmother said those sayings.

She vigorously massaged her thighs and knees like she was infusing them with enough energy to move. Taking a deep breath, she forced herself to stand and walk over to open the door. A familiar face greeted her. It was one of the officers who had been to her home the other night. Both officers flashed their badges. She heard herself mumble, "When it rains it pours."

The familiar officer explained what had happened at her workplace and that they needed her to come with them to the station for questioning. She was not under arrest, just routine.

At their insistence, Julia hurriedly got dressed and left with the officers to go to the police station in D.C. Krystyna had found a note on the kitchen table from her grandmother saying that she was out for a walk. Julia asked her friend to remain at her duplex and wait for Elke to return so that her grandmother would not worry. Krystyna insisted she call a lawyer to meet her at the police station. She was beginning to think that Krystyna thought she was guilty.

Riding in the back of the police cruiser to the Metropolitan

Police Department in D.C., Julia tried to clear her mind and sort out the tangled mess she was in. She remembered her gun was still in her purse. At the police station, they would make her put her purse through the metal detector; an alarm would go off. How would she explain bringing a weapon to the police station? Maybe her best course of action would be to explain her mistake now to the officers.

"Excuse me, Officer Dooley, but I did something very stupid while rushing to accompany you to the police station," she said noticing him staring at her in his rear-view mirror. "Without thinking, I forgot to do something before I left my house."

"Yea, what is that, Miss Bagal?"

"I know this probably happens a lot," she stammered. "It's silly, but I forgot to leave my gun at home."

Before she could feign a laugh, the officer in the passenger seat wheeled around while the officer driving pulled to the curb and hit the brakes. "Hands in the air, now," snapped the passenger officer.

With her feet spread and her hands against the police car, she wondered if Krystyna was right. She should have run. The passenger officer had seized her purse and was now searching it.

Both officers appeared pissed. They instructed her to turn around and face them.

"What is going on here, Miss Bagal?" The passenger officer shoved her purse into her chest.

"It's an honest mistake. I just did not remember to leave my gun at home, like when people go to an airport and get caught with a gun at security." *Oh, shit, that did not come out right.*

"Where is the gun, now?"

She studied both officers in front of her and realized they did not have her gun. Her hand rummaged inside her purse, no gun. "Oh my, I forgot it is in my other purse. I am so sorry. I did not mean to cause trouble." She hoped right now her lying rivaled Elke's.

Back inside the police car, she rechecked her purse thinking somehow the gun might have been missed. Where the hell was her gun? Elke. Always Elke. All her troubles started the day Elke left Harmony. Somehow her grandmother was at the bottom of this.

She was escorted inside the Metro, now named the Henry J. Daly Building in honor of Sergeant Henry J. Daly, a 28-year veteran of the Metro who was killed in 1994 by an armed intruder. It was a tribute to a devoted homicide sergeant. She had feared mobs of reporters would be waiting on the steps of the building shoving microphones in her face and shouting, *did you kill the tattletale office drone?* Her fears were unfounded. The building was bustling with people headed mindlessly to their destination with proverbial blinders on. Nobody knew her or paid any attention to the fact that police officers were escorting her to an office for questioning about a dead body in her cubicle. She had watched too many drama shows on TV.

A female policewoman said, "We heard about you. Funny how trouble seems to follow you."

Julia did not feel like responding. Funny was not the word she would have used. She was sure anything and everything she said would just be fuel for the fire being lit under her. She had no alibi for last night. They knew she had a gun. With her luck, it would match the murder weapon. She needed Elke to hide it.

Sitting behind a desk with a computer, the police officer motioned for her to sit as he started navigating to a screen where he would enter her statement. Nervous, Julia thought she should tell the officer she did hate her supervisor, but so did everybody in the office. Maybe it would help if he knew she was not a violent person and would never use her gun unless she needed to protect herself. Gun. They knew she had a gun, yet did not ask her to turn it over when they came to her home. She decided to keep her mouth shut.

The interrogator behind the desk looked like a grandfather. His head was bald and he wore reading glasses pulled down on his nose. Besides being portly around the middle he did not look like a couch potato. There was an assortment of pictures on his desk of young children. Probably, grandkids.

Prior to initiating questions, he made a lame attempt to establish rapport. He apologized for the inconvenience of having to spend Saturday at the police station. Continuing, he asked about her plans for the day. She just shook her head and told him she needed to get home soon to check on her elderly grandmother who she was taking care of. He feigned interest in her life and said he had a daughter her age living in another state who worked long hours just like she did. She was beginning to like the man until he asked her about the incident the other night at her home where she claimed a man in a Volvo had followed her home. He overemphasized the word claimed too often. He read aloud the statement she gave to the officers that night on why a gun was discharged.

"So it was an accident?"

"Yes. I already gave the information to the officers that night at my home. What does this have to do with the death of my supervisor?" She began fidgeting around in her seat wondering if maybe they found Elke and already had the murder weapon. Her pistol.

"It would be helpful if you knew any reason why your supervisor would be found strangled in your cubicle. Do you think there is a connection with the audit you were working on?"

Strangled? She had assumed her supervisor was shot. Why, she was not sure. Krystyna never told her how Lynda died. The word strangled unleashed images of last night. She remembered the man wrapping his massive arms around Volvo man's neck. Volvo man going limp and slithering from the man's grip.

She shivered and started to respond to the interrogator when somebody started yelling down the hall behind her. A young man with his hands handcuffed was being escorted by two large police officers. He was screaming about police brutality and demanding a lawyer. A woman officer approached and whatever she said calmed him down. Julia turned back in her chair to face the interrogator when something clicked. She twisted back around in her chair and stretched her eyes wide to try to discern a man standing near where the young man had caused a scene. It was him. The man from the subway, the one in her duplex last night was talking to a police officer.

Pointing in his direction, she stood and in a heightened voice said, "That's him."

She started to head toward him when the interviewing officer ordered her to stay seated and let him investigate. "You sure it's him?"

"Positive," she said trying to convince both the officer and herself. If that man was in her place last night and did save her from Volvo man, then it wasn't a dream. But would he confess to it?

The officer, with his hand resting on his gun holster, strolled down the hall over to the dark-haired man. The two men faced each other. After a few exchanges of words, the officer's hand on his holster relaxed and fell to his side. Then the officer turned sideways and nodded in her direction. The stranger looked directly at her. His face gave the appearance he did not recognize her. A good poker face or she was wrong about him in her duplex last night. She wished the officer had allowed her to talk to the dark-haired man.

When the officer walked back to his desk, he had a smug look on his face. "You did say the man following you was driving a black Volvo? This man drives a silver pickup that was broken into last night near a club on the opposite side of town from your home. He says he has never seen you before and, on top of all that, he is a decorated U.S. Army paratrooper."

It was pointless to tell the policeman she meant he was the one who killed the man following her in the Volvo. Her memory was still fuzzy from last night. Explaining what she could not prove would only make her story sound more bizarre and unbelievable. She did not know how this could possibly be connected to her supervisor's murder. But, it had to be since she did not believe in coincidences.

The clock on the wall indicated she had been there forty-five minutes and it looked like it was going to be a lot longer before they had squeezed all the information they felt she was willing to give. The interrogating officer taking her statement wanted a lot of details about the Johnston audit she had just finished working on. Such as who worked on it with her and had she found anything unusual in her audit. While her initial suspicions were wild speculation, Julia was now truly fearing that she was considered a suspect. Or worse yet, the intended victim.

There was no need to have her take a polygraph test. A

noted polygraphist, John E. Reid developed an entire system of questions to ask suspects and watch their reaction. The interrogating officer was more interested in her reactions to the questions than her responses. He must have been trained to identify those who were deceptive in their answers. She remembered rushing to complete the audit so she could check on Elke and perhaps she missed an important detail. A detail that got her supervisor murdered? None of this was making sense. The Johnston Company was large and did international business, but there was nothing in the audit that sent up red flags. After another thirty minutes, she asked to use the ladies' bathroom. There was something she needed to know. She knew just the person to call.

Inside the ladies' room she heard the phone ring twice before he answered.

"Hello Alvin, I have a big favor to ask."

CHAPTER 13

CARVER HAD DISAGREED with Addy about following Julia into the police station when she was taken in for questioning. He told Addy there was a strong possibility, that if spotted, Julia might recognize him from last night even though she had been drugged. Addy, in her usual fashion, did not like hearing her idea was a bad idea. She just instructed him to stay out of her line of sight and find out what the police knew or suspected. Easy for her to say.

Inside the station, everything was working to his advantage until a punk started yelling some bullshit about police brutality and wanting a lawyer. It created such a scene that everyone turned their heads to see what the commotion was about—including Julia. He thought the young brunette missed recognizing him until she turned back around a second time, stood, and pointed in his direction. His military training allowed him to develop an internal strategy as the police officer stopped her from walking over and then moved in his direction. With no way of knowing what she had told the officer or could remember from the night before, he contemplated his options. Mentally, he practiced countermeasures the government had taught him. Be prepared for the unexpected.

The dead body the police were investigating was a woman not a man. He was ready when the police officer approached him. The officer did not mention the incident last night in Julia's home. After a few questions the police officer apologized, shook his hand and headed back in the direction he came.

He used the ruse that his wallet had been stolen out of his truck parked at a bar across town from Julia's place. It was a good plan. Establish an alibi in case she convinced the police he was at her home last night. And his was solid. Since he had been in town, he and the female bartender had become good friends. She was a widow. Two years ago, the police mistook her husband for an armed robber and killed him. If the police checked out his story, he knew she would back his lie.

The police at Metro PD were very helpful, especially after he told them that he served in the 82nd Airborne Infantry Division. One of the officers was also a paratrooper and had served in Afghanistan and did not have any problem freely sharing information about the murder case. Thanking the officer for all his help and saying they should meet some time for drinks and swap Army stories, he left the building. Outside, he pulled out his cell phone and called the woman to let her know what he had found out.

"Where are you?" the woman asked.

"I just left Metro PD," he said.

"Did she see you?"

"Yes. I think she has some recollection of last night."

"I told you not to let her see you."

"And I told you it was not a good idea for me to go inside the station in case she did see me."

"Well, what did you find out?" she demanded in an irritated voice.

"They believe the audit she worked on has something to do with the murder. Seems the company she audited has Russian ties. The janitor who found the dead body emigrated from

Russia fifteen years ago. Heard the CIA mentioned. All of this is locked down tight from the media. Also, I was told they think she knows more about the case than she is telling. She will be there for another hour or so."

"That will be good. Keeps her preoccupied for a while."

"How about the guy stuffed in the trunk of the Volvo?" he asked.

"He's been taken care of," she replied in a matter-of-fact tone.

"Details?"

"You hungry?"

She told him to meet her in ten minutes at an upscale Italian restaurant located on Pennsylvania Avenue not far from Metro PD. She gave him directions and said she would be in a booth in the back where they could talk in private.

He wasn't sure what to expect from an upscale Italian restaurant since he was a meat and potato kind of guy, but he needed answers.

Inside Fiola, the lunch crowd had filled most of the seating. There was one empty bar stool. She told him to head toward the back of the restaurant and look for her sitting in a booth. Many years had passed since he last saw her, however he somehow knew he would recognize her. The woman was unforgettable. He spotted her sitting in a semi curved cream-colored leather booth. A glass of red wine was sitting on the oval table in front of her.

She stood and waved as he moved in her direction. The years had deepened the worry lines and crow's feet around her bright blue eyes. Her thick wavy hair was long and brushed back behind her shoulders. He could tell the woman still had her figure. The light green pullover top and slim gray pants accented her curves.

"You haven't changed," he said. "You look the same as I remembered." He gave her an embrace.

"Bullshit. But, thanks for the attempt at flattery." She was still the spunky woman he recalled. "Would you like a drink? I am afraid they probably don't serve beer?"

He shook his head. "I was surprised to hear from you after so many years," he said as he slid in the booth. "I thought the day you said goodbye would be the last time I ever saw you."

"Life is funny sometimes…how paths cross." She pushed a brown paper bag sitting on the seat next to her toward him. "I needed someone I could trust."

He held the bag under the table and opened it. Inside were a SIG 229 and a white envelope. Leaning forward, he furtively scanned the crowd of people in the restaurant. Grabbing the gun, he tucked it in his pants beneath his jacket. He placed the thick white security envelope on the table.

"Thanks for bringing me a gun. I don't think D.C. is a safe place for law abiding citizens," he said in a tongue-in-cheek manner.

"What do you expect? It's a city full of politicians. Money and power is the root of most of the evil in D.C."

"Most evil?" He kept his focus on her face. "What else is evil in this city?"

"Russians." She took a sip of wine, let it rest in her mouth before swallowing and then told him, "There should be more than enough money in the envelope to pay your expenses."

"Before we continue, I need to know what is going on with you and this girl. I have been tailing her and until last night nothing seemed out of the ordinary. Then a man tries to kidnap her."

"She is a very attractive young lady, don't you think?" He could tell the articulate woman was fishing for something, but he did not plan on falling in the trap.

"Yes. She is very attractive. Is her boyfriend stalking or threatening her?" He continued before she answered, "Last night upped the stakes. All you told me was not to let her out of my sight and to protect her if anyone tried to harm her. Maybe it's time to call the law and get them involved."

A waiter draped in a white apron walked up to the table holding two plates. "Who ordered the Ahi Tuna Caesar Salad and who gets the Rosemary Roasted Beef Tenderloin?"

He faced the woman, drew his brows together and rubbed his chin.

"The beef tenderloin is his." She looked at him and shrugged her shoulders. "Don't look so confused. You always told me you were a meat and potatoes man, so I took the liberty of ordering. I don't have much time before I must leave," she said in a perfunctory manner not allowing him to object.

The meal looked delicious. Normally he would not like having someone order for him, but he would not object this time.

The woman nonchalantly looked around the restaurant as she put a bite of fish in her mouth. She looked back at him and seemed to study his face, as if unsure of what she was going to say next. He thought she might have forgotten his question.

"I have a clandestine op I must complete," she lowered her voice. "The local LEOs are not able to help. This is too big for regular law enforcement officers. It is hard to know who you can trust and Metro PD has been known for corruption. Enough money can easily persuade a person to cross the line and work for the enemy. I am asking you to be patient. A lot is at stake. There is nothing more I can share with you right now."

"Can't or won't?"

"Doesn't matter. I need you." She shrugged. "I know, without a doubt, I can trust you. Money will not influence you. You still have your military values. Loyalty, honor, and integrity flow through your veins. Men like you are not easy to find in this town. Let me track down a few leads and verify the information. Then I will share what I have learned. I need to know you will keep the girl safe. In a week or two, this will all be over and you can return to your gym."

"A week or two? A week or two of surveillance on a good-looking girl who might or might not be involved in a murder where the CIA might be getting their toes wet due to Russian involvement? Sounds like your past. And, obviously your present." He grinned at the woman. "Count me in."

"We both know how the past can haunt you," she said in a warning voice.

"One question," he asked, "what if the police have you on their radar?"

"That's impossible."

"Why is that?"

"Because, I have been declared dead."

CHAPTER 14

HER CELL PHONE didn't have a strong signal inside the police department's bathroom. Julia wasn't sure if the reception was any better in the hall, but she did not want anybody listening to her call. After explaining her situation, Alvin agreed to find out what he could about the Johnston audit. He didn't question the ethics or legality of obtaining the files to review. The only questions to her was she okay and how long did he have to get the needed information?

When she clicked off the call, a rush of guilt accompanied her thoughts. Alvin was doing her a favor that could cost him his job. He liked her and wanted to help. Julia wished she liked him the way he liked her. She wasn't sure how she would ever be able to thank him. Maybe some relationships need time to blossom.

She returned to the desk of the interrogation officer. He was busy talking on the phone and taking notes. Julia sat down and tried to act nonchalant as her eyes strained to see what the officer was writing on the pad. The officer must have noticed because he abruptly ended the call and turned his notepad over. She faked a smile and tried to relax her tense body.

"Do you have all the information you need? I am very upset about the death of my supervisor and need to get home to check on my grandmother. Her health is not good," she said hoping the officer would buy her lie.

"I know this is hard for you, Miss Bagal," the officer said skeptically. "A few more questions and you can be on your way."

She stared at the clock on the wall for a moment, thinking about all the questions she had already answered. At times during the interrogation, she believed it would be wise to get a lawyer. Yet, a voice in her head told her that making a demand for a lawyer might make her look guilty of strangling her supervisor. *How many times had she wanted to strangle the bitch? Now it had happened. And in her cubicle.*

Another thirty minutes of questions.

Some of the same questions were repeated, but in a reworded manner. She hoped she was consistent in her answers. There was nothing to hide. Except maybe her gun. She did promise the officer the other night she would get a gun safe and lock up the gun. What if Elke, during her walk, pulled the gun out and in her confused state shot somebody? Her grandmother had said and done so many strange things lately, who knew what she might be capable of. The other night, she tried to shoot the man sitting in the Volvo. She had to get her gun back as soon as she got back to her duplex.

The dark-haired man who was in her home last night had long since left the Metro PD building or, at least, was not where she could see him. She occasionally stretched her arms upward and moved her head in a smooth relaxed manner and scanned the room in search of the man.

"Are you okay?" the police officer asked.

She looked at him and answered, "Yes, of course. Why do you ask?"

"Well every few minutes you take a full look of the squad room like you're looking for someone. Are you nervous about the man you thought was following you?"

Now was her chance to come clean and tell him the truth. She swallowed hard before answering.

Finally, she said, "No, of course not. It was just that he looked so familiar. And I have a crick in my neck." She carefully rubbed the back of her neck with her fingers to prove her claim.

The police officer nodded, but he did not seem convinced. "How did you hurt your neck?"

Did he not listen when I said "crick" in my neck?

"I didn't hurt it," she assured him. "I just slept on it wrong. And you've had me sitting here for so long, it's making it worse."

"When did you do this? Yesterday?"

Now she saw where he was going with this. The pang of guilt caused distress in the pit of her stomach. Why did she lie? Again. "Do what? Sleep on it wrong? Oh, for crying out—"

Before she could finish, his desk phone rang. He picked it up and then covered the receiver with one hand.

"We are finished, Miss Bagal," he said. "Just review the statement and sign it, then you are free to go. We will contact you if we have any other questions."

She started to give a sigh of relief when he added, "You should be careful. If you remember anything when you get home that you forgot to mention, please give me a call." He handed her his card.

Why did he say *be careful?* Does he think she was the intended victim? She gave the man a thin, nervous smile and nod to acknowledge she understood what he had just said. He uncovered the mouthpiece on the phone and continued to talk to the person on the other line.

She carefully read the statement to make sure she had not incriminated herself. Then signed on the last page attesting her account to be true and accurate. She left the station, anxious to get the hell out of there and return to her duplex to see what Elke was up to and check with Alvin about what he might have discovered in the Johnston audit.

Outside the station, she pulled out her phone from her purse and called Krystyna. No answer. After several more tries she left a message to return her call immediately. When she raised her head, she checked her surroundings. Across the street from her was a man standing in the shadows. His height, broad shoulders, and dark hair were familiar. He gazed down at something in his hand. *Damn. It's him.* Excited, she checked traffic and when it was clear, dashed across the street toward him. As soon as the light uncovered his features, she paused. It was not the man from last night. She did a full 360-degree turn with her body scoping out any impending danger. Nothing unusual.

All she saw were people walking on the sidewalk unaware of the quandary she was in. Frustrated she headed to the Metro station. The police were adamant that she accompany them from her place to the station, but there were no offers to take her back home. She didn't care. She was done being interrogated and feeling guilty whenever she needed to lie. Next time she would get a lawyer. Next time. The words made her heart beat faster.

There could be no next time. She needed to get back to her home. And fast. This whole mess had Elke's name written all over it. It was well past lunchtime and her blood sugar had dropped. A wave of nausea rolled through her. Sweat trickled down the side of her face as she reached the Metro station.

The combination of stress and being hypoglycemic was taking its toll on her. Then she remembered the KIND energy bar she always kept in her purse for times like this. She found the bar and ripped it open when her phone vibrated.

She stopped at the entrance to the station to pull out her phone buried at the bottom of her Hobo bag. After, she swallowed one bite of the bar, she read the text message. *Call me ASAP*. It was from Alvin. She scrolled her contacts and then tapped the screen. It only rang once before Alvin answered.

"Julia. Can you talk?" Alvin's breathy voice made him sound like he had been jogging.

She walked away from the Metro entrance. "The Johnston audit. Did you find out why the police think it has something to do with the murder?"

Even though Alvin worked for another company, he had connections. It was called street talk. People outside your company who found out things before you even had the knowledge.

"No. Not yet," he paused a beat. "Have you seen the news? I don't think the police or the audit are your biggest problem."

"Elke. Is it Elke? Did she shoot somebody? I can't get hold of Krystyna, who is supposed to be waiting at my house for her. Please, tell me." Her voice began to quaver as she felt a moment of panic.

"No, it's not your grandmother. It's the CIA."

CHAPTER 15

DECLARED DEAD.

Words he'd heard too many times while recovering at Walter Reed Army Medical Center. There were casualties from soldiers dying on the operating table and suicide. The gruesome injuries, losing one or multiple limbs and injury to their genitals made the once super heroes fighting a war feel worthless. Mental wounds from war were hard to treat.

He came close to being declared dead himself when he flat lined three times. The doctors told him he was lucky. The woman told him he was too damn stubborn to die. He was sure she was right.

The woman explained she had been declared dead to protect her from the Russians after a covert mission went awry many years ago. She obtained a new identity after the bungled operation forced her to go dark.

He knew her as Addy. The name she used to introduce herself when they first met at his physical therapy while recovering at Walter Reed Medical Center. Addy Bravo.

He gazed across the table at the woman from his past. "I guess your real name isn't Addy Bravo?"

"No."

"Guess you won't tell me your real name?"

"It's just a name. It does not change anything. I am still the woman you knew at Walter Reed."

And she was right. It was just a name. But, she was the woman he credited for saving his life and she had secrets that she was not sharing. She had a nebulous history. Her past was not unlike his. They both worked for the government. Armed and equipped with a license to kidnap, torture, and kill with little or no impunity. He worked for the Army. She worked for the CIA.

"Is Julia involved with the Russians?" he pressed her for information.

"No," she answered and took a sip of wine.

"Does she know you are having her followed?"

"No." She smiled. Her Mona Lisa smile. "And she doesn't need to know, either. Not right now, anyway. We are both trained in interrogation, Derick. I understand you want to know more." She took a deep breath before continuing, "I know the subterranean world of clandestine operatives. Forty percent of the defense budget is secret, as is the budget of the CIA. They operate outside the rules of the law. Without your help, I cannot succeed. The girl must be kept safe."

He did not like being left in the dark about the woman's mission. Addy warned him things could get dangerous. That didn't bother him. He knew about Russians. The CIA's Cold War-era covert action program assisted the Mujahedeen in Afghanistan against the Russians.

Julia was somehow connected to what Addy was involved in. The man he subdued in her duplex had a Russian passport in his jacket pocket. Carver's training told him this was a covert operation. When covert operations go awry, things get messy. He would stick around.

"I have to go," she said as she stood up. "I will contact you soon. If something comes up and you need me," she tapped her phone, "leave me a message."

Carver started to rise, but she told him to wait a few minutes before he left. His eyes followed Addy's slow walk as she exited the room. He had connected emotionally with the woman during rehab. She stood by his side as he learned to walk again. During his darkest moments, Addy seemed to have the words to push away his nightmares. The mysterious woman had cast a spell on him all those years ago. And she was still holding him captive.

The envelope was stuffed full of cash. She had prepaid his hotel room, which was only three blocks from Julia's place. The mini fridge was stocked with beer and snacks. She wanted him to be comfortable, but mostly close to the girl while he was keeping surveillance on her. At first he believed the girl might be related to the woman, but now he wasn't sure.

He could easily give the money back to Addy and return to his gym. That would have been the easy, safe choice. He was not a man who found solace by playing it safe. Agreeing to protect Julia was probably a stupid choice, but he did owe Addy for helping him during his long painful rehab at Walter Reed.

But, there was another reason. A personal reason. He missed the adrenaline rush from the missions.

He loved his life as a paratrooper in the Army. After his recovery, the Army gave him a desk job. He left that job after six months.

At Walter Reed, he remembered Addy telling him about her past. They had jobs for the government with similar goals. Keep America safe.

He was sure there was a potential for serious blowback if the Russians were involved. The company audited by Julia had

Russian ties. Addy said the evil in D.C. was money, power and Russians.

Addy, like him, had special skills. Only her skills were different. She had been trained to lie and deceive in her job with the CIA. She could easily read people to determine their motivations and vulnerabilities. At the Farm, she learned to *spot and assess* potential sources. She became one of their top agents in recruiting foreign agents. Her cover had been blown on an assignment that resulted in the death of an innocent person. She had assumed a new identity and moved to Germany for a brief period. At least, that is what she told him.

Somebody other than himself must also be assisting Addy. That would explain how she knew the movement of Julia and the man who was following her. The body he left in the trunk of the Volvo had not been found.

Addy claimed she could trust nobody but him. She could be playing a role to keep him off track. There were many unanswered questions.

He was a lethal, highly trained soldier. The charming woman had a sinister history and might not be trustworthy.

Maybe he was back in enemy territory.

This time on U.S. soil.

CHAPTER 16

CIA?

The nightmare kept getting worse. She envisioned her grandmother on the national news waving her gun and yelling she was a spy. Krystyna was right. Just run.

"Alvin, what are you saying?" she asked. "What's on the news about the CIA?"

"I wanted to warn you before you heard the news."

"Please tell me it does not involve Elke or my audit."

"I haven't heard anything about your audit. But the CIA just confirmed they arrested a married couple as alleged *sleeper* spies. They're accused of spying for Russia for more than a decade while living in the United States."

"Why would this upset me?"

"The husband worked as a chemical engineer for Johnston."

Julia was confused. "Why would he spy on Johnston? The company is a multinational food company. It's not like Edward Snowden who leaked classified information from the National Security Agency."

"Not all the details are out. I just wanted to give you heads up. Maybe the police think this arrest has something to do with your audit."

"Thanks Alvin. I'm baffled by all this. It's almost overwhelming," she confessed. "I need to get home and check on Elke."

"I'll call you when I have something on your audit. Just be careful. There is something weird about all of this."

Alvin told her to be careful. She was now scared. Moving at a faster pace she entered the Metro station to catch the train home. She hoped desperately Elke and Krystyna were there when she arrived. Boarding the train, she scoped out the car for any suspicious people. There was an old man with a long gray scraggly beard and a worn coat sitting down. Across from him was a woman holding a baby. A group of teenagers laughing and snapping pictures with their phones kept glancing in her direction. Five other passengers on the train were on her radar. She was paranoid. She did not know what to do. Were any of the people on the train targeting her? Not wanting to draw attention to herself she sat down and ate the rest of the energy bar.

At the Forest Glen Metro Station, she exited and used her Uber app to find a driver to take her to her duplex. She instructed the Uber driver to let her out a few blocks past her place.

After the car was out of sight, she backtracked in the direction of her duplex. There were a few cars still parked along the street. Nothing out of the ordinary. She hurried to her door and tried to open it. It was locked. She fished around in her pocketbook and found her keys. When she inserted the key in the lock, her cell phone began to ring. She saw it was Krystyna.

"Where the hell are you, Krystyna? You were supposed to stay here and wait on Elke."

"I had to meet a friend in town. I waited as long as I could. I came back to your house and since Elke was still gone, I decided to circle around and see if I could find her. I found her near the Metro Station. Elke said she was hungry so we are getting a bite to eat. I'll have a taxi take her home in about ten minutes." Krystyna whispered, "Did you have to post bail?"

"I'm not in the mood for your jokes," she answered irritated. "You should have called me so I wouldn't freak out. Why didn't you answer when I called?"

"I never heard the phone ring. It must be on vibrate. This place is very noisy. Elke is sitting next to me. She says hi."

"Oh okay, tell her I said hi." She steadied her voice, "Krystyna, when you dropped Elke off after bingo last night, did you come inside with her?"

"No. I waited in the car outside and watched her go inside. Why do you ask?"

"I was just wondering. I didn't hear her come in. What time did you drop her off?"

"I don't know. Ten, maybe. Is there something you aren't telling me?"

"No. I just wondered."

"How was your morning? Did you enjoy yourself?"

"No. The police aren't talking. I just gave my statement and left." Julia was not ready to tell her friend what had happened or what she thought happened last night. Her friend would have a field day with a possible murder in her duplex and then thinking she spotted the killer at the police station.

"Got to go. Elke is giving me the hand sign to end the call." In a muffled voice Krystyna said, "Don't worry, I won't tell your grandmother that you were hauled down to the police station and interrogated about Lynda's murder."

Clicking off the phone, Julia had a sick feeling in her stomach. *What was going on?*

Her head began to throb again. The man in her place

last night was the same man she saw on the train the other day. Maybe it was a dream. A friend gave her a book about interpreting dreams. It said dreams can be a haphazard mishmash of silly bizarre thoughts we have during the day. Maybe the wine created the kooky illusion. Perhaps. But now there was a real physical dead body. And it was found in her cubicle. She was good at identifying red flags in her work with audits. The big red flag in all of this had to be her grandmother.

Elke, her sweet demented grandmother. It all seemed to begin with her arrival. But why? What could this have to do with her grandmother?

She unlocked the front door and hurried inside. Once inside, she locked the front door and leaned backward against it. She noticed that her grandmother's bedroom door was no longer open. Had Krystyna closed it? She marched over to the closed door, gingerly placed her hand on the doorknob and stopped. It was not her nature to snoop. But, Elke was up to something and she needed to find out what.

She turned the knob and entered the bedroom. The bed was made and there was a mess on the dresser. In the corner was her grandmother's suitcase. She went over and lifted the suitcase. It was light. Inside, it was empty. Next, she pulled out the drawer to the nightstand. Rummaging around she found nothing but medicine bottles. She checked each label. One label read Diazepam. It was used to treat anxiety. Another bottle label said Ambien. A sleeping aide. A bottle of baby aspirin was probably just what older people used in case of heart trouble. She found a large bottle of multi-vitamins. The woman had a regular pharmacy in the nightstand drawer. She opened the closet, rifled through her hanging clothes and still found nothing incriminating. Down on her hands and knees she did a sweep under the bed. "Oh my gosh," she said out loud. "I've got to clean under here. The dust is terrible." *What am I looking for?*

Then she remembered something Elke always told her growing up. *Keep your secrets close to you.* She lifted the pillows off her bed and shook them. Nothing. *Where would Elke keep her secrets?* She lifted the mattress and checked. Still no clues. A voice in her head told her something was wrong. Elke never took vitamins because she claimed all you needed to stay healthy was eat right, exercise and of course have a glass of wine every night.

She went over to the nightstand drawer and retrieved the bottle of vitamins. Inside the bottle was a small piece of paper folded several times to allow it to fit in the cylinder bottle. "I knew it," she yelped. Slipping two fingers down inside the bottle, she pulled out the piece of paper, unfolded it and read the numbers written on it. Three numbers, each two digits, separated by a hyphen. In German were the words, 'Viel Glück', followed by the initials LA. She flipped the paper over searching for more information when the doorbell rang. Startled, she quickly put the paper back in the bottle and screwed on the cap. She threw the bottle back in the drawer and closed it.

Elke was back sooner than she expected. She rushed out of Elke's bedroom, shut the door, but not before inspecting the room to make sure it looked untouched. The second loud knock annoyed her as she stomped to the front door to unlock it.

Swinging the door open she snarled, "Dammit Elke, I waited all day for you to call me and now you can't wait a few seconds for me to get to—"

Her mouth hung open, her words refusing to continue.

Standing before her was the man she saw last night in her duplex.

CHAPTER 17

CARVER WAS NOT able to say a word to the young woman before she tried to slam the door on him. He instinctively shoved his right hand between the door and door jamb to keep it open enough for him to talk to her. Right now, he was not sure he made the right decision. She must have thrown her weight against the door, because his hand hurt like hell. If it had been a man behind the door, he would have broken it down.

"Julia, I am not here to hurt you. I just need to talk. I know you saw me last night."

"I have a gun," she warned. "I saw you murder that man."

"I saved your life. Open the door. Now."

"Step back or I will shoot you." The quavering voice yelled.

"OK. I will step back. But first, open the door enough to let me pull my hand out."

As soon as the pressure from the door lessened, Carver used his shoulder to shove the door open. He heard a thud and a loud moan. First he glanced up and down the street, then hurried inside and shut the front door.

Seeing her sprawled on the floor he asked, "Are you okay?"

She rubbed the back of her head, rolled to her side and stood up. With one hand on the back of her head and the other stretched outward she said, "Get out now or I'm calling the cops."

He took a step back to give Julia more personal space. He raised his hands up to gesture he was not a threat. "Look, I did not come here to hurt you. I just need a few answers."

She was dressed in straight leg jeans, laced brown ankle boots and a long sleeve t-shirt. Her face was pale. Maybe she was just scared. He wasn't very good at seeing details like make-up. The photograph he had been given of her did not do her justice. She had long auburn hair pulled back in a pony-tail. Her eyes were deep bright blue and her lips full. She looked taller than 5'6", probably because she was in a defensive stance.

He lowered one arm to reach inside his jacket when she turned and ran. Damn, she's fast, he thought. But in her panic, she tripped on the rug in the hallway and fell. When he rushed over, she started to crawl toward the room on her right. He leaned down and thrust a picture in her face.

"Will you give me just five minutes and then I will leave?"

She stopped and snatched the picture from his hand.

"Why do you have this picture of me?" She twisted around and faced him. "Are you a stalker? Did you kill the man in my duplex last night? Oh, my God, you killed Lynda too, didn't you?"

"Damn, woman, take a breath and let me talk. I think we can clear some of this up."

"You aren't going to kill me," she said more as a statement than a question.

"Why would I want to kill you?"

He extended his hand and helped her up. She went over to the couch, stared at him a few beats and sat down. He sat in a chair opposite the couch so he would appear less threatening. Then right before he started to explain, she cupped her hands over her face and began to cry.

When it came to emotions, women were so confusing. He was not sure what his next move should be, so he sat there and gave her a few minutes before he spoke.

"Look Julia, I know you have been through a lot. I am not sure why Addy Bravo is having me keep an eye on you. At first, I thought you might have a wacko boyfriend or something."

She stopped crying and looked straight at Carver. The tears caused her mascara to streak down her face. She used her long sleeves to wipe the tears and her nose.

"Who is Addy Bravo?"

He searched her face when she claimed not to know an Addy Bravo. He concluded she honestly did not know Addy Bravo.

"She's a friend." He watched her expressions while he explained, "She contacted me a couple of days ago and asked me to do a favor for her. Addy gave me your picture."

"So, you are some kind of weirdo who follows women around you don't know as a favor for a friend?" Her sarcasm was hard to dispute.

"Addy is not a person who would ask me to do something if it wasn't important. Looks like you are lucky to have her watch out for you."

"Look it has been a long day for me. A long couple of days, actually." She kept sniffing and wiping her nose with her arm sleeve. "My grandmother will be here any minute. I want you to leave."

"Do you live alone?" Carver asked.

"That is none of your business. What *is* my business, did you or did you not kill somebody in my duplex after drugging me?"

"First, I did not drug you. Second, I think you need to ask

yourself why somebody tried to kidnap you and is now trying to frame you for murder."

She bit her lower lip as her eyes grew narrow. She wringed her hands, a confused look spread across her face. He was afraid she was going to start crying again. He thought maybe now he should sit next to her and put his arm around her. Instead, he stood and waited.

Unexpectedly, she rose and faced him. He sensed she wanted to take a swing at him so he took a step back.

In a voice that sounded strong and direct as if she was a prosecutor she said, "I don't know what to think or do. I don't know Addy Bravo. I am just an internal auditor. My father died before I was born. When I was five years old, my mother died of a brain tumor. My grandmother raised me, but now she has dementia. I have no wacko boyfriend. I rarely date. My life is boring." Her voice cracked when she said her life was boring as tears began to fill her eyes.

He wanted to respond with *lady your life is no longer* boring, but better judgment told him to keep that comment to himself.

"Let's just sit down and see about getting to the bottom of this," he tried to sound soothing.

Her shoulders slumped as she accepted his suggestion and slid back down on the couch. He took the cue and sat back down in the chair.

"I met Addy Bravo at Walter Reed Hospital when I was recovering from injuries I sustained in Afghanistan," he explained while he raised his pants leg so she could see his prosthetic leg. "I could talk to her in a way I never could anybody else. She literally saved my life. Then one day she informed me she had to leave. Urgent business. I knew some things about her past so I accepted what she told me. But, I wanted to repay her for her support and kindness. I did not hear from her until a few days ago."

"But, how does she know me?"

"I think she doesn't know you."

"Then why is she having you follow me?"

"I don't know. I suspect she knows something about you which she believes would put you in harm's way."

"That doesn't make sense." She broke eye contact, staring past him toward the living room window. "Is this linked to the audit I worked on? Does Addy what's her name work for Johnston?"

Carver was sure Addy Bravo did not work for the company. He felt what information he had about her employment should not be revealed right now.

"I don't know. She might. Did the police ask you anything about Russian ties with the company you audited?" he asked.

Julia's facial features changed. Her face was tense with lifted brows, and widened eyes.

Her voice was barely audible, "Russians?"

"Yes. Did they ask you about Russians?" He needed her to talk.

"Was the man who tried to kidnap me Russian? The one you...." She let her voice trail off.

"Yes. His identification verified he was. Julia, I need you to help me get to the bottom of this. Things are getting dangerous."

She looked exhausted and continued, "The police never said anything about Russians. Alvin told me on the news a couple was arrested for spying for the Russians. The husband worked at the company I audited. I can't see a connection, but Alvin said he would try and see what the audit might have to do with my supervisor's death."

"Who is Alvin?"

"He's a friend. We went on one date."

"I thought you didn't have a boyfriend?"

Her face told him not to go any further with the questions about Alvin. She said, "I think if we went to the police right now and you tell them what you know, then we can get to the bottom of this. I'm afraid they think I am involved in some way."

"No," his voice was deep and firm. "Not yet. I'm not going to be arrested for murder and thrown in jail."

"I will tell them it was self-defense. You were protecting me."

"Sounds like a good plan to you, does it?"

"Yes. You said yourself this situation is dangerous. The police can protect us."

"There are few problems with your plan." Carver's eyes locked on her face. Maybe Julia was an innocent player in this.

"What? What kind of problems?" Her face gave nothing away.

"To begin with, I lied when the police asked me about following you. Second, there is no body. Third—"

She stood again and leaned forward. "What do you mean there is no body? Like there is no dead body?"

"Addy, or her people, disposed of the body."

"Her people? You make her sound like she works for the mafia."

Before he could think of a good response, her cell phone rang. She placed the phone to her ear. Her body stiffened and she took several shallow breaths as if she was trying to stay calm.

As soon as she ended the call, she said, "We have to leave. Now."

"Who was it? What did they say?" He wanted answers yet he was sure now was not the time to argue.

He got up from the chair and walked over to the window. There was nothing unusual outside that he could detect. "Who was that on the phone, Julia?" No answer. He turned around and did not see her in the room. A moment later, she hurried from what looked like a bedroom with a jacket draped over her arm, her large pocketbook hanging from her shoulder and a duffel bag in her hand.

"I'm crazy for saying this, I know," she told him. "Yet, I think we should take your truck and leave immediately. Where did you park?"

"Down the street." He explained, "I didn't want it parked in your driveway."

"Good. Let's go out my back door and we can cut through the neighbor's yard."

Carver heard in her voice the impending danger she felt was coming their way. He decided he would get answers later. Right now, he would go along with his instinct and trust her.

He followed her to the back door in the kitchen and was about to leave when something caught his eye.

He snatched the paper off the table and tucked it in his jacket as they both hurried out the kitchen door to his truck parked down the street. When he turned the key in the ignition, a car pulled into Julia's driveway. There were two men in jackets getting out of the car and headed to her front door. He immediately pushed her head down and told her to stay down.

Then he eased his truck down the street past the men knocking on her door. One of the men slid something from under his jacket.

A pistol.

CHAPTER 18

JULIA WAS NOT sure why she decided to trust the man driving the truck. She still didn't know his name or why Addy what's her name wanted him to keep tabs on her.

Her grandmother called and told her she had two minutes to get out of the duplex. She was given the code word.

The code word was taught to her when she was a child. It was a word only she and her grandmother knew. There were rules when she heard the word.

It was not unusual for children to be given a code word only known to them and their parents. When approached by a stranger claiming to know their parents, they could ask for the code word. It was designed to prevent abductions. The reality of child abductions was most kids who were reported missing had run away or if truly abducted, most were taken by a family member or acquaintance. But, in this day and age, it was difficult for parents not to fear the world when it came to their children. They were bombarded by news stories about child abductions or crimes committed against children.

The rules when she heard the code word were not to ask questions and do as instructed. This time she was told she had less than two minutes to leave the house. Later a text would tell her where and what time to meet. She followed the rules. Except this time, she left with a stranger. A man she believed killed Volvo man. *What was I thinking?*

She kept her head down and turned it at an angle to look at the man driving the truck. What if the code word meant he was the danger? Now, she was in his truck going who knows where. He told her he had been in the military. Meaning, he knew how to use weapons and how to kill people. However, if he was going to harm her, he would have done it last night.

Back in her duplex, she became overwhelmed with everything going on in her life. Elke, a man murdered in her living room, her supervisor found strangled in her cubicle, and then this stranger saying he was following her as a favor. Sobbing on the couch, she wanted to be comforted. The man just stood there with no compassion.

The stranger drove slow and turned several times. She had to strain to see his features from a face down view. His left leg was a prosthetic limb. It appeared to start just above the knee. At least, she thought it did. It was difficult to determine since he was wearing jeans. She was attracted to this mysterious stranger with the dark, rugged features. The man reeked military. His close cropped dark hair, the way he stood straight and erect with his broad shoulders back. The deep commanding voice.

Alvin was different. He was pleasant looking. Blond hair with a receding hairline. Octagonal rimless glasses sat on a broad nose. Fair skin with red cheeks made him look like his ancestors were Irish. They kissed after he took her home from their date. It was just a kiss. Nothing magical, no sparks. She felt it might be his thin upper lip or the mints he just chewed. Either way, she was not sexually attracted to him.

She turned her head away from the stranger driving the truck. She felt her face grow warm. Inside her body, there was a feeling she had once before. She was in the tenth grade. A boy she had a crush on, asked her to the prom. That feeling of so many years ago had resurfaced.

"Where are we going?" she asked.

"I can't hear you," he said. Sit up."

"I thought you said to stay down."

"That was back at your place."

She straightened up. "You could have told me it was okay to sit up. My back was starting to ache."

The stranger was silent.

What a jerk, she thought.

She repeated her question to him, "Where are we going?"

"My place. We are just about there. I took the long way and made sure we weren't followed."

"What's your name? Don't lie. I can smell bullshit so don't try to make up a name."

"I wouldn't dare." He shot her a quick glance. "Parker Brown."

Brown pulled into the parking lot of a Hampton Inn and shut off the engine.

Surprised, she asked, "Why are you living at a motel?"

"It's temporary. Addy Bravo arranged for me to stay here. She wanted me close to where you live."

"Where do you live?"

"Michigan."

"Michigan?" She was shocked that he lived so far away. "You drove all the way from Michigan because an old friend asked you to do her a favor."

"Yes. We need to get inside," Brown said.

They walked up to a side door of the motel. Brown slid his key card to unlock the door.

She did not move when he pulled the door open and gestured for her to go inside.

"I'm not going to hurt you, Julia. You are safer here than any place right now. Nobody knows about me."

"Except Addy," she corrected Brown.

"Right." He held the door, waiting for her decision.

"I will soon get a text from my grandmother telling me where to meet her. When I do, will you take me?" She thought it was stupid to even ask. He could tell her anything.

"I will."

She stepped inside and followed him to his room.

His motel room looked average. The king-size bed occupied most of the space. There was a chair and desk in one corner. Another corner had an over-sized cloth chair. The room was very tidy with all his belongings put away.

"Have a seat and we can talk." He pointed to the chair.

"I can stand and talk." She wanted to let him know, she was not taking orders.

He grinned and moved toward her.

She stood still, not sure what to do. She thought about fleeing, yet it would be impossible to get by the large man. He stood between her and the door.

She now realized her mistake in agreeing to come inside his motel room as sweat seeped down her back. The muscular man stood in front of her, making her feel small and helpless.

He asked, "Do you mind?"

"Mind what?" she forced herself to sound strong.

"If you aren't going to sit in the chair, I will."

She exhaled with relief and sensed her face getting flush. She felt stupid as she moved aside to allow him to get past her.

After he sat in the chair, he offered her a drink from his mini fridge.

"No, thank you," she said. "I need to know if I'm in danger, then is my grandmother also in danger?"

"Don't know."

"Then we need to warn her."

He sat silent, his eyes boring into her. Finally, he asked, "Why would your grandmother call you and tell you to leave your place immediately?"

"I don't know. Maybe Addy contacted her." She glanced down at her phone in her hand and realized she never told him who had called her. "How do you know it was my grandmother who called?"

"Tell me about your grandmother, Julia."

"Why?" Julia asked as she pulled out the desk chair and turned it to face Brown.

"Just so we know how to protect her if she's in danger too."

"She is a wonderful person. She has dementia." Julia went on the defensive, "I had to place her in a very nice assisted living facility called Harmony."

"How long has she had dementia?" he asked.

"It seemed to come on so fast. I guess I was not paying close enough attention. The doctor said when a person is diagnosed they have had it for around ten years."

"Is she there now? In the facility?"

"No." She frowned at the thought of her grandmother not being in a safe environment. "Three days ago she left and came to my house."

"Hmm," he said as he put his hand in front of his mouth. His eyes seemed to concentrate on what she just said.

"What?" Julia asked. "What are you thinking?"

"If she has dementia, I wonder why you brought her to your place."

"I didn't." She felt her palms sweating. Her jaw clenched.

"Did she just leave on her own?" he questioned.

Taking a deep breath, "Yes. As a matter of fact, she did."

"Why?"

"I did mention she has dementia. There are times she is normal and times she is not."

"So she lives with you?"

"Temporarily."

"Hmm," he said again.

"Would you quit doing that? It is very annoying not knowing what you are thinking."

Her phone beeped. A text appeared on her screen.

She quickly read the message. "I need to answer this text message."

She sensed he wanted to say "Hmm" again, but stayed quiet.

Julia typed her message.

I am fine. I am with Parker Brown, a friend. We are trying to sort some things out. Are you okay?

She did not want to worry her grandmother.

The next text from her grandmother upset her.

Parker Brown is a dog.

CHAPTER 19

EVEN THE NEXT day, Mark Thompson's words of warning still rang in Wagner's ear.

He wanted to know what Thompson meant by saying he was *warning* him. When he tried to coax him, Thompson just clammed up. He refused any details and just advised him not to trust anybody.

He needed time to figure out what was going on. His assistant would discover what rumors were floating around, yet Megan's ability to find secrets long buried were limited. To find out what the Speaker of the House was hiding would require resources. Resources he had.

He thought Thompson must be a victim of extortion and was using the ruse he misused funds to leave office without a bigger consequence. What could be worse? An affair? He was a married man with two teenagers. There was not a whisper of scandal associated with the Speaker. Until now.

Every politician tried to keep a clean record, but everybody, including himself, had secrets. Power brought more than enemies, it brought temptation.

He did not like being in the dark about the situation. Quatterman, a long-time adversary, had always road blocked his proposed legislation. Now the man was championing him for the speakership. Thompson appeared to be sabotaging his own career. He never thought this would be his path to move up in his career.

In college, he was just a kid from the suburbs majoring in economics and political science. His mother pushed him toward a political career. He was sure he did not want to enter the corrupt political world, until he won a second term as president of the student government at Miami University in Oxford, Ohio. He became passionate about leading people and making changes.

His ego wanted to believe hard-work and dedication were the reasons he had a quick climb up the ladder. He modeled himself as a conservative change agent. Deep down he knew doors had been opened for him. Politicians have their backers and supporters. The problem was they usually got their hands too deep in your pocket. In his case, they had his life in their pocket.

There would be challenges as Speaker in governing and legislating. He was excited to give direction and a vision to his party. He already had a lot of ideas to help unite the fractious GOP caucus. This would be an opportunity to define his career goals.

The screen on his cell phone lit up. He picked it up and read the text.

Urgent. Meet me in the park.

Now what? It was from the woman who had called him earlier. They usually communicated by phone calls and text messages. Seldom did he meet with her face to face. She did not want anybody to know about their relationship. It was not an intimate relationship. She was his handler. The one who led him to success in public service. According to her, he was her brightest protégé.

He knew his handler was powerful. The woman had

connections. When he needed anything, she made it happen. He felt the woman watched over him like a big brother. However, most times it seemed like *Big Brother* from George Orwell's book *1984.* She seemed to know too much about him, including his private life. During one conversation, she asked how Abeedah was doing. Abeedah had been his secret lover at the time. She was a Muslin.

His handler instructed him to stop seeing Abeedah. She explained it would not be wise to date a Muslim with the current problems America was having with radicalized Muslims. He did not like the woman spying on him or telling him what to do in his personal life. He refused.

That was when his handler showed him emails and photos of Abeedah. The emails were to a suspected terrorist, her brother. Photos taken of her were with her brother. In the photo was an envelope changing hands between the sister and brother. He regretted not giving Abeedah a chance to tell him she was not a terrorist. His secret lover never knew the reason he stopped seeing her.

When he arrived at the park, his handler was waiting for him on the bench they used for their meetings. He was not sexually attracted to the woman. He preferred dark skin women with dark features. Like his ex-lover, Abeedah or his assistant, Megan. His handler was fair skinned, blue-gray eyes and dirty blond hair. She kept it short making her oblong face look fuller. The black horned glasses gave her the appearance of a librarian. The glasses were probably part of her disguise, just like her wig.

He admired her confident and persuasive manner. His handler would have been an excellent poker player since she was unreadable. Unlike her, he did not know anything about her past. It was her mysterious nature that enticed him.

His handler was assigned to him when he earned his economics and political science degree from Miami University in Oxford, Ohio. Keeping him on track with his political aspirations was her job. In the beginning, he appreciated and welcomed her wise counsel. Later, he realized he had to give up some of his ideals to follow orders. The resentment grew as the puppet strings were drawn taunt.

He sat on the other side of the bench and pulled the brim of his hat low on his forehead. They never acknowledged each other. They were supposed to appear like two strangers sitting on a bench enjoying the day. He pulled out his cell phone, kept his head bowed and pretended to check emails.

"Even the sunglasses do not hide your tired face." His handler's accent was still strong. "Perhaps you need to spend less time at the office."

"I have a job to do," he retorted. "Why didn't you tell me Mark Thompson was stepping down?"

"There was no need. You must look surprised when given news like this."

It irritated him how his handler held all the cards when it was his career and life on the line.

"What is so urgent that you could not tell me on the phone?"

"Are you preparing yourself for your next big step in your career?" she asked.

"I am. Just tell me you had nothing to do with the Speaker being black-mailed. I am able to do my job and get recognized for my accomplishments without your interference."

"So, Alan, you no longer need me. Is that what you are saying?"

"That is exactly what I am saying," he shot back. "I no longer need you."

There was edgy silence.

His handler raised her phone to her ear and pretended to talk to somebody else. "I know you are upset about Thompson. I am very aware you were friends. Yet, you did not know this man. He knew what he was getting into. Did he share his secret with you?"

"No. He did not. What is the secret?" he spoke into his phone to keep up the pretense they were not speaking to each other.

"It is just a small lie he could not hide."

More silence. His handler slowly angled her head in his direction. "He is sterile."

"That's it?" he could not believe this is all she had on the Speaker. "So he and his wife adopted."

His handler spoke in her phone, "His wife has a sordid past. She is clean now. He is willing to protect her and his children at all costs."

Wagner hung his head and spoke in a low voice, "Mark Thompson is a good man. He is a damn good Speaker."

"I need you to focus on the real problem, Alan."

He gritted his teeth and said, "What is the *real* problem?"

"A spy we killed many years ago."

"A dead spy? What the hell do I care about a dead spy?" he asked with sarcasm.

"We believe she has surfaced."

CHAPTER 20

JULIA STARED BOLDLY at the man sitting in the hotel room who just lied to her about his name. Her mouth grimaced and her foot began tapping the carpet. How could she have been so naïve to believe him? And how the hell did her grandmother know Parker Brown was the name of a dog? What was going on?

Quickly she answered the text.

I am okay. I will get back to you in a couple of minutes.

She decided there were two options for her next move. He no longer blocked the motel door. His prosthetic leg would not allow him to move as fast as she could, so it might allow her to escape. Or, she could confront him and find out what was going on.

She cocked an eyebrow at him and blurted out, "You're a liar."

"Was that your grandmother who texted you?" His voice more curious than demanding.

"I trusted you," she said uneasy. "You said you saved my life, and told me you wanted to find out what was going on."

"I do."

"Really," she snapped. "That's why all the bullshit is flowing from your mouth?"

"I am trying to figure this out. Why do *you* think I lied?"

She stood, not sure why she felt the need to stand. Maybe

so she could run if the man made a move toward her.

"I told you in the car I could smell bullshit." She lowered her eyes and demanded, "What is your real name?"

"So you can smell bullshit and that is why you think I lied about my name?"

"Did you?"

"How about you tell me the truth, Julia," he said firmly. "You can't smell bullshit if you stepped in it. It was in the text, wasn't it?"

His words enraged her. She was sure smoke was steaming out her ears. Upset, she began to pace back and forth toward the door.

"You're an ass," she said. "I never liked you from the moment I saw you."

"You mean when you saw me strangle the guy trying to kidnap you?"

She stopped pacing and said. "I saw you shadow me on the train."

"Why don't you just tell me what was in the text?"

"Why don't you tell me how my grandmother knows Parker Brown is the name of a dog?" Her voice was taut.

The man didn't seem surprised when he heard her tell him this. His dark eyes appeared amused as he grinned.

"Because your grandmother and Addy Bravo are the same person."

She sat on the edge of the bed. Her eyes cast downward as she clasped her hands together.

"How is that possible?" she asked.

"Addy is the one who gave me Parker when I was recovering at Walter Reed Hospital. He was my therapy dog."

"Elke hates dogs."

"What do you know about your grandmother?" His voice was too harsh.

She shot him a scathing look. "I know a hell of a lot more than you do. When were you at Walter Reed?"

"Almost two years to this date," he answered.

Her mind raced as she tried to recollect the time frame. She remembered her grandmother was doing a lot of traveling before her mind declined. There were periods when Elke would be gone for months. Her grandmother told her she wanted to see as much of the world before her old bones rebelled.

"My grandmother was traveling in Europe during that time frame so it is impossible she was at Walter Reed Hospital."

"Are you sure? Is it possible she told you that so you would not know where she really was?"

"Elke raised me. She loves me. Why would she volunteer at an Army hospital and not tell me? What would be the point?"

"That is what I need to know Julia. I thought it was a coincidence she was assigned to Walter Reed Physical Therapy clinic. But now I am not so sure," he said.

"I don't believe you. She would have told me."

"Do you have a picture of your grandmother in your wallet?"

Her shoulders hunched. She shook her head.

"So, no picture of your beloved grandma in your wallet? That's odd. I have a picture of Parker Brown in my wallet. Care to see?" His sarcasm made her angrier.

"You carry a picture of your dog in your wallet because you are a pathetic person," her taut voice said.

The man's face caused her to regret her words.

"I do not have a picture of my grandmother," she said, her voice now soft-spoken. "Elke taught me to never have pictures of family in my wallet or on my phone. For safety reasons."

"You mean like having a go bag ready in case you were given some code?"

Startled, she glanced at her go bag on the floor. It was still zipped. She never told him what the bag was for or about the code word. How would he know?

"I never told you I got a code word or what was in my bag," she said.

"You didn't have too. Your phone call was short. You went into a trained mode, like a soldier alerted to danger. Grabbing a bag and doing as instructed. No questions. Just follow orders. Duress codes are used by the military, too."

She felt vulnerable. The man sitting in the room could see through her. She did not like it.

He asked, "Is your grandmother about 5'6", blue eyes, long wavy gray hair, a good looking older woman with an air of confidence?"

"You are attracted to Addy Bravo?" She knew her high pitched voice made the question sound more like *how could you be attracted to a woman you say is my grandmother.*

"The woman could turn heads."

"That is not my grandmother. Even two years ago. She has dementia."

"How do you explain she knew Parker Brown was a dog?" he quizzed.

"I think you told her."

"Think about it. If I told her then I know who she is."

"This could be a set up. I don't know what is going on. Maybe you are taking advantage of an old woman," she reasoned.

"Damn. You're a stubborn woman. You two definitely have

that in common."

She stood up. "I am leaving now. I will call a taxi."

She walked over to her bag, picked it up and headed for the door.

"Julia, Addy told me your parents were killed when her house exploded in Fort Collins, Colorado. You and she were at the park. You had just fed the ducks on the pond."

Paralyzed by an emotion, her hand froze on the door knob. A flashback made her body shudder. She felt unsteady and lightheaded. Then everything went dark.

She could see the clear sky filled with dark smoke and tall yellow flames. The ducks began to quack louder and people were screaming. She was in a park and wanted to run toward the flames, but her feet would not move, so she started to fly. When she looked down from the sky, there was no ground. Frightened, she labored to breath, but there was no air. A feeling of panic that she was being smothered caused her chest to tighten.

She gasped for air and jerked upward. Panting hard, she believed for a moment she was in her bed at home. A haze covered her eyes so she blinked several times and searched the room. *Where am I?*

A large dark featured man walked over to the bed. "Are you okay?"

She blinked again, trying to force tears to coat her dry eyes. "What happened?"

"You fainted."

"How long was I out?"

"About thirty seconds or so."

"I need to call Elke." She rolled to her side and attempted

to put her feet on the ground.

The man took his hands and coaxed her to lay back down.

"You need to rest."

"But Elke. I need to tell her where I am. She will be worried." Her body and mind were exhausted. She saw the man pull a chair up to the bed and sit down.

"Why did you react to what I told you just before fainting?" he asked.

"I don't know. My father died in a helicopter crash while serving in the military. My mother died of a brain tumor when I was a little girl. But..."

"But what, Julia?" The man's voice was soothing.

"What is your real name?"

"Derick Carver."

"Let me see your I.D," she demanded.

He reached around the back of his body with his right hand and slid the wallet out of a pocket. He opened the wallet and turned it so she could read the name on the driver license.

She pretended to study the name and picture. She was curious about Carver. A quick calculation told her his age. He was four years older than she was.

"I wanted to make sure Derick Carver wasn't your pet cat," she said coyly.

Carver laughed. She liked the sound of his deep laugh.

"When you said explosion," she continued to explain, "I could hear it in my mind. Then I remembered turning around and seeing flames in the distance."

"Was it your parents who died in the house that exploded?" he questioned.

"No. I mean... I don't think it could have been them. I was a small child, surely I would have some memory of something that horrifying happening. Besides, Elke told me when I got older what happened to my parents."

"You were just a little girl. Maybe your grandmother did not want to upset you so she told you something else."

"No. I would have remembered something as terrible as that." She felt saying it twice might make it true.

He leaned close, his dark eyes locked with hers. She felt her skin tingle.

"Julia," he cleared his throat. "You did remember that terrible day. Just now."

CHAPTER 21

SINCE CHILDHOOD, SHE had been having a recurring nightmare about being in a park and seeing an explosion in the background. Perhaps the dream was related to a bad experience as a young child. She hated every time the vision appeared in her mind.

As she laid on the bed in his hotel room, she started to feel uncomfortable. He must have felt the same since he stood and pushed the chair back to the corner of the room.

"You should try to contact your grandmother," he said in an abrupt manner.

She was confused. It was as if he was done trying to put the pieces of the puzzle together. Earlier, he claimed her grandmother and Addy were the same person. Now, he wanted her to contact her grandmother. He did not ask her to question Elke about the possibility of her being called Addy.

She swung her legs over the side of the bed and sat up. He no longer gave the impression he cared she was tired or upset. The man who was empathic a minute ago, now seemed cold and distant. He avoided eye contact with her.

"Here's your phone." He stretched out his arm to hand it to her.

She extended her hand too far causing her fingers to brush over his hand. Embarrassed, she quickly retrieved the phone.

She thumbed a text to her grandmother and waited for a

response. The screen did not show an incoming text message. She raised her head and shared her worried look with him.

After five minutes, she began to feel anxious like a parent who thinks his or her child is lost. Think logical, she reminded herself. *Elke could have been distracted. Her dementia might have made her forget.*

Guilt seeped into her conscience as she questioned her judgement. *I should have responded to her right away. Why did I wait?* Stressing over what might be happening with her grandmother, she stood up too fast, dropped her phone as her legs wobbled.

Carver rose from the chair and caught her with his large arms.

"What's wrong?" he asked lowering her to a sitting position on the edge of the bed.

"Elke's not responding." She frowned. "I shouldn't have waited so long to get back to her. Now I can't get hold of her."

He eased back into the chair and rubbed his chin as if he was trying to solve the mystery of Elke not responding. "Does your grandmother always get right back to you?"

"No. But in this case, she would because of her giving me the code word," she explained.

He slipped a phone out from his jacket and said, "I should have thought to check messages on my phone. It is on silent."

"Did Addy text you?" she asked. "Does she know where my grandmother is?"

"Let me check."

He scrolled through his phone, tapped the screen and then placed it to his ear. After a few seconds, she heard it ring.

"Addy. What's going on?"

She tried to listen to his conversation, but Addy must have been doing most of the talking. Perhaps now was the time to call Elke. If they were the same person, then Elke's line would be busy.

It rang and rang and started to go to voice mail when Elke answered.

"Julia, are you okay?"

"Elke what's going on?" She noticed Carver had hung up.

"I have to leave the country for a short time," her grandmother said.

"Leave the country?" Julia massaged her forehead with the tips of her fingers while she tried to make sense of what her grandmother was telling her. Frustrated, she cried out, "My God, Elke, where are you?"

"I am at your house. I want you to stay with Derick. He can keep you safe."

"He says your name is Addy Bravo. Is that true?"

"Yes, dear. That is how he knows me."

Julia, without blinking, glared at the man standing on the other end of the room.

"We need to talk, Elke. Now. I am getting a taxi and will be at my place in a few minutes."

"No," her grandmother said adamantly. "Stay with Derick. He will keep you safe. I love you." Those were her grandmother's last words when the phone call ended.

"Elke. Elke." A loud futile protest. "Dammit."

"We need to disable your phone," he said as he walked over and pulled the phone from her hand.

"Give me back my phone," she pleaded while clawing at his hands.

He dropped the phone on the carpet and with his right foot stomped on it.

She tried to push him, but her attempt was useless. The

large man could not be moved with her body weight.

"I need my phone," she hollered.

"They have tracked your phone," he warned. "We don't have much time. Grab your bag."

"Who would track my phone? I am not going anywhere with you."

He gripped her arm. She tried to pull away when she heard him say one word. The word caused her to standstill.

"How do you know the code word?" she said with her voice cracking.

"You know how," his tone was matter-of-fact.

He let go of her arm, put on his jacket and shoved some items in his bag.

In awkward silence, Julia put on her jacket, got her bag and followed him to his truck.

"Why aren't we destroying your phone?" she asked.

"It's a burn phone."

They drove off in the same direction from which they came earlier that day.

A few miles down the road, she asked, "Is my grandmother safe?"

"Yes."

"I want to go see her."

"Not now. We need to find a safe place to crash for the night."

Exhaustion and low blood sugar from not eating made her lightheaded and irritable. Slouched in the seat, she leaned her head against the passenger window and crossed her arms over her chest. The objects outside blurred as they sped past them.

"Why didn't you destroy my phone earlier if you knew it was being tracked?" she asked.

"I didn't know, until Addy Bravo told me."

"Addy Bravo, who I now know is my grandmother, told you? You need to explain what the hell is going on," she said while placing her hand on her bag on the floorboard. "I have a gun in my bag and will shoot you."

"No, you don't."

"Did you check my bag when I was passed out?"

"No."

"Then you don't know what is in my bag?"

"Julia, I know if you had a gun, I would have seen it by now."

She wished Elke had not taken her gun. Could it be true; the woman she always knew as Elke was also Addy Bravo? Her heart galloped thinking about what she wished were not true.

He wheeled the truck into the parking lot of a sandwich shop. "Let's feed you," he said. "I was warned you get cranky when not fed."

CHAPTER 22

INSTEAD OF DRIVING straight to another motel, Carver turned right into a restaurant parking lot.

"I'm not cranky," she growled.

"Figured you might be getting hungry," he said. It was getting late in the day. Maybe food would help her mood.

The sandwich diner had painted letters on the glass windows that made him turn into the parking lot. *BIG Sandwiches served here.*

He got out of the truck, reached behind the seat and retrieved his pistol. Lifting his jacket to the side, he placed the weapon inside a waistband holster.

"Do you think that's necessary?" she scoffed.

"I do."

"This is a sandwich shop. I don't think we'll get robbed ordering fast food."

"I'm not worried about getting robbed."

Inside the diner, they walked up to the service counter to place their orders. Carver ordered a BIG sandwich with turkey, ham, salami and hot peppers. He got chips and a large drink to go with it. She was still studying the menu hanging on the wall behind the counter. After a minute, she told the young man taking their order to give her the same thing he ordered.

They found a booth near the back of the casual diner. He sat on the bench seat facing toward the door to the restaurant with his back to the wall. The view gave him an unobstructed vantage point of any lurking danger. He was in *relaxed alert* mode.

Facing each other, they ate their food without speaking. He was amazed at how fast and how much she ate. Not once did she slow down except to wash the food down with her large soda. He was impressed.

"When you come up for air, let's talk," he said.

"I feel better. I had low blood sugar."

"So, I've been warned." He grinned. "If you skip a meal, you get cranky."

"How would you know that?"

"Addy told me."

"What else did she tell you about me?" She finished the last bite of her sandwich.

"I think we need to concentrate on what might be going on."

"I thought you knew. Addy Bravo didn't fill you in? Did her dementia kick in?"

"Cut the sarcasm. It gets us nowhere. This started with me doing a favor for Addy."

"You're right. I'm sorry. The last three days have been surreal for me. I was just living a quiet life, and then it started spinning out of control."

"What did Addy, or Elke as you call her, tell you on the phone?"

"She said she had to leave the country. You would keep me safe. She was at my duplex and that she and Addy Bravo are one and the same."

Julia's large blue eyes were captivating. A mix of pale blue and white rays in the iris made her eyes brighter than Addy

Bravo's eye color. They were piercing eyes. Her messy auburn hair hung around her narrow shoulders. She seemed small and vulnerable.

"How did you know?" she asked.

"Know what?"

"That my grandmother was Addy Bravo."

"I didn't. I suspected it."

"When was that?"

"When we left your place, I saw a note on the kitchen table. The handwriting looked familiar. Like the writing in the note she sent to me."

"Why did you lie about your name?"

"It was a way to know for sure if they were the same person. You said your grandmother would text you. I figured you would tell her you were with Parker Brown."

Her head bobbed up and down and her eyes sparkled. Her closed mouth turned up in a slight smile revealing dimples on each side of her cheek. Unlike Addy, Julia could never play poker. All her emotions were on her face.

"What is going on with Elke?" she asked.

"Elke is not the grandmother you think she is."

"What are you saying? She doesn't have dementia? She really is a spy."

He was not sure how much he should tell her. He didn't want to spook her.

"Tell me about your childhood, Julia. What do you remember?"

"Elke raised me after my mother died. She quit her job at a hospital, and we moved to Germany for a while. My grandfather lived there. They were divorced."

"We need to go to Fort Collins," he said.

"Why?"

"Because that is where this all began."

"I thought it began here, three days ago."

He noticed the headlights through the window of the restaurant. The vehicle pulled in the parking lot and parked beside his truck. The lights went off and a tall person stepped out of the car. The figure wore a long dark coat and hat. The parking lot lights were dim, yet there was enough light to let him see the silhouette move around his truck and bend over to peer inside his truck window. Then the person stood facing the picture window of the restaurant. It would be easy for the person to see inside the restaurant since it was already dark outside and lights on the inside illuminated everything. Including him and Julia.

Inside the small diner, a heavy man was sitting at a table drinking coffee absorbed in his iPad. At a table on the other end of the diner was a youthful couple. They were oblivious to the outside world. The teenage girl giggled at whatever stupid thing the teenage boy said. Their hands interlocked on the table top. The table at the other end of the diner sat an elderly man. A face without color or expression. The only other person up front in the diner was the lanky kid behind the counter. Still pubescent. Probably in his late teens. The punk wore a baseball cap with the brim in the back and a red t-shirt with the diner logo on it.

He figured there was one, maybe two other employees in the back. Probably cleaning up so they could go home as soon as the patrons left.

"Julia, don't look around, only at me. Okay?"

She did as he instructed, keeping her eyes only on him.

"I think we have trouble. A car just pulled up."

"Maybe they're coming inside to eat."

"I don't think so. A man got out and was too curious about my truck."

He told her what he needed her to do. He would go in the men's bathroom and wait for two minutes. She needed to create a diversion by going over to the guy behind the counter and keep his attention long enough for him to sneak into the kitchen and out the back door. Then she was to go back to the booth and wait for five minutes before meeting him at his truck.

"Got all that?" he said.

She gave him a sharp nod.

He did not know what he would say to the workers in the kitchen as he dashed toward the exit door. Maybe they would be busy and he could slip past without being noticed. He doubted it would be that easy.

He was surprised nobody was in the kitchen. When he got outside, Carver understood. The worker was taking a smoke break. Only the cigarette was a joint. The startled kid begged him not to tell his boss. A few words exchanged and Carver hurried around the back of the building.

The man standing by his truck was too occupied watching the events inside the diner window. Julia did a good job keeping the guy behind the counter distracted. It had also kept the man in the parking lot looking in the wrong direction.

"Don't move," Carver commanded as he stuck the barrel of his gun into the back of the man.

"Please, do not shoot me." The man raised his arms in the air.

"Put your hands down and don't do anything stupid." He

held the gun against the man's back and patted him down with his other hand. No weapon.

"I am not here to harm you or Julia. I was sent to give you some information."

Julia walked up and stood by Carver.

"Turn around slowly and don't give me a reason to shoot."

She gasped, "I know this man."

CHAPTER 23

JULIA HAD REMAINED silent as Carver outlined his plan to her while they sat in the café booth. He had frightened her when he told her the person who was probably a man was waiting in the parking lot and watching them. She was glad he had his gun on him.

Carver had gotten up and entered the men's bathroom located next to their booth. She unbuttoned several of the top buttons on her shirt and pulled it open. He had instructed her to distract the guy behind the counter. She walked up to the counter where the kid was standing, leaned over and smiled. She was uncomfortable since he was so young, but the age gap didn't seem to bother him.

Out of the corner of her eye, she saw Carver slip into the kitchen. She held the young man's attention a few more minutes and then, as she had been instructed, went back to the booth and sat down.

She fidgeted in her seat, checking and rechecking her watch for the time. After five minutes, she got up, slipped on her jacket and headed to the counter to pay. She told the counter guy she had to get back to her jealous boyfriend who was waiting for her in the truck. The word *boyfriend* tongue-tied the young guy. He nodded, turned his back pretending to be busy. She felt a pang of guilt for leading him on, but that feeling quickly dissipated and was replaced with worry about the situation in the parking lot.

The night air was crisp against her face making her wish she had her knit hat. She was glad the truck was not parked in direct sight of the restaurant. She spotted Carver near his truck standing behind a man. Nervous, she hastened to where he was standing.

With his gun pointed at the man's back, Carver instructed him to turn around slowly and not give him a reason to shoot.

The man's face was familiar to her. She did not know his name, but had seen him many Friday nights.

"What are you doing here?" she asked in a demanding voice.

"You know this creep?" Carver asked her.

"I came as a favor to Elke." The stranger's voice was slow with a thick German accent.

The old man, was tall and thin. His shoulders slumped and his back was slightly hunched. Even in the dim light, she saw his face was timeworn and wrinkled. A small amount of grayish hair stuck out of the wool hat he wore.

"You're the man who works at the bingo hall," Julia said.

"Ya, ya. You remember. That is good. I know Elke long time. Our paths cross many years," the old man explained.

"You worked for the CIA?" Carver asked.

The word *CIA* caused her to cast a questionable look toward Carver.

"Nein. I provide documents to people when they need them."

"What kind of documents?" she asked.

"I create documents that save lives. This how I met your grandmother."

"You're a forger?" Carver asked.

"Most refer to me as the cobbler. I provide new pair of

shoes. Humanitarian reasons. There many bad people in world. I keep good people safe."

"Cobbler," Carver said as he gave the elderly man an intense stare. "The CIA uses the term for a person who provided documents giving a person a new identity."

"Ya. During day, I run bookstore of very rare books. At night, I work in cellar creating new pair of shoes."

"In Germany you did this?" Carver asked.

"My shop is in Wiesbaden," the old man said. "Is very nice. My daughter still run."

"Is that where you met Elke?" She wasn't sure if it was the cool night air making her bounce on her feet or the old man who claimed to know her grandmother.

"The first time. Your grandfather, Milo Wolfgang Fenstermacher and I grow up in same neighborhood in Trier. He visits my shop often. We stay good friends. Then one day he arranges for me to meet Elke. When she walks in my shop, I see why Milo fall in love with her. She very beautiful." The old man opened his palm and held it three feet from the pavement and said, "You, little Julia, just this big."

"Do you and Milo still stay in touch?" she questioned him. "Elke did not like to talk about my grandfather."

"Not so much now. He lives there. I live here. He very old, like me, Julia. Milo not same man after he learn what happened to his daughter."

"So what is your relationship with Elke?" Carver asked keeping his gun trained on the man.

"Elke and Julia given fresh identity. Elke used my services more times after that."

"What are you saying? Fresh identities." Julia shuttered, took a deep breath and let it out very slowly.

"Elke scared. She not trust anybody. Milo tell me, I must help. Your grandmother still held his heart."

"So, you created new identities to protect Elke and Julia?" Carver asked.

"Ya. Keep Elke and Julia safe."

"Why would I, a child, not be safe?" her forehead crinkled in confusion.

"I not know," the old man answered.

"Maybe you need some help with your memory, old man." Carver grasped the man's coat and pinned him against his truck. The barrel of the gun against his chest.

The frightened old man begged to be released.

A murmur of voices came from the diner's door. Carver released his hold on the old man and angled his head in the direction of the sound.

The young couple was leaving the diner. They appeared too occupied with each other to notice what was going on.

Julia looked at the old man and back again at the couple. The couple was laughing, but they stopped at their car and glimpsed in their direction. *Oh, no, they see us.* Before she could react, the couple yelled something and waved. She feigned a smile and waved back. When she turned around, she understood why the couple waved.

Carver holding his gun in the old man's side was waving.

"I suppose people think being friendly means you are not holding an old man at gun point," she said crossly.

"They seem like a friendly couple," Carver sounded amused.

The old man straightened his coat and pulled the collar up around his long neck. A gentle mist chilled the night air.

"I not enemy, Mr. Carver," the old man said. "I come as favor to good friend."

"Is Addy still in town?" Carver asked.

"Addy one of names she goes by. My daughter sent code. I pass information to Elke. We used old ways. I not know where she...."

Carver interrupted as he glanced past Julia down the dark road, "We need to leave now."

She spun around and saw headlights in the distance illuminating the road ahead.

"We need more information." She gestured toward the old man who also stared at the headlights coming their way.

"Mr. Carver correct. Not safe here."

"It's a car. It's a road," she emphasized as she pointed toward the oncoming car. "It could be anybody."

"This old guy was able to track us, then others can too." Carver grabbed her arm and opened the truck door.

"Get your hands off me." She struggled to free herself. "I'm not leaving till I find out what he knows."

"He is right. You should leave," the old man sounded nervous. "Trust no one."

"That means you too, old man," Carver chided.

Carver pushed her into his truck.

"He knows more," Julia pleaded, pushing against Carver with all her strength. "We need him to find Elke."

The old man unbuttoned his coat and reached with one hand inside the heavy coat. Carver swung around and aimed his gun in the old man's direction. Gunshots rang out.

The frail man crumbled to the ground. Blood gushed down his face. His hand still inside his coat.

She muffled a scream with her hand covering her mouth. Shocked, her eyes stunned by what she just witnessed. When the man's body hit the pavement, Carver yanked her out of the truck shoving her downward. She could see the man's lifeless eyes wide open as he laid on the pavement. His head surrounded by a growing pool of blood from the head shot.

Carver was aiming his gun at the car speeding past. In a split second, the car was out of sight. "Fuck," Carver shouted. "Are you okay?"

"No," she managed to say in a shaky voice.

"We can't stay." He reached down and helped her stand. Her legs would not move. All she could do was stare at the dead man on the pavement.

He picked her up, put her in the truck seat and closed the door.

Back in the truck, he started the engine and placed his hand on her trembling shoulder.

"Julia, I need you to hold it together. You can do this. We have to ditch the truck and find another set of wheels."

"Did you kill him?" her low voice asked.

"No. It wasn't me. It was the car that sped by."

CHAPTER 24

THE PARADOX THAT a dead spy could threaten the mission at first amused Wagner. Earlier in the afternoon, when his handler had said, *we believe she has surfaced*, his chest tightened with overwhelming fear. The past was always more dangerous than the present. There was a spy in their midst.

It had been more than two decades since the Cold War. Governments used propaganda to synthesize facts. The Cold War was officially over. The reality was there were more Russian spies in America now. Unlike the CIA, the Russian Foreign Intelligence Service (SVR) was very patient. They would wait twenty years or more before a sleeper was activated.

"Why do you believe a dead spy has surfaced?" he had questioned his handler hours ago while sitting on the bench they shared.

"Have you heard of Operation Ghost Stories?" his handler asked.

"Yes, I know it well. It was a highly publicized case in 2010. The Federal Bureau of Investigation case against Russian operatives that ended with the arrest of ten sleeper agents in the U.S. A prisoner swap deal was reached between Russia and the U.S."

"Correct. The FBI embarrassed our government. It cost our government much time and money. It was thought at the time that Colonel Sergei Tretyakov had been the one who tipped off the U.S. authorities about the illegals."

"I remember Colonel Sergei Tretyakov. He was a double-agent who passed secrets to Washington."

"There were many allegations of a high-level defection. We learned it was not Tretyakov."

An elderly woman walking her dog strolled down the path in front of the bench where he and his handler sat. She stopped several times to let her small dog sniff every bush along the path. He and his handler held cell phones to their ears and continued to talk to each other. The woman with the dog would assume they were not talking to each other since they were sitting near each other on the bench.

"You knew Anna Chapman?" The rising inflection in his handler's voice made the statement a question.

"I met her once at an underground rave party in London's Docklands." He knew not to lie about going to the rave party and meeting Anna. Because his handler already knew. It was frowned upon to attend these large dance parties due to the association of illegal party drugs.

"Anna Chapman was one of our best operatives," his handler explained. "She had begun to develop ties in policymaking circles. But, she became too ambitious and materialistic. There is a decline in the old professional standards we used in the KGB."

He heard his handler tap her foot on the pavement. He wondered if she wanted to make sure he knew what she told him had very serious implications.

His handler continued, "The slip-ups exposed by the FBI strained relations between President Medvedev and the White House. Anna claimed an undercover U.S. agent contacted her using a code only her handler and Colonel Alexander Poteyev knew. The Russian authorities could not find Poteyev. He had escaped to the U.S."

"How does this have anything to do with the dead spy?" he questioned.

"We believe a list with the names of deep cover operatives has surfaced. Poteyev might not have been the source. He was a decoy to protect the real source."

"The dead spy you mentioned."

"Yes. We thought she had been killed and the stolen information destroyed."

"What makes you think this is no longer true?"

"Apparently, Poteyev talks in his sleep."

"Am I in danger?"

"If we do not recover this list, more of our deep-cover sleepers will be exposed. Our leader does not want to deepen hostilities with the American president."

"Why has the dead spy released only some of the names on the list?"

"The Kremlin believed it was to keep us from knowing that the list still exists. We have been able to place people in long term deep cover positions."

He knew Russian spy craft was different today than it was during World War II. Stalin used spies to infiltrate the OSS, U.S. precursor to the CIA. Ethel and Julius Rosenberg were American citizens convicted of passing information about the atomic bomb to the Soviet Union. That was how Russia knew the Americans were working on the atomic bomb. Today's operatives lead normal low-key lives. Today's SVR wanted agents of influence, to make connections. The goal was to influence American policy and opinion.

"They will become operational in a crisis period," his

handler warned with a smirk on her face.

"What kind of crisis period do you speak of?"

"A funeral. Everything is in place."

"A funeral?"

"Do not worry." His handler laughed. "It is not yours?"

He replied in a flat tone, "What is it you expect of me?"

"Continue to wait and be cautious. You will soon be where we need you. This is very important for our country."

"I have always been loyal and worked hard."

"You are one of our most valuable agents of influence."

"When will I be activated?"

"Be patient."

"What is it I will do?"

"You will know when it is time. I only come to tell you to be cautious."

When he got back to his office, he had difficulty concentrating on a bill his party was proposing.

Megan must have noticed something was wrong with him when she had delivered his mail.

"Are you okay, Mr. Wagner?" she had asked. "You look like you've had a rough day."

"I am fine. Just tired," he answered, trying to force a convincing tone in his voice.

"Well, there has been a lot thrown your way." She placed the mail in a tray on his desk.

He studied the dark-skinned woman standing in front of him. Her big eyes were warm and the color of dark chocolate. The red lipstick accentuated her sensual plump lips. He noticed her curvy body dressed in a navy wrap dress. He wondered what she looked like naked.

"Can I get you anything?" she asked in her usual cheerful way.

"Nothing right now. Thanks for asking." He swallowed hard.

As she strolled out of his office his eyes were drawn to the way the dress clung to her backside.

He knew he could never jeopardize their relationship. She was too young for him. All the long hours spent working together had been kept on a professional level. He was not sure why he even thought about Megan in a sexual way, but he did. Maybe it was because he was so frustrated with the conversation he had had with his handler in the park. Or maybe it was because he was feeling so damn lonely.

He turned his leather chair and stared out the window. The cloudy night sky only let a small amount of light dance across the Potomac River. People had long since faded into shadows at the end of the day. He knew soon the sky would be filled with complete darkness. Rain pitter-pattered on the large window.

His handler told him he would be activated soon. She would not tell him what that meant. The speakership was looming on his mind also. So many years of hard work and dedication were paying off. He had won the respect and admiration of his colleagues. Now he needed to make sure he had the support of his colleagues to win the speakership.

A soft tap at his door caused him to swivel his chair around. Megan stuck her head in the door.

"Sorry to bother you, Mr. Wagner, but I am leaving," she paused and stared at him, "unless you have something else you want me to do."

Again, he studied the attractive woman's face. He drew his lips tight together as he straightened in his chair.

A whirlwind of sexual thoughts bombarded his mind. Was she being suggestive? His desires were growing and he knew he could have mind blowing sex with her—one fantasy-filled night. *Should I cross the line? Do I give a shit right now? Maybe, she did not mean anything by what she said.*

Finally, he said, "Thank you Megan. Go home. I won't need anything else today."

She flashed a wide smile. "Have a good night, Mr. Wagner."

"You too."

What he needed was a long, cold shower.

CHAPTER 25

JULIA FELT LIGHT-HEADED as her mind buzzed with the image of the old man lying on the ground with blood seeping from his head. Her lower lip quivered. Numb with shock, she sat motionless staring out the passenger window. With some eerie coincidence or omen, as soon as the old man fell to the pavement, it started sprinkling. Now, it was an all-out deluge.

She had seen Carver wield around with his gun and then the frail man drop dead to the ground. The body bag count had gone up. Her supervisor at work, the man in her duplex and now this old man. Carver said he would protect her. Elke told her Carver could keep her safe. He was a liar. Elke disillusioned.

"Let me out of this truck, now," her quiet voice was barely audible.

"What? What did you say?"

She gulped, opened her mouth and then snapped it shut.

"Julia, I know you are frightened. We've got to get another vehicle. They know I am with you." Carver's deep voice was direct.

"There is no more *we*. I saw you kill that man. He fell as soon as you fired."

"You saw my pistol pointed at the old man and him fall to the ground. I knew he wasn't armed."

"Then why did you point your pistol at him?"

"He reached inside his coat. It was instinct. I never fired my weapon."

"I don't believe you. Let me out now. Stop this damned truck," she said in a frantic high-pitch voice.

He tapped his brakes and made a sudden left turn. The truck bounced from the dip in the road to the entrance of an apartment complex. He drove around back and parked.

Frantically, Julia opened the truck door and reached for her bag on the floorboard. His hand snatched her arm, turned her around so she faced him.

"Give me five minutes and then you can leave."

She stared him straight in the eye and thought about what she wanted to do.

"You've got one minute," she tried to keep her voice steady.

"How many shots did you hear fired?" he asked.

"I don't know how many you fired."

"Was it more than one?"

"Yes. You fired at least three rounds. You bastard."

"I'm former military. Warfare was my specialty. I never need to fire multiple rounds at such close range."

"Then why did you have to fire so many times?"

"Because I didn't. You saw my gun pointed at the old man, right?" He took his gun out of the pants holster and removed the magazine.

"A SIG 229 holds thirteen rounds." He emptied the magazine and put the bullets in the console holder. Then he pulled the slide to the rear to eject the chambered round. He inspected both the chamber and magazine. His hand let the slide go forward and thumbed down the hammer. Then he loaded the magazine with the bullets and counted out loud.

"This is ridiculous. I am leaving now. Your one minute is up."

"Thirteen bullets," he said as if this should have convinced her.

"This proves nothing. You could have reloaded the gun when I wasn't looking." She started to get out of his truck.

"Take this with you." He reached inside the console and retrieved a flashlight. "Look at the side of the truck."

"Why would you want me to look at the side of the truck?"

"Three bullet holes."

The rain slowed.

Staring at his intense eyes she snatched the flashlight from his hand and got out of the cab. Shining the flashlight on the side of the wet truck she searched for bullet holes. After inspection, she climbed back inside the cab.

"You were wrong," she said and handed him back the flashlight. "There aren't three bullet holes. There are five."

He said nothing and started his truck.

"Is there anybody you can trust?" he asked. "We need to get out of town fast."

"There was a bullet hole an inch from where I was sitting. Were they trying to kill me and accidentally hit the old man?" She shook her head in disbelief.

He didn't answer immediately. After several seconds, he finally said, "I don't know."

"Well, think, goddammit," she demanded. "Am I putting other lives in danger?"

"You mean me?"

"I mean anybody within five feet of me. Fifty feet of me. The same county, for crying out loud."

"We need to find a way to the airport."

"I am not calling a friend and endanger their life too."

He did not respond and sat quiet while the truck idled,

windshield wipers sweeping in front of her eyes. Maybe he was starting to see things from her perspective. Both his hands gripped the steering wheel and he stared straight ahead.

"You don't need to call a friend," he said. "This is D.C., there are other ways to travel."

"Like public transportation?"

"Yes."

"Let me see your burn phone," she said.

She stared at the phone unsure of her next move.

"I never lived in the western part of the United States," she stated to him. "The first time I heard about the town Fort Collins was when you mentioned it."

"That is why we need to go there."

"To try to make me remember something that never happened?"

"Julia, search your feelings deep inside. You know why we need to go."

After eyeing the phone for several minutes, she decided what to do.

She brought up a search engine.

"Closest commercial service airport to Fort Collins, Colorado is Denver," she said. "The next flight is tomorrow morning at six A.M."

"Book it," he told her.

"Look Carver. I know you made a promise, but...."

"We're going."

She decided not to argue the point and made the reservations for two.

"Metro will not run early enough for us to get to the airport by 4:30 A.M," she said.

"How about a cab?"

She began searching numbers for cabs on the phone.

"Where do I tell them to pick us up and what time?"

"Right here with enough time to get to the airport by 4:30 A.M."

She turned to check Carver's face in case he was joking.

She said, "You're not serious. How about your truck? You're just going to leave it here in the parking lot of this apartment complex?"

"Hopefully it won't get noticed until we get back."

He zipped his jacket up and turned off the engine. Leaned his head back on the headrest and crossed his arms on his chest.

"I can't sleep in this truck," she protested.

"You can sleep on the plane."

"I need a bath. I need to relax."

"A bottle of Wild Turkey in the glove compartment."

"I was beginning to think you actually had a heart."

He pretended to go to sleep.

"Just for the record, I really do hate you. I am not going to sleep."

She saw a smile creep across his face.

She moaned when Carver shook her body. She blinked, rubbed her eyes and blinked again. After a few yawns, she managed to clear her mind and open both eyes. The rain had stopped. Her face was covered in drool. She sat up and pulled the visor down to look in the mirror.

"I can't go to the airport like this. I look like I have been sleeping in the gutter."

"You can do whatever you need to do in the cab," he said.

"How I envy the women you date."

During the cab ride to the airport she brushed her hair, wiped her teeth with a baby wipe and chewed several mints. Occasionally, she saw the driver looking at her. *He probably thinks I am a prostitute with my John.*

Ronald Reagan Washington National Airport was already bustling at 4:30 with early morning travelers. Carver had already unloaded his SIG before getting in the taxi, locking it securely in a hard-sided case he kept in his truck. The magazine and ammo were locked in a separate case and placed in her duffel bag. Both of their bags had to be checked at the airport.

Waiting at their boarding gate, she broke out in a cold sweat.

"I can't do this," she mumbled to Carver who was sitting next to her.

"Yes you can."

"You don't know me."

"Actually I do."

"I don't even know me." She started biting her nails. "I am going to Fort Collins, Colorado. A place I have never been."

"Addy told me some things about her past. It happened in Fort Collins."

"I'm scared. My body is shaking. I feel like I can't breathe."

"I was at a very dark place once. I didn't think I could do what I knew I had to do."

"How did you find the courage to do it?"

"Addy Bravo."

She had to stand up. This man seemed to know more about her grandmother than she did. Trusting him might be a big mistake. She liked playing it safe.

"You do not know me, Carver. I am not a risk taker."

"If you ever want to find out who you are, then this is not an opportunity you can afford to miss."

She heard the announcement they would start the boarding of the plane. She looked at the gate, then at Carver and back at the gate.

"All right. You win."

Her palms were clammy as she handed the boarding pass to the attendant. The attendant smiled.

She could not return the smile.

She had a strange feeling her life was never going to be the same.

CHAPTER 26

Colorado

THE NONSTOP FLIGHT from Dulles International Airport in D.C. to Denver International Airport took approximately four hours. Washington D.C. was on Eastern time zone and Denver was Mountain time zone so that meant they would gain two hours back when they landed in Denver. Which was good since they needed the extra hours to try and track down clues to find Julia's grandmother.

It was mid-morning when they arrived in Denver. The skies were clear, the sun bright, and the Rocky Mountains provided a beautiful backdrop with their snow-capped peaks in the distance.

The rental car was a newer model Toyota Camry. Carver was not used to all the automation the vehicle offered. A few times he pressed the wrong buttons.

"Damn, these seats are hot. Did you accidentally turn on the seat warmer?" she asked.

He quickly examined the car panel's icons and realized he had indeed pressed the wrong button. He pressed the button again to turn off the heat.

Mockingly, she said, "So, no training in the Army on how to operate a car with lots of gadgets."

"Nah. We just learned how to blow them up."

They burst into laughter. It felt good to see her laugh. Especially doing it together.

"How long till we get there?" she asked.

"Not long. GPS says forty-five minutes."

The Denver airport was located east of the city. Fort Collins was north of Denver. He was glad they did not have to drive through the city. There was enough traffic on Interstate 25.

Not talking made the quiet car even more so. Julia just stared out the side window. Maybe she hoped she would remember something, could remember anything...or maybe not. Addy never gave him many details about her past. He sensed she was always holding something back. The clever woman told him just enough for them to bond. Their talks included pain and regrets.

Julia's crossed leg was bouncing. Anxious and scared, he thought. Hard to believe the woman next to him was related to Addy. Different temperaments. Addy appeared cool on the outside, inside her feelings burned with intensity. Julia could be read like a book. Addy was gutsy, Julia was not.

He did not share with her what the elderly man was reaching for inside his coat just before he was shot. After he pushed her inside the truck, he searched the man's coat and found a sealed manila envelope. The name Julia Bagal was printed on the front. He might have given it to her except for what was written underneath the name.

To be opened upon my death.

Perhaps it was Addy's Last Will and Testament. He doubted it.

When she fell asleep in his truck, he opened the manila envelope. He was not sure what he was looking at. Inside, there was a bingo card with notes he did not understand. Also, there was a note to Julia. It was a hand-written personal note from Addy. At the end of the note were instructions on where to deliver the bingo card in case Addy died. There were two passports and matching credit cards. Probably the handy work of the old man, the cobbler. Indeed, Addy Bravo had thought of everything.

He was sure Julia could not handle the personal note. He'd keep the envelope a secret for now. It did say not to open till they knew Addy was dead.

The word *dead* made him aware of their surroundings. A sense of urgency to find out what was happening made his foot heavy on the accelerator. Addy, the woman who had helped him recover was in danger.

Coming to Fort Collins was a gamble. Addy told her granddaughter she had to leave the country. Same thing she told him. Yet she refused to tell him what country or exactly where she was headed. That was why Fort Collins might be their hope at unraveling this mess. They could be wasting their time. He was not sure there were clues here to help them discover what was going on. Clues to Julia's past, he believed, might answer why people were dying. He needed Julia as much as she needed him.

The Embassy Suites hotel was close to the interstate. He made the decision.

She sat up when the truck made the sudden exit and shot him a quizzical look.

"Where are we going?" she asked.

"To see if we can get an early check-in and clean up."

He saw a smile spread across her face. There was something about her smile. The way she lifted her full lips. Dimples in her cheeks. Her sparkling eyes flashed at him. The smile made him forget his painful past.

"You should do that more often."

"What?"

"Smile."

"You sure are good at giving advice, but not following it," she retorted.

She was Addy's grandchild after all.

Luckily, he was able to secure two adjoining rooms that early in the morning. He gave Julia her room keycard and agreed to meet back in the lobby in an hour.

After cleaning up, he decided to wait for her in the lobby. This hotel was much nicer than the place he stayed in D.C. He located a seat near the check-in counter so he could see her when she got off the elevator. He had thirty-five more minutes before the hour was up.

Exactly one hour from when he told Julia to meet him, she appeared. As soon as the elevator door opened he felt his mouth drop open.

"Damn," he said not meaning to let his thoughts talk.

He was not the only man staring at her. Behind the hotel desk, the clerk's eyes were locked on her.

The messy auburn hair now shining flowed past her shoulders. Her lips a soft pink. A change of clothes she must have packed in her go bag revealed a curvy figure. A short leather jacket, tight jeans and short boots.

Their eyes met and she flashed him a smile. A jolt pierced his body like an electric current.

Carver was mesmerized. He stood as she approached.

"The food. Looks good. I am. Um. Very hungry," his words stumbled out of his mouth.

"What is wrong with you? Have you been drinking?" she

asked.

"No, I just…."

"Well, snap out of it," she said. "I need you to have steady hands."

"Steady hands?"

"Duh. In case you have to shoot somebody."

"Right. Steady hands."

They ate lunch at the restaurant in the hotel and discussed a game plan. She did not remember ever being in Fort Collins. They were both getting frustrated with dead ends.

"You said your grandmother worked at a hospital," he reminded her.

"I don't know which one. I thought it was in D.C. There are probably a lot of hospitals in Fort Collins."

"Maybe if we rode around you would remember something. Like the park Addy told me she had taken you to when there was the explosion."

"I don't know what she is talking about."

"Just tell me what you see in your nightmares."

Her face tightened as she closed her eyes. The memory must have haunted her since the event.

"I see ducks. A lake. A pool with a gate. I always hear a very loud noise. Flames and people yelling. I'm crying, but nobody can hear me." She opened her eyes. Tears one by one rolled down her face.

"It's okay Julia," he said as he placed his hands over hers on the table. "We don't have to continue this."

She hung her head and used the napkin to dry her face.

He did not know how to react. His foundation as a paratrooper was *if brute force fails to solve your problem, you're not using enough.* Since that day in Afghanistan, his foundation gone, he struggled to cope. Addy Bravo kept him strong enough to recover, but she was gone. He vowed to repay her. At first he believed the truth would help protect Julia. Now he was not sure. She might not be ready to discover her past.

"You are right; we don't have to continue this." She pulled her hands out from under his hands and put them in her lap. "I have to continue this."

He inhaled sharply. The courageous face in front of him was ready.

"Let's go then, we're burning daylight."

CHAPTER 27

JULIA AND CARVER took turns quizzing the young clerk behind the hotel desk on local parks and hospitals in Fort Collins. The lanky man's name plate spelled Justin. Justin was not from the area. He knew lots of great places to go hike, local breweries, and a few parks. Justin did not know the names of hospitals in Fort Collins. He told them they could use the media room to look up local hospitals.

They turned to leave when a woman behind them spoke, "How long ago are you taking about, young lady?"

At first, the woman's purple hair and heavy dark framed glasses were all you noticed. She stooped from years of gravity pulling on her bones. A cane in one hand and an over-sized pocketbook hung on her other frail arm.

Carver told the elderly woman they needed to know hospitals and parks in the area from approximately twenty years ago. Julia vaguely remembered she was around the age of five when Elke flew them to Germany. He told her it must be twenty years in the past, give or take a few.

The old woman insisted they call her Iggy. She had moved away, but was back visiting grandkids. Iggy explained the hospital was probably Poudre Valley Hospital (PVH). PVH opened in 1925. But, Iggy explained back then it was called Larimer County Hospital. Her uncle Fred had died in the hospital in 1976. She didn't fancy hospitals. Her children, all

six of them, were born at home. The park was probably City
Park. There was a lake in the park with lots of ducks and geese.
There was a pool in the park, too. Her daughter and son took
their kids there growing up to swim in the pool. Weekends, the
family would pack a basket of food and spend the day in the
park.

Carver grabbed a tourist map of Fort Collins from the front
desk and asked Iggy to show them the location of the hospital
and City Park.

It took a round of thanks before they could steal away from
the woman with her fond memories. Iggy raised her cane and
wished them luck when they headed out of the hotel.

Julia plugged in the address on his prepaid burner phone
for directions to Poudre Valley Hospital. The burner phone
was untraceable. She remembered watching the TV series, *The
Wire*. The drama centered around drug dealers in Baltimore,
Maryland and law enforcement. The television show made
prepaid burner phones famous. Criminals used the phones to
communicate. Ironic, she thought, I am now using one.

At PVH they encountered a construction site. The aging
hospital had deteriorated and demolition was underway for
a hundred-million-dollar expansion. At least that was the
explanation on the sign outside the hospital.

They devised a lie to get information about Elke having
worked there approximately twenty years ago. She hoped a co-
worker might be found in their search who knew more about
the mysterious woman than she knew.

The pretense she used was tracing the lineage of her family
history. She told the middle-aged woman with the short gray
hair in the personnel department that her relatives believed her
grandmother worked at the hospital. She was not sure if her

grandmother went by Elke Bagal, Elke Fenstermacher or Addy Bravo.

The seated woman with her hands poised to type on the keyboard, peered up over her reading glasses perched on her hawk shaped nose.

"How many grandmothers do you have?" the woman mocked with a stern face.

"Just one. I am sorry for all the names. I was adopted at birth. My mother was a drug addict. My father was in prison. The relatives I located gave me several names, she might have used. They said my grandmother was married several times." Julia pouted as she tried to muster up tears. All a pretense, but surprisingly, Carver put his arm around her shoulder as if on cue.

"My girlfriend needs to understand her past." Carver pulled her head down on his shoulder. "Her therapist told her it would help heal her emotional problems," he explained to the woman.

The woman's face softened a little as if she felt an emotional link to Julia's past. Her fingers clicked the keyboard.

"Let me see if I can help in any way. Most of our older files have been scanned into our electronic records. If I find her, all I can do is tell you if she worked here. Privacy laws."

Julia nodded to thank the woman as she freed herself from Carver's arm. She was irritated with him. He must have thought he was funny with his remarks. She wanted to slap the grin right off his face.

After fifteen frustrating minutes of searches, the middle-aged woman shook her head like she was telling a patient they had very little time to live. Disappointed, Julia thanked her and left the office.

She stormed down the hall and out the hospital's automated door. Carver tried to keep up, but trailed behind. Suddenly in the middle of the parking lot, she swung around to face him. "What the hell was that all about?" she asked in an angry tone. "You told her I have emotional issues."

"I got caught up in your lie. It was a good story."

"You went too far. I was handling it."

"Hell, you told her your mother was a drug addict and your dad was in prison."

"How does it help if we had found out she worked here twenty years ago? We still don't have a clue how to find Elke."

"It gives us a pretty good idea she lied to you. A lie hides the truth."

"Damn you." Furious, she threw her arms in the air and rushed to the car.

In the car, she was still too frustrated and pissed off to talk, except to give Carver driving directions to the City Park.

City Park was located on West Mulberry Street. He drove the car around the enormous park, allowing her to see the pool, lake, playground, tennis courts, basketball courts, ball fields, picnic tables, and green spaces full of different species of trees. The whole park was jammed with people out enjoying their weekend.

"Any of this look familiar?"

"I don't know," she snapped back at him.

She inhaled and exhaled loudly. "Maybe Elke never worked at Poudre Valley Hospital, because we never lived here. Maybe you are the one she lied to."

He did not look in her direction keeping his focus on the road. Perhaps she had hit a nerve. Maybe he knew she was right.

He parked the rental and suggested they get out and walk around the park. She agreed since she needed to release her built up emotions. Hearing the loud noise of ducks, she walked toward the lake. Standing near the edge of the lake, she gazed at the ducks splashing in the water, a sense of general happiness was triggered. A small voice of a child asking for bread to feed the ducks sounded familiar. A moment of mental clarity. Deja vu.

"Any luck remembering?" he asked as he stood next to her.

"No. Don't push me." She pointed toward a knoll. "Let's walk in that direction."

On top of the knoll she tried to pull clues from the depths of her mind. She slowly turned 360-degrees hoping there would be something to remind her of her recurring nightmare. Rays of sunlight beamed through the beautiful trees scattered throughout the park. Ash, spruce, scotch pine, maple, oaks, box elder filled the area of green space.

She inhaled and closed her eyes. The fresh scents of the trees and grass filled her nostrils. She once read in a magazine how memory and emotions can be triggered by sensory cues. However, all the noise from the people's activities in the park bombarded her with sensory overload. Her head hurt. She opened her eyes without having a hint of her nightmare.

"It's useless. We don't even know if this is the place." Her voice was low and full of frustration. "I feel we are wasting time. If Elke's life is in danger, we need to find her now."

Carver had his phone in his hand.

"I have been doing a search of past residential explosions in Fort Collins," he told her.

"Was there one around the park?" Her voice was hopeful.

"I can't find shit on this phone," he replied. "There was

no real digital information twenty or so years ago like there is today."

"We need to go to the library and see what they have on file with old newspapers," she said.

"We could spend a lot of time searching when we can't narrow down the year, or even the month," he answered.

"Again, a dead end. This is getting old."

His large hands landed on her shoulders. "That's it."

"What?"

"We need somebody old. Somebody who was here when the explosion happened."

"Oh my gosh. You're right."

As if they had telepathy, they uttered together, "Iggy."

CHAPTER 28

JULIA CLUTCHED THE inside roof handle of the Toyota Camry as Carver weaved between cars to head west toward the interstate.

She broke the silence at the same time Carver punched through the caution light, "Do you think we'll be lucky enough to catch Iggy at the hotel?"

"Don't know," he said as he swung the car into the other lane.

"But, the old woman will know if there was a residential explosion years ago, right?" she asked while holding the handle tighter to keep from being flung toward him when he swerved the car.

"Twenty years, give or take, Fort Collins was not a large city. Even now it is a mid-size college town."

Blowing out her breath, she said, "I wish you would just answer yes or no when I ask you a question."

Carver raised an eyebrow when he turned his head toward her.

"Okay," he said.

She groaned. All she needed him to do was reassure her. A yes or no would be better than it was not a big town. The man frustrated her.

"Wow, Carver. I bet you kept the women enthralled in conversation."

He rubbed his forehead as if he had a headache.

"Not one of my strong points." He slammed the car to a stop just as the light turned red in front of them. His right arm braced her from being flung forward against her seat belt harness.

"Damn. Are you trying to kill us?" She let loose an exaggerated sigh.

"I was distracted for a second." His hands gripped the steering wheel like he was curling them into fists.

When the light turned green he accelerated at a slower speed.

"I like women. Maybe too much. One of my vices." Carver grimaced. "Communicating with women though can be… complicated."

He did not seem to have trouble communicating with her grandmother. Perhaps he meant he had struggled with past relationships.

"Are you married?" she said even though he was not wearing a ring. It was a fishing expedition.

"Not anymore."

"How long have you been divorced?"

"First time, I was twenty. Young. Gullible. I should have seen the knife before she stabbed me in the back. Second time was my fault. I was at Walter Reed Hospital and she came to see me. I blamed it on my injury, but that was just crap. We both knew it."

"That is when you met my grandmother, isn't it?"

"Yep. But, you already knew that."

She was not sure of what to say. She kept her eyes diverted out the car window.

"I know what you're thinking," he said.

"Oh, do you? You tell me you find it hard to communicate with women, yet my grandmother with dementia is a breeze to confide in." The anger in her voice was rising like a tsunami.

"I was an angry man back then. She just helped me through a difficult time, that's all. You're reading way too much in to this."

He drove faster as he merged onto I-25 South.

† † †

The sun began to drain behind the Rocky Mountains. The sky littered with dark and orange strands of clouds created a beautiful backdrop to the mountains in the West. Fort Collins was situated on the Cache La Poudre River along Colorado's Front Range.

She was mesmerized by the silhouette of the Rocky Mountains. *Did she once live in this majestic place and not remember?*

The relationship between Carver and Elke bothered her too much. He was here by her side trying to help and protect her. She needed to concentrate on finding clues. Clues that could lead her to the whereabouts of Elke. The other issue she would have to let go of, for now.

He drove the Camry around to the side of the hotel and parked. The parking lot was starting to fill up with cars from weary travelers ready to find a place to stay for the night.

They entered through the side entrance of the hotel with a room key.

"Should we ask the clerk up front or just wait in the lobby for Iggy?" she asked once they were inside the hallway.

Without a word, he clutched her arm, and pulled her into the stairwell and shut the door. He held her against the wall as he put his finger over her lips.

She could hear the side door open and footsteps pad down the carpeted hall. The footsteps grew faint.

"I think we have company. A Crown Vic has been tailing us since the interstate," he said in a deep whispery voice.

"Why didn't you say something to me in the car?"

"I wanted to be sure. Now I'm sure."

He pointed up the stairwell. They climbed the stairs to the second floor. They waited by the stairwell door. Their rooms were down the hall.

He pulled his gun, eased open the door, and checked the hall. Then he gave her the all clear. Within seconds they were in her room.

He instructed her to pack her go bag. The next stop was his room. With their packed bags, they retraced their steps back to the parked car.

He told her they should put their bags in the car and then check to see if Iggy was still at the hotel. If they felt threatened by the man following them, then they would leave immediately.

Back inside the hotel, they walked over to the hotel front desk. The clerk Justin had been replaced by a young college age girl with a tag inscribed Zoe. The young waif-like girl was at least six feet in height, with long crimped dirty blond hair and heavy eye make-up.

Julia asked Zoe about the sweet old lady they had talked to earlier. They wanted to thank her for the information she gave them.

After a brief physical description, Zoe's eyes lit up. "You're talking about Iggy."

"Yes," Julia replied.

The young lady behind the desk grinned. "We know her well.

She comes and stays every two months to visit grandkids. But, honestly, I think she spends more time visiting with the hotel staff and guests. Her grandchildren are not always available." She shook her head to reveal disgust at the grandchildren not being available.

"Is she still checked in?" Carver asked.

"Right over there." The young lady gestured toward the restaurant inside the hotel. "Same place, same time every visit."

The small elderly woman with the purple hair was sipping what appeared to be wine. Carver and Julia walked over to her table.

"Hello," Julia greeted Iggy. "We are so happy to see you again. Mind if we join you?"

"Be my guest. I figured you two young people might have more questions." Iggy's sunk in eyes smiled through her thick glasses resting on her small nose.

Julia could not hide her expression of surprise. *How could the old woman know they would be back?*

Iggy laughed. "I'm pretty damn good reading people. You two were looking for something that happened around here a long time ago. I was here a long time ago. Not many people are from here like they used to be. Now there are too many transplants. They just don't know much about our history," she boasted with a sly grin.

"You're right. We're doing a story about a past event in Fort Collins. Our editor wants it to be about a tragedy that happened twenty years or so ago. Our detective work is leading us down dead ends," Julia lied.

"So you two are reporters?" the old woman's voice hardened with sarcasm.

They nodded in unison.

"What paper you work for?"

A short hesitation, then Julia muttered, "It is a small paper you probably have never heard of."

"No. I guess I wouldn't have heard of it." Iggy sounded skeptical.

She knows we are lying. Why doesn't Carver help me out?

"I think I'll have a drink," Carver said. "You want one Julia?"

He ordered drinks for them and a plate of appetizers.

"What tragedy are you two *reporters* trying to find out about?" Iggy said with a lot of emphasis on reporters.

"A friend told me about a residential explosion near a park, maybe City Park twenty or so years ago. Killed a husband and his wife," Carver said.

"Well, I do recall an arson fire that gutted a home near City Park."

A wave of panic spread throughout Julia's body. Her eyes glued to the old woman's mouth. Her nightmare coiled in her mind felt like a snake hissing and ready to attack if further provoked.

She felt Carver's warm strong hand cover her trembling hands under the table.

"This was a long time ago. How are you sure you remember the incident?" Carver inquired.

"I am old, young man, but you never forget being upset when you learn a good friend has died."

"What was her name, your friend?"

"I knew her as Uli."

CHAPTER 29

THE OLD WOMAN known as Iggy said she remembered the tragedy because her friend Uli died in the fire. The name meant nothing to him. But, the name must have meant something to Julia. She stared down at the table and fell silent for a moment.

"Uli?" asked Julia. "She was your friend?"

"Yes dear, we were friends," answered Iggy. "Do you need more information about the tragedy for your newspaper article?"

He could see Julia was trying to reconstruct events in her mind and at the same time stay focused on what Iggy was saying.

"We do want to know more about your friend, Uli, and the explosion," Julia replied in a calm voice. "But, if you would excuse me for a few moments, I need to use the restroom." She pushed her chair back, stood and did not walk in the direction of the lobby restrooms, but headed toward the side entrance to the hotel.

He was confused whether to follow or wait, the old woman made his choice.

"Give her a minute. She needs to have privacy for a short time."

He reluctantly sat back down.

"I think your young lady friend knew the people from that tragedy. Is she from here?"

"No. Well, she's not sure." Carver's instinct told him not to lie.

"Your friend Uli, what was her husband's name?" Carver asked.

"I have a good memory. Uli was born in Germany. She never married the father of her daughter. He was not a good man. I knew this not by what she said to me, I knew this by the tone in her voice when she said his name. His name is a German name." Iggy's eyes squinted behind her heavy framed glasses. "For the life of me, I can't think of his name."

Now he had more questions than answers. Elke's past was murky with facts withheld from him and Julia. Elke told him her daughter and son-in-law died in a home fire. She and her granddaughter were in a park when it happened. He was sure he was zeroing in on a piece of the puzzle. Maybe Iggy's episodic memory suffered from old age. The woman, she called Uli had to have died with her husband in the house fire.

"Iggy. I am confused, he said. "You said you remembered the explosion that killed a husband and wife. Yet you told me Uli was not married."

"I'm sorry, young man. I should have corrected you earlier. You are the one confused. There were four people killed in the explosion."

"Four people? I thought there were only two. Are you sure you're not talking about another home explosion?"

"I am quite certain. Home fires caused by arson were not a common occurrence in Fort Collins back then." The old woman stopped Carver from protesting with a wave of her gnarled finger. "There were four lives that perished in the fire. Four innocent victims burned beyond recognition. Uli, my dear friend, her daughter, son-in-law and her sweet young granddaughter she nicknamed Maus."

He should have paid attention to the right information. Elke said she could not be followed. She had been declared dead.

"Was the man Uli had a child with named Milo Wolfgang Fen-something or another?" he asked. Carver remembered the old man who called himself a cobbler telling them this was the name of Julia's grandfather. He could not recall the last name.

"Why yes. I remembered Milo was his name. He had a very long German last name. How is it you know Milo?" Iggy lowered her lids and probed Carver's face. "You are trying to help the young girl in some way."

"Yes," he confessed to Iggy. "It is important. Do you know what caused the fire?"

"Uli's daughter worked for Alcohol, Tobacco, and Firearms. Some people around here believed one of the gang members whom the daughter had arrested and was out on bail, placed a bomb in the home for revenge. He was doing it as a warning."

"So there were four bodies found."

"Yes. Sad to kill so many innocent people. Uli's granddaughter Maus was not yet six years old."

Four bodies were found in the home that exploded. Somebody must have planted two more bodies in the home, Carver speculated. Uli didn't die that day nor did her young granddaughter Maus, now known as Julia. The old man in the parking lot of the restaurant told them he provided false documents for Elke and Julia. Their new identities. The cover up had the smell of the CIA all over it.

But why would Elke take Julia to Germany to meet the man Iggy said she despised?

There was something wrong with the arson-homicide story.

"Please tell me about your friend Uli. Where did she work?"

"You don't believe the arson was gang related either, do you? You think Uli might have been the one they wanted to kill." Iggy's astute observation caused him to wonder if the old woman had some Sherlock Holmes in her.

"Why would you think that? I am just trying to understand what happened."

"You're military, aren't you?" Iggy asked. "I can tell by how straight you sit in your chair. When you walked over here, I saw you had a purposeful and swift stride. You could have lost your leg in a motorcycle or car accident, but you didn't. You communicate quickly, clearly and without any self-doubt. You are constantly monitoring everything around you."

"Paratrooper. 82nd Airborne Infantry Division."

"I knew it." Iggy slapped her hand against the table top. "You have a rugged handsome face too. Is the young lady special to you?"

"Something like that." He glanced around the room to avoid eye contact with the old woman.

"Does she have a personal stake in all of this?"

"She does. I am afraid her life could be in danger if we don't figure out some things fast."

"Servicemen have a strong sense of honor and integrity. I know. Let me see if I can put you two on the right track."

Iggy was full of information about Elke or Uli as she knew her.

"Uli, for the most part, was a private person. Great at helping you with your problems, but did not like you prying into her personal life. I only know about her relationship with Milo because one evening when I was over we had a few too many drinks." She chuckled at the relived memory. "Uli had a secretive side. She said she worked at the hospital. Did you find any helpful information when you visited Poudre Valley Hospital?"

"No. But we were not sure which name to give them."

"Should have told me upfront what you were looking for," Iggy fussed. "I could have saved you a lot of time."

"Wish we had."

"I went to the Poudre Valley Hospital when a friend had cancer. Hate hospitals. They are full of germs and sick people."

Carver gave a sharp nod and raised his arm to check the time on his watch. He scanned the room to see if anybody had interest in their visit with Iggy.

"I decided to visit Uli while I was there. Funny nobody knew who she was. It wasn't like it was a big hospital back then." Iggy paused to sip her wine and then continued, "Later, I asked my friend some questions. She said she studied nursing in New York City. I did not tell her I tried to see her at the hospital. It was her own business. Uli was always leaving town. She said it was for continuing education for nurses. Well, she had to get a lot of education, because she was gone a lot."

"Do you know where she went?"

"Nope, but I suspected it was to Germany to see that no good lover of hers."

"Why would you suspect that?"

"I went to visit her before the last trip she took. You know, the one before she died. On the table in the dining room was a plane ticket. It had Frankfurt on it. I asked Uli if she was going on vacation. She said Milo had some papers for her. Very important papers she needed to get. I did not pry. When Uli did not want you to know something, there was no need to continue a conversation about it."

"So you never knew what papers she was talking about?"

he asked.

"Naw, but the day after she returned to the States, she was dead. If the gang member wanted to kill her daughter, then why not do it at the daughter's home?"

He was impressed with Iggy's logic. Elke was the target all along. Ultimately, it got her daughter and son-in-law killed. The papers she retrieved from Germany might have been part of this sordid tragedy.

"I think you two young people need to leave," Iggy warned.

"I just have a few more questions," he said.

Iggy cautioned, "Earlier there was a man asking the desk clerk about you and the young girl after you left this morning. I pretended not to listen. He said he was your uncle and was supposed to meet you later today."

"Do you see him now?" Carver asked.

"Yep. My eleven o'clock. You two go. I'll slow him down for you."

Carver stood and stole a glance at the man Iggy said had been asking about them.

"Thank you, Iggy, you've been a tremendous help. Take care of yourself." He saw a twinkle in her eye. The old woman would have made a good spy.

He headed in the direction Julia went and intercepted her down the hall. He looped his arm around Julia and led her back to the lobby where they got on the elevator.

"Where are we going? I want to talk to Iggy some more," said Julia as she walked next to Carver.

"Can't. I'll explain later," he said. "Right now we need to get out of here."

On the second floor, they scurried past their rooms to the exit door leading down the stairwell.

Minutes later Carver watched the Crown Vic grow smaller in his rear-view mirror as he hit the gas.

CHAPTER 30

WAGNER QUICKENED HIS pace as the rain battered the ground. He wished he'd called a cab, but now it was too late. What had been a beautiful Sunday afternoon had now turned into a tumultuous night. He should have simply slept on the couch in his office.

The umbrella did nothing to protect his pants now clinging to his legs. His feet squelched in his wet shoes. He clutched his briefcase close to his chest beneath his trench coat.

A passing car splattered a puddle of water across his lower back.

"Asshole," his yell was swallowed in the howling wind and pounding rain.

For a moment, he thought, the weather was a sign of doom. He shivered. His life destined to get swept away like the water gushing down the dark street. He heard the grim echoes of his handler. *You will be activated soon.*

He hated the woman more now than ever. His handler controlled him.

His ambition was to be a history-maker, make his country proud. He just could not remember what country that was until that bitch reminded him.

Between his Junior and Senior years of college, he was encouraged by one of his professors to do a work study program abroad at a school in St. Petersburg, Russia. He became enthralled with Russian culture.

In a bar, he met a beautiful older Russian woman. Their relationship soon grew to an intimate one. At twenty-one, he was in love with Dominika. She was honest, scholarly, and possessed a kindness he had never known. He had grown up with a harsh demanding mother and a weak subservient father. Dominika proposed and nurtured ideas he was eager to absorb. The West was portrayed as a decaying society intent in a quest to expand its influence. She convinced him that Americans were programmed from an early age not to see what was happening to their country. Wagner, young and naive, never suspected the woman worked for the Russian Foreign Intelligence Service (SVR). It was during this time, he surrendered the physical control of his mind.

During his communist indoctrination, he learned his parents posed as ordinary American citizens under assumed stolen identities. They were sleeper spies who would never be activated. He felt his life was not ordinary so when he learned of his parents' identity, he surprisingly didn't feel upset. They were necessary to provide what Russia needed most; a sleeper who would influence the leader of the United States. Himself.

Brainwashing was easier when started with early-age children. Hitler knew children were more easily influenced than older adults. The Hitler Youth indoctrination camps brainwashed boys and girls into supporting the fascist cause. The United States, during the Cold War with Russia, employed techniques to reach children. Bubblegum cards in 1951 had pictures and text saying *Fight the Red Menace*. And now ISIS indoctrinates children through an extremism-based education curriculum to foster them to become future terrorists. The abuse and exploitation of children would secure the radical

Islamic State's future.

Various forms of propaganda dated back to times before the Romans. Technology allowed the use of misinformation to reach a larger population. The printing press helped spread propaganda during the Reformation. Countries during World Wars used propaganda to promote their agenda.

An incessant diet of government propaganda still existed. Only Americans believed they were not guilty. How soon they forget when the United States government and media entities deliberately gave misinformation that Saddam Hussein had weapons of mass destruction (WMDs), and Hussein was in on 9/11. The Cold War between Russia and United States was an example of both nations selling their respective ideologies to the world. Even after the claims proved to be false, Americans plugged their ears.

Panic mongers used fear so effectively to persuade Americans that fear bypassed the rational brain. Stupid Americans. He understood propaganda. Most politicians did, because they all used it to their advantage. He found the manipulation of information fascinating.

The noise from the torrential rain lessened. He was only two blocks from his row home apartment when the rain suddenly stopped. Dark clouds pierced by the moon rays lightened the darkness. The misty air smelled fresh, almost a sweet fragrance. His water-logged body hastened. Beams from an oncoming car made the wet road shimmer. He positioned his umbrella toward the street to shield him from the car splashing through a roadside puddle. Most people did not know splashing pedestrians falls under a section three of the Road Traffic Act 1988. This time he was prepared to protect himself and get the tag number of the vehicle. But, the vehicle slowed, then stopped next to him.

"Mr. Wagner, is that you?" The voice familiar.

He raised his umbrella and recognized the face. "Megan?" She was in the passenger seat. A young male driver smiled at him. In the back seat was another couple. The girl, he thought, looked familiar.

"Can we give you a lift?" she asked.

"Thank you, but I'm only another block away from my apartment. And now that I'm drenched, the rain has stopped. I'll just keep walking." He was sure they thought he was an idiot for walking home in a rain storm.

"Are you sure?"

"I'm sure. Thank you for the offer, though."

"See you in the morning, Mr. Wagner." Megan waved as the car pulled away.

He wondered why Megan never mentioned dating somebody. Then again, he never mentioned he had a handler.

† † †

Inside his historic row-house, he stripped down naked in the entryway underneath the crystal chandelier, letting his soaked clothes crumple on the marble foyer. He padded across the cool floor leaving moist foot prints and climbed the hardwood staircase to his master suite. A shiver hastened his steps to the master bath. He needed a hot shower. The chill from walking home in the rain was still with him.

His luxury row-house, built in 1915, had been beautifully renovated and professionally decorated to fit his bachelor lifestyle. The interior designer had preserved the past character of the home while adding some modern charm. She told him there was a science to blending the old and new. The living area had a 10-foot ceiling, tall windows and a wall accented by a wood-burning fireplace surrounded by floor-to-ceiling plain-sawn cherry wood hearth. Several walls had the original exposed brick. A light cream leather couch adorned with bright colored pillows sat on top of an oriental rug. Modern artwork hung above the couch. He could not figure out what the artist had painted, but he did like the colors. Mounted on a wall facing his favorite chair was a large screen HD TV. His office, with multiple black stained bookshelves, a mahogany desk and high back leather chair, was located across the foyer from the living area. He did not spend much time in either of these rooms. Most of his time was spent at his Capitol Hill office.

It wasn't the beautiful molding, the cozy courtyard, the impressive staircase, or the historic charm that made him open his wallet and buy the over-priced home. The two things that sold him on the place was its location and the gourmet kitchen. He wanted to be able to walk to work and this location was perfect. When the realtor showed him the home, he did not notice the crystal chandelier in the foyer. But the moment the realtor showed him the kitchen, his inner chef began to visualize the meals he could prepare on the six-burner commercial grade range. The Sub-Zero refrigerator was awesome. The kitchen was clad with premium finishes and fixtures along with a pantry large enough to stock food for a year. He signed the contract that evening.

Abeedah taught him how to prepare Dam Kay Boti Kabab in this kitchen. He learned about Halal food and Islamic customs through her eyes. Abeedah was an American Muslim. Their candlelight meals were followed by wonderful conversations. He loved waking up the next morning, her lying next to him.

She was a strikingly beautiful and intelligent woman who made him feel alive. *I should have stood up for her when the handler made accusations. I let my ambition blind me.*

The hot pulsating spray from the shower ran across his skin allowing his muscle fibers to loosen and relax. The earlier meeting with his handler caused him to tighten the muscles in his neck and shoulders so much they began to ache.

He felt a tinge of jealousy about Megan. He assumed because of the long work hours, she would not have a personal life. Now he realized how much he did not know about her.

It must be wonderful to have a personal life you do not have to share.

His handler on the other hand knew every skeleton in his closet. His financial status, every woman he had dated, his favorite food, his mother's hoarding, even that his right foot had Morton's neuroma.

His handler had overstepped her authority. She was necessary in the beginning of his career, but now he did not need her. His loyalty was not to her. It was to his country. A strong country.

Yes, Russia had declined after the demise of the Soviet Union. The President of Russia knew that future military power would soon be capable of actions on a global level once again. Bases in Cuba and Vietnam closed in 2002, under a pretense of improved relations with America. The economic decision tricked the Americans. Putin never intended to leave Cuba or Vietnam for good.

Cyprus president Nikos Anastasiadis now allowed Russian aircraft to land on a Cypriot airbase near Paphos and the Russian navy could use the port of Limassol. Money could buy many things. The Kremlin was now negotiating the usage of already existing military bases with Venezuela, Nicaragua,

Algeria Singapore, Cuba and Vietnam. This would be a means of defense and a tool to support additional territorial claims in these regions. The next stop for Russian presence would be in the Arctic. Soon Russia would have thirteen air bases and ten radar stations in the Arctic Region.

He was sure he knew his role.

Not foreign policy. America would focus on Russia's strengthening military defenses. They would not see the real danger was the non-military tactics. Americans were incapable of registering the reality of the real threat. It was not a lack of information, but a lack of thinking outside the box. When the truth was right under their noses, fear could cause people to focus on the wrong issue.

The tool Russia would employ would be clever. They would not have to launch a military war against America. No, that would not be necessary.

Russia would promote and fund radical movements.

They would use minority populations to gain strength in the anti-government environment.

He was a spy with power to influence and undercut the United States President's agenda.

CHAPTER 31

THE RENTED TOYOTA headed southbound out of town.

Headlights flickered on the highway and traffic was heavy on I-25 southbound toward Denver. Carver, at the wheel speeding along, passed cars and big rigs barreling down the road.

As soon as dusk descended into night, the warmth of the sun's rays was replaced with a pleasant coolness.

Julia stared blankly out the window. She earnestly believed she was prepared to discover the truth in Fort Collins.

She was not.

When she heard the name Uli, it sounded so familiar. She needed a few moments to try to remember why the name stirred her emotions. Julia walked outside the hotel as her brain tugged at a memory she was afraid to remember. This was where it began, just like Carver had told her.

Outside, she stood looking in the direction of the Rocky Mountains and knew the truth about what had happened to her parents. The nightmares she suffered since childhood were part of her past.

The truth had not set her free, it made her feel like she was suffocating, unable to swallow the gut-wrenching reality. Her past was a fraud, made up of lies fed to her by the one person in life she trusted.

Elke.

Her parents had been killed in a house explosion in Fort

Collins. The echoes of truth fueled her anger toward Elke. Her grandmother was now a person she did not know.

Julia wet her chapped lips with her tongue and sighed. *Why did you lie to me Elke?*

Carver reached over and gently squeezed her shoulder.

"How you doing?" he asked.

"Fine." She turned away in a vain attempt to hide her real feelings.

"I thought it would help."

She felt the car surge when Carver stomped harder on the gas.

"Help who? Me? Was that your real reason?" she challenged.

"I thought you would remember things to help us figure out what was going on."

"Now that we know Elke is not the person I knew, and my past is not what I believed for over twenty years, does that help?"

"We need to find Elke," Carver said. "I have called her several times. No answer."

"I don't care anymore. I just want to go home."

He gave her an *are you kidding* stare. "You can't go back. Not to your home."

"You going to stop me?"

"If I have to."

"I'm done with this masquerade." She ran her fingers through her hair like she was combing it. "I have to get back to my job."

"Your job? Have you forgotten there was a dead body found in your cubicle at work? There is an ongoing investigation."

"When I tell the police what I know now, about you, Elke and my past, they can help us."

"Elke is in danger. *You* are in danger," his deep voice rose in a no-nonsense tone.

She knew he was right. Elke should have contacted them by now. She needed to make a call.

"I need the burn phone." Julia shoved her open palm toward him.

He reached in his front pocket and passed the phone. She thought he would object demanding to know who she was going to call, yet he drove without protest.

She did not have Alvin's number. It was lost when Carver smashed her phone into pieces. She did a white page search and did not see a listing for him. *Who could I call that would have his number?*

The time zone difference might be a problem. Denver on Mountain time. D.C. on Eastern Time. Two hours' difference. It was too late to try his work. Then she remembered. He had friended her on Facebook before they began dating.

After logging in to Facebook, she sent him a message.

I need to talk to you. What is your number?

Two minutes later his number showed up.

On the phone keypad, she thumbed the digits.

"Julia, where are you?" Alvin's voice sounded panicky. "I've been worried. Are you okay?"

"I'm fine." For some reason, she did not feel comfortable telling Alvin where she was. "I need to know if you have any new information about the Johnston audit?" She hoped the audit she worked on would provide a clue.

"Still a lot of hush-hush surrounding this case, but I have a friend in the FBI who was able to do some snooping. This is really weird."

"Alvin, just get to the information." She realized her voice sounded desperate.

"Sorry," Alvin said. "The FBI apprehended two passengers before they boarded a flight to Moscow. They worked for a large Russian agricultural company that does crop research to develop seeds. In their suitcase, buried in microwave popcorn boxes were 300 small manila envelopes, all cryptically numbered-A35, A36 and so on. Each envelope contained one single seed."

"They were stealing seeds?" she interjected.

"Yes. Seeds that were tested and found to be genetically modified hybrids. The FBI traced the seeds back to their development with guess who? Johnston."

"So, the FBI thinks that is why my supervisor was murdered in my cubicle. For a few GMO seeds? My audit dealt with financial statements."

"I don't know any more than that. I am worried about you."

"There is no need for you to worry. I'm fine. I will contact Krystyna about any gossip she has heard at work."

"Hmm, well there is…" Alvin paused before continuing, "more bad news Julia."

She felt a lump in her throat. Her heart beat like the thrumming wings of a hummingbird. *Please don't tell me she has been murdered.*

"My FBI friend heard Krystyna went missing. When they went to her apartment, she was not there. They have her place under surveillance."

"What?" She was sure her friend was dead.

"Let me help you," Alvin pleaded. "Tell me what to do."

"I'll call later. Right now, I am staying at a friend's place in D.C. Thanks Alvin."

She quickly ended the call. Then she thumbed another

number. The phone call went to voice mail. *Krystyna where are you? Please be okay.*

She shuttered. Her trembling hands thumbed another number. Again, the phone call went to voice mail. "Answer me, Elke. God sakes, answer," she said loudly.

After clicking off, she stared at the phone in her hand.

"I think I know where Elke went," Carver said as if the thought just occurred to him.

His statement caught her off guard. It was devoid of emotion.

Julia, overwhelmed with the magnitude of the crisis, studied his face.

"Where?"

"Germany."

"Did Iggy tell you something to make you think this?"

"Yes."

"You want me to make reservations to Germany?" she asked.

"Yes, but under different identities."

Carver explained to Julia about finding the envelope inside the coat of the old man at the restaurant in D.C. Elke knew there was a good chance they would figure out where she went. To protect Julia, Elke must have asked the cobbler to provide new identities for them. A safety precaution.

He exited the interstate and rolled the rental car into a gas station. She was angry he had not shared this information with her. He rendered an apology and tried to justify his actions. She rebuked it.

At the airport, he parked the rental in long term parking. He rationalized if they did not turn in the rental, then nobody could discover they were back at the Denver airport.

"An airport, has a lot of video surveillance," she said, "What if the authorities are waiting for us at the airport?"

"I'm hoping the man who followed us to Fort Collins thinks we are still in our hotel room or still in town. If he is FBI or CIA, they will have alerts to know if we purchased tickets out of Denver."

She used their new passports and credit cards to purchase two nonstop tickets to Frankfurt, Germany that evening for an overnight flight. She hoped the card had a high credit limit since the tickets were almost $3,000. The woman behind the United Airlines counter, checked the passport picture against Julia's and Carver's face. She smiled, handed them back their passports and said, "Have a good flight Mr. and Mrs. Thompson."

She rolled her eyes at Carver.

Security was always a problem for Carver. His prosthetic leg took extra scrutiny. She admired the way he remained calm during the screening. Ever since 9-11, TSA security had increased. Amputees faced longer screening than non-amputees.

When Carver removed his jacket, he rolled up his shirt sleeves. Julia had not seen the tattoos adorning both his arms. The TSA agent recognized one and knew Carver was a paratrooper. He nodded and the screening went without any further delays.

Seated on the plane, she tried to relax. So far, they were still alive and able to leave the country.

Carver's broad shoulders invaded her seat. His shoulders

also protruded into the aisle.

"We have time now to rest and discuss everything we know up to this point on the long flight," he told her.

A man headed to the back of the plane, caught her eye and bumped Carver's shoulder as he passed.

"Excuse me, sir," he said in a deep accent.

Russian.

CHAPTER 32

THE STRONG ACCENT from the man who bumped Carver caused Julia to look up at him. Her eyes focused on the upper portion of his face—disfigured from a large scar. The piercing eyes from the tall muscular man fixed upon her face lasted a beat too long. Was this the man tracking them in Fort Collins? She never saw the face of the man in Fort Collins.

When he was out of earshot she whispered to Carver, "Is that the man who followed us in Fort Collins?"

Carver craned his neck to get a look at the man headed to the back of the plane.

"No," he replied.

"Are you sure?"

"The man in Fort Collins was about five foot eight with a head full of black hair. He had dark Italian skin and a disheveled appearance. If you put a rumpled beige trench coat over his suit and a cigar in his hand he could pass for Columbo."

"Who's Columbo?"

"Guess you never saw reruns of the television series about a homicide detective with the Los Angeles Police Department. Peter Falk played the detective."

"Peter Falk? Never heard of him."

She slid down in her seat and peeked through the space between the seats to see if she could locate Scarface. In the back of the plane, she saw him place a briefcase in the overhead bin before taking a seat.

Poking Carver in the arm, she said, "The man is Russian."

"What man?"

"The man who bumped into you."

"This is an international flight, Julia."

"He recognized me."

"Is this a gut feeling?"

"Yes. I just can't put my finger on it."

"Gut feelings are usually right," he agreed.

"Should we try to get off the plane?" She gave him a worried look.

"No." He shook his head. "He can't have a weapon. Probably surveillance for somebody. We stick with our plan. Go to Germany and try to figure out what is going on."

Peeking through the seats, she told him, "Let me have your phone for a minute."

She raised up and leaned against Carver, her arm extended with the phone out front like she was taking a selfie of the two of them. The camera angled above their head, she saw the real intended target.

"Look, a selfie of our honeymoon trip to Germany." Her voice loud enough to be heard by surrounding passengers. After snapping several shots, she slipped back in her seat.

"What the hell was that all about?" he asked.

Her fingers enlarged several of the pictures. Satisfied, she passed the phone to Carver. "Look, that is him."

"Okay." Carver shrugged. "He probably has our picture too, so only fair we have one of him."

She reached under the seat in front of her to retrieve her pocketbook. Her hand fetched a steno pad along with a pen.

"I spend a lot of time at my job reviewing documents to

uncover problems in a company's business practices. There is always something to find, if you are diligent." Her enthusiasm animated her hands and gestures.

She opened the pad, drawing lines and labeling columns.

"All right Sherlock, give me a clue why your job as an auditor can help us."

She went on the defensive. "We need to look at every angle of this problem. The reason some auditors never find fraud is they focus all their attention on the same items in the same way year after year. Clients know their auditors and know what areas will be tested."

"We aren't conducting an audit."

"You said we need to go back to the beginning. To where it began. We discover clues to find Elke. But to find Elke, we must know her motivation. We need to go deeper than the surface to unravel the clues. If my clients knew what part of their system I would test, they would make sure it was without error. What do most auditors test? The large dollar transactions. But, most of the issues in a company are the small issues. The ones that never draw attention."

"You want to translate in English."

"Small things add up to big clues. We need to harness everything we know and see if it leads to something."

"All right. Tell me what you know."

"No. You need to start. I don't even know my past. I suspect you know more about it than I do."

Her pen poised over the notebook.

He said, "For starters, you tell me why you call me by my last name and then I'll start."

She paused and then answered, "I'm not sure."

She lied.

Elke called him Derick so even though it was silly, she decided to call him by Carver. "If it bothers you, I can call you Derick."

"No. Carver works for me." She was sure he was smiling even though his face had no expression.

He began, "Elke told me she worked for the CIA when she was younger. Her daughter and son-in-law died in an explosion in Fort Collins. I could tell she still struggled with guilt."

Scribbling on the pad, she quizzed, "Why would my grandmother feel guilty?"

"That I don't know. It had something to do with the fact that there was a cover-up"

She stopped writing, tilted her head forward, and gave him a slight frown. "Cover-up. What are you saying?"

"Something Iggy told me when you went outside."

Her lips tightened, "When were you going to share this with me?"

"You were still upset."

"What did Iggy say?"

"She said Uli was her best friend. And Uli died in the explosion."

"I already know that. Hearing the name Uli evoked a memory. I felt like it was yesterday. I was in a park and heard the explosion. Uli died and I saw the flames." Tears streamed down her cheek. Carver found a tissue in his pocket, placed it in her hand.

"Julia, who do you think Uli is?"

"I believed Elke when she told me my mother's name was Grace. But, when Iggy said Uli, I knew that was my mother's real name. She always comforted me when I was little. I felt it that moment I heard it."

The announcement from the flight attendants said they were cleared for take-off. The airplane flaps and slats extended, the engines strong acceleration created a loud noise inside the cabin. The landing gear groaned from the brakes as the wheels stopped before they retracted into the wheel wells.

She stiffened in her seat, grasped the arm rest and took deep breaths to relax.

"You don't like flying?" he asked.

"No. I don't like it. Makes me feel like I'm not in control."

The plane climbed and the aerodynamic noise increased in the cabin.

"If it helps. You aren't in control." He laughed. "We'll level off soon."

The laugh soothed her tensed body.

"I need to tell you something that will upset you," he said with a shake of his head. "Maybe now is not the time."

"Upset me," she mocked. "Are you frickin kidding me? Ever since Elke, then you, came into my life, I have been upset. There is not one damn thing you can say to make my life more upset."

"Uli is Elke."

How could that be? Why wouldn't I remember my mother's name?

The strong hand in her lap kept her seated. She felt ill. He checked inside the seat back pocket in front of him and handed her the barf bag. He turned the overhead air vent on high and rang the call light. He asked the attendant for Ginger Ale and a cold, wet towel. Gently he placed the wet towel on the back of her neck.

"Better?" he asked.

"Yes. A little. Thanks." She felt as limp as the towel around her neck.

After a few minutes, he spoke, "I think the reason you believed Uli was your mother's name was because the explosion that killed your parents traumatized you."

"Why wouldn't Elke tell me she used to be called Uli?"

"There were four bodies found in the charred ruins of Elke's home."

"I don't understand," she tried hard to comprehend what he was telling her.

"Elke worked for the CIA and whatever information she had acquired, the Russians wanted it destroyed. Your grandmother faked her death and your death. Elke needed the Russians to believe both of you died in the explosion along with your mother and father. Therefore, her name Uli was changed and your birth name also."

"It was a cover up to protect us," she exclaimed. "That is why we went to Germany to get new identities."

"Yes. I believe that is what happened."

It was hard to process that her grandmother worked for the CIA. Elke in her demented state talked about being a spy. Could it be true, her grandmother used to work for the CIA?

"My parents were collateral damage. They were just in the wrong place at the wrong time."

"It appears that way," he said in a low tone.

Elke should have told her the truth. She had been living behind a mask for over twenty years and didn't even know it.

The nine-hour, thirty-five-minute nonstop flight was long enough to flesh out the facts they shared with each other.

"This all seems to have started when Elke went into the assisted living facility," Carver said.

Julia suggested, "Maybe there is an underlying purpose Elke became vocal about being a spy. Her babble might have a hidden motive. Perhaps it was to force somebody she needed out of hiding."

Carver agreed, "It appears Elke had an unfolding plan. Your grandmother did not know who was tainted in her own agency, therefore she found me to protect you. Right now, we all are in the epicenter of this storm."

She closed the steno pad, "We know more now. Maybe we are right or maybe we got it wrong. So, where do we go from here?"

"There are three possible scenarios we should consider," he offered. "One, Elke is running from danger to protect you. Two, Elke is on the trail of information she recently learned. Third, Elke is back on CIA's payroll."

"Which of those do you think is the most plausible?"

"Right now. All three."

CHAPTER 33

Frankfurt, Germany
Early morning

AFTER EXITING THE plane at their arrival gate, Julia and Carver were directed to Passkontrolle, or passport control. After they had their passports stamped, Carver directed Julia over to the side wall. He disclosed his plan to wait outside the woman's restroom, while she went inside. The Russian who Julia called Scarface was still in line to have his passport stamped. Carver preferred his target in front of him. Not behind.

A tall man with a deep scar across his cheek appeared in the crowd of passengers deplaning flights. He quickly assessed the man, from the expensive leather jacket, the shoes, even the wristwatch he wore. The mannerisms of the man did not warrant suspicion. Scarface held a cell phone against his ear with one hand, carrying a briefcase in the other, never once glimpsed in Carver's direction.

Julia walked out of the bathroom and stood next to him. "Has Scarface walked by?"

"Just up ahead."

"What do you think?"

"I don't like him."

"Gut instinct?"

He raised an eye brow. "You can wipe that grin off your face," he said. "We need to be careful."

They followed Scarface just close enough to see where he was headed.

Frankfurt Airport, a major international European airport was bustling with passenger traffic even this time of morning.

Unexpectedly, Scarface surged deeper in the herd of people ahead of them. Carver clenched Julia's hand leading her as they weaved through the mass of people. He heard her say *Entschuldigen uns* when they bumped people that needed to move out of their way. She pointed at a man that looked like Scarface on the escalator headed down to baggage claim. He was sure they would catch up before Scarface collected his checked bags.

People had already begun to gather around the baggage carousel waiting for their bags when they got there. He felt they could be at any busy international airport. Airports all possessed the same personality. A man with a jawbone attached to his ear, a woman wearing a neck pillow, business men with their leather briefcases, moms with young children tired and crying. All the noise of announcements and people except the dominance of the German language.

He swept the crowd hoping to locate Scarface. Julia was stretching on tiptoes in a frantic search to locate the Russian as well.

"I don't see him," he said.

"We assumed he checked a bag since he headed in this direction," she said. "Maybe he just had the carry-on."

"Stay here," he instructed. "I will walk around the carousel and see if I can find him."

He strolled around groups of people in position to grab

their bags. The conveyor belt began moving, dropping an assortment of luggage on the carousel. Swarms of people began to scoot right up to the edge and retrieve their bags. The packed crowd made it difficult to spot Scarface.

If he isn't waiting for us here, he might have left the terminal. Maybe my gut instinct was wrong.

The moment he turned to walk back to Julia, he halted. In his peripheral, Scarface stood next to another man near an exit door. He could not identify the features of the other man whose hat was pulled low on his forehead. The man facing Scarface was doing all the talking. It appeared he was giving instructions to Scarface. What he saw next convinced him Scarface was probably up to something.

Scarface bent over to gather his briefcase on the ground next to his left leg. In one swift motion, he leaned passed his briefcase, and picked up the briefcase by the other man's feet. Scarface slowly turned his head and caught Carver's stare. A second later, there was no trace of either man.

He and Julia claimed their bags, passed through the custom area, and then followed the blue signs in the airport to the train station. He lied to Julia. He told her there was no trace of Scarface so he probably was not following them. Right now, he needed her to stay focused and calm. She was doing a good job with all she had been through in the past few days.

While on the plane, they figured that if they wanted to find Elke they needed to find Milo. The closest friend to Milo was dead now. He wanted to check out Frankfurt's directory for a Milo Wolfgang Fen-something or other. He could not recall Milo's last name because when the old man pronounced the name it rolled deep in his throat coating it in a thick German accent. The German language sounded harsh with words ridiculously long. Like Milo's last name. Germans put several words together to form one complex word. Perhaps it was their way to be efficient.

Unlike him, Julia could recall Milo's last name. She sounded German when she pronounced the name.

"I think we have a better chance of finding Milo in Wiesbaden not Frankfurt," she told him. "The old man said Milo would visit his bookstore often. His bookstore is in Wiesbaden." She held up crossed fingers. "Let's hope there is an old local there like Iggy who can help us. We need to check it out."

"That was a long time ago. The bookstore might have closed."

"He said his shop *is* in Wiesbaden, not *was*." Her astute memory of that small fact impressed him.

"Yes, I remember that now. And he said something about his daughter running the bookstore. We need to find an information desk to figure out how to get to Wiesbaden," he said.

"We can go to the Reisezentrum and ask for the most direct train to Wiesbaden."

"The what?" he asked.

"What you said, information center."

"You speak German?"

"Ja, ich spreche flieBend Deutsch."

"Well, you could have told me earlier when we were sharing all the facts."

"Since you and Elke had such intimate conversations, I figured you knew." She flipped her long hair over her shoulder.

Carver knew better than to say anything. He followed the signs to Reisezentrum.

† † †

Jet lag always made him feel fatigued. And with it, the usual accompanying headache started to throb on the sides of his temples. The lack of space between seats kept him from being able to sleep more than a half hour.

The easiest way to get to Wiesbaden was to jump on a train and arrive forty minutes later. Even though many Germans spoke English, Julia's fluent German expedited the ability to quickly find everything they needed before hopping on the next train to Wiesbaden, including the purchase of a cell phone at the airport.

He was relieved to get away from the bustling airport of Frankfurt.

Before boarding the train, he told her he needed to check on Parker Brown, his dog. He dialed an international number. The voice on the other line said, "What is your emergency?" He placed a finger in his ear and headed away from Julia and the crowd. Carver hoped Julia would not follow.

"Parker Brown," he responded.

"One moment," the voice said. Two minutes, a woman on the other line asked for a code. After he gave it to her she said, "You made a promise. You should not have contacted me."

Carver spoke, "We have a situation. Where are you?"

The tone in the voice on the other end was angry, "Your instructions were to disappear with her and keep her safe. Not follow me."

"We have disappeared. She is safe. You leaving the country to chase down something will not keep them from trying to get to her."

"Bullshit. You get her on a plane now. Leave immediately."

"How do you know where we are?"

"I have my ways."

"They want her as bait," he warned. "They know it is the only way to get what you are after or already have. I need to know what this is about and where you are."

"The more you know, Derick, the more it endangers her."

He heard lots of background noise and then a female voice he did not recognize greet Elke.

The line went dead.

He slipped the phone inside his jacket before walking back to Julia.

"Did you find out how your dog is doing?"

"He's doing fine," he said looking in another direction to avoid eye contact with her.

Onboard the train, she said, "I need to eat when we get to Wiesbaden. I feel my blood sugar dropping."

"Sounds good. I could eat a giant hamburger right now."

He stretched out his legs, leaned his head back against the headrest. He saw her eyes examining his prosthetic leg. "Wondering how I lost my leg?" he asked.

"No. I wasn't thinking about how you lost it."

"Funny," he said. "That's usually the first thing people ask me."

"Accident or in war?"

"I like the fact you say in war. Seems a lot of Americans don't know we are at war."

"I know you were in the Army. You lost it in war."

Carver visibly flinched. The moment was scorched into his memory.

"What was your mission?" she asked.

He took a deep breath.

"I'm sorry. I have no right to pry into your past," Julia murmured.

Carver shrugged. "I was in Afghanistan almost six months when I was injured. I was leading my unit on a dismounted patrol to clear IEDs from an area where U.S. troops were soon to open a school for 2,000 children. Taliban had closed the school because the local village elders allowed girls to be educated. When we approached, the villagers were everywhere. They knew what was going on. So did I. When I raised my rifle, and started to squeeze the trigger to yell *ambush*, it happened."

"IED?"

He nodded.

"So, what is a *dismounted* patrol?"

"By its simplest definition, a patrol on foot…as opposed to a motorized patrol, which is usually in an armored vehicle, like the Humvee."

"You sacrificed a lot for your country, are you bitter?"

"Angry. I lead my men into a trap. I lost two good men that day."

"You followed orders. Did you think about the lives you saved that day?"

Damn. Addy Bravo and his therapist had said the exact same thing to him. So many soldiers coming home had survival guilt. Addy wasn't a soldier, yet she had survival guilt. Addy told him she should have been the one to die in the explosion. Not her daughter.

He was surprised how easy it was to talk to Julia about this.

"I'm glad Elke supported you at Walter Reed," Julia said. "I'm sure it seemed at times the public and even our government doesn't care about the sacrifices our soldiers make."

"At times, but there was one young politician who visited

MATC Physical Therapy clinic at Walter Reed. We became good friends during my recovery. It's been a few months since we last connected."

He peered into her pleading eyes. She was a lot like him in many ways. In one instant, their lives were changed forever. They both were struggling with anger. They both had to deal with the hand dealt them. A connection between two people brought together by a woman who had saved both their lives in very different ways. He felt a strong attraction to her.

"Julia. I am not sure what is happening...", his words stuck at the sight of the image in the train car.

"What is happening?" she questioned.

"Damn. We are popular people today."

"What are you talking about?"

"Pretty sure I just saw Columbo climb the stairs."

"The man following us in Fort Collins?"

"Only now he's wearing the rumpled trench coat."

"Are you sure? How could he know where we were going?"

Carver shook his head and muttered, "Elke."

CHAPTER 34

ELKE? IS THAT what Julia heard Carver say? He was holding back information from her and she didn't like it.

Abruptly, he stood. "Stay here. I think it's time to find out who this guy is."

"What about Elke? I tried to call her in Frankfurt. The call went to voice mail. Did you talk to her?"

Ignoring her question, he stalked toward the train stairs.

"Carver, I'm going with you."

He turned so sudden, she collided into his large chest.

"I need you to stay put. Do I make myself clear?"

"You go, I go. Don't try to stop me."

He hesitated and then finally nodded. "Just stay behind me. Let me make sure it's him first. Copy that?"

"Uh-huh."

At the top of the stairs, the man Carver called Columbo was seated with his back to them. A laptop was open on the table top in front of him. Carver walked up, shoved the man over to the next seat with his shoulder and sat down. She slid in a seat facing both men.

"Hey, what are you doing?" the voice of the man in the rumpled raincoat was American. He did not have a distinct accent, but she could hear a hint of a southern drawl.

The description Carver gave her on the plane was dead on. The man across the table had a thick black mop of hair, sleepy eyes, cleft chin, and a weathered dark complexion. She guessed he was in his fifties. Propped next to Carver he looked small in stature.

"Let's start with you telling me why you've been tailing us. I spotted you in Fort Collins," Carver gravelly voice frightened the man.

The man's voice quivered, "You're mistaken, mister. I've never been to Fort Collins."

She was ready to beg forgiveness and leave, then the man's face grimaced.

"I can easily break your hand if you lie. So, I'll ask only one more time. Why are you tailing us?" Carver demanded.

Carver was hurting the man. She knew he was inflicting pain in some manner underneath the table. Maybe she should protest. The man didn't look threatening.

"I'm telling the truth," Columbo said weakly.

The man yelped causing passengers to look in their direction.

"Next lie and I break your hand." Carver's face frightened her.

"No. Please. My job. I need my hands."

"One second," Carver warned.

"I am doing a favor for a friend," the man confessed. The grimace left his face.

"Your friend have a name?"

"She said this mission was important to the security of our nation."

Another grimaced face.

"Please stop that," the man begged.

"Two seconds," he roughly reminded Columbo.

"Same person you're doing a favor for…Addy Wilson."

"You mean Addy Bravo?" Julia voice filled with excitement.

Carver released his stronghold. The man's torso sagged slightly and he quickly placed his shivering hands on the table.

"You call her Addy Bravo?" Columbo asked. "She uses several variants of several names to change identities like a chameleon. She told me Addy Wilson. Nevertheless, she's the same person."

Carver kept a steady gaze on the man and asked, "Where is she now?"

"I don't know." The man recoiled from Carver. "I promise. We have never met. She helped me find work after the agency canned me."

"What agency?"

"CIA."

"You worked for the CIA?" Julia said in a low voice as she leaned across the table.

"Yes, many years ago. It was the good ol' boy network. Still is. Addy worked for the Clandestine Service and the analytic arm was where I worked. The former had case officers in charge of spies and directing covert operations. The analysts were responsible for interpreting whatever secrets or other data were fed into the Agency from abroad."

"So why would they fire you? Did you do something illegal?" Julia queried.

"No, not illegal in the sense you are thinking. I had heard of Addy while I worked at the agency. She had a reputation as one of the best covert CIA officers. Before she could meet and share classified information with the CIA director, an attempt on her life was made and all evidence destroyed."

"What was the assignment?" Carver asked.

"I was never privy to that information. Addy was deep undercover to gather intelligence. My job was to sanitize all evidence that she survived."

Carver asked, "Why the cover-up?"

"The agency felt her life would be in danger if the Russians knew she was still alive."

"So why were you fired?" Julia asked. "I'm confused."

"My nickname at the agency was Fly. I got it because I can find out things without people realizing I was listening. You know, like a fly on the wall."

"Yeah, so what was it you heard?" Carver said not seeming impressed.

"I learned there was a mole in the CIA who blew Addy's cover. I figured out a way to contact her and let her know what I knew."

"The CIA found you broke agency protocol," Carver said.

"Something like that. They claimed I failed my drug test."

Carver continued to drill for information, "Did the agency find out who the mole was?"

"Years later, he was arrested and charged with espionage. In his testimony, he confessed to compromising the identities of CIA and FBI human sources. Sent to prison for life."

"So he is the one who blew Elke, I mean Addy's cover?" Julia asked.

"Addy thought so. He mysteriously died in the prison hospital."

The train announcement for the next stop Wiesbaden was heard throughout the train.

"How are you tracking us?" Julia asked. "You can't be using our cell phones."

"No." He looked at Julia. "Addy put the tracker in your bag."

"Oh my gosh, our bags." She sprang from her seat, ran and took the stairs two steps at a time. The bags were still in the overhead bin. She snagged her bag, unzipped it, and rummaged through it. Hooked on the inside was a tiny bag with a small device inside. Damn Elke.

Zipping the bag shut, she saw Carver descend the steps with the man in the rumpled trench coat leading the way. Carver pushed him toward her.

"Fly is coming with us."

"Fly?"

"Tell her your birth name."

"Brailsford Troup Nightingale, Jr."

"Okay, Fly it is. Let's get going."

† † †

There were plenty of fast food places inside the Wiesbaden train station. After ordering fast food at McDonald's, Julia found a taxi to take them to the first bookstore from a list of the ten best Googled bookstores in Wiesbaden.

During their express lunch, Fly sat next to her forcing Carver to sit on the opposite side. She figured Fly wanted as much distance as possible between him and Carver.

"What exactly is your mission Fly?" Carver's unblinking stare made Fly nervous.

Fly began to stutter, "Mr. I...I... am...am a friend, an analyst. Plea...Please believe me."

Carver blinked. His interrogation tactic changed.

"I believe you. Fly," Carver continued in a less intimidating tone, "you can relax. We need to know what you know."

The man slumped back in the seat. He took a bite of his hamburger.

"Addy Wilson contacted me three days ago," Fly explained.

"She told me there was a national crisis and needed somebody she could trust."

Carver added, "Sounds familiar. I'm beginning to wonder how many people this woman trusts."

"Not many. Believe me. The man she trusted at the agency betrayed her. He compromised her identity *and* the documents she acquired from a KGB defector. This betrayal got her daughter and son-in-law murdered."

"So, Addy is having you tail us?" Carver asked.

"Surveillance. When you left for the airport, an old lady tried to mislead me into thinking you were going to your room."

"Iggy," Julia said.

"I was going to head to my room when I realized I forgot my cigarettes in my rental."

"You saw our car was missing." Carver was beginning to figure out how Fly got to Germany so fast.

"Yep. I informed Addy. She told me what to do. First class, late gate check."

"Shit," said Carver as he gulped down his soda. "You flew first class while I was cramped back in the plane." She thought Carver was going to punch the man.

She asked Fly to give her Addy's contact information.

"I'm afraid I can't. I lost contact with her when I arrived in Frankfurt."

CHAPTER 35

THE MIDDLE-AGED taxi driver was reluctant to dedicate his cab solely to them for the day until Carver counted out enough Euros to seal the deal. A German native, he spoke broken English. When Julia attempted to communicate in his native tongue, he would wave his hand saying, "English, please. I speak English."

There were ten bookstores that specialized in rare books in Wiesbaden. After each visit to a bookstore, the driver would take them to the next one on the list. The salt and pepper haired taxi driver's pronunciation of many English words made it difficult to understand all the encyclopedia facts about his beloved city, Wiesbaden. The German taxi driver, proud of his speaking ability, had a captive audience.

Wiesbaden was famous for its architect and hot springs. Fourteen hot springs still flowed today. A modest city of 273,000 inhabitants, 20,000 were Americans, most of them with the United States Army. Carver added he had never been stationed here.

If they had not been pressed for time to find Elke, or Addy Wilson as Fly called her, she would have gone to the hot springs the driver mentioned to relax. She envisioned herself melting into the steamy hot water, muscles relaxing as she surrendered all her stress. But, right now she needed to find the bookstore the old man told them about before he was gunned down. She feared they were running out of time and options.

They had already checked out nine bookstores without success. Not one store owner had heard of Milo Wolfgang Fenstermacher. She attempted a description of the old man who told them he owned a rare bookstore in the town. The shopkeepers would shake their head and say, "Nein, ich kenne ihn nicht." *No I don't know him.*

Back in the taxi, Carver asked, "How many more stores on your list, Julia?"

"One more. I don't know what we will do if this is a dead end."

The taxi pulled up to the curb letting them out in front of a shop with a sign hanging over the doorway that read, *Der Letzte Buchhandlung.* The old stone building had a picture window filled with books displayed in a chaotic manner which could have passed for a storage unit. A clinging evergreen vine wrapped the rough facade suggesting a place warm and inviting. In Europe, people let the ivy cover their building to keep it cool in summer and insulated in the winter. A bicycle propped against the storefront had a wooden crate attached to handle bars.

"This has to be it." Julia believed the name of the store, *The Last Bookstore* ironically conveyed her last hope. The three paraded up to the open door.

Inside the shop, wooden shelves stretched from the floor to the ceiling holding a bounty of books. Old volumes of books were scattered helter-skelter across the floor. Some of the piles were more than knee high like a stack of firewood. A wooden ladder leaned against one shelf that appeared to prevent an avalanche of jam-packed books from devouring the customer standing next to it.

She loved the smell of these antique bookstores. She ran her fingers along the spine of several old books filled with tales from the passage of time. The tranquil feeling of the shop was like sitting around a campfire mesmerized by the flames.

"Hey, is anybody tending shop?" Carver's deep voice filled the shop.

"Maybe, the shopkeeper is at lunch," Fly said.

"Why would they leave the shop unattended?" Julia asked him.

Carver yelled a few more times. Julia and Fly chimed in.

After several attempts to locate the owner, she turned toward Carver and asked, "Now what?"

"Maybe the old man deliberately misled us," Carver said.

Her face slackened and her brows furrowed. A feeling of defeat caused her shoulders to slump. She was afraid her grandmother would be snatched from her life just like her parents.

Carver and Fly retreated toward the taxi. She stopped in the doorway to the shop, turned around and again shouted, "Ist jemand hier?"

From behind a shelf, she heard a gruff voice. "Ja, ja ich bin hier." *Yes, yes I am here.*

Excited, she yelled to the others, "He's here. He's here."

The man was as old as many of his books. The tall thin man had a head full of white hair, thick eyebrows and a long white beard. His long thin crooked fingers held a pipe in one hand and a stack of books in another. Along with his wrinkled clothes and sleepy eyes he might just be the legend Rip Van Winkle.

The old German spoke excellent English. He seemed disappointed he did not know their friend. All his regular customers were locals from Wiesbaden and did not have the name of the person they sought. Julia showed him the list of Googled bookstores with rare books and asked if there were any others in town.

"Ya, there is one other very small bookshop that carries antiquarian books. Very old, out-of-print books, not used books like many of the ones on your list. I do not think the person you described is the shopkeeper now. It is very close to here."

"Please would you give us the address so we can go there?" Julia asked.

"Ya, but it is closed for a few days. The owner's father has died and she is waiting for his body to be shipped home for the funeral."

Julia asked, "Where did he die?"

"In your country. America."

"Do you know how he died?" Carver chimed in.

"Rumors I hear. Say he was killed by an American military man."

She felt a lump in her throat. "When is the funeral?"

"I am sorry, I do not know," the old bookstore owner said.

Carver, Julia and Fly hurried out the store. Carver told the taxi driver they would walk, shoving a few more Euros at the driver. They followed the directions the bookstore owner gave them. The location was around the corner.

"The bookstore is closed," Fly said walking beside Julia. "Why are we bothering to go there?"

"For information we might find. There could be something on the closed sign. We might see something in the window." Julia was breathing hard. Carver was walking fast. Even with his prosthetic leg, she was trotting to keep up.

After rounding the corner and crossing the street, they continued down the sidewalk another block before realizing they had gone too far. Not one of the buildings had a sign to indicate a bookstore or a window displaying books.

"I never saw a bookstore and we should have seen it by now according to the directions," Carver said.

She studied the address on the piece of paper. The old man from the bookstore made it seem like the store was just around the corner. They never saw a shop or the address.

"We should have stayed with the taxi driver," Fly said in a tone that was too much like I told you so.

"You want your phone and laptop back in one piece, you better shut up," Carver said.

"You have his phone and laptop?" she asked.

Before Carver could answer, she pivoted on her heels toward a smell of fresh bread and pastries that filled her nostrils. She hurried toward an old woman in front of a bakery sweeping the sidewalk with a broom made of corn husks attached to a long handle. She handed the paper with the address on it to the old woman and asked if she could help locate the shop. The woman nodded, spoke in German as she pointed toward an alley they had passed. Julia said, "Danke" and darted back across the street.

The barren narrow alley did not have many store fronts. There were several odd shape doors. One looked like a door to a medieval castle along with a stone archway surrounding a thick wooden door adorned with a weathered brass knocker and hinges.

The bookstore's door was a rustic old world arched door with raised panels. There was a front window with a collection of leather bound books displayed around an assortment of relics of the past. A vintage typewriter, an inkwell pen holder with a feathered pen quill on antique parchment style paper, and an oil lamp. The display of books was strategically placed, unlike the last bookstore. The painted lettering on the show window read, Aicher's Buchgeschäft. Julia quickly interpreted the note written in German on the door out loud.

"Store closed due to death in family. Sorry for your inconvenience. Signed Liese Aicher."

"Now I guess we need to find out where she lives," Fly suggested.

"Maybe the woman at the bakery will know," Julia added.

Carver pounded the door with his fist. "He said at night he worked in the cellar. That means he probably lived here. Which means Liese probably lives here."

She cupped her hands around her eyes, leaned against the glass to peer in the window. Inside darkness filled the outline of bookshelves. She strained to adjust her eyes when she caught a glimpse of a shadow move behind a shelf of books.

"Carver, I think I saw somebody in there."

"Yeah, well if she won't answer the damn door, I'm gonna bust it down."

"You can't do that."

Carver readied his body to charge the door and hit it hard with his shoulder. Julia held her hands up in protest. They began to argue about the best way to find Liese. Julia thought the bakery woman could be of help. Carver wanted to use brute force on the door and if it failed break the glass shop window.

They stopped arguing back and forth when Fly, in a high-pitched voice, interrupted, "Have you checked to see if the door is locked?"

Julia and Carver stared at Fly. It would be ridiculous if the door was not locked.

Carver lumbered over to the door, placed his hand on the handle and twisted the knob. It turned.

He gave a slight push inward.

The door opened.

CHAPTER 36

THE RUSTY HINGES of the door creaked when Carver slowly pushed it open. A musty scent greeted him upon entering the bookstore. Daylight streamed in from the open door allowing him to scan the unlit room. Floor to ceiling ornate shelves outlined the walls intersected with several free-standing shelves between them. All the space on the shelves was occupied with tightly packed vertical books with titles in German. The shop had two chairs, a counter with a lamp and a computer for making sales. The floor unlike the other bookshop was devoid of clutter.

Standing in the doorway, Julia tapped his back and whispered, "Should we call out her name?"

Shaking his head, he mouthed to her and Fly to stay put. His two fingers told her to keep eyes on the door and Fly to watch the back of the store. Then he began his search of the building. If the owner was inside, he planned on finding her.

Carver did not like being unarmed, but he knew Germany had one of the most stringent gun control laws in Europe. He shipped his SIG 229 to his home in Michigan from the Denver airport. He wasn't sure how he would obtain a gun in Germany, until Julia said they should go to Wiesbaden. An old Army buddy stationed at the U.S. Army Garrison in Wiesbaden might help him out. He tried several times to contact her, but ended up leaving a message.

Julia said earlier she saw movement in the shop. The fact the door was not locked was another red flag. He again signaled to Julia and Fly to stay near the front of the store. *That damn girl is stubborn.* She and Fly had moved further inside.

He moved stealthily toward the back of the store sweeping his vision back and forth across the room. In his peripheral, he saw movement. A free-standing shelf's books were flying out like blocks of ice breaking loose from an iceberg. He yelled back to Julia and Fly who were standing beside the tumbling shelf. He charged back to help block the weight of the shelf before it trapped them.

Julia's scream filled his ears.

Before he reached the falling shelf, a fist popped out from an aisle between two bookshelves. A hard-solid blow on the side of his face caused him to wobble. The shadowy figure lunged forward wrapping one arm around his neck. The man exerted pressure with his strong bicep and forearm on Carver's carotid arteries. He had eight to thirteen seconds before he would lose consciousness. He used both hands to pull down the shadow's forearm and bicep allowing him to gasp for air and bend his chin next to his chest. Carver grunted, bolted upward like a machine lifting weights and executed an elbow strike to the shadow's ribs. The opponent released the choke hold as Carver heard a popping sound from the punch accompanied by a yelp. The shadow on the ground scrambled to his feet. Light shining through the shop window reflected off the barrel of a gun pointed directly at Carver's torso. The shadowy figure pushed the gun out advancing toward his target. Carver began talking and slowly started to raise his hands as if surrendering. In a swift movement, Carver moved his body sideways, stepped in, simultaneously grabbed the shadow's wrist with his left hand

and pushed down with his right. Holding the shadow's gun, Carver told him to put his hands behind his head and turn around.

"Carver, help. We're trapped." Julia's frantic voice from under the fallen bookshelf.

He surveyed the area and saw two bodies wedged under a large wooden shelf with hundreds of books littered across the room. He raised the butt of the gun to smash the back of the head of the shadow when a bullet whizzed past his ear. He flinched, dropping his arm as the shadow swirled around. He jerked back his left fist and slammed it into the shadow's gut. When the shadow bent forward, he saw another shadow pointing a gun at him. Carver fired at the armed shadow and leaped behind the counter as bullets struck all around him.

"Shit." The bullet grazed his arm, but the pain felt like being scalded with a hot iron. Warm blood oozed down his arm. His back against the counter, adrenaline coursed through his body.

A shower of bullets struck the counter and a bookshelf behind him. He was glad the counter was thick and solid. Splinters of wood flew into the air and rained down like confetti from a parade. The suppressive fire now had him pinned down. He readied his weapon and waited for his opportunity to turn the tide of the firefight. He listened for movement from the attackers to determine his tactic. Raising up would make him a target. He heard scuffling feet retreating. He moved to the far side of the counter and began firing. The two shadows were racing out the store. A car squealed to a halt, and the assailants jumped in.

A second later, they were gone.

✝ ✝ ✝

"Julia, are you okay?" Carver shouted.

"Get us out. Fly isn't moving. Hurry."

He hurried to the voice trapped under the bookshelf.

"Julia, can you move your arms?"

"I think so."

He shoved books out of his way, walked around the case to assess the situation. He could lift the case high enough for Julia to climb out, but Fly was unconscious.

"If I raise the case high enough for you to climb out, can you drag Fly out?"

"I'll try."

The solid aged wooden bookshelf consisted of seven horizontal shelves. The case was eight feet tall and twice as wide. It was not the weight of the case that presented the problem. Carver could dead lift over 450 pounds. It was the massive size of the bookcase. Trying to push the case all the way upright would not work.

"Get ready," Carver instructed, bending down locking his hands under the top lip of the bookcase.

A grunt, his hulk like biceps raised the case three feet off the floor. Enough clearance for her to crawl out.

A moan. She tugged on Fly's trench coat. Carver could see her struggle beneath the case. She was unable to nudge the dead weight of the man. He could not reach Fly and hold up the case at the same time. He knew she would not be able to lift the heavy wooden case. Maybe Fly was dead.

"Just crawl out. I'll figure how to get Fly out after you are clear."

She crawled from under the case and sat up. She moaned several more times.

"Do you have any broken bones?"

"No. I don't think so. But, my back hurts."

"Let me check you."

"We need to get Fly out first," Julia said. "I'm okay. That shelf must weigh a ton. I think the fallen books protected me."

He spied a wooden chair in the corner and put the chair next to the case.

"When I lift the shelf, can you prop the chair under?"

"I can do that."

With the chair holding up the wooden case, he managed to stretch his arms out and grab Fly's trench coat dragging him clear of the case.

"Is he alive?" She sounded scared.

Fly moaned, his eyes fluttered open. He sat up and gasped, "Ow."

The man appeared dazed. Julia held his arms and asked, "Are you okay?"

"I remembered books hitting me and then everything went totally dark. My head is throbbing. It feels like a jackhammer went off inside."

She checked Fly's head. "I don't see blood or an open wound. You need to take it easy."

Fly gave Julia a weak nod.

"Carver, who attacked us?" she asked.

"I couldn't see his face. He wore a black ski mask and was dressed in black. I'd be willing to bet he was the Russian on our flight."

"If you didn't see his face, then how do you know it was him."

"The watch. When he walked by us at the airport, I noticed the expensive gold watch he was wearing."

"Should we call the police now? Fly might need medical attention."

"We call the police, they arrest us. We need to do a quick check of the store and get the hell out of here. You and Fly check up front. I'll try to find the cellar."

She tried protesting that Fly should not start moving around, but Fly assured her he would be fine.

"What are we looking for?" Fly questioned.

"A reason to kill," Carver grumbled.

They began searching the store.

Traversing around a bookcase, Carver found a small room. He lost the rays of light peeking through the front door and window. He patted his hands along the cold stone wall that had the feel of a dungeon. A faint light shone across the floor from beneath a door.

"That must be the door to the cellar." Julia was standing behind him.

"Dammit, Julia," he fumed, "I thought I told you to help Fly search the front of the store."

"Who put you in charge of this search? There is nothing in the front of the store. I'm going down to the cellar with you."

"You're the most headstrong woman I've ever known," Carver said as he turned abruptly and reached for the door handle. He swung the door open and a draft swept across his face. The door did not creak like the front door. Probably because it was protected from the weather.

Carver had to keep his head low with his right hand holding the pistol as he descended the narrow stairs. The windowless room was lit with light bulbs encased in wire cages dangling from the ceiling. The dank subterranean cellar reeked of stale cigarette smoke. Thick stone walls were lined with rustic handmade wood workbenches. A machine that looked like a printer was perched on a shelf in the corner. A workbench directly in front of Julia had bottles of glue, razor knives, and a task lamp surrounded by an assortment of different colored passports. The weathered cellar afforded a glimpse into the past of the cobbler who tried to warn them at the diner before he was murdered.

While she searched through the items on the workbenches, he kept the gun aimed ahead and skulked around the back side of the chilly cellar when the smell filled his nostrils. Lying face down was a woman's body splayed across the floor. Her arms spread above her head cradled a gun in her hand. Blood soaked her blouse and a liquid pooled around her body.

The smell was urine caused by the muscles in her body relaxing right after death. He reached down and touched her body. She was warm and rigor had not set in, therefore he figured she had not been dead very long at all.

He glanced over his shoulder and did not see Julia. He debated on how to handle the situation. Julia had not handled the death of the old cobbler very well. Maybe he could just tell her he did not find anything and they could leave the store. He knew Julia would get suspicious if he lingered too long out of her view.

He needed time to check out something recessed in the stone wall next to where the dead body was lying.

A vault.

CHAPTER 37

JULIA CAREFULLY RUMMAGED through the items on the workbench down in the bookstore cellar. Several of the passports appeared legitimate with one exception, the photo was missing. A sheet on the table had a list of people's full names, social security numbers, addresses, dates of birth and dates of death. A credit card, driver license and birth certificate were in a folder along with several copies of a 2 x 2-inch photo of a man. Julia noticed at the end of one bench was a camera and computer. The cobbler's shop was still active.

Finally, Julia concluded there was no hint of a clue where Milo might be staying. Frustrated, she shouted, "Carver, I can't find anything to help us locate Milo. I'm not even sure what I am looking for. Have you seen anything?"

"No," he shouted back. He paused and then continued, "If you want to go check on Fly, I'll be right up and we can get out of here."

If I want to check on Fly? Carver was up to something.

She spun around inspecting the room. *Where did he go? What was he up to?*

She crept around the stairs toward the back of the basement. The L-shaped room had less lighting in the narrow space of the back corner. A caged light bulb dangling from the ceiling was casting a shadow on Carver. His arms were raised in what look like an attempt to pry open a door with a long black object.

Immediately after spotting the body of the dead woman lying on the ground, she stopped in her tracks. She stared silently at the body for a few seconds forcing her mind to comprehend what she saw.

"Oh my God. Is that the store owner?"

Carver did not turn around. He was busy pounding the large metal object on what appeared to be a vault door.

"Pretty sure it's her." He tried to jam the metal bar in the seam around the vault. A loud clink sound echoed in the room.

"There's a weapon in her hand," she said knowing Carver had already seen the gun.

"Don't touch it," he commanded. "Still loaded and we don't want our fingerprints on it."

"What are you doing?" She stood next to Carver trying to get a look at the object he was trying to pry open.

"The owner must have refused to open the safe," he said. "She died trying to protect something contained inside. I found this piece of iron. Hoped it would slip in the door gap so I could try to pry it open," Carver said as he stepped back. "This thing is made with steel and concrete. It's no use trying to get inside."

She insisted, "We have to open it."

"Negative. Without the right tools or the combination, we're shit out of luck."

"Combination. Numbers, right?" She stared at the locking mechanism.

He threw the piece of iron down on the floor and took her by the arm, "We need to get out of here before somebody calls the cops."

"The name on the store door was Liese Aicher? Right?"

"Affirmative. And I'm pretty sure that's her." Carver pointed to the body lying by the safe.

She pulled her arm free from Carver's hand and refused to budge. "I can open it."

"Julia, you can't do it without the combination. We need to go."

Stepping forward, she placed her slim hand on the combination. Her fingers turned the locked backwards several times before landing on a number. She completed the sequence and heard an unlocking sound. A satisfied smile spread across her face when she saw the surprise on Carver's face.

"How in the hell did you know the combination?"

She told him about searching Elke's bedroom and discovering a vitamin bottle with a folded piece of paper inside.

"I'm good at remembering numbers. On the note were three numbers, each two digits separated by a hyphen. Beneath the numbers, were the words, 'Viel Glück', which means 'Good Luck' followed by the initials LA. When I read LA, I thought it was Los Angeles or something. I did not put it all together until you said combination. Then I knew LA stood for Liese Aicher. She had given the combination to Elke. I think Liese was the cobbler's daughter and was following in his footsteps."

"Very impressive detective work. Elke would be proud." Carver patted her shoulder.

Together they pulled on the heavy door opening it to reveal the contents. The vault was full of documents on one shelf. Another shelf held a cache of guns. A metal box occupied a shelf on the bottom of the vault.

"We don't have much time. What should we do?" Julia's anxious anticipation caused her to bounce on her toes like a teenybopper waiting in line to get a peek of her idol.

He retrieved the documents on the top shelf and handed

them to her.

"Take these to the bench up front where there is better lighting and see what you can discover. I'll see what else I can find in the safe."

He removed a pistol and tucked it in the back of his pants.

"Why are you taking a pistol?" she asked. "You already have one."

"Never can have enough weapons."

She was happy to move as far from the body as possible. The sight of the woman on the floor made her feel like she was falling down a dark bottomless shaft. Elke was in danger and time was running out. She rushed back to the other side of the basement to try to discover needed clues.

"Hey, what's taking so long down there?" called Fly as the sounds of mournful creaks could be heard on the old wooden stairs.

Fly approached her and asked, "Where's Carver? I could not find anything helpful upstairs."

"He'll be back in a moment. I need you to help me. These documents are in German. Can you understand German?"

"A few words. Not fluent. I think we need to get out of here." Fly's head kept turning like he expected somebody to show up on the stairwell.

She knew he was right. It was only a matter of time before somebody passed by the store and got nosy. She also worried the assassins would return.

Carver walked over while she tried to speed read the documents.

"Find anything Julia?" he asked.

"There is just too much to sift through," she said. "Nothing that would lead us to Milo. Inside a manila envelope, I found a tiny metal case that turned out to be a USB flash drive. It might have something interesting on it. Also inside the envelope is a picture of a man and woman on a park bench."

"Elke?" Fly asked.

"No. I don't recognize her and the man has on sunglasses and a hat. His face is not visible."

"Keep the flash drive and contents in the envelope. When we have time, we'll check it for possible clues. Right now, we need to get out of here." Carver clutched his right arm.

"Are you okay?" She nodded toward his clutched arm.

"Affirmative. Bullet grazed my arm."

"Bullet. Somebody was shooting at you?" Fly sounded scared. "I was hired for surveillance only. Surveillance is all I was supposed to do. I don't like this."

"I don't like you, Fly. We've got no choice right now, but stick together and figure this out. So how about you shut the fuck up." Carver's biting tone caused Fly's eyes to dart around the room as if he were searching for a place to hide.

"Both of you stop it. It doesn't help acting like children."

She almost missed the picture inside an envelope. She slipped it out, held the photo in her hand and scrutinized the man in the picture. Her intuition told her she knew this man. He was old, his timeworn face was weather beaten. His feet, no longer able to transport him were replaced by a wheel chair. The lush-winter white hair was unkempt making him look like a mad scientist. The sad droopy eyes seemed to have given up on life. There was nothing familiar about his face, except a distinctive handlebar mustache. A memory of sitting on her grandfather's lap, twirling the ends of the mustache came to light.

"Look. This picture might be Milo," her voice excited. "I

can't remember his face. It was so long ago, but I remembered he had a mustache."

"Fly, do you know what Milo looks like?" Carver asked.

"No. I have never seen the man in this picture."

She turned the picture over. The writing on back was in German so she translated, "My friend, we end where we began. Signed Milo."

She leaped in the air and threw her arms around Carver. Finally, a clue. The cobbler from the diner told her where he and Milo grew up as children.

Trier.

CHAPTER 38

AFTER HE WAS sworn in by the longest-serving member, Democrat Samuel Whitney from Pennsylvania, the gavel was passed to the newest Speaker of the House, Alan Wagner. During his speech, he spoke of the great accomplishments of former speaker, Mark Thompson. He told the members Thompson was a man of character who led the house through many turbulent times with dignity.

He asked the members of the House to join him in thanking Thompson one last time. A round of applause followed.

He thanked his colleagues saying he would continue the path to lead the way for reform on legislative goals. He reminded the audience, "We are obligated by those who put us in office to work together to solve problems for the greater good of our country." A loud cheer and standing ovation erupted from the chamber.

When his speech concluded, Wagner stepped away from the podium to speak privately to Mark Thompson.

"Congratulations, Alan. I'm glad you stepped up to be the Speaker of the House," said Thompson as he gave him a firm, hardy handshake.

"Thanks Mark. That means a lot. I have some big shoes to fill."

"Funny Alan. I am only 5'6" with these damn lifts in my shoes. The right man was elected to the speakership. You have the balls to act on policy goals that these dumb asses in our own party will try to stall for the sake of their political career. Many are incompetent and would serve our country better flipping hamburgers."

He started to pull his hand out from the handshake with Thompson, but Thompson gripped it tighter and leaned in closer.

"Just remember you have no true friends when you have power." Thompson stared in his eyes. A hardened stare. Then he released Wagner's hand and walked away.

Wagner never thought he would be Speaker of the House under these circumstances. He had sacrificed all social life and dedicated his life to honing his skills in a demanding career. He had not considered the job of Speaker at this point in his career until Congressman Quatterman told him Thompson was stepping down from the position. At first he was sure dirty politics was the reason his friend was calling it quits.

Thompson's confrontational, bullish, overbearing style was not well received by many of the house members. Yet, the man got results.

It was when Thompson and he talked in the cafeteria that Wagner knew there was never a witch hunt. The groundwork had been laid for Wagner to be the Speaker of the House. His handler confirmed it in the park. The dirt on Thompson came from the Russians. They needed Wagner as Speaker to spy on the president and influence policies.

He wanted to smile and soak in the glory of the moment, yet watching Thompson walk away, caused his stomach to feel queasy as his eyes tersely glanced around the room. The Russians did not care whose life they ruined to accomplish their mission. Innocent people, like Thompson, were disposable.

And if they were disposable, then he too would be when they got what they wanted.

† † †

"Congratulations Mr. Wagner on being the newest Speaker of the House," Megan clapped as she gleamed at him. Then, she gave him a hug.

"Thank you, Megan. Looks like our early days and late nights will continue. I might have to join the *cot club* even though I don't live that far from here."

Cot club was a term used for members of Congress who used their office as housing during times Congress was in session. Many members criticized the *cot club* as using their office as taxpayer-subsidized housing. He slept on his couch many nights, but rented a row house to avoid the stigma.

"Will you be moving to the former speaker's palatial suite?" Meagan asked. He thought he detected a glint of excitement in her eyes.

"I don't think so, Megan. As much as I like Mark Thompson, he was a chain smoker and that office reeks of stale cigarette smoke. This office is smaller, but it has a great view. We'll stay put for now."

"I kind of figured you wouldn't want to make an office move, but thought I'd better make sure. Did you ever find out any more about why Congressman Thompson stepped down as speaker? Was there more to it than an ethics charge?"

He knew he could not tell Megan the truth, that his Russian handler had blackmailed Thompson with details about his wife's sordid past. Thompson gave up the speakership to protect his family not himself.

"No, I believe the ethics charge brought against him was the only reason he decided to vacate."

He could tell Megan knew this was a lie, just like he knew it when he first heard. Yet she would not challenge what he told her. She had good insight and knew to leave it alone.

"Hold all my calls this afternoon so that I can concentrate on the policy proposals. I need to focus on the nuts and bolts of what is causing the opposition to move forward."

"Do you need me to do anything for you? Research?"

"Not right now. Thanks."

She left the room, leaving him to debate the ideas floating around in his mind. He had never been a violent man, but right now he wanted to strangle his handler for destroying the career of Thompson. He could not deny his handler had opened so many doors for him in his political career and that being Speaker of the House was something he wanted.

He swiveled his desk chair so the view outside his office window was in front of him. The leaves were changing from their summer green to the vibrant hues of orange and scarlet. People wrapped in sweaters and light jackets strolled down the street unaware of what had happened within their own government.

It was time to think about his future as Speaker of the House.

Now that he was Speaker, he wanted to know exactly what his main mission was supposed to be. When he questioned her about being activated, his handler just said be patient. When he asked her what he was supposed to do, she just said that he would know when it was time.

She said there would be a crisis period which had something to do with a funeral. When he asked about it, she laughed and in a mocking tone told him not to worry, it was not his funeral. He wondered who had to die. Perhaps it was the spy who had resurfaced.

He was Speaker of the House, a major instrument of influence and his handler did not trust him with what they were planning. *Does the Soviet intelligence question my loyalty?*

Suddenly, he wondered if his office was bugged. Thompson hinted it might be. If there was a listening device in his office, he was sure who planted it. Soviet intelligence.

All these years the only thing that kept him working so hard at his career was the idea of being able to serve his country. He detested that his country would question his loyalty. There could be only one reason his loyalty would come into question.

His handler.

The blood drained from his face and raw anger radiated from his thoughts. He was the handler's puppet.

It was time to cut those strings.

CHAPTER 39

IT WAS SUNSET when they fled the bookstore. Streaks of light lingered in the sky as the sun's last rays slowly sank beneath the horizon. The day's warmth had disappeared and Julia wished she had her go bag, which they had stored earlier in the train locker. She shivered as the brisk evening air brushed across her body.

Julia, Carver and Fly did not speak while they quickly threaded their way down the cobblestone alleys back to the main street. Village shops were closing their doors while the hum of outdoor cafés buzzed with activity. The smell of food emanating from the cafés made her stomach growl.

The growing sound of the police sirens determined the path they needed to take—or rather avoid. They traveled in the opposite direction from where they had entered the narrow alley. A few more zig-zags and they were back at the opposite end of the main street where the old woman sweeping the sidewalk in front of her bakery had given them directions.

Down the street, were two police cars parked in front of the bakery. One of the policemen was talking into his collar radio. The old woman must have heard the news and called the cops to give a description of them.

Her pulse pounded in her ears when she saw Carver ease the pistol out of his back holster.

"What are you going to do with the pistol?" she asked while

keeping her eyes trained on the street.

Carver motioned with his head in the direction of the policemen.

"My God, no Carver," she said as her muscles tensed.

Fly paced back and forth. She was sure he would bolt any minute.

"You can't kill police officers," barked Fly. "I won't be a part of murder."

"I'm not going to murder anyone. I just want to make sure they don't kill us."

"Why would they try to kill us?" questioned Fly. "We can tell them we didn't break into the bookstore. It was already open when we got there."

"They would probably think we killed the shop owner," Carver said.

"What? What are you saying? There was no dead body in the store." Fly looked shell-shocked.

Julia and Carver both gave Fly a look telling him, *yes there was a dead body.*

"That's frickin crazy. Why didn't you tell me?"

Carver barked, "There was no point. She was dead."

"We have to get back to the train station and get out of here. Julia, call a taxi, now," Fly's voice was frantic.

"We can't call a taxi," Carver said. "There's probably the German version of a BOLO alert out on us. They have a description of what we look like."

"We could split up," Fly suggested while he paced and kept his hands in his trench coat pockets.

"They're already one step ahead of us," Carver informed Fly.

She felt like an animal being hunted by a lion, but she did

not run. The idea of cops arresting them for murder and Carver refusing to surrender was a horrific image. They were trapped and now there was no way out.

"I feel sick." Fly leaned against the building they were huddled by.

She hesitated a few minutes and then said, "Carver, should we just turn ourselves in?" At the moment, she did not know what else to say.

The phone in Carver's jacket buzzed.

✝ ✝ ✝

Minutes seemed like an eternity as they pretended to window shop while waiting on Carver's army buddy to pick them up. People with stern expressions passed by them without a nod or smile. She would have thought they were rude, except Elke had told her Germans just did not like small talk.

She jumped back when the sound of car tires screeched to a stop on the other side of the street. Carver locked his arm around her waist and they briskly crossed the street where the Mercedes was idling. Carver climbed in the front seat, Julia and Fly in back. The car sped off leaving the wailing sirens and the bookstore behind.

"Thank you, Major Taber for helping us out," Carver said to the driver.

"Derick, we know each other well enough for you to call me Peggy," she chastised Carver with pouty lips covered in pink lip gloss.

"I got your message this morning to call, but I was in a meeting," Peggy said.

The tall redhead, her hair pulled in a tight bun, drove them to a friend's apartment off base. Her friend was away on business and apparently, she had a spare key. Peggy explained it would be better to stay at her friend's place, because going on base would raise eyebrows. The news of the murdered shop keeper had already circulated throughout the community.

The friend's apartment was tastefully furnished and looked expensive. The glances shared between Carver and her and the fact she had a key to a man's apartment caused Julia to surmise the woman had no problem with lovers.

Peggy was an officer stationed at the U.S. Army Garrison in Wiesbaden. The mid-thirties woman was still wearing her military uniform. Her service jacket, knee length skirt and shiny black pumps did little to camouflage the woman's shapely figure. Her knobby knees and big feet were flaws Julia knew Carver never noticed. He probably never got past the woman's chest. She was convinced Carver and Peggy at one time had a close relationship. They were too chummy.

Peggy ordered Carver to strip to the waist so she could administer first aid to his wound. She told him to sit in a chair in the kitchen while she gathered the things she needed. It surprised Julia that Carver did not object. Carver might not like Fly, but she did not like this woman.

Carver's bare, chiseled chest and huge arms revealed more than defined muscles and tattoos, there were noticeable physical wounds. He had told her how he lost his leg in the war on their train ride from Frankfurt to Wiesbaden. Now she examined the jagged scars left from the shrapnel that ripped and pierced his skin when he stepped on the IED.

She saw in Carver's eyes he was working out in his head what she must be thinking about his scarred body. She wanted to yell, *you almost died in Afghanistan, why are you here risking your life for me?*

Peggy returned with her red hair now hanging freely around her shoulders, her dress jacket off and the sleeves of her dress shirt rolled up. She walked with the confidence of a person of authority. Julia was sure the woman caught her staring when she lifted an eyebrow. Peggy cleaned Carver's wound with hydrogen peroxide, applied an antiseptic and covered it with a square of gauze.

"Julia would you mind putting pressure on this so I can tape it." Peggy's grin riled her.

Julia narrowed her eyes at Carver, "As soon as you patch Carver up, we need to get to the train station and retrieve our bags from the locker. Then we are headed to Trier."

"Derick told me about your situation," Peggy said. "I already sent somebody to retrieve your bags."

Julia' drew in a deep breath, her eyes flashed with contempt at Carver.

"It was too risky for us to go to the train station, Julia," Caver elucidated. "Peggy offered and I accepted."

She was seething. "You should have told me."

"It isn't his fault Julia. I can be pushy at times. Comes with being a female in a good ol' boys' club."

Peggy's words were not helping the situation. She knew Carver was right, but he should have asked her and Fly first.

"If you will accept, all of you are welcome to stay the night. I had my friend pick up some food for us on his way back from the train station. You must be exhausted. Tomorrow, I can take all of you to Trier."

Julia realized her blood sugar had dropped. She felt edgy. Fly was already asleep on the couch. No complaints from him. Perhaps she was being jealous and not practical. Food and a good night's sleep was an offer hard to pass up.

After supper, Carver suggested they look at the flash drive
Julia had found in the basement of the bookstore. Peggy let
them use the computer in her friend's apartment.

"We can use Fly's laptop," Julia told Peggy.

"I have a large monitor, which would make viewing the
contents on the drive easier," Peggy suggested.

"Thank you," Julia answered trying to sound sincere.

Julia sat in front of the computer and everybody gathered
behind her. Once it loaded, she said, "There is a video on here."

The video was difficult to view all the details. The person
who shot the footage kept moving the camera too fast. The
man always had his head bowed while he talked on his cell
phone. The face of the woman was that of a stranger.

Julia angled her head and looked up at Carver, "I'm not sure
what this is about. Do you think this is what the Russians were
trying to get?"

"Shh, listen. Are they talking?" Carver leaned over her
shoulder.

"Turn up the sound," Fly chirped in as he crowded inward.

The audio was poor quality with the interference from the
sound of blowing wind and people walking by. They played
the video several times and could only understand a few things
said. *Crisis period, activated, agents of influence.* Fly told them the
person doing the surveillance was an amateur. They were
probably using a cell phone and did not get close enough to
the subjects."

Peggy interrupted, "The words we can understand from the

video are disturbing. I have a friend who specializes in this kind of technology. He might be able to extract more information from the video."

Julia pulled out the flash drive and handed it to Peggy. "Can he keep it confidential?"

"He can…and will."

††††

The guest bedroom contained a queen size bed, neatly made with a nightstand and table lamp. Peggy had laid out something for her to sleep in on the bed. She was surprised to see the flannel pajamas were gray, dotted with pictures of purple cows jumping over a moon. When she walked over to turn on the lamp she discovered Fly was sacked out on the floor using his trench coat for cover. She took a pillow from the bed and placed it under his head.

Julia worried the Russians might have followed them to the apartment. She eased the curtains back, peeked out the window and was sure she saw a man under a street light with a scar across his face. A woman stepped out of the shadows of darkness to give the Russian a shiny object. The long hair blew away revealing her face. It was Peggy. She was giving the Russian the flash drive. She bolted to the door to warn Carver. When she swung the door open, Carver stood at the entrance. He wasn't wearing a shirt. His broad muscular chest and bulging arms were inked with different tattoos.

She had no idea what he was doing at the door or what he planned to do. She tried to speak, but he was suddenly so close to her, she felt dizzy. His arms swept her up and carried her to the bed. He gently lowered her onto the bed. Her face felt warm.

The room began to spin. Her heart was pounding. Carver's dark eyes never let his gaze leave her face. He started to unbutton her top. She thought he might laugh at the ridiculous sight of her in the flannel pajamas. He just smiled and tenderly kissed her lips. She wondered if he minded the pink lip gloss she was wearing.

Then she remembered Fly was on the floor by the bed. Panic filled her mind as she started yelling, "No, no, no."

"Wake up, Julia, wake up."

She jolted awake, her breathing labored, and eyes blurry.

Carver's face slowly came into focus.

"You have on a shirt," she mumbled.

"Are you okay? You were having a bad dream. I heard you moaning and then yelling."

"Yeah," she answered very slowly. "I'm okay." Her eyes raced across the floor, but Fly was not there. The dream melted away as she rubbed her sleepy eyes.

"Were you having the nightmare about the explosion?"

"The explosion," she said trying hard not to reveal what she had just experienced. "Um, yes it was the same nightmare."

CHAPTER 40

THE COUNTRYSIDE VIEW was enchanting as the car accelerated down the road toward their destination. Hill-hugging vineyards and alpine villages were scattered along the serpentine route. Julia was mesmerized by the stunning views outside her car window.

A red-orange glow of a new morning peeked over the horizon. The air was crisp as it waited on the sun rays to radiate back from the earth. Inside the car, the heater had not warmed up the back where Julia and Fly sat. Fly was wearing his trench coat. She wondered if he ever took it off. She zipped up her jacket, folded her arms and feigned a smile when she noticed Peggy looking at her through the rear-view mirror.

"Julia, are you cold? I can turn up the heat?"

Oh, I bet you can. "No. I'm fine," she answered.

At breakfast, Julia had avoided eye contact with Carver. The dream of him last night left her rattled and feeling guilty. At the table, he asked her too many times if she was okay. She snapped back that she was just tired. He raised an eyebrow, shook his head, and frowned. She slumped her shoulders and looked away. Today she had to stay focused on finding Milo, her grandfather.

In the backseat, Fly was helping her locate nursing homes on his phone. Carver had returned Fly's cell phone right before they left for Trier. She suspected Carver had gone through Fly's cell phone messages, emails and contacts. Carver, like Elke, did not trust anybody. She figured his paranoia was a result of his military days. She asked Carver why he was dragging Fly along with them. Carver told her he felt better being able to keep an eye on him.

Fly's search found over a dozen nursing homes located in Trier. It would take all day if they were to go to everyone on the list, so they decided to call them. After a couple of calls, Julia discovered the nursing homes would not reveal the names of their residents without the permission of the person staying there or their caretaker.

"How sure are you that he is in a nursing home and isn't living in a private residence?" Carver asked.

"In the picture, there is a building in the background with a courtyard. The place looks like a facility of some sort. He is in a wheelchair and I remember his old friend told us at the diner that he was in bad health." An image of the old man lying dead in the parking lot of the diner washed across Julia's mind. She felt responsible for his death. If he had not come to warn her and Carver, then he would still be alive.

She jotted down the list of nursing facilities located in Trier on a tablet as Fly read out the names and locations. After giving her information on six facilities, Fly stopped.

"What's wrong, Fly?" she asked.

"We can't find your grandfather by calling these listings and it is going to take too much time going to every one of them. We could get lucky and it could be at the top of the list or it could be at the bottom, like the bookstore in Wiesbaden."

Fly asked to see the picture of the old man in the wheelchair. Holding the picture, he tapped it and said, "This building in the picture might be on the nursing facility's website. Let me start checking websites."

"Thanks Fly. That's a great idea." She rubbed the nape of her neck to relieve the aching pain. She had not shared her doubts with Carver or Fly. She was not sure if the picture meant Milo had gone back to live in the city where he was born. The words on the back of the picture we end where we began could mean something else. It was a long shot. If they did find Milo, would he know where Elke was? Would her grandfather even remember her? The last time she saw him she was a little girl.

"Eureka," whooped Fly.

He held the phone up so she could see the image on it. Her eyes brightened, there it was, she was right.

She pumped her fist in the air and yelled, "Yes. We found it."

Carver turned around to share his grin with her.

It felt good to know they were headed in the right direction. This was the break she needed.

✝ ✝ ✝

It took less than two hours to get to Trier. During the drive, Peggy revealed her love of history. Trier, the oldest city in Germany, was situated on the Moselle River. Founded in 16 B.C. under Emperor Augustus it became part of the Roman Empire. At least eight Roman emperors ruled there. Trier had some of the best preserved Roman ruins in the entire world.

Peggy had a heavy foot, and traffic was light so they arrived at Trier sooner than Julia had calculated.

She felt she had been transported back in time as they drove into the city.

"I feel like I'm in Rome." Elke had taken her to Italy when she was a teenager.

Peggy laughed, "Trier is known as *Rome of the North*, therefore Julia, it is Rome."

After a moment, the sights in the ancient city relaxed her body helping to release some of the built-up tension. There was so much history in this city and some of it was her grandfather growing up here. She imagined what life was like for Milo as a young boy playing in a city where Roman rulers once lived.

Peggy pointed at a landmark, "That is the Porta Nigra. It is the best preserved Roman city gate from antiquity."

The market square was filled with people, fruit stands, flowers, painted facades, and fountains. A market cross, Peggy explained was from 958 AD and used to celebrate the trading rights given to the town by King Otto the Great.

"I didn't know you were such a history buff," remarked Carver to Peggy.

A buzzing cell phone, Peggy answered, "Hello, Lieutenant General Piagno."

Most of the conversation, Peggy just answered, "Yes sir," or "No sir."

When she clicked off, her face was no longer rosy colored.

"Looks like we have a shit-storm brewing," said Peggy. "I have to report to base immediately for a debriefing. General Duttweiler has been advised that an American, possibly former military, might be involved in the murder of a local bookstore owner. The owner seemed to have possible ties to terrorists."

"Do they know we are with you?" Carver asked.

"Not yet."

"What can we do to help?"

"Get what you need in Trier and disappear."

CHAPTER 41

Trier, Germany

THE SUNNY MORNING rays warmed Julia as she stood in the nursing home courtyard, her breathing rapid and shallow. She stared at the picture in her hand and the building in front of her and felt a rush of intense feelings. Elke would not talk about her grandfather so every time Julia asked about him, the subject changed. The man inside the nursing home was a ghost of a memory, nothing more.

The last and only time she saw Milo was when she was about five or six years old. At the time, she believed Elke took her to Germany to meet her grandfather. The visit confused her and upset her when they returned to the United States.

The impending meeting with her grandfather triggered a memory long ago forgotten. Julia closed her eyes to visions of plump brunette curls bopping when she skipped into his outstretched arms. He raised her up to have a seat on his lap. A sound of laughter when her fingers twirled his handlebar mustache. Cuddled next to the tall man's chest with his big arms wrapped around her small body made her feel that a void had been filled. The feelings of abandonment when her parents died left her depressed and longing for what her friends had, a mother and father. In this moment sitting on her grandfather's lap, her troubled mind felt everything was more normal. Then they left Germany, and she never heard from her grandfather again. He vanished from her life just like her parents.

Never a visit, a call or letter from Milo, which confirmed in her mind that he did not care about his granddaughter. Elke tried to make up for the missing pieces in her life, yet her grandmother struggled with her own grief. Julia's loneliness, isolation and depression had only gotten worse. A lost soul whose coping mechanism was being an over achiever.

"Are you nervous?" Carver standing beside her asked.

She opened her eyes now moist, "It's just been a long time."

Carver's neck cranked toward Fly, "You stand guard outside. If you even feel like there is a hint of trouble headed this way, call."

"How will I know if people are going to be trouble?"

"You do surveillance for God's sake." Carver's lethal stare made Fly shake. "And take off that stupid trench coat. It's like a bull's eye is painted on it."

Walking up to the front door of the Ziegler Haus, she said, "I know you don't like Fly, but was that necessary?"

She turned around and saw Fly taking off his trench coat just like Carver had instructed.

"There is something about him," Carver said as he opened the door to the nursing facility. "Not sure we can trust him."

Inside the Ziegler Haus was a large glass window separating the dining room from the entry. A large aquarium filled with multi-colored fish was encased in the glass divider. She strolled up to the desk, greeted a woman with a pleasant face seated behind the counter and stated she was here to visit Milo Wolfgang Fenstermacher. In English, the woman asked her name, then picked up a phone. "Sie haben einen Besucher. Ya. Julia Bagal," spoke the woman to the person on the other line.

When the woman hung up the phone, she pointed, "He is in room 101. Take a left and down at the far end on the right is his room. Have a nice visit."

They walked down a hall lined with a patchwork of colorful carpet and mounted wooden handrails for people unsteady on their feet. The doors to most of the rooms were wide open, elderly people sat alone in their rooms, watching a television set, some staring in a trance-like state. She wondered if some of the residents who were no longer able to enjoy life wouldn't welcome death if given the opportunity. An elderly woman pushing a walker passed by greeted them, "Guten morgen."

"Guten morgen," replied Julia.

The door to room 101 was pulled shut, she lightly rapped, then heard a feeble voice tell her to come in. An elderly gray headed man with a handlebar mustache sat slightly hunched in his wheel chair parked in front of a window with a nice view of evergreen trees. His arthritic hands were nestled on a blanket spread across his lap. Milo's eyes were sunken, his hands covered with dark age spots. The clothes he wore were old and frayed on the ends.

There was a peculiar odor lingering, a combination of stale air and Ben Gay. The small unkempt room had an unmade bed along one wall, a handicap bathroom, a kitchen with barely enough room for a refrigerator and sink, and two chairs in the far corner. A small dresser was covered with too many pill bottles to count, a water pitcher, Kleenex box, and no personal items. The room temperature uncomfortably warm caused them to remove their jackets upon entering.

"Hello, Milo. It is me, Julia Bagal. Your granddaughter." She held her breath, afraid the old man would not recognize her.

His eyes took her in, then in a voice slow and unsteady, "I

remember. You are grown now."

That is what happens when you don't see somebody for over twenty years. She felt her face heat up.

He raised a hand and pointed toward Carver, "You, I do not know."

She mustered self-control and soundly said, "Milo, he is here to help. Elke sent him."

"Please, sit down," Milo said waving his crooked finger toward two chairs against a wall.

After they sat down, Milo smiled warmly at her. She could not return the smile. "We need your help to find answers."

Milo's droopy eyes narrowed at Carver. "Julia said Elke sent you?"

"She asked me to keep Julia safe. I met Elke when I was recovering at Walter Reed Army Medical Center. She was volunteering there at the time."

Milo snorted a giggle, "Elke did like the ruse of volunteering at hospitals for her cover. You know she was going to nursing school when the CIA recruited her. She was one of the best they had. Elke could seduce a man with her eyes."

She was sure this would be more information than she wanted to know about her grandmother. Her hands began to clasp and unclasp each other as she fidgeted like a child sitting in a chair outside the principal's office.

Carver interrupted, "Have you seen Elke in the last few days?"

Milo ignored the question. His eyes full of despair locked on her face. He looked like he was about to speak, yet was not sure what to say.

"We need to find Elke, Milo." She was afraid the old man might have dementia.

"I thought I would never see my beautiful granddaughter before I died. I am old, Julia, my dreams are now regrets. But being able to see you one last time...it has brought me great joy."

The words from the man she detested created a strange feeling inside her. She did not recognize his voice which was now brittle. A part of her wanted to remember his face, to recapture a past moment. Time had robbed her of this. Only a memory of sitting in his lap and twirling his mustache with her fingers was left.

As if Milo read her thoughts he said, "Do you remember sitting in my lap and playing with my mustache? It was not white then."

"I do remember, Milo."

"You called me Papa. I liked that."

She did not care what this old man liked. She reminded him, "Please, tell us about Elke, Milo."

Milo's heavily lined face crumpled when she again called him Milo. She did not care. Milo had twenty years to connect with her. He made his choice.

"The moment I saw Elke, I lost myself to love. She was working at the Rhein Haus in Frankfurt." Milo's mind seemed to drift to another time as a tiny smile crept across his face.

She was sure this was a mistake. Milo would not be able to help them. A part of her wanted to just get up and leave, but she sat and listened as Milo talked.

"She was wearing a blue dress. Her long golden brown hair wrapped up in a bun, her fair skin was smooth and her eyes as bright as the bluest sky. When her eyes gazed at me it made my heart go thump." Milo patted his heart with his arthritic hand. "I carry those months we spent together in my heart."

Milo lowered his head and when he raised it, tears trickled down his cheeks.

"Elke wanted to go to America to live. I was so much older than her and could not understand her dreams. I made a stupid choice, Julia. I let her go."

"Let her go?" Julia's chest felt as tight as her clenched fists. Then without control, her pent-up emotions spewed like a volcano that had erupted. "I understand why Elke never talked about you. You were never around for your own daughter or me. My mother died and never knew her own father. Don't try to act pitiful and want forgiveness. Forgiveness is no longer an option."

Carver reached for her hand squeezing it tight. She pulled away.

With downcast eyes, Milo said, "Things are never truly black and white, Julia. You were too young to know the truth."

"The truth?" Her nostrils flared and her lips quivered, "How can a father abandon his own child?"

"When he does not know she exists."

CHAPTER 42

JULIA WAS STUNNED as her brain tried to process the words she heard Milo say; *When he does not know she exists. What did he mean by that?*

Milo fixated again on Julia, reluctant to speak at first, but when he started, it was like he was in a confessional to get repentance for his sins.

"Elke and I began to argue about her desire to go to America. Finally, we decided to go our separate ways. I never knew I had a daughter until Elke brought you to Germany."

"You never knew about your child during all those years?"

"Nein. Not until Elke told me I had a granddaughter."

"Why would she not tell you? I... I don't understand."

"Elke is a proud woman. Do not be angry with her. Elke knew I would not be a good father. I had a bad temper when I was young. Parents make the best decisions we can at the time for our children. She did the right thing. After many years, we lost touch with each other."

Milo became animated as he continued, "It started with the explosion that happened many years ago, child. When the Russians blew up Elke's home, they thought all evidence was destroyed. That was the moment it started. Elke felt responsible for the death of your mother and father. She was —"

Carver interrupted, "Milo, what evidence did the Russians think they had destroyed?"

"Documents. Files smuggled out of Russia by a senior

KGB official which revealed sleeper agents and weapon caches in the West."

"What? My grandmother, Elke, a CIA agent, had acquired classified documents from a Russian? This can't be true." Julia's stomach drew in knots, causing cramps.

Carver leaned forward in his chair, "So if the documents were destroyed, why would Elke have to change identities?"

"You don't know, do you?"

"Know what?" Carver and Julia shared a quizzical look.

"Elke is special. She has a unique trait. She has an eidetic memory."

Shocked, she said, "You are saying, Elke memorized all the information in the files containing the names of the Russian sleepers." She recalled while growing up, Elke would glance at her spelling words and quiz her later without looking at the list of words. Elke's recall was always off the chart.

"Ya. That is exactly what I am saying. The Russians found out about Elke's eidetic memory because of a mole working deep in the CIA."

"Elke did not know who the mole was at the time of the explosion, therefore she disappeared with Julia to keep them safe," Carver concluded.

"Ya. That is why she faked her death." Milo nodded toward her. "And yours. Elke knew there was a leak. She did not trust anybody. When she came to me and explained everything, I helped you disappear."

Her life was beginning to sound like a fictitious novel. She was not Julia Bagal. Her identity had been changed. Her mother and father were murdered when the Russians blew up her grandmother's home. Elke used to be an agent for the CIA, stealing secrets from the Russians. Milo, her grandfather never knew he had a daughter until he met his granddaughter.

She felt lightheaded, like she had been playing the game where somebody turns you around in a circle quickly several times and then you stop suddenly. She held both hands against her throbbing temples.

"Milo, when I first met you, I was five or six years old." The image replayed itself in her mind. "You made me feel like you loved me, but I never heard from you after Elke and I came back to America."

"I am so sorry Julia. I loved you so much." Milo overtaken with emotions broke down, covering his face with his hands.

She continued to challenge Milo, "I was just a child and my whole life had been torn apart. I needed you. Don't you understand?"

"There were so many times, I wanted to hold my sweet Julia again or simply hear her voice. But, I could not endanger your life. The Russians knew Elke and I had a past. We were afraid. I would have given them the breadcrumbs."

She witnessed the death-longing eyes of a tormented old man. A rush of guilt filled her thoughts of the anger she had held on to for so many years. The people she was so angry with, were only trying to keep her safe.

"I promised Elke I would find the person responsible for your mother and father's death. All I have done these past years is track down leads. I lost my job, my home and my friends. This revenge consumed me, the way it has consumed Elke. If I could never know my daughter, then I would know her killer."

When Milo finished talking, she was overpowered by emotions. Before she walked in Room 101, she was convinced of how she felt about Milo and angry with Elke lying about the past. An anguish of grief ignited by Milo's recounting past events was painful.

"Julia, do you need to get some air?" Carver asked.

She could not respond, so he asked again.

She slowly shook her head.

Carver said, "Milo, how did you know Julia would come here?"

"You are very smart. Elke was wise to have you keep her safe. I told you, for many years I searched for the Russian responsible for killing my daughter. No luck. Every time, I find something, it leads nowhere. My friend, Otto, tried to help as well as his daughter. They are very good at this. Then I find out the Russian is living in the United States. Still working. I want revenge, but I am an old man in very bad health. Before I die, I felt I must tell Elke."

"She came here to see you?" Carver asked.

"Ya. Elke said Julia would find me. She said I should tell her the truth. Elke did not want our granddaughter to hate me."

Julia's eyes fixed and unblinking said, "You know where she is?"

"Nein." Milo shook his head several times.

"Elke is in danger. You need to tell us," she said.

"Julia, you must not try to find Elke. She is smart and will be safe. You must disappear. I have a friend in Wiesbaden who can help you."

"Liese Aicher? Is that your friend?" Carver asked.

"Ya. But how do you know her name?"

"We found the bookstore in Wiesbaden. Liese is dead. Your friend Otto is dead. He was gunned down trying to warn us."

Milo averted his gaze and his hunched body trembled, while he reached for one of the bottles on the dresser. "I need my medicine." Shaking, he poured a glass of water from the pitcher.

He was having difficulty breathing making his unsteady hands spill the water in the glass he tried to raise to his mouth.

She went over and took the glass from his cold arthritic hands. She gently held it to his lips and let him sip enough water to swallow his pills. Before she could return the glass to the dresser, Milo reached up and wrapped his hands around hers holding the glass.

"Thank you." Milo's doleful eyes met hers.

She swallowed hard, quickly put the glass back on the dresser.

"Milo, I need you to do this for me. Elke's life is in danger. This time she might not be so lucky. You can help us save her."

"I cannot help you. She did not tell me where she was going."

"Elke's life is in your hands, Milo. I know you still love her."

His head sunk into his chest and he shook it, "Elke would never forgive me. You are all we have left."

She edged closer to Milo's wheelchair and lifted his wet chin with her hand. Her eyes fixed with Milo's eyes. Life had already left the weathered man's face like it would soon leave his body, yet he was still trying to protect her.

"I never knew it until now what my purpose in life was. Elke has been preparing me for this all my life. She knew this day would come. You cannot protect your children from the truth. We found you, Milo, so that we could help Elke. Many people have already died. Do not let Elke, the woman you love and my grandmother, die because we did not try to help her." She stepped back and with a strong voice, "I beg you, Milo."

It seemed an eternity before Milo spoke in a resigned voice, "I will help you."

Milo began laying out in detail how he managed to contact Elke to tell her he had found the Russian agent responsible for their daughter's death. Otto's daughter was the conduit to Elke. She sent a coded message to her father, Otto. Otto worked at the bingo parlor and passed the coded message to Elke on a bingo card.

Otto was part of a network of retired spies using the old ways to gather information. They did not trust modern technology.

"Why did Elke go live in the assisted living facility and carry on about being a spy if she wanted to keep her identity secret?" she asked.

"The Russians had discovered she was still alive. She tried to act like she was crazy and had lost her mind so they might believe she was no longer a threat."

"But, then she learned you found the Russian assassin responsible for my mother and father's death," she added.

"Ya. Elke came to see me and wanted to know what I had discovered. I told her the information was stored in the safe house."

"The safe house?"

"That is what we call the bookstore cellar. The safe is used by the old spies."

"Did you give Elke the combination to the safe?"

"No. I think Otto's daughter, Liese sent it to her."

"Where is Elke now?"

"Elke went to Wiesbaden to see the picture of the Russian who is responsible for the death of our daughter. Elke called from Frankfurt and said she was going to Fort Collins to visit her friend, Iggy. She thanked me and said she could rest now knowing the face of the killer. I know she lied to me so I wouldn't worry. She will never stop until she finds this woman."

"How long ago did Elke call you, Milo?" Carver inquired.

"Late last night, right before I took my pills for bed."

"What?" Julia slapped her leg. "That means we probably just missed her at the bookstore."

She expelled a short breath as she moved toward Milo, "The name, Milo. What is the name of the Russian responsible for the death of my mother and father?"

"I do not have a name. It was never known. There was a picture and a movie."

"Movie? You mean a video."

"Ya. Ya. That is what it is. I am afraid Elke will not wait for others to help her."

"We have to hurry, Milo. Elke is not that far ahead of us."

"Please, Julia, be careful."

She stood facing her grandfather, a man she never got to know. A part of her wanted to hug the man, yet he was still only a stranger.

Milo nodded. "It is okay Julia. You owe me nothing."

The old man was like a Jedi from *Star Wars* who could sense the feelings and unrest of people around them.

Bending down, she wrapped her arms lightly around his frail shoulders whispering, "Thank you." She kissed him on the forehead.

Exiting the room, a brittle voice called out to her, "Lisa Saitow."

She pivoted and stood in the doorway. "That is the name of the Russian assassin?"

"Nein, dear, that is your name. Your birth name."

CHAPTER 43

CARVER REACHED OVER and squeezed Julia's hand when Milo recounted the past, but she jerked her hand away and wrapped her arms around herself. He wasn't sure why he even tried to appear compassionate.

She didn't speak when they left Milo's room and walked down the hall of the nursing home and out the front door. They did not forge a plan or share a look. He began to think she might shut down as reality sunk in.

Warm rays of the sun were now blocked by a sky full of dark, silver-gray clouds. A thin drizzle stirred a chill in the air. They pulled on their jackets while they scanned the courtyard for Fly.

"Where is he?" she asked in an alarmed tone.

"That bastard. I knew he could not be trusted."

"Maybe he's inside, using the bathroom and we just missed him."

"Or maybe he took off."

On the bench in the courtyard, she saw it first. "Oh no. It's Fly's trench coat." She swooped it up and searched the pockets. Nothing. Right in front of the bench, lying on the brick pavement was his cell phone. He saw her face go from concern to panic after she examined the phone.

"I think Fly's in trouble," she said. "He would never leave his trench coat. The man practically lived in it. He must have dropped his phone when something bad happened to him."

Carver scanned the grounds and said, "Let's get the hell out of here. No matter what happened, it can't be good."

They went back inside the Ziegler Haus and asked the lady behind the counter to call them a taxi.

Within five minutes, a taxi pulled up to the Ziegler Haus. He instructed the taxi driver to drop them at a car rental in Trier.

"Why don't we take the train back to Frankfurt?"

"Two reasons. One, the train goes through Wiesbaden and we don't want to chance the police looking for us there. And two, per my Goggle search, we can bypass Wiesbaden and it will be quicker getting to Frankfurt."

She clutched Fly's trench coat like she had just lost a child. He was convinced she believed Fly had been captured by the Russians, but he was sure that was not the case. The Russians would have simply killed Fly and waited until they walked out of the nursing home and then kidnapped Julia. Fly and he would be nothing more than collateral damage.

"Julia, check Fly's phone record and see if you can find the last call he made."

"Here it is." She read the number out to him. "Looks like it is an area code from the D.C. area."

"Try calling it."

She tapped the phone. "It's ringing and ringing. I think it is going to voice mail."

After hanging up, she said, "Well, it seems Fly has a surveillance agency. The recording said, *Nightingale Investigation, please leave your name, number, a brief message and we will get back to you within twenty-four hours.*"

"We need to find out about this joker." Carver was certain there was more to Fly than helping Elke keep tabs on them.

"Let me see your cell phone," she said. "I can call my friend, Alvin."

The snippets he had heard from the conversation made him question the whole mutual friendship thing.

"I am fine, Alvin, honest." Pause. "No, thank you, I have been staying with a friend. I am fine, please no need to worry. Did you hear any more information about the audit?"

She shook her head at him.

Her so called friend did not have any more information for her about the audit. The guy seemed willing to stick his neck out to ask his friend, who worked for the FBI, to check out Fly. She said Alvin offered to let them stay at his place outside the city until things settled down.

He did not think it was an option he wanted to consider.

At the Trier car rental agency, he told the agent they were staying in Trier and needed a car to explore the country side. He was not sure at this point who might track them back to the car service. A half hour later, he pulled out of the car lot.

Since it was almost noon, he asked her if she was hungry. She snapped with a quick *no*, which sounded more like *if you do not feed me now, I will bite off your head,* so he swerved the car into the first cafe he spotted after passing a sign that read Karl Marx Haus. Seemed Trier was famous for more than just having the best preserved Roman ruins in the entire world. Crowds of Chinese tourists were standing in front of the Marxist building, snapping pictures.

She was not hungry, she was starving. He knew when her blood sugar dropped, she was not somebody you wanted to be around. It reminded him of the Snicker's commercial on TV. Maybe he should buy some Snickers and keep them in his pocket.

After she scarfed down the last bite on her plate, she apologized, "Sorry I was so short with you earlier. I just had a lot thrown at me by Milo."

"Not the best way to learn about your past."

"I feel bad Elke dragged you into this mess."

"You got it all wrong, Julia. I knew what I was signing up for."

"Did you?"

He rubbed a hand over his dark stubble. "I knew things about Elke's past. When she asked me to keep you safe, it was probably something I needed in my life at the time."

"Welcome to my crazy screwed up world. I hope it was everything you hoped it would be," she mocked.

"As much as you don't want to accept it, I want to be here."

Her eyes stared back at him, "I sound ungrateful. It's just I don't know why anything is what it is right now. I am angry. At my life...and at myself."

She propped her hand under her chin resting her elbow on the table and glanced out the cafe window.

The unexpected silence was awkward and he was stumped on what to say next. He could kill a man with his bare hands, lift more weight with one leg than most men with two, yet he felt helpless to make things better for her. She was wounded and emotionally volatile. Right now, maybe he needed to let the dust settle. She was right, he sucked talking to women.

† † †

Over an hour passed, without much conversation, as they sped down the highway toward Frankfurt Airport. Julia made the necessary airline reservations for them from Frankfurt to

Washington, D.C. on the burn phone.

The trip to Germany had unlocked many clues to Julia's past, however he was not sure she wanted to hear the truth. It might take time for her to digest it.

The buzzing noise from the console stopped him from drumming his fingers on the steering wheel. He quickly placed the cell phone to his ear.

"Peggy, I'm glad you called. You'll be happy to know we're not sticking around." Carver did not want to say too much in case somebody was listening.

"On a secure line. I don't know what you've gotten involved in, but the word is out about three Americans, man with a prosthetic leg, a young woman and your trench coat friend, Columbo, being involved in murder and possible espionage."

"Do authorities believe we are still local?"

"You've got about twenty-four hours. Then there is no way out of the country. Forget Wiesbaden. Right now, the local authorities believe you are somewhere on the military base."

"Anything on the flash drive?"

"My friend was able to capture more sound from the video. He said whoever took it was not a professional. Said it reminded him of his grandma trying to use a cell phone to take a video."

He remembered Milo had told them, *Otto was part of a network of retired spies using the old ways to gather information.* Maybe one of those old spies must have tried to use modern technology.

"So what did he hear?"

"There was a lot of wind noise, but the words he could distinguish were disturbing."

"Julia, can you write this down for me?" he asked. She reached in her bag and pulled out a pad and pen.

"Ready. Give them to me." He repeated the words as Peggy

spoke them, "Dead spy, recover list, deep cover positions, crisis, a funeral, when will I be activated."

"Derick, I know you like the girl, but you are getting in deep over your head. I need to run this up the food chain to national security."

"No," Carver's tone was emphatic. "Not yet. Give me some time to get you more information. There is a life at stake and if it gets out, we will probably lose our opportunity to shut it down."

"I shouldn't do this. I don't like it, but I owe you. Forty-eight hours and then I will push it up the ladder. Otherwise, this could cost me my career."

"I will make sure that doesn't happen, Peggy. I promise."

He knew he couldn't keep that promise if they didn't find Elke.

Forty-eight hours.

They could not afford to miss their flight out of Frankfurt.

The drizzle turned into a howling rain.

CHAPTER 44

Flughafen Frankfurt am Main
Frankfurt International Airport

CARVER DID NOT turn the rental car in at the Frankfurt airport. Instead, he parked the rental in long term parking. At their gate, he asked her for Fly's cell phone. He held her arm, guiding her to the gate where the outbound flight to Denver, Colorado would soon depart.

Her face twisted with a scowl. "What are you doing? Our flight is to D.C. We already determined from the photo of the Russian agent, the bench is probably in a park in the D.C. area. Milo told us he did not believe Elke was headed to Fort Collins."

He scanned the people at the Denver gate, waiting for their flight to be called.

"I think we are being set up."

"Set up? Why are you so paranoid?"

"You found Fly's trench coat and phone outside the nursing facility. Why take Fly? Why not wait and get the prize? You."

"Maybe Fly put up a fight and attracted too much attention."

"Or maybe Fly left his phone to make us think that happened. Or maybe Fly has a tracking device in his phone."

"That's crazy. If that were true, why wouldn't Fly just stay with us instead of leaving a tracking device in his phone?"

He hesitated, "I don't know, but there is something not right about this."

"What are you going to do?" She was not convinced he was right about Fly.

He explained they were going to plant the phone unknowingly on an airline passenger headed to Denver. That would hopefully mislead the Russians or whoever was trying to follow them if the phone was bugged.

✝ ✝ ✝

The Boeing 777 was a nine-hour flight to Washington, D.C. Once she had consumed her gin and Coke, she relaxed enough to reflect on her life, as she now knew it. There were moments when she wanted to crawl in a hole or at the very least stay in bed with the covers pulled over her head and wait for someone to save her. Ironically, her anger had been misdirected all these years. Elke and Milo had good intentions, yet she struggled to find solid footing in all of this. Betrayal was the emotion eating away inside her.

She could feel Carver's stare. *He doesn't understand. How could he?*

With her head hung low she said, "Why me? Why did this happen to me?"

"Pretty much same reason I lost my leg."

He was so unsympathetic.

"This is not the same," she said turning her face toward him.

"Your parents were in the wrong place at the wrong time. I was in the wrong place at the wrong time. There is no *why me.*"

"So, it's that simple? Shit happens?"

"Don't you think there are thousands of people wondering why me when bad things happen to them?"

"Elke should have told me. I had the right to know."

"I understand, but you fail to recognize something."

"Don't defend her, Carver. I recognize exactly what she did."

"No, you don't. Milo and Elke did what they thought was best for you at the time. They did it out of love. Love for you. Nothing more."

"It is hard to forgive."

"Forgive?" he asked. "A better word is accepting."

She stared out the window.

"Julia, are you okay?"

"Sure. Well no, look at me. I thought I had my whole life planned. I believed I was Julia Bagal."

"It's just a name," he said. "You can plan out your life, but you have no idea what's going to happen in the future to cause you to change your direction."

She looked at his prosthetic leg and knew he had to accept his circumstances.

"Just feeling sorry for myself," she said.

"You're gonna be fine Julia. Just give yourself some time."

Changing the subject, he said, "I did not see Scarface or Fly at our gate or board our plane.

Do you think we have been able to evade being followed?" she asked.

"Not sure. If there is a tracking device in Fly's phone, then maybe."

"Our only lead now is the photograph of the Russian agent on a park bench in D.C. with a man we cannot recognize next to her. We have a few words from the audio on the flash drive that your friend, Peggy managed to get off the recording. So how will any of this help us locate Elke?"

"We will check all the locations we know Elke might visit. Bingo hall, your duplex, and Harmony Assisted Living facility."

"I tried calling Elke before we boarded," she said. "The call went to voice mail."

She reached over and cupped Carver's hand which caused a wrinkle of surprise to spread across his forehead.

Her eyes narrowed, cold, hard while she held his gaze, "Carver, we're going to find Elke and hunt down that Russian assassin."

He did not respond. His eyes darted down at her hand on top of his and then back to her face.

She quickly withdrew her hand. "This is the moment I need you say something encouraging, Carver."

"Yes, we will."

"Damn it Carver. Are you now talking in code? How about, let's nail that bastard."

He chuckled, "Never thought I'd say this, but it's good to have the old sarcastic Julia back."

"What do you think the conversation recovered from the flash drive means?" She pulled out her pad and read the list back to Carver. "Dead spy, recover list, deep cover positions, crisis, a funeral, when will I be activated."

"The dead spy could be reference to Elke. Recover list could be the document Milo told us about. Deep cover might be the guy on the bench with the Russian woman. The man said *when will I be activated*. That might mean he is a Russian sleeper. A crisis and funeral are unknowns."

"Yeah. I think you're right. The question, *when will I be activated* makes me believe something is going to happen soon."

"We have forty-eight hours to find out minus about twelve."

"What do you mean?"

"Peggy told me she will keep a lid on this information for forty-eight hours and then she will elevate it up to national security. About twelve hours will have passed by the time we get to Washington."

"When we land in D.C., we should split up and check every place we think Elke could be. If we don't find her, then we must eliminate the threat ourselves," she said.

"The Russian woman responsible for your parent's death?"

"Yes."

They tried to catch some shut-eye on the long flight from Germany. They decided that they needed to be as rested as possible before landing in D.C. She woke with her head leaning on Carver's shoulder, drool on the side of her face, and a crick in her neck. She was certain he never slept.

Her ear's popped and she yawned out loud to relieve the pressure. A grinding noise made her hands grip the arm rest.

"Just the landing gear, Julia."

Out the window, she could see vehicles on roads, big city high rises, trees whiz by as the aircraft made its approach with the tires bouncing on the runway. The Boeing 777 taxied slowly to the arrival gate.

"You can loosen your grip, we're on the ground," he said with a quick wink.

She instantly became aware of her white knuckles hands wrapped around the armrest. She let go and scooped up her bag under the seat in front of her. The warmth on her face was more than being silly about her fear of flying. His wink made her feel self-conscious of how she must look.

He said they should get another burn phone for her in case

they got separated.

"I thought we agreed to split up to cover more ground faster," she protested.

"No. You said that. I never agreed. We stay together."

They exited the plane and walked out to the arrival gate. A shuttle took them to U.S. Customs and Border Protection. Standing in line, she glanced over her shoulder at the long line of passengers behind them. She turned back around, tilted her head back from one side to the other and swung around directing her focus on a man back in the line.

She yanked on Carver's jacket sleeve. "It's him. Don't look. I am sure it is him."

"Who? Fly?"

"No. Scarface."

"How the hell could he have followed us? I know he wasn't on our flight."

Whispering, she said, "I'm pretty sure it's him. What do we do?"

"Once through customs you bolt for transportation. Get a taxi. I will wait on him and eliminate the threat. Then I will take a taxi to pick up my truck at the apartment complex."

"No. You just said we don't split up."

"Yes. But you said we should, circumstances have changed, so we're going with your plan."

"I don't like it."

"Just meet me at Harmony. You can check with the residents while waiting and see if you can find out anything about where Elke might be."

She did not like the plan now that the Russian was involved, but maybe he was right on this one.

Once through customs, she exited with long-legged strides

directly to the lower level of the Main Terminal where taxis were available. She was nervous about leaving Carver to deal with the Russian. Would Carver push the Russian in a bathroom stall and strangle him? She didn't want to know.

She was rushing so fast toward the exit doors, she almost missed what was standing in front of her. She stopped dead in her tracks when she read the sign the man in the chauffeur hat and dark sunglasses held.

Addy Bravo.

The man in the business suit approached her. She backed up, unsure of her next move.

He pulled off his sunglasses.

"Julia, it's me. Fly."

CHAPTER 45

**Ronald Reagan Washington National Airport
Washington D. C.**

CARVER KNEW HIS gait and mobility would slow Julia down after they hustled through customs. His plan was to delay the Russian long enough to give Julia enough time to get to the lower level, take a cab and meet him later at Harmony assisted living. Her long legs could out walk most of the people in the terminal. He noticed her long legs when he first followed her in D.C.

After formulating a quick plan, he stopped by a flight board and pretended to read it. That was about as far ahead as he planned. The next move would be in Scarface's court.

A batch of travelers from different backgrounds power-walked past him like they were late for work. Cell phones glued to their ears made Carver invisible as he stood with his eyes trained on the one passenger he knew would see him. He was not sure how long it would take Julia to reach the lower level. All he needed was enough time for her to get a taxi and head toward the assisted living facility. Maybe ten minutes. Five minutes had already passed.

A young exhausted mother pushed a screaming child in a stroller and carried a toddler on her hip. She stopped a few feet from Carver frantically searching for something inside a large bag hanging from her shoulder. Maybe a bottle to quiet the upset infant in the stroller.

Without warning, Carver's plan for Scarface derailed.

The mother lowered the child on her hip to the ground hanging on to his small hand. She continued her search in the over-sized bag, pulled out a bottle and a toy. The instant the bottle fell out of her hand, she released the grip on the toddler. A split second later, the toddler bolted into the swirling chaos of people. The mother's face, full of horror, met Carver who tried to keep his stare on the passengers flowing his way.

He spun back in the direction the toddler ran, pushed people aside and lumbered to catch the mini-sprinter. People cursed and threatened him as he made his way toward the child. When the crowd opened, he spied the toddler standing next to a man he recognized, Scarface.

Both men glared at each other, their eyes burned with hatred.

Unexpectedly, a grin crept across the ugly Russian's face.

He decided to storm toward the toddler, and nail Scarface at the same time.

It would have worked except that Scarface picked up the child and threw him into the path of an oncoming golf cart like vehicle. With mere seconds before the child was crushed, Carver dove for the cart, landed beside the startled driver, viciously yanked the steering wheel hard right. The cart careened into the wall as a frenzy of yelling travelers jumped out of the way. The dazed black woman driver shouted at him until she saw the toddler being lifted by a woman. She kept repeating, "Mercy me. Thank the lord."

Carver, having lost his balance, was still on the ground when a man offered his hand thanking him for what he did.

The toddler's mother gave him a big hug. Security swarmed the area forming a perimeter around Carver preventing him from following Scarface.

Every minute he was delayed by the questions from security lessened his chance of catching Scarface. He thought about telling them what happened, but was sure it was not a good idea. He claimed he just saw the toddler stumble in front of the golf cart and reacted. He begged off praise, then continued to the lower level.

Shit. Now the Russian might catch up to Julia. Next time we meet; I will put a bullet in his head.

On the lower level, he did not locate her or Scarface. He was not sure whether to be relieved or worried. After exiting the lower level, he prepared to get a taxi, when an elderly man with a fringe of gray hair approached him.

"Sir, excuse me, but I think you forgot your coat."

Draped over the man's arm was a beige trench coat.

"No. That's not mine. Thanks, buddy, but I'm in a hurry."

"Please just look at it. I am sure you will recognize it." The weathered man thrust the coat at him.

"What the hell?" He realized the trench coat was Fly's and the only person who would have it was Julia. "Who are you and where is Julia?"

"She is safe. You do not have much time. A silver Mercury Grand Marquis will pull up in less than five minutes." The senior man left and entered the terminal.

The silver Mercury sedan pulled to the curb with the passenger window down.

"Hop in, mate." A deep baritone voice said.

Carver threw his bag in the back seat and climbed in the front seat next to the driver. The voice did not fit the small frame man wearing a tweed herringbone newsboy cap and wire rim glasses. He wore a hearing aid attached by a wire wrapped around his large protruding ears. Carver figured he could not be taller than 5 feet since he could barely see over the steering wheel.

The elderly man did not drive slow, like Carver expected. The car sped out of the airport, with an occasional angry fist shaking at other drivers who were in his way.

"My name is Leo."

"Hello Leo, my name__"

"Carver, I know. The lassie is safe. We got her out a tad before that Russian showed up."

"You are saying Julia is safe?"

"Abso-bloody-lutely," Leo exclaimed.

Carver figured the thick accent was British.

Leo abruptly changed lanes weaving the Mercury between cars, hitting his brakes when he got too close, the Mercury tires screamed filling the air with the smell of burned rubber. Several drivers honked, gave him the bird, while they mouthed obscenities. Leo's fist would shake violently as he continued to speed along. Carver held tight to the door handle as he swayed back and forth in the seat. *This old man is crazy.*

He tried to protest, "Leo, you can stop driving like Mario Andretti. Wherever we're going, I'd like to arrive alive."

"Sorry mate. I figured you being a bloody paratrooper and all, you'd fancy a tad of speed." Leo snickered. "Besides, mate, we have company." Leo was staring in his rear-view mirror.

"The same Russian you saw at the airport?"

"Just a few bloody minutes and we'll lose him."

"I can't believe he can keep up with you." Carver spotted the taxi in his side view mirror. "Is he in the taxi three cars back?"

"Indeed. Grab your bag and be ready to do exactly as I tell you."

He was not sure he was going to like what the old crazy man called Leo wanted him to do. At this point, he was wondering why he even got in the car.

"I am going to swing into an apartment complex in a short time. You have thirty seconds to get the bloody hell out and climb into the boot of a Toyota Corolla."

"Boot?"

"Sorry mate. I forgot you Americans call it the trunk."

"Wait, the trunk? You want me to climb into the trunk and I don't know who the hell you really are."

"Your gun is in the glove compartment. Get it and if you want to keep Julia safe then don't cock it up."

Carver opened the glove compartment and found his favorite weapon, a SIG 229. He never got the chance to ask Leo exactly what was going on or where the Toyota would take him.

† † †

The ride in the trunk took over thirty minutes until it came to a stop. Carver was glad the driver of the Corolla was not speeding and weaving like Leo. After a nine-hour flight from Europe, he was tired and now very uncomfortable. He wondered if Julia was with Fly or had she found Elke.

The trunk popped open and a slender hand reached inside to help him straighten up right. At first he thought it might be Julia, but the girl looked like a teenager.

"You okay, Mr. Carver? I know my grandpa Leo drives kind

of reckless."

"Yes. Thank you. Where am I?"

"This is a house where you will stay for a few days. You will be safe here. Julia is inside waiting on you."

"What happened back there when I got in the trunk?"

"There were ten of us helping on this mission. Grandpa Leo had a man similar in height to you ride with him. He drove off in one direction and the rest left at different intervals to confuse the man tailing you. I was picked to bring you here since I look like a teenager. Old people and young people don't look suspicious." She snickered just like Leo had earlier.

Mission? Who are these people?

"Just go on up to the house, they are expecting you."

"Why aren't you staying?"

"I have homework I need to do."

"You're in high school?"

"No. Junior at college. Nice meeting you." The young girl shook his hand, climbed in the car and backed out of the driveway.

He began to feel like he had entered the *Twilight Zone*. He inspected the neighborhood as the young girl drove away.

Nice meeting me? I was in the trunk of your car most of the time.

The house, obscured from the street, might have been nice once, but now the paint had blistered from years of pounding sun causing large flakes to lift from the wooden frame. There was rotten wood around windows covered in Castilian wrought iron. A neglected garden was over grown with weeds. Down the street he heard police sirens and an ambulance wail.

He instinctively checked his SIG in the back of his pants, just in case he had been set up. He plodded up to the entry, partially hidden by bushes and brambles, keeping his eyes

trained on the windows and front door. There did not appear
to be a welcoming party. No Julia. No Russian.

A few raps on the front door, a curtain slid to the side and
then the sound of locks began to click. A lot of locks.

He slid the SIG 229 out, held it by his side and shifted
sideways, away from the door.

The door opened in slow, small jerks.

"Carver, don't shoot. It's me. Fly."

CHAPTER 46

When Julia heard Fly's screams, she wrapped a towel around her wet body, and stormed down the creaky staircase to the entry hall.

Fly had his arms up, surrendering against a wall with Carver's hand around his neck and the gun in his other hand. Sweat glistened on Fly's forehead, his body trembled.

"Carver, let him go," she yelled.

Carver released his grip, letting Fly slither to the floor.

"I tried to explain, but he wouldn't listen," Fly's voice was croaky as he massaged his neck.

"I thought Fly set me up."

Carver's gaze dipped to her towel-wrapped body. She tightened her grip on the towel.

"Damn, Carver. You have to give a person a chance to talk, before you beat them up."

"I thought you might be in danger."

"Next time, ask. Now, help Fly up. After I get dressed, I'll be back down so we can talk."

She scampered back upstairs and wasted no time with make-up or drying her hair. After she rammed her bare feet into her jeans and pulled on a long sleeve t-shirt, she joined Carver and Fly downstairs. Fly expelled a breath like he was relieved she had joined them. Carver sat erect in a chair across from Fly with a beer in his hand.

"I see you found the refrigerator."

"Fly told me there was beer in the fridge."

She sat next to Fly on the couch. "Carver, do you want to take a shower?"

"First, why don't you fill me in on what the hell is happening. I didn't get much intel from the geezer gang. Leo is one pissed off driver who gets demented enjoyment from scaring his passengers shitless. And I didn't get an opportunity to chat with his granddaughter, since I was locked in the trunk of her car."

"For starters, you were wrong about Fly. Elke had him stage leaving his trench coat and phone in hopes we would stay longer in Germany looking for him."

"There was no tracer in the phone?"

Fly scratching the back of his head said, "Yea. I did put a tracer in my cell. Elke thought it would be a good way to keep tabs on both of you."

"Then why aren't you in Denver?"

A familiar voice trailed from the kitchen, "Because I knew you found evidence at the bookstore that would lead you here."

The sound of Elke's voice caused all the pent up worry and anger to evaporate from Julia's mind. She leapt from the couch rushed over with arms spread wide, "Elke, I am so happy you are okay. I've been so worried."

Elke brushed Julia's hair out of her face, and planted a kiss on her forehead. "I'm very happy you are safe." Elke's eyes bored into Carver, "You promised me you would stay with Julia and keep her safe."

Julia interjected, "He did stay with me, Elke, until the Russian tried to follow us. Carver stayed behind to intercept Scarface so I could get away. We were going to meet up later."

"Yeah? How did that work out?" Elke's sarcasm was directed toward Carver.

"Not too damn good." Carver took a slug of beer.

"That's right. The Russian would have followed you to Julia, therefore I had a few friends intervene."

"Elke, Milo told me about my past," said Julia. "I wished you had told me."

"You were only a child when it happened. You had to believe your new identity to stay safe."

"Why can't I remember my past? Did you have the CIA brainwash me?"

"Sit down, dear." Elke led her over to the couch and they sat next to each other. "In the first place, I knew there was a mole in the CIA when the Russians blew up my home. I did not trust the agency, even though there were a few trustworthy agents willing to help me."

"Was Fly one of those agents?"

"Yes, in addition to a few others. In reality, a mole can be the person you trust the most."

"Why didn't I remember my name, my mother, or my father?"

"You had what is called traumatic amnesia. I did not do anything to make you forget. Nor did I do anything to help you remember."

"Why did you disappear Elke? I was so worried. You could have called or answered my texts."

"It was necessary to keep you safe. I did not want you to follow me to Europe, even though you did." Elke's face tightened, "In other words, Carver, you put my granddaughter in harm's way."

"In the first place, Elke, Julia's life was already in danger when the Russians discovered you were still alive. The best way to keep her safe would have been to tell me what the hell was going on."

"Can we stop this bickering for a moment?" Julia demanded. "I smell food." She headed for the kitchen.

"You were right about the low blood sugar, Elke. When the hunger creeps in, you better feed her or the tiger's claws come out."

"I'm not deaf, Carver, I can hear you," she yelled from the kitchen.

Elke erupted in a loud chuckle.

† † †

The kitchen had a small table for four that rocked if you leaned on it. The fast food was hot and tasty and immediately made her feel better.

She sat, silently soaking in how Elke and Carver interacted with each other at the kitchen table. She felt silly for thinking Carver was attracted to Elke. However, there still lingered a tinge of jealousy about their relationship. And for what reason, she couldn't understand.

The next hour was a question and answer session. Carver and Julia had most of the questions, since Fly had filled Elke in on what they knew.

"How safe are we at this place, Elke?" Carver asked.

"On the positive side, we are safe here for a couple of days."

"On the negative side?"

"Keep your go-bag with you at all times. Did Leo give you the gun?"

"Yes. Glad you remembered my favorite weapon is the SIG

229."

"I remember all your favorites."

Julia frowned at Elke showing her disapproval.

"Why exactly did you bring us here, Elke?" Carver inquired.

"In short, to keep Julia safe. Fly suggested it would be better to work together on this mission. Of course, I will lead it."

"What mission are you talking about? Revenge?" Julia asked.

"Revenge is a peculiar thing, Julia," Elke explained. "If you believe you cannot get revenge, you try to move on. But, when you know you can exact retribution, you think about it all the time."

"This is mad, Elke," Julia said. "The Russians know you are alive. We need to go to the authorities and tell them what we know. They will keep us safe."

Elke and Fly stared at each other.

"What? What are you thinking?" Julia's fingers flew apart with palms up.

"We can't do that now, Julia," Elke said.

"Why not? The mole in the CIA is no longer a threat."

Carver spoke up, "It is no longer just about revenge, is it Elke?"

A smug look appeared on her grandmother's face.

"No. It has gotten much bigger than revenge," Carver continued. "Was Liese already dead when you got to the bookstore?"

Julia was astonished by Carver's revelation.

Julia's bare feet tapped the wood floor underneath the kitchen table. She added, "The masked killers were in the store when we got there and Liese was already dead, therefore Liese had to be alive when Elke was at the bookstore."

"Or died while Elke was there," Carver added.

"Oh, my God Elke, what happened?" Julia's eyes pleaded.

"The Russians murdered her in cold blood. Elke closed her eyes and swallowed, "She saved my life."

Her grandmother slowly opened her eyes before continuing in a steady, measured voice, "I made a mistake. Liese showed me the information from the safe in the basement. When we heard the banging on the door upstairs, we put everything back in the safe and Liese told me to hide behind the staircase while she checked to see who it was. I heard the footsteps, a man with a deep voice spoke German. He followed her down the staircase with a gun stuck in Liese's back. When they cleared the stairs, I aimed my gun at his head and ordered him to drop his gun which he did." Elke hung her head.

"Are you okay Elke?"

"Yes, I am all right." Elke placed her elbows on the table, raised her intertwined finger to her chin, diverted her eyes downward.

"My back was to the top of the stairs. I recognized the voice speaking from the top of the stairs the instant I heard it."

Without hesitation, Julia pleaded, "Who? Who was it?"

"Your friend, Julia."

"My friend? What friend do I have in Germany?"

"Krystyna."

CHAPTER 47

KRYSTYNA?

"What? No, Elke, you're wrong. There's...there's no way Krystyna could be involved in any of this. She's my friend."

Carver interjected, "Why would Elke lie about a thing like that?"

"That's right," Elke agreed. "Why would I lie?"

She pulled her hand away and pointed at her grandmother. "Because you hate Russians. You've always hated Russians—and Krystyna is Russian."

"Yes, she is," Elke said. "But, she is also your friend and I wouldn't intentionally say something hurtful to you about your friend just because she was Russian unless I had good reason. Julia, search your feelings, how much do you know about Krystyna? She played you."

Julia couldn't believe what was happening. Could it be that her friend had lied to her all this time? "Dammit it, Elke." She slammed her fist on the kitchen table so hard the legs rocked, knocking over her glass of water. Fly fetched a towel from the counter and began soaking up the water while Carver and Elke pushed back from the table to keep from getting wet. "You didn't actually see her though, did you? You only heard someone who sounded like Krystyna, right? I mean, you could be wrong."

"Julia, I know you don't want to believe it. It's always

difficult to accept when you've been betrayed. But, this is my line of business. It *was* Krystyna. Of that, I am positive. And remember, I never forget anything."

Julia hung her head. "I'm sorry. I just…I just thought I knew her." She looked up at Elke. "Did Krystyna kill Liese?"

"Yes. Liese dove for the gun on the floor. Before she could return fire, Krystyna fired, striking Liese. I returned fire after taking cover. The Russian rushed up the stairs and they escaped out the door. Liese was dead before she hit the ground. There was nothing I could do, so I left."

"The Russians returned before we got there and tried to break into the safe," Fly added.

"I still don't understand why we can't just go to the authorities and let them handle this."

Carver leaned toward Elke, "A bit of a moral dilemma, isn't it Elke? Why don't you tell your granddaughter the reason you can't involve the CIA?"

Julia snapped, "What the hell is going on?"

Elke's sardonic grin took on a vengeful glare as she said, "I believe we should let Derick tell us."

"What is the moral dilemma, Carver?" Julia asked.

"I believe Elke went to Germany to learn the identity of the Russian assassin who killed her daughter—your parents, Julia. She did not expect to learn more than the identity of the assassin, but Liese showed her something besides the picture, didn't she Elke?"

"She shared a great deal of information."

"Liese was upset by the information and wanted to give it to the authorities. The network of old spies tracked down the Russian assassin and found they had stumbled onto something much bigger. You told Liese to wait before she gave the flash drive to anybody. Perhaps, you told her you needed time to gather more intel."

"It is a little more complicated than that."

"No. It's not. If the CIA were to get their hands on the disk, they would use your Russian assassin for bait. Perhaps even cut a deal with the agent. To put it another way, keep you from your real objective, killing the assassin. I believe you plan on preventing whatever it is the assassin has in the pipeline, and then...."

Elke exploded with anger, "I will not be denied justice, goddammit, they killed my daughter." She stormed from the room.

Julia found it difficult to hear what Elke planned to do. This was a side of her grandmother's personality she had never seen until now.

"How did you know what was going on?" she asked Carver.

"It was something Fly told us on the train. He said Elke was the CIA's best covert officer."

"Don't make this twenty questions, Carver. How did you know? Have you been in contact with Elke and...."

Fly interjected, "You should have been an analyst for the CIA, Mr. Carver."

"How so, Columbo?"

Fly ignored the sarcasm and continued, "You knew if she was the CIA's best covert officer, then once she learned the identity of the assassin, the killer would be dead. Elke said we have a mission so you deduced the Russian assassin was still alive. Very good. This is a moral dilemma for her."

"Because Elke won't let something bad happen to this country, so the assassin is the bait."

"Yes."

"And then, she will kill the assassin."

"Yes."

"That is illegal," Julia said. "We can't let her do it."

Fly put his hand over his mouth, muffled a laugh, "Illegal? We are talking about the CIA. Don't be misled when the government says they operate by a set of rules and regulations. Drone wars, assassinations, night raids, they are all authorized, but that doesn't mean it is legal."

"We're talking about domestic activities, here in the United States," Julia argued.

"The CIA is prohibited from conducting spying operations on U.S. soil against US citizens," Fly explained. "You think that doesn't happen? September 11 attacks created fear. Fear created Executive Order 13470 which allows the CIA to conduct covert action activities approved by the President. The lines are blurred on what exactly is authorized."

"What intel does Elke and her network of spies have for this mission?" asked Carver.

"Back in 2000, a former Soviet spy testified at a congressional hearing that during the Cold War, Russian intelligence operatives placed weapons and communication caches in the United States. Before 9-11, it was not so difficult to bring illegal weapons in from other countries."

"Fly, this is public knowledge," said Carver sounding frustrated. "The former Soviet spy you mentioned was in the federal Witness Protection Program and never was able to identify a specific location of one of the sites."

Fly agreed, "You're right. The network heard rumors about this activity even when they were active agents. Lack of proof does not mean it did not happen. The flash drive recording leads us to believe something is going to happen soon, caches will be used and it involves a high-level politician."

"Us?" Julia asked. "So, you are a member of the old spies?"

Elke's voice from the kitchen doorway interrupted, "We have a network of agents, most of whom are retired." She was wearing a jacket with a large pocketbook hanging from her shoulder.

"Where are you going?" Julia asked.

"I have a meeting with an asset downtown at a D.C. hotel."

"I'm going with you." Julia stood and walked around the table to where Elke was standing.

"No. I need you to stay here. A Russian official has agreed to meet with me. This could be the intel we need to discover what the bastards are up to."

Julia nervously glanced over her shoulder at Carver. She searched for confirmation, he gave her nothing. *He wants me to make the decision.*

She sucked in her lips, leveled her gaze to let her grandmother know how serious her next words were, "Sorry, Elke. We're going with you."

"So, I assume if I refuse to let you go with me, you will follow anyway? Hmmm? Of course you will," Elke said and exhaled a sigh.

Julia, Carver and Fly nodded their heads in unison.

"You are very stubborn, just like your…"

"Grandmother," Carver said loudly.

✝ ✝ ✝

Fly drove his Acura out of the slum neighborhood where graffiti-laden, dilapidated, boarded-up houses with yards of overgrown weeds dominated the street. The dreary sky was littered with gray clouds threatening rain.

When Elke instructed everybody to take their go bags, just in case, Julia got nervous. Just in case what? The Russians try to kill *them*?

While they drove in tense silence, Julia's mind shifted to Krystyna. Nagging thoughts asked what if Krystyna showed up at the hotel? And would Krystyna, her friend, try and kill her?

Carver interrupted the silence, "Elke, where exactly are we headed?"

"Not far, you will see when we get there."

"Your lack of information is impressive," he said. "Does your informant have a name?"

"The asset is Mikhail Lesin, a prominent Russian millionaire and former minister of the press."

"Does Lesin have information to help decipher the intel on the flash drive."

"That is what I will find out."

"I think I should go in with you, since Fly has a gun phobia," Carver said.

Elke turned around in her seat, her face red, eyes icy cold. "Excuse me, but, you are staying in the car protecting Julia like you agreed to do."

"Elke, Carver is right. You need somebody who can help if things go wrong," Julia argued.

Carver placed his hand on Julia's lap, "Elke is right on this. We'll stick to the plan."

The sedan pulled along the side of a curb, a block from the luxurious five-star hotel. Several hotel porters in uniforms stood guard under the wide portico entrance.

Elke briefed everybody on their assignment roles. Carver

and Julia were to wait in the car. Fly would be stationed inside the lobby. Everybody had burn phones and were to text if they saw anybody or anything suspicious.

If the mission was compromised, Carver and Julia were to take the car, Fly and Elke would get a taxi and meet back at the house. Elke had everybody add the address to their phone and Leo's number for backup. They agreed not to wait longer than thirty minutes for Elke to return.

Fly, dressed in a business suit without his signature trench coat, carried a briefcase and cruised in the direction of the hotel. Five minutes later, Elke sashayed across the street where she was greeted by a porter who held the large glass hotel door open and then she disappeared.

Julia and Carver got in front, she sat in the driver seat.

"Julia, she'll be all right." Carver's attempt to comfort her was not going to work. How did Elke do this for so many years? *I never knew she did such dangerous things.*

The buzz of Carver's phone startled her. "Something is wrong," she told him. Her heart raced, eyes locked on Carver as he answered the cell phone.

"She is right here." He handed the cell phone to her saying, "It's Alvin."

"Alvin, what's up? I am fine, yes, that was the man I'm staying with. He's only a friend."

Carver arched a brow when he heard her last comment. She mouthed, *stop it* to him and continued to listen. A few minutes into the conversation, she gave Carver a burning hard stare.

"Thank you, Alvin. This is very helpful. No, I'm not in trouble. Yes, yes. Thank you for the invitation. I have to go." She clicked off.

"What's wrong? You look a bit more than pissed off."

300   DJ STEELE
"It's Fly. Carver, you were right. I think he might be a double agent or something like that."

"What did Alvin tell you?"

"Alvin said Fly was fired from the CIA, not for failing a drug test, but because he leaked classified information to a reporter that, in turn, damaged national security. Fly failed the polygraph test, one of dozen given to him. Not only that, Fly told us he had never been to Fort Collins, but guess where he lived after he was fired? Yep. Fort Collins."

"I knew there was something about that sneaky bastard."

"We need to call and warn Elke," she told him. "Fly might have set her up."

He hit the number on the cell phone. The number rang without being picked up. He kept the phone to his ear while it continued to ring and said, "Get a pistol out of my go bag, Julia."

"A pistol?"

"Elke gave me several extra weapons, just in case. You know how to use one. Elke taught you."

"Targets. I have only shot targets, not people. I can't shoot a person."

"You might not have a choice," he cautioned her as he kept the phone to his ear. "Get the pistol. Be careful, it's loaded."

She twisted her body, reached back between the seats to the rear floor board, dipped to unzip Carver's go bag when the rear window shattered. Carver's hand held her down, and she heard the engine start.

"Stay down, put your foot on the brake," he spoke in a low, rough voice.

Her body still contorted, she stretched her leg and managed to press the brake with her left foot.

"Stay down, Julia until I tell you to move."

She felt a cramp move from her left foot to her side.

"The car is in gear," he said. "Swing around, mash the gas and drive."

She did not have a chance to argue with him. She spun around, captured the steering wheel, slammed the gas pedal, and blasted down the road. Carver poised his weapon in the direction they left behind.

"Why are they trying to kill me? I thought the Russians wanted me to lure Elke out of hiding," her panicky voice commanded.

"They were probably trying to take me out. Head toward the safe house."

"What about Elke? We can't leave her."

"We're being followed."

"What, what do I do?"

"Lose them."

She drove faster, weaving through traffic, determined to put distance between them. Carver's head bobbed back and forth when she yanked the steering wheel to miss cars in her way. A Mercedes horn blared as she slithered in front of the car, nearly clipping the front end. The green and yellow lights were a blur as they blasted through them. Barreling down the road, the car still taunting them, Julia wondered, *where are the cops?*

The car following was growing smaller in the mirror. Her eyes flickered back and forth from the rear-view mirror, the road ahead, to the side mirror. She took several more turns, found a parking garage, swung in and pulled into an empty stall.

"Who facilitated the meeting for Elke at the hotel?" She sounded like she was trying to catch her breath.

"Fly."

"He set her up," Julia's voice was furious. "We know he lied to us about the reason he was fired from the CIA and never having been to Fort Collins."

"We need to get back to the hotel, Julia."

"Try calling her again," she said. "Then we can decide our next move."

She eased the car toward the exit for Carver to get a signal on his phone."

"Hang on. I have a text from Fly."

"What does it say, hurry, read it to me."

"Blown."

CHAPTER 48

WAGNER BELIEVED HIS handler had bugged his office, home and phone. It would be her way of controlling everything in his life, from political to personal. He swiveled his chair back around and studied the room he could call home. There were more hours spent in this room than his row house. First thing he did was cut a small piece of paper and tape it over the camera eye on his laptop. Then he did a meticulous sweep of his office to detect anything that seemed out of place. He ran his hand along the lampshade, the picture on his desk and unscrewed the mouthpiece on the land line phone.

The couch cushions were pulled up and checked. *I spent too many nights sleeping on this couch.*

He pulled items off the bookshelf and inspected them. Nothing. Then he noticed something different, he had never paid attention to before. The eagle ornament on top of the flag in the stand next to his desk was crooked.

He approached the flag stand and quickly unscrewed the finial and finding what he suspected, a small listening device. He left the device in place, screwed the ball back on when his cell phone vibrated in his pocket.

His handler. *Shit, what does she want? Maybe I am being activated.*

"Yes. Of course, I am excited to be the Speaker of the House. Why wouldn't I?"

He found it difficult to be pleasant with the condescending

woman. His handler always started their conversation with small talk. Weather, health, friends or anything else he knew she did not give a damn about. The small talk was a smoke screen for the real reason she called him.

"Problem? What problem?" He figured it was the issue with the dead spy who had miraculously resurfaced.

"Yes, I know of Mikhail Lesin. He was the minister of the press in the Soviet Union."

The handler explained Lesin, now an activist, was suspected of being in Washington, D.C. to meet with a CIA agent.

"Why would he do that? It is not for money. He is a very rich man."

Lesin had knowledge of the crisis period that the Russians had been planning and was of the opinion it was an unethical and a dangerous objective even for his country. His handler continued to explain that the spy they were searching for was the one meeting with Lesin today. The Russia Foreign Intelligence Service (SVR) had intel the American spy was meeting Lesin at a hotel in downtown D.C.

"So you will be able to neutralize this spy?"

His handler said that the spy would easily be apprehended and Lesin would pay for his disloyalty to the Kremlin.

He knew what she meant, Lesin would die and the spy would disappear and never be heard from again.

When the rumors surfaced on Capitol Hill of this incident, they were to be reported immediately to her.

Clicking off, he vigorously rubbed his hands together while he paced back and forth. Rumors? What rumors would circulate after Lesin was murdered and the spy captured?

Ironically, the Russian handler had used the eagle finial on top of the American flag to plant a listening device. He would have to be very cautious what he said out loud. The handler was listening. Of course, he could destroy the listening device, or he could leave it and use it against her. He was a politician and who better to use disinformation to their advantage?

He pressed the intercom button on his desk, "Megan, would you please set up an appointment with Congressman Quatterman for three o'clock in my office." He figured Quatterman would know any gossip of the incident by then. If you had Quatterman promise not to share a rumor, he was the man to spread it on the Hill.

✝ ✝ ✝

He kept checking the NBC top stories on the Internet. He called a few members in his *brain trust* under the pretense he needed their input on some of the bills being proposed by Congress. The *brains trust* began as a term for a group of close advisers to a politician, prized for their expertise in particular fields. He kept his inner circle small and guarded.

There was no information leaked to him about what the Russian millionaire, Lesin was doing in Washington or if there had been an incident. He would have to wait and speak with Quatterman later at three. He had about an hour before the meeting.

He tried to concentrate on a bill his party was planning on passing. His strategy was to try to placate his own party without letting them realize he was supporting the former speaker's agenda. Many of the members were too radical to realize you must compromise to get things done.

The intercom beeped, "Mr. Wagner, Congressman Quatterman is early. He wants to see..." Wagner could hear the booming annoying adenoidal voice. A second later, his door opened.

"Sorry Alan. This can't wait."

"Always an emergency. Come on in. I'm just trying to figure out how we can fix a broken House of Representatives."

"This won't take much of your time."

"Have a seat Dan and tell me what has you so riled up."

"I just heard through the grapevine that a Russian official died of a heart attack in a downtown hotel."

He wanted to tell the windbag he didn't have the scoop on what had happened, but he needed to know what the American authorities believed.

"That's it? Do we know why this official was visiting Washington?"

"No. The Russians aren't talking. His relatives back in Moscow claim he suffered from heart disease. Rumors have it, he was going to pass classified info to an American source."

"Do we know the American source? CIA agent?"

"No, the gossip is it might have CIA involvement. This Russian guy was a big shot as head of a media giant, one of the largest media groups in Russia and Europe."

"Is there any suspicion he did not die of natural causes?"

"It's the Russians for God's sake, Alan. Of course, we don't believe he died of natural causes."

He looked up at the American flag by his desk and spoke in a clear voice, "Russians cannot be trusted, even by their own country." He hoped his handler boiled over with anger when she heard him say this. "But, even Russians die of natural causes. Sometimes even when they are visiting foreign countries."

"You're right, Alan. But, this could become an international issue if not handled with care."

"Thanks for the information, Dan. Keep me abreast if you hear of any new developments."

"Certainly. You'll be the first to know. Now, what is it you wanted to meet with me about?"

He had forgot he called the meeting, until Quatterman reminded him.

"I'm planning on holding a series of private meetings ahead of Congress reconvening for the next session and would like for you to be there." He knew it was wise to feed Quatterman's ego. The man could be very useful in the future.

"Wow, Alan. Even though we have had our differences on policy, I would be honored to be a part of the meetings. Thank you."

Quatterman was a successful suck up. He despised the man.

As Quatterman stood, pivoted, and strode out the office door, Wagner debated texting his handler and filling her in on what Quatterman had told him. *Why bother? She just heard everything.*

He knew a call was necessary to keep up the ruse, but he just wasn't in the mood to talk to her again. Now that he knew his handler had his office and probably home and phone bugged, he needed a plan to get rid of her. He just did not know how. Perhaps, she could die of a heart attack.

His phone vibrated in his pocket.

A text. It was probably her, his handler.

He was surprised to see the text was not from her. She was the only one who contacted him on this phone. The message was short.

A time and place to meet. He was not to be late. The name on the text was from a man he had heard his handler speak about in the past.

Why would Igor Buryakov want to meet with him? Igor worked in Moscow as a member of Russia's Foreign Intelligence, SVR.

CHAPTER 49

"BLOWN? WHAT DOES that mean?" Julia's voice was shaky.

"The clandestine meeting didn't happen. We have to assume Elke had to get out quick and Fly is letting us know."

"Why didn't Elke let us know? Do you think this is part of Fly's deception?"

"At this point, I don't know what to think."

"I'm going back to the hotel. Elke might need our help."

Carver was convinced Fly had already taken a taxi back to the safe house. The weasel might have the Russian waiting to take Julia hostage. Fly would probably put a bullet in his head. For all he knew, Fly might be a sniper and used the pretense he didn't like guns. *I get my hands on you Fly, you are a dead man.*

She drove a different route to get to the hotel. The car following them earlier was nowhere in sight.

A block from the hotel, they saw it at the same time. A swarm of people crowded the entrance to the hotel, the street blocked by whirling blue and red lights.

"Christ," she uttered. "Something has happened to Elke."

"Don't panic." He squeezed her arm. "We don't know anything yet. Just make a slow U-turn and head back to the safe house."

"No. I need to go see what is going on. I'm not going to leave her."

"You have to Julia. This is not the time to let your emotions block reason. It's already too late to prevent whatever happened inside the hotel. We need to get to the house and find out what Fly knows."

"You mean beat the crap out of Fly until he tells us everything we need to know."

He crossed his arms over his chest, and suppressed a curse.

"All right. Let's go find Fly," she said as she wheeled the car around in the opposite direction.

He was surprised she agreed to get out of the car a block before they reached the safe house. He told her the plan would be to park the car in the driveway close to the house, blocking the view from the living room window. She was to approach from the blind side on foot, keeping a watch on the upstairs window, just in case. "Anything suspicious, anything at all and you are to get out fast."

"The pistol," she said when she opened the car door and handed him the keys.

"What?"

"The weapon you wanted me to get out of your go bag, when we were parked across from the hotel. I need it to cover you."

He nodded, as he climbed out to get in the driver's seat. He retrieved his go bag, unzipped it, and handed her a semi-automatic weapon.

"Be careful. Keep the muzzle pointed down and your finger off the trigger and outside the trigger guard until you have made a commitment to fire."

"A Smith and Wesson M&P 9mm." The self-defense classes

and time spent at the firing range with her grandmother when she was growing up gave her confidence handling a weapon. Julia pointed the pistol toward the ground, racked the slide to the rear and released it, chambering a round. "I'm a bit rusty, but with seventeen rounds I should hit something."

She tossed her hair over her shoulder, smirked, and scurried in the direction of the house.

"Use that woman instinct shit. If your gut says it's a trap, get the hell out," Carver hollered before climbing into the driver seat.

He rammed the car in gear and sped to the house. He wanted to get there and neutralize any threats before she arrived.

The curtain in the window upstairs was closed as was the one in the living room; there was no noticeable movement. So far so good. He lumbered up to the front door with his weapon by his side. The door knob twisted freely. The door was unlocked.

He stepped back, checked the upstairs bedroom window. No movement. The living room curtain still shut.

He turned the knob, pushed hard, the door swung wide open.

Standing to the side of the door he called out, "Fly, are you in there? It's me Carver."

A foot over the threshold, he did a quick sweep of the room with his SIG aimed. The room appeared empty. His hunch told him there was somebody inside. He raised the gun toward the top of the stairs and listened. Nothing. He put his back to the staircase wall and placed a step on the stairs. A thumping and scratching noise from the kitchen distracted his attention from upstairs. He swung his weapon toward the direction of the sound. The kitchen.

"Fly, show yourself." *So, I can put a bullet ibetween your eyes.*

He backed down the step to check if Fly was indeed hiding in the kitchen. Without warning he spotted the noise and reeled back. The mouse heard him approaching, stayed still till his foot was almost on top of him and then scrambled. He was not sure his hunch was right, unless Fly was hiding in the bedroom upstairs. When he got to the foot of the stairs, it was too late.

Fly appeared at the top of the stairs braced against the wood railing with a gun pointed at Carver's head. "Drop your weapon. Drop it, or I will shoot."

"You said you don't like guns." Carver's hands were in the air, one holding the SIG.

"I don't like guns, but I don't like dying either. Where's Julia?"

"Why don't you ask your Russian friend?"

"Drop the gun," Fly repeated, only this time there was agitation in his voice.

Carver lowered the SIG to the floor.

"Kick it far away."

"You been watching too much TV."

"Do it."

Carver kicked the SIG across the room. Fly kept the gun pointed toward Carver's head, and commanded him to move into the living room. Slowly, Fly descended the creaky stairs, the pistol directing Carver to continue to move further back into the room.

"You better hope I don't get a chance to put a hand on you. Cause I will beat the shit out of your lying ass."

"I had to leave the hotel. I knew you would not understand."

"Damn right, I don't understand."

"Just listen to what happened," Fly started to continue.

"Drop your weapon, Fly." Julia aimed the M&P at Fly's head.

Fly lowered the gun, Carver took three steps, and knocked him to the ground. "Where is the Russian and Elke? Lie and I'll kill you."

"I don't know. You got to believe me, I don't know."

"Get up."

He pulled Fly to his feet by his shirt. His fist pounded Fly in the gut. He dropped to his knees, wrapped his arms around his stomach, coughed, sucking in air, and threw up. Carver yanked him up again by his shirt.

"Carver, stop it," Julia yelled.

"He knows something."

"You can't beat it out of him."

"Oh, hell yes I can."

"Not this time." She pointed the pistol at Fly's head and asked, "Where is Elke? Did you set her up?"

"No. Honest, Julia. I figured Elke would be here after the meeting was blown."

"Carver, what exactly did you tell me about the hair trigger on this pistol?" The M&P bullet shot passed Fly's head and lodged in the wall.

Fly ducked with his hands covering his head, and collapsed to the ground.

Carver inhaled a sharp breath, his pulse picked up. *Damn, I misjudged Julia.*

"Julia, I would never do anything to harm Elke, you've got to believe me." Fly trembled, he struggled to breathe.

"I won't kill you like Carver over there. I will aim for your legs, arms or maybe your ass. You got one minute. Time him,

Carver."

Whoa, this is a whole different side to Julia I hadn't seen. I like it.

With his hands still covering his head, Fly rapidly said, "In the lobby, I positioned myself to keep an eye on the elevator and the front door. Elke came in and took the elevator up to the eighth floor where she was to meet Mikhail Lesin. I saw no threat after she went up. Then a few minutes later, the fire alarm began wailing, people covered their ears, scrambled out the exits and front door. I didn't know what to do. That is when I saw the woman and the man with the scar on his face rush through the lobby and exit out the front door."

"Scarface," she sounded surprised. "Maybe the woman was Krystyna."

"Why didn't you go up and see if Elke needed help?" Carver said still sounding pissed off.

"I don't know. Things were too chaotic, I left and sent the text. That is what Elke told us to do."

"You're a liar. You set Elke up," Carver said in a deep, loud aggressive voice.

"No. I would never do that. Elke helped after I got fired from the agency."

"Are you a liar and a coward?"

"I was scared. I told you what happened."

"We know the real reason you got fired from the CIA, Fly," said Julia. "You were fired for leaking classified information to a reporter which damaged national security. And you told us on the train you had never been to Fort Collins, but in fact you lived there after you were fired."

"Maybe the Russians paid you to set Elke up," Carver moved closer to Fly. "Is that what you did?"

"No. I would never do that."

"You're a liar," Julia said.

CHAPTER 50

SHE AIMED THE Smith and Wesson at Fly's leg. She wasn't sure if this was the right thing to do. What if she shot Fly in the leg and he still claimed he did not know anything? Would she have to shoot his other leg and so on till he bled to death? On the other hand, time was crucial and maybe he did know something. He had lied to them about his past. Was he still lying?

Her finger rested on the trigger, only a light squeeze would discharge a round.

"Fly, you will tell us where Elke is." Her hand tightened on the grip of the pistol.

"Shit," Fly hollered while he appeared to hyperventilate. "I don't know where Elke is."

"You lying bastard," Carver said.

She slowed her breathing, a bead of sweat dripped from her nose. She ran the *what ifs* through her mind and decided she had no choice.

"What the hell is going on?" A loud voice bellowed from the kitchen entrance. Elke had managed to come in the back door without being heard.

Julia's face looked like a deer in the headlights as she exclaimed, "Elke, how on earth did you get in?"

"Why are you pointing a pistol at Fly?"

"We thought he set you up. He has lied about his past. He

can't be trusted."

"Of course he lied, he worked for the CIA. We all lie for a living."

"You knew why he was fired?"

"Fly had a weakness for a very attractive reporter. Too much pillow talk, I'm afraid."

"He didn't set you up?"

"Probably not. He knows I'd kill him if he tried."

Fly moved quickly away from Carver and Julia and stood close to Elke.

"Carver and I saw the police had surrounded the entrance of the hotel," she explained to Elke. "Then, we got a text from Fly saying the mission was blown. We just assumed he had betrayed you. He should have stayed at the hotel and helped you."

Elke dropped her go bag on a chair and said, "Fly did what he was supposed to do. I told everybody if the mission was compromised, we were to meet back at the safe house."

"The mission was compromised?" Julia lowered the S&P and placed the pistol on the hutch. "What happened?"

"Let's sit down in the living room," suggested Elke. "I'm tired."

Then Elke continued, "The Russians got to him first. I took the elevator to the eighth floor, and climbed the stairs to the ninth, just to be cautious. I saw a man come out of Lesin's room and scan up and down the hall. It was the Russian you called Scarface. It was a trap. He was waiting on me, so I pulled the fire alarm. I waited until Scarface and a woman left the room. When they were out of sight, I hurried down to Lesin's room, but he was already dead. I did a quick search and left."

"Was it Krystna?"

"It happened so fast and there were too many people running from their rooms. I'm not sure."

"We were so scared something had happened to you, Elke. Why didn't you text us?" asked Julia.

"I was a little busy trying to stay alive at the time. I knew you would figure it out soon enough."

Julia apologized to Fly for pointing a gun at his head and discharging a round. Fly complained his ears were still ringing. Carver told Fly he was lucky he hadn't fired the round. He wouldn't miss.

"You missed? I am disappointed all the firearms training didn't pay off." Everybody laughed at Elke's joke, except Fly.

"You could have killed me," Fly grumbled, his fingers massaged his ears.

Elke's source was dead, there were no more leads. Carver told them in twenty-four hours, the flash drive would be turned over to the authorities by his friend in the army, Peggy.

Carver asked, "Can your network help us find out what the Russians are planning?"

"The last thing they were able to do was put me in touch with Lesin." Elke, sitting on a chair, crossed her legs and continued to explain, "Now they are tracking down the Russian handler. I'm afraid we will need more help. She usually contacts her agents by phone. It was rare for her to risk a meeting in person with an agent we suspect has a high profile."

Carver pushed for more information, "Can he be identified by the person who took the video and pictures?"

"No, she was unable to get close enough and the man kept his head down, wore sunglasses and a hat."

"Any physical description?" Julia pressed.

"Tall, not thin or heavy, maybe muscular. He wore an

expensive suit. She believed he was not old."

"High profile means he could be CIA, FBI or a politician. The House of Representatives has 435 members; the Senate has 100. Since the House and Senate are both in session, we need more than the guy is not old, tall and a good dresser." Julia slumped on the couch stretched her arms up and let out a yawn.

The loud sound was glass shattering in the living room, as a bullet continued its course and ricocheted off the hutch cabinet and traveled till it struck the adjacent wall.

Carver shoved Julia to the floor, Elke and Fly dove to the floor.

Lying on the floor, her eyes nervously scanned the room, then she got down on all fours crawling toward the hutch where she had placed her weapon. A volley of bullets pierced the air, causing her to flatten to the floor. Carver instructed her to stay down until he returned fire.

Panting, she watched Carver and when he began firing, she quickly continued crawling across the floor. At the hutch, she stayed low, reached up with one hand and retrieved the M&P.

She saw Elke crawl to the kitchen, unzip her go bag, take out a Glock, load a magazine, and chamber a round. "I have the back door covered," yelled Elke.

Oh. My. God. Nobody will believe this. I'm in a firefight with my grandmother.

"Fly, get your weapon, help Elke protect the back of the house," Carver barked orders like he was back in the army.

"Elke, anything out back?"

"Not yet."

Carver said, "I estimate there are at least two shooters out front, less than a hundred meters away."

The gunshots hit the house in short bursts. Carver instructed everybody to hold their fire unless they saw a target. No need to waste bullets.

"Somebody will hear the shots and call the cops, right?" Fly's shaky voice asked.

"Not in this neighborhood," said Elke. "Nobody wants the cops to come around here." She added, "Besides, the residents here are used to hearing gunshots."

"Should we call the cops?" Fly asked.

A creak on the stairs, Carver swung around, took aim, and fired, killing one of the assassins on the top of the stairwell. The dead body crumbled, then fell from the banister and flipped over and over until he hit the floor with a thud.

The silence was more terrifying to Julia than the gun fire. She stooped to the floor and was going to reposition near Elke when a volley of fire erupted, splintering the walls and furniture inside.

"Elke, we need back up. Now." Julia sighted her M&P pistol up the stairs.

Julia could hear Fly whimpering. He won't be any help. The guy is in shock.

"How many still out there, Carver?" Julia sensed their situation was becoming hopeless.

"One less than before."

"Elke, is anybody coming to help?" Julia pleaded.

Gunfire again rained through the house, only now it was coming from all directions.

Carver yelled, "Fly, get off your ass and give Elke some cover. Now, or I'll shoot you."

The rounds of gunfire had them pinned down.

"Carver, we've got to call the cops," Julia felt the strain in her voice. "We don't have a choice. There is no way to get out of this alive."

"Where's your phone?" he asked.

She realized her cell was in her purse, which was in the car.

"No, it's in the car. Do you have your phone?"

He had his phone in his hand when they heard a siren approaching. It sounded like an army of sirens roaring down the street.

Immediately, the gunfire ceased, people rustled in the dark, car doors slammed and the sound of rubber squealed on the pavement.

Her body was losing its stiff posture and her breathing began to slow down. She slumped against the wall and said, "Thank God somebody called the police."

CHAPTER 51

THE POLICE SIRENS stopped.

Julia eased up, peered out the broken window panes into the street. Her body began to shake as she strained to see through the inky darkness. An almost full moon was casting eerie shadows from the overgrown shrubby on the driveway.

"Where are the police?"

"Get your bags and let's get out of here." Elke held her go bag in her hand and headed for the front door.

"What about the police? Did they pursue the Russians?"

Carver chuckled under his breath, "Those old spies got a lot of tricks up their sleeves, huh, Elke?"

"What?" Julia was annoyed. Carver and Elke communicated like twins, speaking in their own language. Twin Telepathy. She didn't like it.

"It will only take them a few minutes to figure out they were tricked, and then they'll come back," Elke warned.

"Tricked?" She was not sure why the police would be tricking the Russians.

"It's the *Bridge Club*. I named them," Fly sounded like he had just won a spelling bee contest. "They have lots of tricks up their sleeves, like police sirens attached to their cars," Fly explained to Julia.

Fly's car that Carver had parked in the driveway was miraculously undamaged except for the earlier gunshot cracking the back window. Carver took the wheel and headed in the direction Elke told him.

When Fly climbed in his car, he saw the back window of his Audi was cracked from a bullet hole. "The Russians shot out my car window," he stated with surprise.

"Oh no," she responded hearing Carver muffle a chuckle. She did not want to explain what had happened back at the hotel.

"Where are we headed Elke?" Carver inquired as he increased the car speed, causing Julia and Fly to bump into each other in the back seat with every sharp turn.

Elke was busy talking on her phone, more listening than talking. The phone glued to her ear, she gave Carver short directions.

Once Elke clicked off the phone, she said, "We'll go to another safe house for now and regroup. The watcher team has eyes on the handler. So far she has not made physical contact with the man we saw in the video sitting on the bench."

"Watcher team is the Bridge Club spy network?" Julia asked.

"Partially. Watcher team is a surveillance team assigned to this target. She is a high priority so we have brought in other resources. This is too important not to make certain we shut it down."

"What are the other resources?"

Julia remembered from her childhood, whenever Elke said more than she intended, she would ignore your question, which was what she did now.

"Pull to the curb, keep the engine running. I will signal if the safe house has not been compromised and you can meet me there, otherwise we will keep on moving." Elke took her weapon, phone and binoculars when she exited the car.

Julia wondered where they were as she stared out the car window surveying the homes around them. As far as she could tell they were out of the slums and now in an upscale neighborhood. One that obviously would call the cops if shots were fired. That somehow made her feel safer. She watched Elke cross the street and disappear between two houses. Her grandmother was in great shape, probably in better shape than she was.

"Elke called the last place a safe house, but I didn't see any technology or security." Julia remembered watching the movie, *Safe House*, a few years back.

"The type of safe house shown in movies is over-glorified. Safe houses should be easily and quickly changed when the location has been compromised. A safe house has to be portable," Fly said as he peered through binoculars pointed in the direction Elke went. She was sure they were high quality binoculars and expensive since Fly's line of work was surveillance.

Fifteen minutes seemed like thirty to her. She constantly bumped the cell phone to register the time since Elke had left the car. "What is taking her so long?" She was antsy now that Murphy's Law seem to be following them every step of the way. "Should I go look for her? Just in case."

"It hasn't been that long, Julia. She'll be careful," Fly said, never removing the binoculars from his face. "She has to do surveillance of the safe house to make sure there isn't anything suspicious going on."

"Why doesn't she call them and ask? They could use a code word to alert her."

"They might not know they are being watched."

"Ten more minutes, Fly, and then you go find out what is

going on. You are the surveillance..."

The handle on the car door pulled, startling Fly and Julia whose attention was in the other direction. Julia did not see any reaction from Carver in the front seat.

Elke jumped in, "Let's go."

"Is it okay to go there?" Julia asked.

"No. Take a right turn at the next intersection, Derick."

"The Russians were there?" Julia busied snapping her seat belt expecting Carver to keep her and Fly in motion with his speed and turns. "You saw them Elke?"

"No."

"Then what are we doing? Why aren't we going to the safe house?"

Elke explained, "I thought everything was okay, until the porch light was turned on. That was a signal not to come inside."

"Now where are we going to regroup? Does the Bridge Club have any other safe houses, Elke?" Carver asked.

"We need a place on the outskirts of the city," Elke said.

Julia remembered Alvin's offer to let her stay at a place he had outside the city. "I know a place we can use."

"I think it's a bad idea," replied Carver.

"You haven't even heard what I'm going to suggest."

"Alvin's place. Right? We don't need his place."

"Actually, we do," replied Elke. "Julia, can you call and set it up. Make sure he knows that if he says anything your life could be in danger." Elke tilted her head so everybody in the car would hear her say, "We are in a time crunch. If we don't identify the handler's sleeper very soon then the crisis might happen before we can stop it."

† † †

Alvin seemed happy Julia was taking him up on his offer to let him help by providing her and her friends a place to stay. He promised not to say a word to anybody and would be over tomorrow after his early morning conference meeting. He told Julia where to find the hidden key. After locking himself out multiple times, he kept a key hidden.

His place was not large, more cottage size. The middle-class single-family neighborhood probably had an HOA or home owner association, because the lawns were all manicured, the homes in the same color pallet, and Alvin didn't seem the type who would ever do yard work.

The inside of his house had a clean look with white walls, modern modest furnishings and was devoid of clutter. Fly immediately threw his bag down and flopped on the couch, only to move as soon as Carver sat down next to him. The poor guy was still scared of Carver. Probably her too, since she discharged her pistol near his head at the safe house.

Carver had a beer in his hand, obviously, a man with no problem helping himself to whatever was in the refrigerator.

"Do you think you should be drinking a beer?"

"Yeah, I do. Alvin has good taste in beer."

She snooped around the house, making the excuse she needed to make sure the place was secure. She wanted to know what kind of place Alvin lived in when he wanted to relax outside the city. Right now, she was not sure why the curiosity. The place was as she expected, except the exercise bike being used as a clothes rack in the bedroom.

Back in the living room, Carver and Elke were in an argument about something. Sounded like they had gotten some news.

"I don't like it." She heard Carver tell Elke.

"It is our best chance, right now. We have this information and have to assume it's correct," Elke argued.

"What don't you like and what do we know?" She sat on the couch next to Carver and faced Fly and Elke.

Carver picked up the conversation, "Elke has a SITREP."

"A what?" Julia asked.

"SITREP. Situation report. The watcher team has intel that the handler is meeting somebody tomorrow mid-morning that they suspect might be the sleeper agent we are looking for."

"That is good news. We can get both at the same time. Where's the meeting?"

"Same spot," Elke said when she got up and walked toward the kitchen. "We hope."

"What don't you like, Carver? This is what we hoped would happen."

"Elke wants to go alone."

CHAPTER 52

CARVER HEARD IT first.

The sound of a car pulling into the driveway. Alarmed, Julia scooted to the window to check to see if it was a black Prius. Alvin's car. There was not a clear view of the driveway, since shrubbery and Fly's Acura blocked the line of sight. The grinding noise was the garage door being opened.

"Alvin said he was staying in the city, since he has a conference meeting first thing in the morning. But, it must be Alvin, who else would have the garage door opener?" asked Julia with the room full of eyes staring at her.

Carver did some hand commands to tell everybody where to move and wait. The lock on the door to the garage clicked and the door opened. Standing in the doorway, Alvin's jaw went slack, his arm released the bag he was holding sending it crashing to the floor. Carver shifted from around the back side of the door and pressed the barrel of his gun to Alvin's head. Julia and Elke kept their weapons trained on Alvin.

"Anybody with you? Could you have been followed?" Carver asked the questions so fast, Alvin was unable to answer them separately.

"No, no. It's just me. I was very careful driving here," a shaky voice stuttered.

Carver pushed Alvin into the room and headed out into the garage. A minute later he yelled, "Clear."

Julia lowered her weapon and hastened over to Alvin, "I'm so sorry Alvin. You said you were staying in the city." She wrapped her hand over his arm and felt him tremble. "Come on in and sit down. We're just being cautious."

"I thought I would bring you some food. I couldn't remember what I had here, so I cancelled my conference for tomorrow. It has been awhile since I've been here."

Alvin sat close enough to Julia on the couch that their legs touched lightly, maybe to feel safer or maybe to let her know he still liked her. She told him most of what had happened in the past week. He told her what his friend with the FBI was willing to share, but there was not much more information he had to give her. Except, one of Julia's co-workers who was also a friend of Alvin's told him that Krystyna had called another co-worker where Julia worked and asked if she had heard from Julia. Office gossip could spread faster than a prairie fire with high winds fueling it. His friend did say they heard rumors Julia had left town because she might be guilty of killing her supervisor. *There goes my job.* You could also be convicted in an office setting without a trial.

Elke was back on her cell phone again, listening and shaking her head most of the time. When she clicked off the phone, her face looked more wrinkled than usual. She thought maybe her grandmother was tired or the phone call had upset her.

"Is something wrong Elke?" she asked.

"One of our watcher team agents was found dead a half hour ago."

"Oh no. Elke, I'm so sorry."

"It gets worse." Elke's stern face did not give away her emotion. "The agent was tortured before she was murdered. Then her body was dumped next to a dead drop location scheduled for today."

The woman was stoic, not revealing how things affected her. Julia remembered as a child being amazed because her grandmother never cried, always strong no matter what was going on in their lives. When a friend of Elke's died in a car accident, Julia did not see a tear escape from her grandmother's eyes when the friend's husband came to the door to tell her that his wife—her best friend—was dead. The man broke down and Elke put her arms around him. Always the shoulder for those in need. She believed as a child that the woman was a super hero, incapable of being hurt until one night she had a nightmare and ran to be consoled by Elke. In the bedroom, she witnessed her grandmother sobbing and shaking as she laid on her bed. It was at night when she was all alone that Elke grieved.

"What does this mean?" She stood up and walked toward Elke.

"It means we don't know for certain if she talked."

"Who are these people?" Alvin asked.

"Russians."

"Funeral," I remembered on the video that the handler mentioned a funeral. This is it. I think the crisis has already begun," Julia said.

"You might be right," Elke agreed and placed her arm around Julia holding her tight. "The Russian handlers are activating their network of sleepers to crush their enemies."

Alvin leaned forward and sat near the edge of the couch, his elbows propped on his legs and hands clasped. "It sounds like you are saying the Russians are starting another Cold War like we had after World War II."

"No," Elke's tone was sober. "The Russians are not starting

another Cold War, because the Cold War never truly ended."

"You know," Alvin said. "I remember my FBI friend talking about a Robert Hanssen, who was a former FBI agent and spied for Soviet intelligence services for twenty-two years. He was finally arrested in 2001. It was crazy, but the FBI transferred him to the Soviet analytical unit responsible for capturing Soviet spies. And he was the spy all along."

Julia moved back to the couch and Elke sat in a chair across from her and Alvin.

"Elke, why don't you give the CIA the names of the sleepers you know about? I know you have an eidetic memory. Milo told me you memorized the names from the documents that you got from a Russian official. The list had names of sleeper agents and weapon caches in the West."

She could not read the expression on Elke's face from what she just said. Her grandmother just folded her hands in her lap, stiffened in her chair and said, "That day your mother and father died, I vowed never to return to the line of work that took so much from me. I feared any leak of names would let the Russians know I was still alive and this would put your life in danger also. There was a mole in the CIA and I did not have a name for him. It does not matter what side these people are on, you cannot trust anybody." Elke heaved as if she was glad these secrets were no longer just her secrets. She continued, "After many years, it was necessary to leak names, but I did it through dead drops, no personal contact with the agency that betrayed me. Many of the old sleepers have since died and were never activated." She pointed to her head. "I kept some of this information, as collateral."

"Wow," Alvin said. "Julia, I never knew your family was so fascinating."

"Neither did I until a few days ago," Julia said as she thought about Milo and wondered if he was okay. When she left Milo in Trier, she was not sure how to feel about a man, her grandfather who was never a part of her life growing up. Later, she would like to go back to visit him.

If she lived through this.

CHAPTER 53

JULIA, STILL HALF asleep, stretched out her body as she walked toward the smell of fresh brewed coffee coming from the kitchen. She didn't sleep much last night. There was something about today's mission she felt they had missed. Maybe she was letting her nerves rattle her or getting paranoid like Carver.

Everybody was already sitting at the kitchen table, drinking coffee and talking. Even Fly, who usually said very little, had a vocal opinion.

"Good morning. I wish somebody had awakened me earlier," she said while walking toward the counter with the coffee pot.

"Let me get that for you Julia." Alvin eagerly got up, walked over to the coffee pot and poured her a cup. "Just cream, right?"

Standing next to Alvin, she noticed the look on Carver's face and smiled, "You remembered. Thank you, Alvin."

"I was going to wake you up Julia, but you were sleeping so soundly," Fly said apologetically.

"Yeah, you were sawing some logs," added Carver. "Since we have been spending nights together, I haven't gotten much sleep with all your snoring."

She wanted to spill her hot coffee in Carver's lap for his smart aleck remark. He said it for Alvin's benefit.

"All right kids." Elke laid a map on the center of the table. She opened it, refolded it and then drew a circle around an area. "We need to concentrate on today and make sure we know our roles. This is the park. Intel says the handler and the Russian agent will make contact this morning. It is believed that they will meet on the same park bench as before."

"How can you be sure of that?" Julia questioned.

"We can't, most of this is based on a pattern and we don't have much of one to make a definitive decision. Therefore, we will need everybody to spread out and use phones to communicate if we identify our target."

Alvin gulped a sip of coffee and then asked, "If we see the person in the photo you showed me, then what? Just let you know?"

"You're not going Alvin," Julia chimed in.

Carver leaned backward in his chair, almost tipping it over. "Julia, we need as many eyes on this area as possible. Alvin can just be our jogger in the park." He cut his eyes at Alvin. "You can jog?"

"Six to ten miles, four times a week."

Alvin's remark kept Carver quiet for the next few minutes.

"What are we going to do when we surround the target?" Fly's fingers strummed his cup of coffee.

"We kidnap them," Elke said.

They spent the next forty-five minutes debating the moral issue about what they planned to do. Carver had no problem with it. He said the CIA, FBI and police would waste time unraveling what was going on, besides arresting Julia, Fly and him on suspected murder charges from Germany. That reminder must have made Fly nervous, since his foot tapping got louder and more annoying. Alvin on the other hand, acted like he was being cast for an exciting role in a TV series.

"Is everybody on board?" Elke asked as her eyes went around the table. Carver gave a thumbs-up, followed by Alvin and then Julia. Fly squeezed his hands together several times and then finally gave a thumbs-up.

"Good," Elke said.

She used her pen and circled sections of the park. She assigned each of them an area to conduct surveillance in the park. Elke ended her instructions, "Fly you ride with me. Julia, Carver and Alvin go in Alvin's car."

† † †

Julia instructed Alvin to pack a go bag for himself, just in case. She didn't like the idea of placing Alvin's life in danger. He didn't hesitate to agree to help, even after all the information she recounted to him about almost getting killed. She tried to reason with herself that nothing dangerous would happen in the park. They were just identifying the handler and the Russian agent. The kidnapping part was on Elke's shoulders. She was sure Carver would be more than happy to assist.

The clock on her cell phone indicated that they had ten minutes before they needed to leave. The drive to the park would take thirty-five minutes. The palms of her hands started to sweat and she could not shake the chills running down her spine. She hoped Alvin and Carver wouldn't notice how nervous she felt right now.

"Is your weapon ready?" Carver's question only heightened her anxiety.

"I thought we were doing surveillance," she said. "Why do I need my weapon on me?"

"There are a lot of ifs about this operation today. We need to be prepared for anything."

"Like what?" Alvin asked as he came up behind Julia.

"Like the agent who was tortured letting the Russians know about today. It could be a trap," Carver said. "Do you know how to shoot a weapon, Alvin?"

"Yes."

"How accurate are you?"

"I can shoot a moving thirty-inch circle at twenty-one yards," Alvin remarked with a confident tone.

"Skeet shoot?" Carver asked him. "Are you talking about skeet shooting?"

"Yes, I am. I use a pump action shotgun."

Carver reached in his backpack and removed a weapon. "Come here, Alvin. This is a 9mm Glock. It has a 17-round magazine. The only way this handgun can be fired is for the trigger to be pulled fully to the rear." Carver put the Glock back in the clip-on holster and handed it to Alvin. "Can you handle this?"

"He doesn't need a gun," Julia interrupted.

"No. It's okay Julia. Just in case, I can always fire it in the air," Alvin said as he carefully clipped the holster to the back side of his pants.

Her icy glare melted when Carver said, "Listen to me, both of you. This is very important. If either of you must pull your weapon, do not hesitate to fire at the target. Hesitation will get you killed. Do you understand? These people won't hesitate to put a bullet in you."

She rubbed her sweaty hands on her pants and quickly went outside. A few minutes later, Carver and Alvin joined her. Elke and Fly had already left for the park.

"Here are some ear buds Alvin has for us to use with our cell phones," said Carver as he handed a pair to Julia.

Carver drove while she gave him directions to the park. The sunlit clouds drifted in the sky highlighting a beautiful fall day with just enough nip in the air to allow them to wear jackets to conceal their weapons.

Alvin didn't appear nervous. Perhaps, it was because all he knew was TV and movie violence. Unless it was the news, the entertainment industry liked to have the good guys always win. This was not a *Dirty Harry* movie. She glanced at Carver and thought the man was a beast. Maybe he was a little like Clint Eastwood in *Dirty Harry.* She could see that in him. The only people experienced with guns and killing were Carver and Elke. Fly never did field work with the CIA. She prayed the handler in the park did not have a weapon.

Carver interrupted her thoughts, "Did you notice that Fly was more jittery than usual?"

"I thought the same thing," she answered.

"His foot tapping got loud when Elke asked if he was in on this," Alvin added.

"There is something just not right about this," Carver said. "Something Elke is lying about."

"Would your grandmother lie to you, Julia?" Alvin asked.

In unison, she and Carver answered, "Yes."

She added, "She worked for the CIA."

Carver continued, "I think she is sending us to the wrong park."

"Why would she do that?" Alvin asked.

Carver explained, "Because she has a vendetta. Once she has the sleeper agent, she plans to terminate the handler."

"Which is why Fly was so nervous this morning. He knows,"

Julia added. "But, now we don't know which park and there are a lot of parks in this area."

"Shit. I should have figured it out sooner. She argued with me yesterday about going alone and then changed her mind too fast." Carver slowed the car and pulled to the curb, letting the car idle. "Julia, look at the picture of the handler on the park bench to see if anything looks familiar."

She opened her go bag and removed the picture. She studied the picture, searching for a clue. "I don't see anything I recognize in this picture."

Carver blew out his breath and said, "Give it to Alvin. He jogs all the time, maybe he'll recognize the surroundings."

Alvin held the picture, mumbled something and said, "No. The picture only focuses on the bench. The stuff around the bench could be any park in D.C. Sorry." He handed the picture to Julia but then clamped tight, refusing to let go.

"Wait. The bench. Let me look again." Alvin held the picture close to his face and then next to the window letting the sunlight shine on it. "Here. Look here." His finger tapped the picture. "On the bench you can see a dedication plaque. I do know this park."

CHAPTER 54

"You know which park? Are you positive?" Carver knew they did not have time to be wrong. Elke and Fly could already be at the park positioned and waiting on the Russian handler and sleeper agent to show up. If they did not get there in time, Elke might kill the handler, the woman she believed was responsible for Julia's mother and father's death. Cold blooded. He didn't have a problem with her motivation, although he feared this was a trap and Elke's life might be in danger.

Alvin told him to turn around. The park he recognized in the photo was in the opposite direction.

"What's our ETA?" Carver asked Alvin while spinning the car in the other direction.

"Twenty minutes, no more," replied Alvin.

That would take too long. He had to get there faster.

"Do you know a shorter way?" Carver asked as he increased the car speed.

"Let me check Google Maps," Alvin answered with his phone already in his hands.

Julia was staring at him, "You think Elke is in danger, don't you?"

He decided not to answer. She already knew the answer and lying was not going to help the situation.

He did not like the idea of staying at Alvin's house. The guy seemed to like Julia and he felt a tinge of jealousy. Maybe more than a tinge. Alvin was not model material, maybe 5'10" in height, a runner's body, wire rimmed glasses, and fair features. Just as opposite of him as you could get. But deep down he had to admit the guy was amicable, willing to help, and did not complain. He owned two homes, had a successful job, and was probably a good communicator with woman. Husband material. Something he would never be.

Julia was scrolling her phone for alternative routes also.

"Come on guys, give me something." Carver tried to stay within the speed limit with occasional burst of speed. The last thing they needed was to be pulled over by the cops. Every one of them was packing a firearm. He had a concealed-carry permit and Julia probably had one too. Elke would have made sure of that. But, he doubted Alvin had one. It would not be necessary for skeet shooters.

"Turn right at the next light," yelled Alvin as he glanced up from his cell phone. "It's not shorter, but there should be less traffic than on the main road."

Carver slowed for the red light and then accelerated a sharp right. He increased his speed, changing lanes often and squeezing in front of cars. He slammed on the brakes when a dog ran into the road causing the vehicle to slide sideways for a short distance. The smell of burning rubber drifted into the cab of the car when it came to a stop.

Pounding his palm to hit the horn several times, he spooked the dog that retreated to the sidewalk.

"Close call, good reaction Carver," said Alvin as he took several deep breaths.

Carver continued to follow Alvin's directions, staying off the main roads and trying to avoid as much traffic as possible for D.C. He wondered why anybody with a choice would live in this city. There were too many people and too much traffic. Alvin instructed him to take a right at the next light, but Carver slowed when he saw the blue lights blocking his turn.

"What are we going to do? We can't make a run for it." Julia was going into her dooms day thought process.

"It looks like a wreck. Alvin, now what? How much further?"

"Just keep going and I will tell you when to turn. About two more blocks. I'd estimate about five minutes to the park from here."

"Where do I park the car? Is there a parking lot?" Carver asked Alvin who was still watching his phone.

"No parking lot. Parallel parking along the street. Since it's a weekday, we should find a parking space," he said, nodding his head.

Carver and Julia spotted the car at the same time. "Elke and Fly are here," Julia exclaimed pointing in the direction of the car.

"Nobody inside. Hopefully we got here in time." He located an empty parking spot, about six cars down from Fly's car.

A small knoll blocked the view of the city park from the car. Carver turned half way in his seat so he could see both Julia and Alvin.

"Since we don't have a com system, we will use the ear buds Alvin gave us and conference call our cell phones. Alvin, since you know the location of the bench, you go first. Julia and I will follow. As soon as you have a visual, pretend to tie your shoe, and give a fix on the bench. I'll give Julia instructions on which direction she needs to go. We need to circle like vultures and I will make sure I got your six." Carver paused to make sure he was understood and then continued, "Be on the lookout for Elke and Fly. Keep eyes peeled for anybody and I mean anybody paying too much attention to our target area." He checked his weapon and put it back in the holster.

"Should we approach Elke and let her know we are here?" Alvin was breathing like he had run his eight to ten miles.

"Negative. Stay back. I will assess the situation. We don't want to cause a scene that might alert the target."

Alvin climbed the knoll with Carver not far behind. Julia lingered near the car waiting for him to tell her which direction to head. On the other side of the knoll, Alvin turned left and walked toward a paved path lined with benches. He stopped twenty yards from the path, bent down like he was tying his shoes and said, "To my right, four benches down. Can't see the plaque, but I'm sure it's the one." He raised up and began a slow almost uncoordinated jog. Carver was sure he was deliberately trying to look like a newbie to jogging. *Good job, Alvin my man.*

"Julia, Alvin is going north along the path. You take the path and move south."

"Roger that," her voice was steady.

"Be careful," he added.

"Worried about me?"

"We could have company, keep eyes scanning area on both sides of the path." He did not want Julia to suspect he was worried about her, Alvin, Elke and even Fly. This park had people walking and jogging on the path and lots of places for an ambush.

Carver could see the park bench Alvin said he recognized from the picture with the handler meeting the Russian agent. There was a woman sitting on that bench with her back to him. He doubted it was their target and began to question if Alvin remembered the right bench. The handler had dirty blond hair, this woman had long curly red hair. Her phone was glued to her ear. Maybe the redhead was already on the bench when the handler arrived, forcing the handler to find another bench.

His eyes scoped the benches right and left of the one the redhead occupied. There were empty benches and a few benches had people resting or relaxing on them. An elderly man wearing a black brim hat with dark glasses was sitting on a bench nearest to the redhead. He held a red-tipped cane in one hand and a leash attached to a guide dog laying patiently by his feet. Further down from the blind man was a young woman with two children running circles around the bench. Elke and Fly were nowhere in sight.

They had to be in the wrong place. "Any sign of Elke or Fly?"

"No," Alvin said. "Should I continue moving down the path?"

"Could you have picked the wrong bench?"

"I've checked the plaques on every bench I've jogged past and it's none of them," Alvin relayed to Carver.

"Me too," Julia chimed in. "I checked the benches I walked past and did not see the one we want."

Carver knew he was missing something. Where were Elke and Fly? Did Elke get new intel that the handler was meeting the agent somewhere else?

"Stay put Alvin. I'll get back to you."

"Julia, I want you to go another quarter of a mile and see if you see anything?"

"Roger," Julia said. "If I don't see anything, I'm turning around. We have to be in the wrong place."

Carver kept scanning the path when the redhead on the bench turned her head in the direction of a jogger. He got a good enough look at the redhead's face to recognize her as the handler in the picture.

"It' her. I have eyes on the target," Carver uttered into his phone.

CHAPTER 55

JULIA'S WALK SPED up until she was in a full-fledged jog along the paved walkway. The gun in the holster clipped to her pants was heavy…or maybe she was just out of shape.

Her eyes constantly checking each side of the path, hoping to spot Elke and Fly. She felt her fingernails with her thumbs and realized she had bitten them down to the quick. A nervous habit. One she'd picked up over the past few days. Sitting in her cubicle at work would be a welcomed relief right now instead of running through a park with a gun strapped to her backside.

After a quarter mile, she checked in with Carver.

"Carver, nada. Nothing," she tried to hide her heavy breathing.

"Julia, go check Fly's car. Maybe we missed them," he said. "Alvin, start a slow jog back this way."

"Roger that." Julia thought Alvin sounded proud he was using military slang.

She left the paved path and headed back to where they saw Fly's car parked. Elke wouldn't leave the park, unless she was forced. Carver warned them it could be a trap. The handler could have been the bait. She reached behind her jacket to check the gun in her holster and continued toward the car.

Something appeared in her peripheral that made her heart skip. Unsure what to do, she ducked behind a large oak tree to hide herself from the woman. She rubbed her arms vigorously up and down with her hands attempting to calm herself. On the chance she was wrong, she did not say anything into her phone.

To make sure her suspicion was correct, she leaned her head out from the tree to verify the identity of the young woman. The tall woman dressed in slim black pants, a short black leather jacket, and a wide brim hat and sunglasses was walking toward the target Carver just said he identified. Her red hair blowing in the breeze. It was Krystyna.

"Shit," she heard Carver say in her ear piece. "We have a problem."

She was puzzled how Carver recognized Krystyna. Then when he spoke, she knew it was not Krystyna who was the only problem.

"A jogger just sat down next to the handler. Looks like Elke," he said.

"Elke?" Her heart beat so hard it hurt. She left the tree cover, leaned low to make herself less noticeable, all the while keeping a distance between her and Krystyna. *What is she up to?*

"What's Elke doing?" she whispered.

He hesitated a beat and in a low commanding voice said, "Stay back, the handler has a weapon trained on Elke."

The word weapon was still shocking her mind when Julia saw Krystyna reach in her jacket and brandished a gun with a silencer. Krystyna held it beside her leg, as she continued to move closer to the bench. Carver was standing on the other side of a large oak tree and would not be able to see Krystyna's approach from his blind side.

A loud popping noise caused Julia to spin around toward the street, only to realize it was a car backfiring.

"Carver..." was the only word to leave her mouth when she

whipped back around in time to see Krystyna raise her weapon and fire.

She started running toward Krystyna, at the same time her hand retrieved the gun from her holster clipped in the back of her pants.

"Behind you, Carver. Four o'clock." Her short breaths stopped when a man lunged out of nowhere, yelling "Elke" as he charged toward Krystyna.

Krystyna's gun fired in the direction of the bench as the man tackled her to the ground. It was Fly. They wrestled, tussling back and forth.

She bent and squared her knees gripping the pistol with two hands, waiting for an opportunity to get a clean shot. They rolled and Krystyna ended on top of Fly. Now. Her finger, already wrapped around the trigger, was ready to squeeze when Krystyna went flying backward, landing on the ground, apparently unconscious.

Fly had knocked her out with a right uppercut to the head.

"Fly, are you okay," she cried out.

He struggled to his feet, and turned to face the park bench. "Is Elke okay?" he asked.

There had been no more communication with Carver. Her earbuds had fallen out. She started to put them back in as her eyes focused on the danger.

Krystyna was standing, holding a gun pointed at her.

Chills ran down Julia's spine when she saw the cold hard stare from the woman she believed was her friend. "Stop, Krystyna. It's over."

Without warning, Krystyna aimed her weapon towards Fly.

"No," Julia screamed. "Don't do it." She raised her weapon at Krystyna and fired at the same time Krystyna fired at Fly.

Fly was hit in the back by Krystyna's bullet. He staggered a few steps and fell to the ground.

Krystyna, lying on the ground, groaned as she clutched the bullet hole in her chest. Blood gushed as her ribcage heaved in and out with each labored breath.

Julia rushed over to Fly lying on the ground, bleeding. She cradled his head in her hands, yelling into her microphone, "Carver, Fly has been shot."

His eyes were open wide; like he could not believe his fate either.

"Hang on, Fly," she pleaded. He tried to speak, then his eyes went blank.

Krystyna's moans were gone and she laid motionless on the ground. Blood no longer pumped from her lifeless chest.

Julia's eyes—full of tears—widened in panic as Carver had not responded to her screams. Jumping up, she ran, gun in hand as fast as she could to the bench. The handler, slumped on the bench was dead. Elke was laying on the paved pathway clutching Carver's shirt. Alvin's hand was keeping pressure on her blood-soaked wound. Carver pressed his ear close to Elke's mouth as she spoke to him.

Julia yelled, "Oh, my God" and raced to her grandmother's side. She was overcome with fear; was her grandmother dying?

† † †

Elke told Carver enough for him to understand the gravity of the crisis that the handler and Russian agent spoke about on the video. He had to act fast, but people in the park were already on their phones, pointing in their direction. Soon the place would be swarming with cops. Alvin was the one who came up with the plan. He slipped his gun to Carver and told him he would stay with Elke and mislead the police.

Alvin started yelling at the people approaching them, "Did you see that dark-skinned man with the beard?" He used his hands to demonstrate the length of the beard. "He shot these women. The dark-skinned man with the long beard." He pointed in the opposite direction.

One of the onlookers yelled, "Terrorist," and said he thought he saw him. Another guy took off running in the direction Alvin had pointed.

Alvin was a clever guy. People tended to believe things that didn't happen if a false seed was planted. Many people believed that memory records events that happened, but memory could be constructed, reconstructed, influenced, and altered. It was not hard to contaminate a memory. In many cases, people's memory changed or a new one was created.

Carver pulled Julia up and locked his arm around her waist since he was not sure if she was going to faint.

"We have to get out of here fast," he said to her in a low voice.

"I can't leave her."

"We have no choice. The ambulance and police are on their way."

"Is Elke going to die?"

"No. The shooter's aim was off. First shot hit the handler in the head, but the second shot missed and struck Elke low. She is lucky."

"Her aim wasn't off Carver," Julia said as they walked away.

He tilted his head and wondered if she was in shock.

"Krystyna had Elke in her cross hairs, but Fly tackled her. It cost him his life."

He did not know how to respond until they reached the car, "I was wrong. He wasn't a coward. He was a hero."

They climbed in the car and Carver started driving, staying within the speed limit and trying desperately not to garner attention. He needed to put as much distance as he could between them and the park. Time was not on their side, but neither would be the police.

Police cars, with their sirens wailing, blasted past them.

"Julia, I know what the crisis is now. Elke milked it from the handler."

"Why would the handler tell her?"

"The handler planned on killing Elke. I think she enjoyed taunting her, but Elke was smarter."

"Oh my God. What's the crisis?"

"I believe some of it has already happened. It's a funeral."

"A funeral? Who died?"

"The vice president's wife. The funeral is in forty-five minutes."

"If she's dead, then we're too late."

"She's not the target. It's the President and Vice President of the United States, they are the targets."

Julia argued that they should go to the authorities. This was now over their head and beyond their control. They had lost their chance to discover the identity of the Russian agent since his handler was dead.

"I don't know if we have time to convince the CIA, FBI or Secret Service that the President's life is in danger. All we have are two dead women and a retired spy who has been in a memory care unit and unverifiable claims that the Russians are going to kill the President and Vice President at a funeral," he explained to her. "Who's going to believe us? They'll arrest us and by the time everything is sorted out, it will be too late. The President and Vice-President will be dead."

"Call Peggy," Julia suggested. "Tell her what we know."

He hit the number on his cell phone for his friend, Peggy who was stationed in Germany. The phone rang and finally went to voice mail. He left a message to call him immediately. It was urgent.

"Think she's in a meeting?" Julia asked.

"No. It is a six-hour difference from here. She's off work by now. I don't know. She could be anywhere."

"We need a miracle." Julia sunk low in her seat. "I can't believe we can't stop what's going to happen. I thought I was content being an auditor for an accounting firm, but right now I'd give anything to have enough influence that the Secret Service would listen to me. People just don't..."

Carver interrupted, "I know somebody who the Secret Service will listen to and the President himself."

"Who?"

"Alan Wagner, Speaker of the House."

CHAPTER 56

WAGNER KNEW HIS handler was upset that he was late for their prearranged meeting. Her usual arrogant and calm demeanor had slowly morphed into a fury that had contorted her face. He imagined the vibration from his cell phone in his pocket was her trying to get hold of him. Foolish woman.

His meeting yesterday with Igor Buryakov of the SVR was an answer to his wishes. Igor told him his handler's cover was blown and all ties to her must be severed for his own safety. Wagner was told to arrange a meeting with her at their usual bench. A Russian agent would take care of the rest. They would remove her from the country immediately.

He could not resist returning to the park and witnessing the surprise on his handler's face when she was told her services were no longer needed. He only wished she could see the pleasure on his face when that happened.

It didn't play out like he thought it would.

At first, he believed the older woman jogger who sat down on the bench next to his handler was the Russian Agent. They seemed to know each other. He knew his handler's personality. She would not like to be told that she was being sent back to Russia. Yet, his handler smiled and laughed with the woman as if they were old friends. The jogger woman's hands tightened into fists, like she wanted to pummel his handler. He wished he could have been a bee buzzing around their bench so he could hear what they were saying. Why was his handler so smug about what was happening to her?

If anybody was watching his face, they would have known he was not blind when his handler's head sprayed a fine pink mist into the air and she collapsed on the bench. He could not hide his shock and surprise. Before he could escape from the park, the jogger sitting next to his handler fell to the pavement. She was bleeding from her torso. Then he heard gunfire coming from a tree near the knoll in the park. Something had gone wrong. He needed to get out of there.

His fake seeing eye dog was barking and growling. He took his cane and tugged at the leash of the dog and walked away from the scene. It wasn't easy to keep pretending he was blind, since his hands were shaking and all he wanted to do was run.

Back inside the sanctum of his office, he tried to regain his composure. The Russians had killed his handler and the jogger. What was going on? Would he be their next target? He stared at the eagle finial on top of the American flag. He walked over, unscrewed the finial and removed the microscopic listening device. His handler would not need this anymore, he concluded, as he dropped it on the floor and smashed it with the heel of his shoe.

He had opted out of attending the funeral for the Vice-President's wife this afternoon. He had scheduled a speaking engagement with a local chapter of the National Federation of Independent Businesses. The speaking engagement was in an hour, just enough time, he hoped, to calm his nerves and clear his head.

He opened the folder on his desk, and forced himself to review his notes for the presentation. The urge to check the news was blurring the words on the page in front of him. He could not concentrate. The blood bath in the park kept replaying in his mind.

An unexpected beep on the phone intercom caused him to involuntarily jerk in his seat. He took in a few deep breaths and answered.

"Mr. Wagner, I am sorry to interrupt you," Megan said. "I know you said no calls, but there is a man on the line who claims he is a friend and said it is urgent he speak with you."

He racked his brain, wondering what this could be about. "What is the man's name?"

"Derick Carver. He said you two met when he was recovering at Walter Reed Army Medical Center."

He remembered initially meeting Carver at Walter Reed Hospital while he was visiting wounded veterans. The remarkable young man made quite an impression on him. They went to dinner several times and became friends. He gave Carver his business card with all his contact information and told him to call if he ever needed anything or was in the area. They last spoke just a few months ago. What could be so urgent?

"Put Mr. Carver through Megan."

After the standard pleasantries, Carver gave him a synopsis of why he called.

Carver told him a group of retired CIA spies who called themselves the Bridge Club, had uncovered a disk with audio and visual evidence of a Russian handler and Russian sleeper spy who were preparing to create a crisis in the United States. The handler was murdered by a Russian assassin to keep the identity of the sleeper unknown.

"Do you know who the Russian sleeper is?" Wagner hoped

he sounded innocent.

"Agent of influence is all we know at this juncture. A person who could threaten our national security at any level."

"That means the Russian sleeper could be with the FBI, or CIA."

"Exactly," replied Carver. Wagner listened for any audible cues that Carver suspected him.

He was stunned when Carver said he was in the park during the shoot-out. He never saw him, meaning the man showed up after he left. His hands were shaking from what happened, yet Carver's voice was steady and calm. The man had been an Airborne soldier and a platoon leader. He had been trained to fight by the U.S. government. But how much did Carver know?

"We are fairly certain," Carver continued, "that the Russians are planning to assassinate the President and Vice-President at the funeral just forty minutes from now."

Wagner lurched, hoping Megan knew CPR, because right now he felt like he was having a heart attack. "Are you positive about this Derick? That would be impossible. The security surrounding this event would make an assassination attempt virtually impossible...especially a double assassination. Even for the Russians. Everybody in attendance would be checked for weapons," he paused, "If you're right Derick, this would lead to a nuclear war. Your source has to be wrong."

The pounding in his chest began to hurt. He understood now what his handler meant when she told him he would know when it was time for him to be activated. Would the Russians be so brazen to kill the President and Vice President of the United States? Did they deliberately withhold this from him so his reaction to the event would be genuine shock? Like what he was feeling now?

Carver reminded him that dozens of high-profile Russian politicians, human right activists and journalists had been murdered by the Kremlin leaders. And he said, "Those are just the figures whose deaths made international headlines."

He was right. Wagner wondered why he did not figure out that the funeral his handler mentioned was the Vice-President's wife. It was because nobody would believe Russia would go this far. Until now.

Carver's clever source already knew the Russians would not take the blame. Even with blame pointed in their direction, there would be no proof. The soldier emphasized time was running out and it was on Wagner's shoulders to prevent the planned attack.

He told Carver that he would do everything within his power to prevent anything from happening to the President and Vice-President. What else could he say?

There were only thirty minutes to figure out what to do. If he stalled and pretended to alert the Secret Service and President, would Carver figure it out? It had to appear that he did everything possible to stop the Russians from carrying out this attack. Otherwise, he could become a suspect also. Igor Buryakov of the SVR would know what to do. He would probably arrange for Carver and all his retired CIA spy friends to disappear.

Wagner had always been loyal to Russia and worked very hard in his profession. His handler told him that he was one of Russia's most valuable agents. Now, his handler was no longer needed, so she was murdered today in the park. He did not like the woman handler and had wished her dead on more than one occasion, but he had never truly considered it. The world could be a cold, cruel place filled with people who only had their own interest in mind. Now, he too would be like that.

He studied his watch on his wrist, the second hand ticked so fast. There was no more time to hesitate.

He needed to make the call before Carver figured things out.

Epilogue

Med STAR Washington Hospital Center
Washington D. C.

IT HAD BEEN three days since her grandmother had been shot in the torso. Elke had been moved out of ICU after twenty-four hours, her critical condition was upgraded to stable. Julia was relieved Elke was going to fully recover, but it was still difficult seeing the woman who had raised her, hooked up to so many tubes and machines. An IV drip kept a steady flow of liquid from a bag hanging on a stand near Elke's hospital bed. A bedside monitor that looked like a TV screen continuously displayed wave forms. She sat in a chair beside the hospital bed, holding her grandmother's hand while she slept. Only two weeks ago, she believed Elke had dementia and was delusional claiming to be a spy. How could she have believed this sweet face would have worked in the sordid world of espionage?

The Secret Service agents guarding the door and the warmth of her grandmother's hand were reminders this was not a dream, although it had seemed like a nightmare.

This was real.

Everything had happened in such a short amount of time. This was the first moment she had had to reflect on the shocking events.

Her grandmother learned that the Russians had discovered

she was still alive. Elke said the Russians still wanted the sleeper list she had memorized so many years ago. That was when her grandmother devised a plan to pretend she had dementia and was so convincing that even Julia believed it. The ruse was to convince the Russians she was no longer a threat. It might have worked except for the audit and Elke discovering the identity of the killer of her mother and father.

It still hurt to believe that her friend, Krystyna had betrayed her. The Director of the CIA told her that Krystyna was deep undercover as part of a Russian spy ring. Oleg, the janitor at her auditing firm, was arrested for the murder of her supervisor. The CIA believed Oleg was also part of the spy ring and was snooping in her files when the supervisor came along and caught him in the act. Her supervisor probably threatened to report Oleg so he strangled her. The thought of her dead supervisor's body in her cubicle was haunting.

It made sense to her now that the Russians believed that there was a connection between the Johnston audit and the list of Russian sleepers Elke obtained twenty years ago. The name of the Russian spy working for Johnston was on the list. The Russians believed Elke must have given the list to her granddaughter before she lost her memory. Ironically, it was only by sheer coincidence that the Johnston paper audit trail led to the Russian spy. Lucky for the FBI, unlucky for her supervisor.

When her grandfather in Trier, Germany sent Elke a message that the *Bridge Club*, as Fly called them, had discovered the name of the killer of their daughter, Elke left for Germany. Her grandmother did not trust anybody after being betrayed by a mole in the CIA so Elke asked Carver, a wounded warrior and a man she trusted, to keep Julia safe.

What her grandmother didn't count on was Carver and her tracking down clues to discover Elke's real mission. The sweet grandmother she knew wanted cold revenge for the deaths of her daughter and son-in-law, Julia's parents.

It seemed that the Bridge Club had been using their skills as retired spies to collect information on the Russian Illegal Program in the United States. They did not trust modern technology and used old Cold War tactics to collect and disseminate information. All intelligence was being kept in the bookstore cellar in Wiesbaden. It was the Bridge Club that sent the video to the safe house and told her grandfather about it.

The bingo parlor was used by the Bridge Club to pass information on bingo cards. It was a clever way. An old-school way.

She did not understand why she never realized that Krystyna was not a friend, but rather a cold-blooded killer. She killed Otto's daughter at the bookstore in Wiesbaden, murdered the Russian handler, shot and killed Fly, and tried to assassinate her grandmother.

After learning the news of Fly's death, especially when told Fly sacrificed his life to save her, Elke did something Julia had never seen her grandmother do in front of people before—cry.

Her grandmother received intel that the sleeper agent would not show up so she confronted the handler on the bench, telling the handler that it was over, she had been caught. The Russian handler laughed at her grandmother. Elke said she probably would have killed the handler right then, but the handler was already pointing a gun at her. If her grandmother had killed the handler, then the outcome could have been drastically different. A twist of fate.

Julia still had trouble believing that she had been the one

who killed Krystyna. It took less than a second for her to pull the trigger and end her friend's life. An act she believed she was incapable of. She could not remember making the decision, it was instinct. Before, she had never thought about what it would be like to take a life or how people felt afterwards. Did Krystyna have a family in Russia mourning her death?

She rested her head on her grandmother's arm and began to sob. The light rap on the hospital door caused her to raise up, and wipe her eyes.

"Hey, Julia, are you okay?" Alvin stood in the doorway.

"Yes. Come on in."

Behind Alvin was Carver. "Wow," Julia said plucking a tissue from the tissue box and blowing her nose. "Carver, you shaved."

"I wanted to look my best for the President," he said with a wide grin on his face.

"The President of the United States?" She picked up the mirror on the dresser. "I look terrible. How much time before we meet him?"

Carver and Alvin moved to the far side of the room to allow the man behind them to enter.

The President, dressed in a deep navy suit, white shirt and light blue tie, looked like he was ready to address the nation or meet some important dignitary. Yet, here she stood in jeans, a crumpled shirt and her hair pulled back in a ponytail.

No wonder Carver and Alvin were on the other side of the room. She wanted to choke both of them.

"Julia Bagal, it is my pleasure and an honor." The President extended his hand. "I wanted to personally thank you, your grandmother, Mr. Derick Carver and Mr. Alvin McCallister." He looked at Elke and asked, "Is she still asleep?"

"Yes, Mr. President. She should wake up any time now." She tried to straighten her shirt and smooth her hair. "We are so thankful that you," she motioned, "Mr. President, and the Vice-President are safe." She could not believe she was being congratulated by the leader of the United States.

"I am just learning all the details of what happened and the people responsible for the plot against our country and its leaders. I regret we didn't have this intel earlier. The Vice-President's wife's autopsy and toxicology examination have revealed her death to be under suspicious circumstances. It was previously believed that her existing heart problems and high blood pressure caused her fatal heart attack."

"She was poisoned?" she asked the President.

"The results have not been released but, suffice it to say, it now appears that she did not die of natural causes."

"Were the authorities able to identify the sniper at the funeral?" Carver asked the President.

"I am afraid not. At least, not yet. When the FBI closed in, the sniper detonated his suicide vest."

"Suicide vest?" Alvin questioned. "Isn't that unusual for Russians? That is what we expect of the radical Muslims."

"Yes, it was very unusual. We still haven't analyzed all the evidence. It is imperative we do not leak any information to the public. This could cause serious diplomatic relationship problems with Russia if not handled with discretion."

"Mr. President, with all due respect," said Carver, his face becoming tense, "the Russians tried to assassinate you and our Vice-President."

"Mr. Carver, I appreciate what you have done for your country, saving my life and that of the Vice-President, but Russia has added forty new intercontinental ballistic missiles to its nuclear arsenal this year. We must proceed with caution. At this point we have nothing concrete with which to accuse the Russians. The dead Russian spies are not proof of an attempted assassination. We do not want to fuel an already volatile situation."

Julia gulped and said, "Have you identified the Russian agent who was supposed to meet with the dead handler in the park?"

"No. Not yet, I have created a task force assigned to use every tool at their disposal to identify him. His deep cover will not keep him safe for long. I have personally entrusted this task to a man who will study all known and rumored sleeper agents in this country. I have the greatest confidence he will find him."

"Mr. President," the man was winded. "I am sorry I'm late, but I got held up in a congressional meeting."

The President spun around, shook the man's hand and said, "Right on time as usual Alan, we were just talking about you. Mr. Carver, I believe you two have met. Let me introduce the man who I've entrusted to leave no stone unturned in his search to find the Russian sleeper who could connect the Russians with the assassination plot, Speaker of the House, Mr. Alan Wagner."

It had been a long day when Carver finally told her he needed to get on the road. He had to get his truck and head back to Michigan. She asked Alvin to wait for her in Elke's room while she walked Carver out of the hospital.

"So, you are leaving town so soon," she knew her voice sounded disappointed.

"I have a gym to run and Parker Brown is waiting."

"Oh yeah, that's right. Parker Brown. Your dog."

His dark eyes and the warm smile across his face made her do something that surprised both of them. She tugged his arm to stop walking, leaned close and kissed him on the mouth. A long tender kiss.

"Wow. You're making it difficult to leave."

She placed her palms on his chest and gazed into his dark eyes. "Carver, you need to go back to your gym and check on Parker Brown. Right now, I have a lot of things to figure out about my life. Alvin said there is a job opening at his company that I qualify for."

"Then the kiss was ...?"

"So, you will remember me."

"Julia Bagal, I could never forget you."

They turned and walked down the hospital corridor.

She said, "So my grandmother really was a spy?"

"Is a spy."

"And she isn't crazy?"

Carver stopped and looked her in the eyes. "I never said she wasn't crazy."

WELLINGTON
PUBLIC LIBRARY
WELLINGTON, CO 80549

ACKOWLEDGEMENTS

First and foremost, I would like to express my gratitude to my husband who motivated and guided me through the process of writing my first novel. He did more than give support and encouragement, he edited, offered input, kept me organized with timeline events, and published my book. This project would never have happened without him. We are still married.

In addition, I personally want to thank the real Derick Carver who inspired the character Derick Carver. My original idea for the tagline was to have a military veteran who had lost a leg in war and had incredible upper body strength and is handsome. I was introduced to Derick. He gave me an understanding of the struggles, physically and emotionally, soldiers have when they return from war.

A special thanks to my beta readers for their input and edits. Terence Traut, Artie Lynnwood and Cheryl Duttweiler. You guys are awesome.

A big thanks to the following for allowing me to use their names for fictitious characters in my book. I hope you enjoyed your character: Derick Carver, Peggy Taber, Addy Bravo, Lisa Saitow and, believe it or not this is his real name, Brailsford Troup Nightingale, Jr. His nickname is fictional.

AUTHOR NOTES

I have been told there is no such thing as original ideas, creative ideas are inspired. Mark Twain, in a letter to Helen Keller, called all ideas second-hand, consciously and unconsciously drawn from a million outside sources.

My novel was inspired by facts woven into a story of fiction. I listed some of the facts used to develop my thriller.

Prologue: Major Vasili Mitrokhin in 1992 defected to the British embassy in Riga, Latvia carrying his documents in a suitcase full of dirty clothes. He offered the files to the U.S. embassy first, but was turned away. The senior KGB archivist had 25,000 pages of files on operations dating back to 1930. Included were names of Russian *Illegals* and Soviet weapon caches hidden in major cities across the western world.

Captain Derick Carver was a platoon leader in the Army 82nd Airborne Division in Afghanistan on patrol to open a school for 2,000 Afghan children (the school was closed because local village elders allowed girls to be educated) when his platoon was ambushed. Carver was hit by an IED, which resulted in the amputation of his left leg. Most of his recovery was at Walter Reed Army Medical Center where he required multiple surgeries and months of rehab. Derick is now a sponsored athlete winning the world's strongest adaptive athlete-seated and is cofounder of the team Some Assembly Required (SAR).

Derick's passion is coaching athletes to compete and win.

Operation Ghost Stories: FBI arrested ten Russian *Illegals* in the U.S. and conducted a prisoner swap between Russia and the U.S. on July 9, 2010.

Mikhail Lesin was a media executive and an adviser to president Vladmir Putin. He died in a Washington, DC hotel room under unknown circumstances in 2015.

Robert Hanssen: former FBI agent, spied for Soviet intelligence for twenty-two years. He was given the task to look for a mole in the FBI in 1987. Ironically, he was looking for himself. He is currently serving fifteen consecutive life sentences at a federal super max prison near Florence, Colorado.

CPSIA information can be obtained
at www.ICGtesting.com
Printed in the USA
FFOW02n0022170817
38902FF